W9-AYO-068

CONTENTS

The daughter of a town marshal, **Linda Lael Miller** is a #1 *New York Times* bestselling author of more than one hundred historical and contemporary novels, most of which reflect her love of the West. The "First Lady of the West" lives outside Spokane, Washington, where her rescued horses, dogs and cats live the high life. Published since 1983, Linda was awarded the prestigious Nora Roberts Lifetime Achievement Award in 2007 by the Romance Writers of America. She was recently inducted into the Wild West Heritage Foundation's Walk of Fame for her dedication to preserving the heritage of the Wild West.

LINDA LAEL MILLER

A *McKettrick*
Christmas
Special

HQN™

Recycling programs
for this product may
not exist in your area.

ISBN-13: 978-0-373-30809-5

A McKettrick Christmas Special

Copyright © 2016 by Harlequin Books S.A.

The publisher acknowledges the copyright holder of the individual works as follows:

A McKettrick Christmas
Copyright © 2008 by Linda Lael Miller

An Outlaw's Christmas
Copyright © 2012 by Linda Lael Miller

This edition published by arrangement with Harlequin Books S.A.

For questions and comments about the quality of this book, please contact us at CustomerService@Harlequin.com.

Printed in U.S.A.

A McKETTRICK CHRISTMAS

For all those people, everywhere, who make a
loving space for pets in their hearts and their homes.

Chapter One

December 22, 1896

Lizzie McKettrick leaned slightly forward in her seat, as if to do so would make the train go faster. Home. She was going *home*, at long last, to the Triple M Ranch, to her large, rowdy family. After more than two years away, first attending Miss Ridgely's Institute of Deportment and Refinement for Young Women, then normal school, Lizzie was returning to the place and the people she loved—for good. She would arrive a day before she was expected, too, and surprise them all—her papa, her stepmother, Lorelei, her little brothers, John Henry, Gabriel, and Doss. She had presents for everyone, most sent ahead from San Francisco weeks ago, but a few especially precious ones secreted away in one of her three huge travel trunks.

Only her grandfather, Angus McKettrick, the patriarch of the sprawling clan, knew she'd be there that very evening. He'd be waiting, Lizzie thought happily, at the small train station in Indian Rock, probably at the reins of one of the big flatbed sleighs used to carry feed to snowbound cattle on the range. She'd warned him, in her most recent letter, that she'd be bringing all her belongings with her, for this homecoming was permanent—not just a brief visit, like the last couple of Christmases.

Lizzie smiled a mischievous little smile. Even Angus, her closest confidant except for her parents, didn't know *all* the facts.

She glanced sideways at Whitley Carson, slumped against the sooty window in the seat next to hers, huddled under a blanket, sound asleep. His breath fogged the glass, and every so often, he stirred fitfully, grumbled something.

Alas, for all his sundry charms, Whitley was not an enthusiastic traveler. His complaints, over the three days since they'd boarded the first train in San Francisco, had been numerous.

The train was filthy.

There was no dining car.

The cigar smoke roiling overhead made him cough.

He was never going to be warm again.

And *what* in God's green earth had possessed the woman three rows behind them to undertake a journey of any significant distance with two rascally children and a fussy infant in tow?

Now the baby let out a pitiable squall.

Lizzie, used to babies because there were so many on the Triple M, was unruffled. Whitley's obvious annoyance troubled her. Although she planned to teach, married or not, she hoped for a houseful of children of her own someday—healthy, noisy, rambunctious ones, raised to be confident adults and freethinkers.

It was hard, in the moment, to square the Whitley she was seeing now with the kind of father she had hoped he would be.

The man across the aisle from her laid down his newspaper, stood and stretched. He'd boarded the train several hours earlier, in Phoenix, carrying what looked like a doctor's bag, its leather sides cracked and scratched. His waistcoat was clean but threadbare, and he wore neither a hat nor a sidearm—the absence of both unusual in the still-wild Arizona Territory.

Although Lizzie expected Whitley to propose marriage once they were home with her family, she'd been stealing glances at the stranger ever since he entered the railroad car. There was something about him, beyond his patrician good looks, that constantly drew her attention.

His hair was dark, and rather too long, his eyes brown and intense, bespeaking formidable intelligence. Although he probably wasn't a great deal older than Lizzie, who would turn twenty on her next birthday, there was a maturity in his manner and countenance that intrigued her. It was as though he'd lived many other lives, in other times and places, and extracted wisdom from them all.

She heard him speak quietly to the harried mother, turned and felt a peculiar little clench in the secret regions of her heart when she saw him holding the child, bundled in a shabby patchwork quilt coming apart at the seams.

Whitley slumbered on, oblivious.

There were few other passengers in the car. A wan and painfully thin soldier in a blue army uniform, recuperating from some dire illness or injury, by the looks of him. A portly salesman who held what must have been his sample case on his lap, one hand clasping the handle, the other a smoldering cigar. He seemed to have an inexhaustible supply of the things, and he'd been puffing on them right along. An older couple, gray-haired and companionable, though they seldom spoke, accompanied by an exotic white bird in a splendid brass cage. Glorious blue feathers adorned its head, and when the cage wasn't covered in its red velvet drape, the bird chattered.

All of them, except for Whitley, of course, were strangers. And seeing Whitley in this new and disconcerting light made *him* seem like a stranger, too.

A fresh wave of homesickness washed over Lizzie. She longed to be among people she knew. Lorelei, her stepmother, would be baking incessantly these days, hiding packages and keeping secrets. Her father, Holt, would be locked away in his wood shop between ranch chores, building sleds and toy buckboards and dollhouses, some of which would be gifts to Lizzie's brothers and various cousins, though the majority were sure to find their way onto some of the poorer homesteads surrounding the Triple M.

There were always a lot of presents tucked into the branches of the family's tree and piled beneath it, and an abundance of savory food, too, but a McKettrick Christmas centered on giving to folks who didn't have so much. Lorelei, Lizzie herself, and all the aunts made rag dolls and cloth animals with stuffing inside, to be distributed at the community celebration at the church on Christmas Eve.

The stranger walked the aisle with the baby, bringing Lizzie's mind back to the here and now. He glanced down into her upturned face as he passed. He didn't actually smile—as little as she knew about him, she *had* figured out that he was both solemn and taciturn by nature—but something moved in his eyes.

Lizzie felt a flash of shame. *She* should have offered to spell the anxious mother three rows back. Already the child was settling down a little, cooing and drooling on the man's once-white shirt. If he minded that, he gave no indication of it.

Beyond the train windows, heavy flakes of snow swirled in the gathering twilight, and while Lizzie willed the train to pick up speed, it seemed to be slowing down instead.

She was just about to speak to the man, reach out for the

baby, when a horrific roar, like a thousand separate thunder-heads suddenly clashing together, erupted from every direction and from no direction at all. The car jerked violently, stopped with a shudder fit to fling the entire train off the tracks, tilted wildly to one side, then came right again with a sickening jolt.

The bird squawked in terror, wings making a frantic slapping sound.

Lizzie, nearly thrown from her seat, felt the clasp of a firm hand on her shoulder, looked up to see the stranger, still upright, the baby safe in the curve of his right arm. He'd managed somehow to stay on his feet, retain his hold on the child *and* keep Lizzie from slamming into the seat in front of her.

"Wh-what…?" she murmured, bewildered by shock.

"An avalanche, probably," the man replied calmly, as though a massive snowslide was no more than he would have expected of a train ride through the rugged high country of the northern Arizona Territory.

Whitley, shaken awake, was as frightened as the bird. "Are we derailed?" he demanded.

The stranger ignored him. "Is anyone hurt?" he asked, of the company in general, patting the baby's back and bouncing it a little against his shoulder.

"My arm," the woman in back whimpered. "My arm—"

"Nobody panic," the man in the aisle said, shoving the baby into Lizzie's arms and turning to take the medical kit from the rack above his seat. He spoke quietly to the elderly couple; Lizzie saw them nod their heads. They were all right, then.

"Nobody panic!" the bird cawed. "Nobody panic!"

Despite the gravity of the situation, Lizzie had to smile at that.

Whitley rubbed his neck, eyeing the medical bag, after tossing a brief, disgruntled glare at the bird. "I think I'm hurt," he said. "You're a doctor, aren't you? I need laudanum."

"Laudanum!" the bird demanded.

"Hush, Woodrow," the old lady said. Her husband put the velvet drapery in place, covering the cage, and Woodrow quieted instantly.

The doctor's answer to Whitley was a clipped nod and, "Yes, I'm a physician. My name is Morgan Shane. I'll look you over once I've seen to Mrs. Halifax's arm."

The baby began to shriek in Lizzie's embrace, straining for its mother.

"Make him shut up," Whitley said. "I'm in pain."

"Shut up!" Woodrow mimicked, his call muted by the drapery. "I'm in pain!"

Lizzie paid Whitley no mind, got to her feet. "Dr. Shane?"

He was crouched in the aisle now, next to the baby's mother, gently examining her right arm. "Yes?" he said, a little snappishly, not looking away from what he was doing. The older children, a boy and a girl, huddled together in the inside seat, clinging to each other.

"The baby—the way he's crying—do you think he could be injured?"

"My baby is a girl," the woman said, between groans.

"She's just had a bad scare," Dr. Shane told Lizzie, speaking more charitably this time. "Like the rest of us."

"I think we's buried," the soldier exclaimed.

"Buried!" Woodrow agreed, with a rustle of feathers.

Sure enough, solid snow, laced with tree branches, dislodged stones and other debris, pressed against all the windows on one side of the car. On the other, Lizzie knew from previous journeys aboard the same train, a steep grade plummeted deep into the red rocks of the valley below.

"Just a bad sprain," Dr. Shane told Mrs. Halifax matter-of-factly. "I'll make you a sling, and if the pain gets to be too bad, I can give you a little medicine, but I'd rather not. You're nursing the baby, aren't you?"

Mrs. Halifax nodded, biting her lower lip. Lizzie realized with a start that the woman was probably close to her own age, perhaps even a year or two younger. She was thin to the point of emaciation, and her clothes were worn, faded from much washing, and although the children wore coats, frayed at the cuffs and hems and long since outgrown, she had none.

Lizzie thought with chagrin of the contents of her trunks. Woolen dresses. Shawls. The warm black coat with the royal blue velvet collar Lorelei had sent in honor of her graduation from normal school, so she'd be both comfortable and stylish on the trip home. She'd elected to save the costly garment for Sunday best.

She went back up the aisle, still carrying the baby, to where Whitley sat. "We need that blanket," she said.

Whitley scowled and hunched deeper into the soft folds. "I'm *injured*," he said. "I could be in shock."

Exasperated, Lizzie tapped one foot. "You are *not* injured," she replied. "But Mrs. Halifax is. Whitley, *give me that blanket*."

Whitley only tightened his two-handed grasp, so that his knuckles went white, and shook his head stubbornly, and in that moment of stark and painful clarity, Lizzie knew she'd never marry Whitley Carson. Not even if he begged on bended knee, which was not very likely, but a satisfying fantasy, nonetheless.

"Here's mine, ma'am," the soldier called out from the back, offering a faded quilt ferreted from his oversize haversack.

The peddler, his cigar apparently snubbed out during the crash, but still in his mouth, opened his sample case. "I've got some dish towels, here," he told Dr. Shane. "Finest Egyptian cotton, hand-woven. One of them ought to do for a sling."

The doctor nodded, thanked the peddler, took the quilt from the soldier.

"If I could just get to my trunks," Lizzie fretted, settling the slightly quieter baby girl on a practiced hip. Between her younger brothers and her numerous cousins, she'd had a lot of practice looking after small children.

Dr. Shane, in the process of fashioning the fine Egyptian dish towel into a sling for Mrs. Halifax's arm, favored her with a disgusted glance. "This is no time to be worrying about your wardrobe," he said.

Stung, Lizzie flushed. She opened her mouth to explain why she wanted access to her baggage—for truly altruistic reasons—but pride stopped her.

"I'm in pain here!" Whitley complained, from the front of the car.

"I'm in pain here," Woodrow muttered, but he was settling down.

"Perhaps you should see to your husband," Dr. Shane said tersely, leveling a look at Lizzie as he straightened in the aisle.

More heat suffused Lizzie's cheeks. It was cold now, and getting colder; she could see her breath. "Whitley Carson," she said, "is most certainly *not* my husband."

A semblance of a smile danced in Dr. Shane's dark eyes, but never quite touched his mouth. "Well, then," he drawled, "you have more sense than I would have given you credit for, Miss…?"

"McKettrick," Lizzie said, begrudging him even her name, but unable to stop herself from giving it, just the same. "Lizzie McKettrick."

About to turn to the soldier, who might or might not have been hurt, Dr. Shane paused, raised his eyebrows. He recognized the McKettrick name, she realized. He was bound for Indian Rock, the last stop on the route, or he would not have been on that particular train, and he might even have some business with her family.

A horrible thought struck her. Was someone sick? Her papa? Lorelei? Her grandfather? During her time away from home, letters had flown back and forth—Lizzie corresponded with most of her extended family, as well as Lorelei and her father—but maybe they'd been keeping something from her, waiting to break the bad news in person....

Dr. Shane frowned, reading her face, which must have drained of all color. He even took a step toward her, perhaps fearing she might drop the infant girl, now resting her small head on Lizzie's shoulder. The child's body trembled with small, residual hiccoughs from the weeping. "Are you all right, Miss McKettrick?"

Lizzie consciously stiffened her backbone, a trick her grandfather had taught her. *Keep your back straight and your shoulders, too, Lizzie-girl, especially when you're scared.*

"I'm fine," she said, stalwart.

Dr. Shane gave a ghost of a grin. "Good, because we're in for a rough patch, and I'm going to need help."

As the shock subsided, the seriousness of the situation struck Lizzie like a second avalanche.

"I have to check on the engineer and the conductor," Dr. Shane told her, stepping up close now, in order to pass her in the narrow aisle.

Lizzie nodded. "We'll be rescued," she said, as much for her own benefit as Dr. Shane's. Whitley wasn't listening; he'd taken a flask from his pocket and begun to imbibe in anxious gulps. The peddler and the soldier were talking in quiet tones, while Mrs. Halifax and her children huddled together in the quilt. The elderly couple spoke to each other in comforting whispers, Woodrow's cage spanning from one of their laps to the other like a bridge. "When we don't arrive in Indian Rock on schedule, folks will come looking for us."

Her father. Her uncles. Every able-bodied man and boy in Indian Rock, probably. All of them would saddle horses, hitch up sleighs, follow the tracks until they found the stalled train.

"Have you looked out the window, Lizzie?" Dr. Shane asked, sotto voce, as he eased past her and the shivering child. "We're miles from anywhere. We have at least eighteen feet of snow on one side, and a sheer cliff on the other. I'm betting heavily on first impressions, but you strike me as a sensible, levelheaded girl, so I won't spare you the facts. We're in a lot of trouble—another snowslide could send us over the side. It would take an army to shovel us out, and one sick soldier does not an army make. We can't stay, and we can't leave. There's a full scale blizzard going on out there."

Lizzie swallowed, lifted her chin. Kept her backbone McKettrick straight. "I am not a girl," she said. "I'm nearly twenty, and I've earned a teaching certificate."

"Twenty?" the doctor teased dryly. "That old. And a school-marm in the bargain."

But Lizzie was again thinking of her family—her papa, her grandfather, her uncles. "They'll come," she said, with absolute confidence. "No matter what."

"I hope you're right," Dr. Shane said with a sigh, tugging at the sleeves of his worn coat in a preparatory sort of way. "Whoever 'they' are, they'd better be fast, and capable of tunneling through a mountain of snow to get to us. It will be pitch-dark before anybody even realizes this train is overdue, and since delays aren't uncommon, especially in this kind of weather, the search won't begin until morning—if then."

"Where's that laudanum?" Whitley whined. His cheeks were bright against his pale face. If Lizzie hadn't known better, she'd have thought he was consumptive.

Dr. Shane patted his medical bag. "Right here," he answered. "And it won't mix with that whiskey you're swilling. I'd pace myself, if I were you."

Whitley looked for all the world like a pretty child, pouting. What, Lizzie wondered abstractly, had she ever seen in him? Where was the dashing charm he'd exhibited in San Francisco, where he'd scrawled his name across her dance card at every party? Written her poetic love letters. Brought her flowers.

"Aren't you even going to examine him?" Lizzie asked, after some inward elbowing to get by her new opinion of Whitley's character. Oddly, given present circumstances, she reflected on her earlier and somewhat blithe conviction that he would settle in Indian Rock after they were married, so that she could teach and be near her family. He'd seemed casually agreeable to the idea of setting up house far from his own kin, but now that she thought about it, he'd never actually committed to that or anything else. "He might truly be hurt, you know."

"He's fine," Dr. Shane replied curtly. Then, medical kit in hand, he moved up the aisle, toward the locomotive.

"What kind of doctor is he, anyhow?" Whitley grumbled.

"One who expects to be very busy, I think," Lizzie said, not looking at him but at the door Dr. Shane had just shouldered his way through. She knew the car ahead was empty, and the locomotive was just beyond. She felt a little chill, because there had been no sign of the conductor since before the avalanche. Wouldn't he have hurried back to the only occupied passenger car to see if there were any injuries, if he wasn't hurt himself? And what about the engineer?

Suddenly she knew she had to follow Dr. Shane. Had to know, for her own sanity, just how dire the situation truly was. She moved to hand the baby girl to Whitley, but he shrank back as if she'd offered him a hissing rattlesnake in a peck basket.

Miffed, Lizzie took the child back to Mrs. Halifax, placed her gently on the woman's lap, tucked the quilt into place again. The peddler and the soldier were seated together now, playing a card game of some sort on the top of the sample case. The old gentleman left Woodrow in his wife's care and stood. "Is there anything I can do?" he asked, of everyone in general.

Lizzie didn't answer, but simply gave the old man a grateful smile and headed for the locomotive.

"Where are you going?" Whitley asked peevishly, as she passed.

She didn't bother to reply.

A cold wind knifed through her as she stepped out of the passenger car, and she could barely see for the snow, coming down furiously now, arching over the top of the train in an ominous canopy. The next car lay on its side, the heavy iron coupling once linking it to its counterpart snapped cleanly in two.

Lizzie considered retreating, but in the end a desperate need to know the full scope of their predicament overrode common prudence. She climbed carefully to the ground, using the ice-coated ladder affixed to one end of the car, and stooped to peer inside the overturned car.

It was an eerie sight, with the seats jutting out sideways. She uttered a soft prayer of gratitude that no one had been riding in that part of the train and crawled inside. Clutching the edge of the open luggage rack to her left, she straightened and crossed the car by stepping from the side of one seat to the next.

Finally, she reached the other door and steeled herself to go through the whole ordeal of climbing to the ground and reentering all over again.

The locomotive was upright, however, and the snow was packed so tightly between the two cars that it made a solid path. Lizzie moved across, longing for her fancy new coat, and stepped inside the engine room.

Steam huffed forlornly from the disabled boiler.

The conductor lay on the floor, the engineer beside him.

Dr. Shane, crouching between them, looked up at Lizzie with such a confounded expression on his face that, had things not been at such a grave pass, she would have laughed.

"You *said* you might need my help," she pointed out.

Dr. Shane snapped his medical bag closed, stood. He looked so glum that Lizzie knew without asking that the two men on the floor of the locomotive were either dead or mortally wounded.

Tears burned in her eyes as she imagined their families, preparing for Yuletide celebrations, unaware, as yet, that their eagerly awaited loved ones would never return.

"It was quick," Dr. Shane said, standing in front of her now, placing a hand on her shoulder. "Did you know them?"

Lizzie shook her head, struggling to compose herself. Her grandfather's deep voice echoed in her mind.

Keep your backbone straight—

"Were they—were they lying there, side by side like that?" It was a strange question, she knew that, even as she asked. Perhaps she was still in shock, after all. "When you found them, I mean?"

"I moved them," the doctor answered, "once I knew they were both gone."

Lizzie nodded. Just the act of standing up straight and squaring her shoulders made her feel a little better.

A slight, grim smile lifted the corner of Dr. Shane's finely-shaped mouth. "These rescuers you're expecting," he said. "If they're anything like you, we might have some hope of surviving after all."

Lizzie's heart ached. What she wouldn't have given to be at home on the Triple M at that moment, with her family all around her. There would be a big, fragrant tree in the parlor at the main ranch house, shimmering with tinsel. Dear, familiar voices, talking, laughing, singing. "Of course we'll survive," she heard herself say. Then she looked at the dead men again, and a lump lodged in her throat, so she had to swallow and then ratchet her chin up another notch before she could go on. "Most of us, anyway. My papa, my uncles, even my grandfather—they'll all come, as soon as they get word that the train didn't arrive."

"All of them McKettricks, I suppose."

Lizzie nodded again, shivering now. The boiler wasn't putting out any heat at all. Most likely, the smoke stack was full of snow. "They'll get through. You wait and see. Nothing stops a McKettrick, especially when there's trouble."

"I believe you, Miss McKettrick," he said.

"You must call me Lizzie," she replied, without thinking. He had, though only once, and she needed the normality of her given name. Just the sound of it gave her strength.

"Lizzie, then," Dr. Shane answered. "If you'll call me Morgan."

"Morgan," she repeated, feeling bewildered again.

He went back to the bodies, gently removed the conductor's coat, then laid it over Lizzie's shoulders. She shuddered inside it, at once grateful and repulsed.

"Let's get back to the others," Morgan said quietly. "There's nothing more we can do here."

Their progress was slow and arduous, but when they returned to the other car, someone had lighted lanterns, and the place had a reassuring glow. Most of the passengers seemed to have regained their composure. Even Woodrow had ceased his fussing; he peered alertly through the bars of his cage, his snow-white feathers smooth.

Whitley had emptied his flask and either passed out or gone to sleep, snoring loudly, clinging possessively to his blanket even in a state of unconsciousness.

"I'd better take a look at him," Morgan said ruefully, stopping by Whitley's seat and opening his kit, pulling a stethoscope from inside. "My preliminary diagnosis is pampering by an overprotective mother or a bevy of fussy aunts or spinster sisters, complicated by a fondness for strong spirits. I've been wrong before, though." But not very often, he might have added, if his tone was anything to go by.

Lizzie could not decide whether she liked this man or not. He certainly wasn't one to remain on the sidelines in a crisis, which was a point in his favor, but there was a suggestion of impatient arrogance about him, too. Clearly, he did not suffer fools lightly.

She approached the Halifax family and found them still burrowed down in the faded quilt. The peddler had lighted another cigar, and the soldier was on his feet, trying to see out into the night. Darkness, snow and the reflected light of the lanterns on the window glass made it pretty much impossible, but Lizzie understood his need to be doing something.

"Some Christmas this is going to be," he said, turning when Lizzie came to thank him for giving up his quilt to Mrs. Halifax and her little ones. "Nothing to eat, and it'll get colder and colder in here, you'll see."

"We'll need to keep our spirits up," Lizzie replied. "And expect the best." Lorelei said things generally turned out the way folks *expected* them to, Lizzie recalled, so it was important to maintain an optimistic state of mind.

"Reckon we ought to do both them things," the soldier

said, his narrow, good-natured and plain face earnest as he regarded Lizzie. "But it wouldn't hurt to prepare for some rough times, either." He smiled, put out a hand. "John Brennan, private first class, United States Army," he said.

"Lizzie McKettrick," Lizzie replied, accepting the handshake. His palm and fingers felt dry and hot against her skin. Did he have a fever? "Do you live in Indian Rock, Mr. Brennan? I grew up on the Triple M, and I don't think I've ever seen you before."

"My wife's folks opened a mercantile there, six months ago. I was in an army hospital, back in Maryland, laid up with typhoid fever and the damage it done, for most of a year, so my Alice took our little boy and moved in with her mama and daddy to wait for my discharge." Sadness flickered in his eyes. "Reckon my boy's all het up about it bein' almost Christmas and all, and lookin' for me to walk through the front door any minute now."

Lizzie sat down in the aisle seat, and John Brennan lowered himself back into the one beside the window. Lorelei had written her about the new mercantile, pleased that they carried a selection of fine watercolors and good paper, among other luxuries, along with the usual coffee, dungarees, nails and tobacco products. "What's your boy's name?" she asked, "And how old is he?"

"He's called Tad, for his grandpappy," Mr. Brennan said proudly. "He turned four last Thursday. I was hoping to be home in time for the cake and candles, but my discharge papers didn't come through in time."

Lizzie smiled, thinking of her younger brothers. They'd be excited about Christmas, and probably watching the road for their big sister, even though they'd surely been told she'd arrive tomorrow. She consulted the watch pinned to her bodice; it was almost three o'clock. The train wasn't due in Indian Rock until six-fifteen.

She imagined her grandfather waiting impatiently in the small depot, right on time, hectoring the ticket clerk for news, ranting that in his day, everybody traveled by stagecoach, and by God, the coaches had been a hell of a lot more reliable than the railroad.

Shyly, John Brennan patted her hand. "I guess you've got home-folks waitin', too," he said.

Lizzie nodded. "Will you be working at the mercantile?" she asked, just to keep the conversation going. It was a lot less lonely that way. And a lot easier than thinking about the very real possibility of another avalanche, sending the whole train toppling over the cliff.

"Much as I'm able," Mr. Brennan replied. "Can't do any of the heavy work, loading and unloading freight wagons and such, but I've got me a head for figures. I can balance the books and keep track of the inventory."

"I'll be teaching at Indian Rock School when it reopens after New Year's," she said.

Mr. Brennan beamed. He was one of those homely people who turn handsome when they smile. "In a couple of years, you'll have my Tad in first grade," he said. "Me and Alice, we place great store by book learnin' and such. Never got much of it myself, as you can probably tell by listenin' to me talk, but I learnt some arithmetic in the army. Tad, now, he'll go to school and make something of himself."

Lizzie remembered how Mr. Brennan had given his quilt to Mrs. Halifax, even though he was obviously susceptible to the cold. He'd wasted during his confinement, so that his uniform hung on his frame, and plans to help out at the mercantile or no, he might be a semi-invalid for a long time.

"If Tad is anything like his father," she said, "he'll do just fine."

Brennan flushed with modest pleasure. Sobered when he glanced toward the front of the train, where Whitley was awake again and complaining to Dr. Shane, who looked as though he'd like to throttle him. "Is that your brother?" he asked.

"Just someone I knew in San Francisco," Lizzie said, suddenly sad. The Whitley she'd thought she'd known so well had been replaced by a petulant impostor. She grieved for the man she'd imagined him to be—the young engineer, with great plans to build dams and bridges, the cavalier suitor with the fetching smile.

Morgan left Whitley and came back down the aisle. "I'm going out and have a look around," he said, addressing John Brennan instead of Lizzie. "If I don't come back, don't come searching for me."

Lizzie stood up. "You can't go out there alone," she protested.

Morgan laid his hands on her shoulders and pressed her back into the hard, soot-blackened seat. "Mrs. Halifax might need you," he said. "Or the children. Or the old folks—the husband has a bluish tinge around his lips, and I'm worried about his heart." He paused, nodded toward Whitley. "God knows, that sniveling yahoo up there in the blanket won't be any help."

The peddler opened his sample case again, brought out a pint of whiskey, offered it to Morgan. "You may have need of this," he said. "It's mighty cold out there."

Morgan took the bottle, put it in the inside pocket of his coat. "Thanks."

"At least take one of the lanterns," Lizzie said, anxious wings fluttering in her stomach, as though she'd swallowed a miniature version of Woodrow.

"I'll do that," Morgan answered.

"Here's my hat," Mr. Brennan said, holding out his army cap. "It ain't much, but it's better than going bare-headed."

"I have a scarf," Lizzie fretted. "It's in my handbag—"

Morgan donned the cap. It looked incongruous indeed, with his worn-out suit, but it covered the tops of his ears. "I'll be fine," he insisted. He went back up the aisle, leaving his medical kit behind, and out through the door at the other end.

Lizzie watched for the glow of his lantern through the window, found it, lost track of it again. Her heart sank. Suppose he never came back? There were so many things that could happen out there in the frigid darkness, so full of the furious blizzard.

"I don't think your interest in the good doctor is entirely proper," a familiar voice said.

Lizzie looked up, mildly startled, and saw Whitley standing unsteadily in the aisle, glowering down at her. His cheeks were flushed, his eyes glazed.

"Be quiet," she said.

"We have an understanding, you and I," Whitley reminded her.

"I quite understand *you*, Whitley," Lizzie retorted, "but I don't think the reverse is true. Unless you mean to make yourself useful in some way, I'd rather you left me alone."

Whitley was just forming his reply when the whole car shuddered again, listed slightly cliffward, and caught. The peddler shouted a curse. Mr. Brennan launched into the Lord's Prayer. Mrs. Halifax gave a soblike gasp, and her children shrieked in chorus. Woodrow squawked and sidestepped along his perch, and the elderly couple clung to each other.

"We're all right," Lizzie said, surprising herself by how serenely she spoke. Inside, she was terrified. "Nobody move."

"Seems to me," observed the peddler, having recovered a

modicum of composure, "that we'd all better sit on the other side of the car."

"Good idea," Lizzie agreed.

Whitley took a seat very slowly, his face a ghastly white. Lizzie, the peddler, and John Brennan crossed the aisle carefully to settle in. So did the old folks and Woodrow.

Outside, the wind howled, and Lizzie thought she could feel the heartbeat of the looming mountain itself, ponderous and utterly impersonal.

Where was Morgan Shane?

Lost in the impenetrable snow? Buried under it?

Fallen into one of the treacherous crevasses for which the high country was well known?

Lizzie wanted to cry, but she knew it was an indulgence she couldn't afford. So she cleared her throat and began to sing, in a soft, tremulous voice, "'God rest ye merry gentlemen, let nothing you dismay...'"

Slowly, tentatively, the others joined in.

Chapter Two

Morgan hadn't intended to wander far from the train—he'd meant to keep the lantern-light from the windows in view—but the storm was worse than he'd thought. Cursing himself for a fool, his own lantern having guttered and subsequently been tossed aside, he stood with the howling wind stinging his ears, bare hands shoved into the pockets of his inadequate coat. It was as though a veil had descended; he not only couldn't see the glow of the lamps, he couldn't see the train. All sense of direction deserted him—he might be a step from toppling over the rim of the cliff.

Be rational, he told himself. *Think.*

For the briefest moment the wind collapsed to a whisper, as though drawing another breath to blow again, and he heard a faint sound, a snatch of singing.

He pressed toward it, blinded by the pelting snow, blinked to clear his eyes and glimpsed the light shining through the train windows. Seconds later he collided hard against the side of the railroad car. Feeling his way along it, grateful even for the scorching cold of bare metal under his palms, he found the door.

Stiff-handed, he managed to open it and veritably *fall* inside. He dropped to his knees, steadied himself by grasping the arm rest of the nearest seat. His lungs burned, and the numbness began to recede from his hands and feet and face, leaving intense pain in its wake.

Frostbite? Suppose he lost his fingers? What good was a doctor and sometime surgeon without fingers?

He hauled himself to his feet and found himself face-to-face with a wide-eyed Lizzie McKettrick. He could have tumbled into the blue of those eyes; it seemed fathomless. She draped something around him—a blanket or a quilt or perhaps a cloak—and boldly burrowed into his coat pocket, brought out the pint the peddler had given him earlier.

Pulling the cork, she raised the bottle to his lips and commanded, "Drink this!"

He managed a couple of fiery swallows, waved away the bottle. His vision began to clear, and the thrumming in his ears abated a little. With a chuckle he ran a shaky forearm across his mouth. "If you have any kindness in your soul," he said laboriously, "you will not say 'I told you so.'"

"Very well," Lizzie replied briskly, "but I *did* tell you so, didn't I?"

He laughed. Not that anything was funny. He'd seen little on his foray into the blizzard, but he *had* confirmed a few of his worst suspicions. The car was off the tracks, and tipping with dangerous delicacy away from the mountainside. And *nobody*, McKettrick or not, was going to get through that weather.

If any of them survived, it would be a true miracle.

★ ★ ★

Once Morgan stopped shivering, Lizzie returned the quilt to Mrs. Halifax and went forward again to sit with him. Whitley glared at her as she passed his seat.

She'd gotten used to wearing the conductor's coat by then; even though it smelled of coal smoke and sweat, it was warm. She considered offering it to Morgan, but she knew he would refuse, so she didn't make the gesture.

"I heard you singing," Morgan said, somewhat distractedly, when she sat down beside him. "That's how I found my way back. I heard you singing."

Moved, Lizzie touched his hand tentatively, then covered it with her own. His skin felt like ice, and his clothes were damp. Once he dozed off, not that he was in any condition to stop her even then, she'd make her way back to the baggage car. Raid her trunks and crates, and Whitley's, too, for dry garments. And the freight car might contain food, matches, even blankets.

Lizzie's stomach rumbled. None of them had eaten since their brief stop in Flagstaff, hours before, and she'd picked at her leathery meat loaf and overcooked green beans. Left most of it behind. Now she would have devoured the sorry fare happily and ordered a cup of strong, steaming coffee.

Coffee.

Suddenly, she yearned for the stuff, generously laced with cream and sugar—and a good splash of brandy.

Morgan's fingers curled around hers, squeezed lightly. "Lizzie?"

"I was just thinking of hot coffee," she confessed, keeping her voice down, "and food. Do you suppose there might be food in the freight car?"

He grinned at her. "I watched you in the restaurant at the

depot today," he said. "You barely touched your meat loaf special."

"You were watching me?" She found the idea at once disturbing and titillating.

"Hard not to," Morgan said. "You're a very good-looking woman, Lizzie. I did wonder, I confess, about your taste in traveling companions."

Lizzie felt color warm her cheeks, and for once, she welcomed it. Every other part of her was cold. "You seem to have formed a very immediate, and very poor, impression of Mr. Carson."

"I'm a good judge of character," he replied. "Mr. Carson doesn't seem to have one, as far as I've been able to discern."

"How could you possibly have reached such a conclusion merely by *looking* at him in a busy train depot?"

"He didn't pull back your chair for you when you sat down," Morgan went on, his tone just shy of smug. "And you paid the bill. It only took a glance to see those things—I saved the active looking for you."

"Mr. Carson," Lizzie said, mildly mortified, "is making this journey as my *guest*. That's why I paid for his meal. He is, I assure you, quite solvent."

"Planning to parade him past the McKettricks?" Morgan teased, after a capitulating grin. "I've only met one of them—Kade—a few weeks ago, in Tucson. He told me Indian Rock needed a doctor and offered me an office in the Arizona Hotel and plenty of patients if I'd come and set up a practice. Didn't strike me as the sort to be impressed by the likes of Mr. Carson."

All kinds of protests were brewing in Lizzie's bosom, but the mention of her uncle's name stopped her as surely as the avalanche had stopped the train. Though she wasn't about to admit it, Morgan's guess was probably correct. Kade, like all the other McKettrick men, judged people by their actions rather than their words. Whitley could talk fit to charm a mockingbird out of its tree, but he plainly wasn't much for pushing up his sleeves and *doing* something about a situation. There was no denying that.

"I'm afraid you're right," Lizzie conceded, bereft.

Morgan squeezed her hand again.

The wind lashed at the train from the side that wasn't snow-bound, rocked it ominously back and forth. Lizzie spoke again, needing to fill the silence.

"Did you practice medicine in Tucson?" she asked.

Morgan shook his head. "Chicago," he said, and then went quiet again.

"Are you going to make me do all the talking?" Lizzie demanded after an interval, feeling fretful.

That smile tilted the corner of his mouth again. "I'm no orator, Lizzie."

"Just tell me something about yourself. Anything. I'm pretty scared right now, and if you don't hold up your end of the conversation, I'll probably prattle until your ears fall off."

He chuckled. It was a richly masculine sound. "All right," he said. "My name, as you already know, is Morgan Shane. I'm twenty-eight years old. I was born and raised in Chicago—no brothers or sisters. My father was a doctor, and that's why I became one. He studied in Berlin after graduating from Harvard, since, in his opinion, American medical schools were deplorable. So I went to Germany, too. I've never been married, though I came close once—her name was Rosalee. I practiced with my father until he died—probably would have stayed put, except for a falling-out with my mother. I decided to move west, and wound up in Tucson."

It was more information than Lizzie had dared hope for, and she felt her eyes widen. "What happened to Rosalee?"

she asked, a little breathless, for she had a weakness for romance. Whenever she got the chance, she read love stories and sighed over the heroes. The woman must have died tragically, thereby breaking Morgan's heart and turning him into a wanderer, and perhaps the experience explained his terse way of speaking, too.

"She decided she'd rather be a doctor than a doctor's wife and went off to Berlin to study for a degree of her own. Or was it Vienna? I forget."

Lizzie's mouth fell open.

Morgan grinned again. "I'm teasing you, Lizzie. She eloped with a man who worked in the accounts receivable department at Sears and Roebuck."

She peered at him, skeptical.

He laughed. "Your turn," he said. "What do you plan to do with your life, Lizzie McKettrick?"

"I mean to teach in Indian Rock," Lizzie said, suddenly wishing she had a more interesting occupation to describe. A trapeze artist, perhaps, or a painter of stately portraits. A noble nurse, bravely battling all manner of dramatic diseases.

"Until you marry and start having babies."

Lizzie was rattled all over again. What *was* it about Morgan Shane that both nettled her and piqued her interest? "My uncle Jeb's wife is a teacher," she said defensively. "They have four children, and Chloe still holds classes in the country school house he built for her with his own hands." Jack and Ellen, living on the Triple M, would attend Chloe's classes, because the distance to town was too great to travel every day.

Morgan's eyes darkened a little as he assessed her, or seemed to. Maybe it was just a trick of the light. "How does Mr. Carson fit into all this?"

Lizzie sighed. Looked back over one shoulder to make sure

Whitley wasn't eavesdropping. Instead he'd gone back to sleep.

"I thought I wanted to marry him," she answered, in a whisper.

"Why?"

"Well, because it seemed like a good idea, I guess. I'm almost twenty. I'd like to start a family of my own."

"While continuing to teach?"

"Of course," Lizzie said. "I know what you think—that I'll have to choose one or the other. But I don't have to choose."

"Because you're a McKettrick?"

Again, Lizzie's cheeks warmed. "Yes," she said, quite tartly. "Because I'm a McKettrick." She huffed out a frustrated breath. "And because I'm strong and smart and I can do more than one thing well. No one would think of asking *you* when you'd give up being a doctor and start keeping house and mending stockings, if you decided to get married, would they?"

"That's different, Lizzie."

"No, it isn't."

He settled back against the seat, closed his eyes. "I think I'm going to like Indian Rock," he said. And then he went to sleep, leaving Lizzie even more confounded than before.

"I have to use the chamber pot," a small voice whispered, startling Lizzie out of a restless doze. "And I can't find one."

Opening her eyes, Lizzie turned her head and saw the little Halifax girl standing in the aisle beside her. The last of the lanterns had gone out, and the car was frigid, but the blizzard had stopped, and a strangely beautiful bluish light seemed to rise from the glittering snow. Everyone else seemed to be asleep.

Recalling the spittoon she'd seen at the back of the car, Lizzie stood and took the child's chilly hand. "This way," she whispered.

The business completed, the little girl righted her calico skirts and said solemnly, "Thanks."

"You're welcome," Lizzie replied softly. She could have used a chamber pot herself, right about then, but she wasn't about to use the spittoon. She escorted the child back to her seat, tucked part of Mr. Brennan's quilt around her.

"We have to get home," the little girl said, her eyes big in the gloom. "St. Nicholas won't be able to find us out here in the wilderness, and Papa promised me I'd get a doll this year because I've been so good. When Mama had to tie a string to my tooth to pull it, I didn't even cry." She hooked a finger into one corner of her small mouth to show Lizzie the gap. "Schee?" she asked.

Lizzie's heart swelled into her throat. She looked with proper awe upon the vacant spot between two other teeth, shook her head. Wanting to gather the child into her arms and hold her tightly, she restrained herself. Children were skittish creatures. "I think *I* would have cried, if I had one of *my* teeth pulled," she said seriously. She'd actually seen that particular extraction process several times, back on the ranch—it was a brutal business but tried and true. And usually quick.

"My papa works on the Triple M now," the little girl went on proudly. "He just got hired, and he's foreman, too. That means we get our own house to live in. It has a fireplace and a real floor, and Mama says we can hang up Papa's socks, if he has any clean ones, he's been batching so long, and St. Nicholas will put an orange in the toe. One for me, and one for Jack, and one for Nellie Anne."

Lizzie nodded, still choked up, but smiling gamely. "Your brother is Jack," she said, marking the names in her memory by repeating them aloud, "and the baby is Nellie Anne. What, then, is *your* name?"

The small shoulders straightened. "Ellen Margaret Halifax."

Lizzie put out a hand in belated introduction. "Since I'll be your teacher, you should probably call me Miss McKettrick," she said.

"Ellen," Mrs. Halifax called, in a sleepy whisper, "you'll freeze standing there in the aisle. Come get back under the quilt."

Ellen obeyed readily, and soon gave herself up to dreams. From the slight smile resting on her mouth, Lizzie suspected the child's imagination had carried her home to the foreman's house on the Triple M, where she was hanging up a much-darned stocking in anticipation of a rare treat—an orange.

Having once awakened, Lizzie found she could not go back to sleep.

The baggage and freight cars beckoned.

Morgan, the one person who might have stopped her from venturing out of the passenger car, slumbered on.

Resolutely, Lizzie buttoned up the conductor's coat, extracted a scarf from her hand luggage and tied it tightly under her chin, in order to protect her ears from a cold she knew would be merciless.

Once ready, she crept to the back of the car, struggled with the door, winced when it made a slight creaking sound. A quick glance back over one shoulder reassured her. None of the other passengers stirred.

The cold, as she had expected, bit into her flesh like millions of tiny teeth, but the snow had stopped coming down, and she could see clearly in the light of the moon. The car was still linked to the one behind it, and both remained upright.

Shivering on the tiny metal platform between the two cars, Lizzie risked a glance toward the cliff and was alarmed to see how close the one she'd just left had come to pitching over the edge.

Her heart pounded; for a moment she considered rushing back to awaken the others, herd them into the baggage car, which was, at least, still sitting on the tracks.

But would the second car be any safer?

It was too cold to stand there deliberating. She shoved open the next door. They would all be better able to deal with the crisis if she found food, blankets, *anything* to keep body and soul together until help arrived.

And help *would* arrive. Her father and uncles were probably on their way even then. The question was, would they get there before there was another snowslide, before everyone perished from the unrelenting cold?

Lizzie found her own three steamer trunks, each of them nearly large enough for her to stand up inside, stacked one on top of the other. A pang struck her. Papa had teased her mercilessly about traveling with so much luggage. *You'd never make it on a cattle drive,* he'd said.

God, how she missed Holt McKettrick in that moment. His strength, his common sense, his innate ability to deal ably with whatever adversity dared present itself.

Think, Lizzie, she told herself. *Fretting is useless.*

Chewing on her lower lip, she pondered. Of course the coat and her other woolen garments were in the red trunk, and it was on the bottom. If she dislodged the other two— which would be a Herculean feat in its own right, involving much climbing and a lot of pushing—would the inevitable jolts send the passenger car, so precariously tilted, plummeting to the bottom of the ravine?

She decided to proceed to the freight car and think about the trunks on the way back. It was very possible, after all, that orders of blankets and coats and stockings and—please, God, *food*—might be found there, originally destined for the mercantile in Indian Rock, thus alleviating the need to rummage through her trunks.

Getting into the freight car proved impossible—the door was frozen shut, and no amount of kicking, pounding and latch wrenching availed. She finally lowered herself to the ground, by means of another small ladder, and the snow came up under her skirts to soak through her woolen bloomers and sting her thighs. She was perilously close to the edge, too—one slip and she would slide helplessly down the steep bank.

At least the hard work of moving at all warmed her a bit. Clinging to the side of the car with both hands, she made her precarious way along it. Her feet gave way once, and only her numb grip on the iron edging at the base of the car kept her from tumbling to her death.

After what seemed like hours, she reached the rear of the freight car. Somewhere in the thinning darkness, a wolf howled, the sound echoing inside Lizzie, ancient and forlorn.

Buck up, she ordered herself. *Keep going.*

Behind the freight car was the caboose, painted a cheery red. And, glory be, a *chimney* jutted from its roof. Where there was a chimney, there was a stove, and where there was a stove—

Blessed warmth.

Forgoing the freight car for the time being, Lizzie decided to explore the caboose instead.

She had to wade through more snow, and nearly lost her footing again, but when she got to the door, it opened easily. She slipped inside, breathless, teeth chattering. Somewhere along the way, she'd lost her scarf, so her ears throbbed with cold, fit to fall right off her head.

There *was* a stove, a squat, pot-bellied one, hardly larger than the kettle Lorelei used for rendering lard at home. And on top of that stove, miraculously still in place after the jarring impact of the avalanche, stood a coffee pot. Peering inside a small cupboard near the stove, she saw a few precious provisions—a tin of coffee, a bag of sugar, a wedge of yellow cheese.

Lizzie gave a ranch-girl whoop, then slapped a hand over

her mouth. Raised in the high country from the time she was twelve, she knew that when the snow was so deep, any sudden sound could bring most of the mountainside thundering down on top of them. She listened, too scared to breathe, for an ominous rumble overhead, but none came.

She assessed the long, benchlike seats lining the sides of the car. Room for everyone to lie down and sleep.

Yes, the caboose would do nicely.

She forced herself to go outside again—even the sight of that stove, cold as it was, had warmed her a little. The freight car proved as impenetrable from the rear door as from the first one Lizzie had tried, but she was much heartened, just the same. Morgan, Whitley and the peddler would be able to get inside.

She was making her way back along the side of the train, every step carefully considered, both hands grasping the side, when it happened.

Her feet slipped, her stomach gave a dull lurch, and she felt herself falling.

She slid a few feet, managed to catch hold of a tree root, the tree itself long gone. Fear sent the air whooshing from her lungs, as if she'd been struck in the solar plexus, and she knew her grip would not last long. She had almost no feeling in her hands, and her feet dangled in midair. She did not dare turn her head and look down.

"Help me!" she called out, in a voice that sounded laughably cheerful, given the circumstances.

Morgan's head appeared above her, a genie sprung from a lamp. "Hold on," he told her grimly, "and *do not* move."

She watched, blinking salty moisture from her eyes, as he unbuckled his belt, pulled it free of his trousers and fashioned a loop at one end. He lay down on his belly and tossed the looped end of the belt within reach.

"Listen to me, Lizzie," he said very quietly. "Take a few breaths before you reach for the belt. You can't afford to miss."

Lizzie didn't even nod, so tenuous was her hold on the root. She took the advised breaths, even closed her eyes for a moment, imagined herself standing on firm ground. Safe with Morgan.

If she could just get to Morgan....

"Ready?" he asked.

"Yes," she said. Still clinging to the root, which was already giving way, with one hand, she grasped the leather loop with the other. Morgan's strength seemed to surge along the length of it.

"I've got you, Lizzie," Morgan said. "Take hold with the other hand."

After another deep breath, she let go of the root.

Morgan pulled her up slowly, and very carefully. When she crested the bank, he hauled her into his arms and held her hard, both of them kneeling only inches from the lip of the cliff.

"Easy, now," he murmured, his breath warming her right ear. "No sudden moves."

Lizzie nodded slightly, her face buried in his shoulder, clinging to the fabric of his coat with both hands.

Morgan rose carefully to his feet, bringing Lizzie with him.

"The caboose," she said, trembling all over. "There's a stove in the caboose—and a c-coffeepot."

He took her there. Seated her none too gently on one of the long seats. "What the *hell* were you thinking?" he demanded, moving to the stove, stuffing in kindling and old newspaper from the half-filled wood box, striking a match to start a blaze.

"I was looking for food...blankets—"

Morgan gave her a scathing look. Took the coffeepot off the stove and went out the rear door of the caboose. When he came back, Lizzie saw that he'd filled the pot with snow. He set it on the stove with an eloquent clunk. "You could have been killed!" he rasped, pale with fury.

"How did you know to...to come looking for me?"

"John Brennan woke me up. Said he'd seen you leave the car. At first, he thought he was dreaming, because nobody would do anything that stupid."

"*You* left the car," Lizzie reminded him. "What's the difference?"

"The *difference,* Lizzie McKettrick, is that you are a woman and I am a man. And don't you *dare* get up on a soapbox. If I hadn't come along when I did, you'd be at the bottom of that ravine by now. And it was the grace of—whoever—that we didn't *both* go over!"

He found a tin of coffee among the provisions, spooned some into the pot, right on top of the snow.

Lizzie realized that he'd put himself in no little danger to pull her to safety. "Thank you," she said, with a peculiar mixture of graciousness and chagrin.

"I'm not ready to say 'you're welcome,'" he snapped. "Leaving that car, especially alone, was a damnably foolish thing to do."

"If you expect an apology, Dr. Shane, you will be sorely disappointed. Someone had to do something."

The fire crackled merrily in the stove, and a little heat began to radiate into the frosty caboose. Morgan reached up to adjust the damper, still seething.

"Don't talk," he advised, sounding surly.

Lizzie straightened her spine. "Of course I'm going to talk," she told him pertly. "I have things to say. We need to bring everyone from the passenger car. It's safer here—and warmer."

"*We* aren't going to do anything. *You* are going to stay put, and *I* will go back for the others." He leveled a long look at her. "So help me God, Lizzie, if you set foot outside this caboose—"

She smiled, getting progressively warmer, catching the first delicious scent of brewing coffee. She'd probably imagined that part, she decided.

"Why, Dr. Shane," she mocked sweetly, batting her eyelashes, "I wouldn't *think* of disobeying a strong, capable man like you."

Suddenly he laughed. Some of the tension between them, until that moment tight as a rope with an obstreperous calf running full out at the other end, slackened.

It gave Lizzie an odd feeling, not unlike dangling over the side of a cliff with only a root to hold on to and the jaws of a ravine yawning below.

She blushed. Then her practical side reemerged. "I tried the door on the freight car," she said. "But I couldn't get in. If we're lucky, there might be food inside."

"Oh, we're lucky, all right," Morgan responded, his amusement fading as reality overtook him again. The sun was coming up, and Lizzie knew as well as he did that even its thin, wintry warmth might thaw some of the snow looming over their heads, set it to sliding again. "We're lucky we're alive." He studied her for a long moment. Then he snapped, "Wait here."

Frankly not brave enough to risk another plunge over the cliff-side, McKettrick or not, Lizzie waited. Waited when he left. Waited for the coffee to brew.

He brought the baby first.

Lizzie held little Nellie Anne and bit her lip, waiting.

Next came Jack, riding wide-eyed on Morgan's shoulders, his little hands clasped tightly under the doctor's chin.

After that, Mrs. Halifax. Her arm still in its sling, she fairly collapsed, once safely inside the caboose. Lizzie immediately got up to fill a coffee mug and hand it to the other woman. Mrs. Halifax trembled visibly as she drank, her two older children clutching at her skirts.

Whitley appeared, having made his own way, scowling. Still clutching his blanket, he looked even more like an overgrown child than before. When Mrs. Halifax gave him a turn with the cup, he added a generous dollop from his flask and glared at Lizzie while he drank. She'd seen him empty the vessel earlier; perhaps he had a spare bottle in his valise.

She did her best to ignore him, but it was hard, since he seemed determined to make his stormy presence felt.

The peddler arrived next, escorting the old woman, his jowls red with the cold. He'd brought his sample case, too, and he immediately produced a cup of his own, from the case, and poured a cup of coffee at the stove. "Hell of a Christmas," he boomed, to the company in general, understandably cheered by the warmth from the fire and probably dizzy with relief at having made the treacherous journey between cars unscathed. He gave the cup to the elderly lady, who took it with fluttery hands and quiet gratitude.

Finally, John Brennan came, on his feet but supported by Morgan. The old man accompanied them, carrying Woodrow's covered cage.

The peddler, after flashing a glance Whitley's way, conjured more cups from his sample case, shiny new mugs coated in blue enamel, and gave them to the newer arrivals.

"I'm starving," Whitley said petulantly. "Is there any food?"

"Starving!" Woodrow commented from his cage.

The grin Morgan turned on Whitley was anything but cordial. "I thought maybe we could count on you, hero that you are, to hike out with a rifle and bag some wild game," he said.

Whitley reddened, looked for a moment as though he might fling aside the coffee mug he was hogging and go for Morgan's throat. Apparently, he thought better of it, though, for he remained seated, taking up more than his share of room on the benchlike seat opposite Lizzie. Muttered something crude into his coffee.

Lizzie stood, approached Morgan. "I was thinking if we could find a way to—well, *unhook* this car from the next—"

"Stop thinking," Morgan interrupted. "It only gets you in trouble."

Lizzie felt as though she'd been slapped. "But—"

Morgan softened, but only slightly. Regarded her over the rim of his steaming coffee. "Lizzie," he said, more gently, "it's a question of weight. As shaky as our situation is, if we uncoupled the cars, we'd be *more* vulnerable, separated from the rest of the train, not less."

He was right, which only made his words harder for Lizzie to swallow. She averted her eyes, only to have her gaze land accidentally on Whitley. He was smirking at her.

She lifted her chin, turned away from both Whitley and Morgan, and set about helping Mrs. Halifax make a bed for the children, using John Brennan's quilt. That done, she turned to the elderly couple.

Their names were Zebulon and Marietta Thaddings, Lizzie soon learned; they lived in Phoenix, but Mrs. Thaddings's sister worked in Indian Rock, and they'd intended to surprise her with a holiday visit. Having no one to look after Woodrow in their absence, they'd brought him along.

"He's a good bird," Mrs. Thaddings said sweetly. "No trouble at all."

Lizzie smiled at that. "Perhaps I know your sister," she said.

Mrs. Thaddings beamed. "Perhaps you do," she agreed. "Her name is Clarinda Adams, and she runs a dressmaking business."

Lizzie felt a pitching sensation in the pit of her stomach.

There was no dressmaker in Indian Rock, but there *was* a very exclusive "gentleman's club," and Miss Clarinda Adams ran it. Cowboys could not afford what was on offer in Miss Adams's notorious establishment, but prosperous ranchers, railroad executives and others of that ilk flocked to the place from miles around to drink imported brandy, play high-stakes poker and dandle saucy women on their knees.

Oh, Miss Adams was going to be surprised, all right, when the Thaddingses appeared on her doorstep, with a talking bird in tow. But the Thaddingses would be even more so.

Lizzie felt a flash of mingled pity and amusement. She patted Mrs. Thaddings's hand, still chilled from the perilous journey from one railroad car to another, and offered to refill her coffee cup.

Once they'd finished off the coffee and started a second pot to brewing, Morgan and the peddler set out to break into and raid the freight car.

As soon as they were gone, Whitley approached Lizzie, planted himself directly in front of her.

"If I die," he told her, "it will be *your fault*. If you hadn't insisted on bringing me into this wilderness to meet your family—"

Despite a dizzying sting—for there was truth in his words, as well as venom—Lizzie kept her backbone straight, her shoulders back and her chin high. "After staying alive," she said, with what dignity she could summon, "my biggest problem will be *explaining* you to my family."

With a snort of disgust, he turned on one heel and strode to the other side of the car.

And little Ellen tugged at the sleeve of the oversize conductor's coat Lizzie had been wearing since the day before. "Do you think St. Nicholas will know where we are?" she asked, her eyes huge with worry. "Jack's had a mean hankerin' for that orange ever since Mama told us we could hang up stockings this year."

"I'm absolutely certain St. Nicholas will know *precisely* where we are," Lizzie told Ellen, laying a hand on her shoulder. "But we'll be in Indian Rock by Christmas Eve, you'll see."

Would they? Ellen looked convinced. Lizzie, on the other hand, was beginning to have her doubts.

Chapter Three

The caboose, although not much safer than the passenger car, was at least warm. When Morgan and the peddler returned from their foray, they brought four gray woolen blankets, as many tins of canned food, all large, and a box of crackers.

"There was a ham," the peddler blustered, red from the cold and loud with relief to be back within the range of the stove, "but the doc here said it was probably somebody's Christmas dinner, special-ordered, so we oughtn't to help ourselves to it."

Everyone nodded in agreement, including Ellen and Jack, her younger brother. Only Whitley looked unhappy about the decision.

There were no plates and no utensils. Morgan opened the tins with his pocket knife, and they all ate of the contents— peaches, tomatoes, pears and a pale-skinned chicken—forced to use their hands. When the meal was over, Morgan found an old bucket next to the stove and carried in more snow, to be melted on the stove, so they could wash up.

While it was a relief to Lizzie to assuage her hunger, she

was still restless. It was December twenty-third. Her father and uncles must be well on their way to finding the stalled train. She yearned for their arrival, but she was afraid for them, too. The trip from Indian Rock would be a treacherous one, cold and slow and very hard going, most of the way. For the first time it occurred to her that a rescue attempt might not avert calamity but invite it instead. Her loved ones would be putting their lives at risk, venturing out under these conditions.

But venture they would. They were McKettricks, and thus constitutionally incapable of sitting on their hands when somebody—especially one of their own—needed help.

She closed her eyes for a moment, willed herself not to fall apart.

She thought of Christmas preparations going on at the Triple M. There were four different houses on the ranch, and the kitchens would be redolent with stove heat and the smells of good things baking in the ovens.

By now, having expected to meet her at the station in Indian Rock the night before, her grandfather would definitely have raised the alarm....

She started a little when Morgan sat down on the train seat beside her, offered her a cup of coffee. She'd drifted homeward, in her musings, and coming back to a stranded caboose and a lot of strangers was a painful wrench.

She saw that the others were all occupied: John Brennan sleeping with his chin on his chest, Ellen and Jack playing cards with the peddler, Whitley reading a book—he always carried one in the inside pocket of his coat—Mrs. Halifax modestly nursing baby Nellie Anne beneath the draped quilt. Mrs. Thaddings had freed Woodrow from his cage, and he sat obediently on her right shoulder, a well-behaved and very observant bird, occasionally nibbling a sunflower seed from his mistress's palm.

"Brennan," Morgan told Lizzie wearily, keeping his voice low, "is running a fever."

Lizzie was immediately alarmed. "Is it serious?"

"A fever is *always* serious, Lizzie. He probably took a chill between here and the other car, if not before. From the rattle in his chest, I'd say he's developing pneumonia."

"Dear God," Lizzie whispered, thinking of the little boy, Tad, waiting to welcome his father at their new home in Indian Rock.

"Giving up hope, Lizzie McKettrick?" Morgan asked, very quietly.

She sucked in a breath, shook her head. *"No,"* she said firmly.

Morgan smiled, squeezed her hand. "Good."

Lizzie had seen pneumonia before. While she'd never contracted the dreaded malady herself, she'd known it to snatch away a victim within days or even hours. Concepcion, her stepgrandmother, and Lorelei had often attended the sick around Indian Rock and in the bunkhouses on the Triple M, and Lizzie had kept many a vigil so the older women could rest. "I'll help," she said now, though she wondered where she was going to get the strength. She was young, and she was healthy, but her nerves felt raw, exposed—strained to the snapping point.

"I know," Morgan said, his voice a little gruff. "You would have made a fine nurse, Lizzie."

"I don't have the patience," she replied seriously, wringing her hands. They'd thawed by then, along with all her other extremities, but they ached, deep in the bone. "To be a nurse, I mean."

Morgan arched one dark eyebrow. "Teaching doesn't require patience?" he asked, smiling.

Lizzie found a small laugh hiding somewhere inside her,

and allowed it to escape. It came out as a ragged chuckle. "I see your point," she admitted. She turned her head, saw Ellen and Jack enjoying their game with the peddler, and smiled. "I love children," she said softly. "I love the way their faces light up when they've been struggling with some concept and it suddenly comes clear to them. I love the way they laugh from deep down in their middles, the way they smell when they've been playing in summer grass, or rolling in snow—"

"Do you have brothers and sisters, Lizzie?"

"Brothers," she said. "All younger. John Henry—he's deaf and Papa and Lorelei adopted him after his folks were killed in Texas, in an Indian raid. Lorelei, that's my stepmother, sent away for some special books from back east, and taught him to talk with his hands. Then she taught the rest of us, too. Gabe and Doss learned it so fast."

"I'll bet you did, too," Morgan said. By the look in his eyes, Lizzie knew his remark wasn't intended as flattery. Unless she missed her guess, Dr. Morgan Shane had never flattered anyone in his life. "John Henry is a lucky little boy, to be a part of a family like yours."

"We've always thought it was the other way around," Lizzie said. "John Henry is so funny, and so smart. He can ride any horse on the ranch, draw them, too, so you think they'll just step right off the paper and prance around the room, and when he grows up, he means to be a telegraph operator."

"I'm looking forward to meeting him, along with the rest of the McKettricks," Morgan told her. His gaze had strayed to Whitley, narrowed, then swung back to Lizzie's face.

Something deep inside her leaped and pirouetted. Morgan wanted to meet her family. But of course it *wasn't* because he had any personal interest in her. Her uncle Kade had encouraged him to come to Indian Rock to practice medicine, and the McKettricks were leaders in the community. Naturally, as a newcomer to town, Morgan would seek to make their acquaintance. Her heart soaring only moments before, she now felt oddly deflated.

Morgan stood. "I'd better go outside again," he said. "See what I can round up in the way of fuel. What firewood we have isn't going to last long, but there's a fair supply of coal in the locomotive."

Lizzie hated the thought of Morgan braving the dangerous cold again, but she knew he had to do it, and she was equally certain that he wouldn't let her go in his stead. Still, she caught at his hand when he would have walked away, looked up into his face. "How can I help, Morgan?"

His free hand moved, lingered near her cheek, as though he might caress her. But the moment passed, and he did not touch her. "Maybe you could rig up some kind of bed for John, on one of these bench seats," he said quietly. "He used up most of his strength just getting here. He's going to need to lie down soon."

Lizzie nodded, grateful to have something practical to do. Morgan left.

Lizzie sat a moment or so longer, then stood, straightening her spine vertebra by vertebra as she did. Fat flakes of snow drifted past the windows of the train, and the sky was darkening, even though it was only midday.

Papa, she thought. *Hurry. Please, hurry.*

Lizzie made up John Brennan's makeshift bed on one of the benches, as near to the stove as she could while still leaving room for her or Morgan to attend to him. He gave her a grateful look when she awakened him from an uncomfortable sleep and helped him across the car to his new resting place. Using two of the four blankets from the freight car as pillows, she tucked him in between the remaining pair. Laid a hand to his forehead.

His skin was hot as a skillet forgotten over a campfire.

"I could do with some water," he told Lizzie. "My canteen is in my haversack, but it's been empty for a while."

Lizzie nodded. "Dr. Shane brought in some snow a while ago. I'll see if it's melted yet."

"Thank you," Mr. Brennan said. And then he gave a wracking cough that almost bent him double.

"Is he contagious?" Whitley wanted to know. He stood at her elbow, his book dangling in one hand.

"I only wish he were," Lizzie answered coolly. "Then you might catch some of his good manners and his generosity."

"Don't you think we should stop bickering?" Whitley retorted, surprising her. "After all, we're all in danger here, the way that sawbones tells it."

"Are you just realizing that, Whitley?" Lizzie asked. "And Dr. Shane is not a 'sawbones.' He's a *physician,* trained in Berlin."

"Well, huzzah for him," Whitley said bitterly. Apparently, his suggestion that they make peace had extended only as far as Lizzie herself. *He* was going to go right on being nasty. "I swear he's turned your head, Lizzie. You're smitten with him. And you don't know a damn thing about the man, except what he's told you."

"I know," Lizzie said moderately, "that when this train was struck by an avalanche, he didn't think of *himself* first."

Whitley's color flared. "Are you implying that I'm a coward?"

The peddler, Ellen and Jack looked up from their game.

John Brennan went right on coughing.

Woodrow, back in his cage, spouted, "Coward!"

"No," Lizzie replied thoughtfully. "I've watched you play polo, and you can be quite brave. Maybe 'reckless' would be a better term. But you are selfish, Whitley, and that is a trait I cannot abide."

He gripped her shoulders. Shook her slightly. "Now you can't 'abide' me?" he growled. "Why? Because you're a high-and-mighty McKettrick?"

A click sounded from somewhere in the car, distinctive and ominous.

Lizzie glanced past Whitley and saw that the peddler had pointed a small handgun in their direction.

"Unhand the lady, if you please," the man said mildly.

Ellen and Jack stared, their eyes enormous.

"Don't shoot," Lizzie said calmly.

Whitley's hands fell to his sides, but the look on his face was cocky. "So you're still fond of me?" he asked Lizzie.

"No," Lizzie replied, watching his obnoxious grin fade as the word sank in. "I'm not the least bit fond of you, Whitley. But a shot could start another avalanche."

Whitley reddened.

The peddler lowered the pistol, allowing it to rest on top of his sample case, under his hand.

"I'm catching the first train out of this godforsaken country!" Whitley said, shaking a finger under Lizzie's nose. "I should have known you'd turn out to be—to be *wild*."

Lizzie drew in her breath. "'Wild'? If you're trying to insult me, Whitley, you're going to have to do better than *that*." She jabbed at his chest with the tip of one index finger. "And kindly *do not* shake your finger at me!"

The peddler chuckled.

"Wild!" Woodrow called shrilly. "Wild!"

The door at the rear of the caboose opened, and Morgan came in, stomping snow off his boots. He carried several broken tree branches in his arms, laid them down near the stove to dry, so they could be burned later. His gaze came directly to Lizzie and Whitley.

"I'm leaving!" Whitley said, forcing the words between his teeth.

"That might be difficult," Lizzie pointed out dryly, "since we're *stranded.*"

"I won't stay here and be insulted!"

"You'd rather go out there and die of exposure?"

"You think I'm a coward? I'm *selfish?* Well, I'll show you, Lizzie McKettrick. I'll follow the tracks until I come to a town and get help—since your highfalutin *family* hasn't shown up!"

"You can't do that," Morgan said, the voice of irritated moderation. "You wouldn't make it a mile, whether you followed the tracks or not. Anyhow, in case you haven't been listening, the tracks are *buried* under snow higher than the top of your head."

"Maybe you're afraid, *Dr.* Shane, but I'm not!" Whitley looked around, first to the peddler, then to poor John Brennan. "I think we should *all* go. It would be better than sitting around in this caboose, waiting to fall over the side of a mountain!"

Ellen raised a small hand, as though asking a question in class. "Are we going to fall over the mountain?" she asked. Jack nestled close against his sister's side, pale, and thrust a thumb into his mouth.

"You're frightening the children!" Lizzie said angrily.

Morgan raised both hands in a bid for peace. "We're *not* going to fall off the mountain," he told the little girl and Jack, his tone gentle. But when he turned to Whitley, his eyes blazed with temper. "If you want to be a damn fool, *Mr.* Carson, that's your business. But don't expect the rest of us to go along with you."

Little Jack began to cry, tears slipping silently down his face, his thumb still jammed deep into his mouth.

"Stop that," Ellen told him, trying without success to dislodge the thumb. "You're not a baby."

Whitley grabbed up his blanket, stormed across the car and flung it at Ellen and Jack. Then he banged out of the caboose, leaving the door ajar behind him.

Lizzie took a step in that direction.

Morgan closed the door. "He won't get far," he told her quietly.

"Come here to me, Jack," Mrs. Halifax said. She'd finished feeding and burping the baby, laid her gently on the seat beside her; Nellie Anne was asleep, reminding Lizzie of a cherub slumbering on a fluffy cloud.

Jack scrambled to his mother, crawled onto her lap.

Lizzie felt a pinch in her heart. She'd held her youngest brother, Doss, in just that way, when he was smaller and frightened by a thunderstorm or a bad dream.

"I have some goods in the freight car," the peddler said, tucking away the pistol, securing his case under the seat and rising. He buttoned his coat and went out.

Lizzie helped Ellen gather the scattered cards from their game. Mrs. Halifax rocked Jack in her lap, murmuring softly to him.

Morgan checked the fire, added wood.

"He'll be back," he told Lizzie, when their gazes collided.

He was referring to Whitley, of course, off on his fool's errand.

Lizzie nodded glumly and swallowed.

When the peddler returned, he was lugging a large wooden crate marked Private in large, stenciled letters. He set it down near the stove, with an air of mystery, and Ellen was immediately attracted. Even Jack slid down off his mother's lap to approach, no longer sucking his thumb.

"What's in there?" the little boy asked.

The peddler smiled. Patted the crate with one plump hand. Took a handkerchief from inside his coat and dabbed at his forehead. Remarkably, in that weather, he'd managed to work up a sweat. "Well, my boy," he said importantly, straightening, "I'm glad you asked that question. Can you read?"

Jack blinked. "No, sir," he said.

"I can," Ellen piped up, pointing to a label on the crate. "It says, 'Property of Mr. Nicholas Christian.'"

"That," the peddler said, "would be me. Nicholas Christian, at your service." He doffed his somewhat seedy bowler hat, pressed it to his chest and bowed. He turned to Jack. "You ask what's in this box? Well, I'll tell you. *Christmas.* That's what's in here."

"How can a whole day fit inside a box?" Ellen demanded, sounding at once skeptical and very hopeful.

"Why, child," said Nicholas Christian, "Christmas isn't merely a *day.* It comes in all sorts of forms."

Morgan, having poured a cup of coffee, watched the proceedings with interest. Mrs. Halifax looked troubled, but curious, too.

"Are you going to open it?" Jack wanted to know. He was practically breathless with excitement. Even John Brennan had stirred upon his sickbed to sit up and peer toward the crate.

"Of course I am," Mr. Christian said. "It would be unthinkably rude not to, after arousing your interest in such a way, wouldn't you say?"

Ellen and Jack nodded uncertainly.

"I'll need that poker," the peddler went on, addressing Morgan now, since he was closest to the stove. "The lid of this box is nailed down, you know."

Morgan brought the poker.

Woodrow leaned forward on his perch.

The peddler wedged one end of it under the top of the

crate and prized it up with a squeak of nails giving way. A layer of fresh wood shavings covered the contents, hiding them from view.

Lizzie, preoccupied with Whitley's announcement that he was going to follow the tracks to the nearest town, looked on distractedly.

Mr. Christian knelt next to the crate, rubbed his hands together, like a magician preparing to conjure a live rabbit or a white-winged dove from a hat, and reached inside.

He brought out a shining wooden box with gleaming brass hinges. Set it reverently on the floor. When he raised the lid, a tune began to play. "O little town of Bethlehem…"

Lizzie's throat tightened. The works of the music box were visible, through a layer of glass, and Jack and Ellen stared in fascination.

"Land," Ellen said. "I ain't—" she blushed, looked up at Lizzie "—I *haven't* never seen nothin' like this."

Lizzie offered no comment on the child's grammar.

"It belonged to my late wife, God rest her soul," Mr. Christian said and, for a moment, there were ghosts in his eyes. Leaving the music box to play, he plunged his hands into the crate again. Brought out a delicate china plate, chipped from long and reverent use, trimmed in gold and probably hand-painted. "There are eight of these," he said. "Spoons and forks and butter knives, too. We shall dine in splendor."

"What's 'dine'?" Jack asked.

Ellen elbowed him. "It means eating," she said.

"We ain't got nothin' to eat," Jack pointed out. By then, the crackers and cheese Lizzie had found in the cupboard were long gone, as were the canned foods pirated from the freight car.

"Oh, but we do," replied Mr. Christian. "We most certainly do."

The children's eyes all but popped.

"We have goose-liver pâté." He produced several small cans to prove it.

Woodrow squawked and spread his wings.

Jack wrinkled his nose. "Goose liver?"

Ellen nudged him again, harder this time. "Whatever patty is," she told him, "it's vittles for sure."

"Pah-tay," the peddler corrected, though not unkindly. "It is fine fare indeed." More cans came out of the box. A small ham. Crackers. Tea in a wooden container. And wonderful, rainbow-colored sugar in a pretty jar.

Lizzie's eyes stung a little, just watching as the feast was unveiled. Clearly, like the things stashed in her travel trunk, these treasures had been intended for someone in Indian Rock, awaiting Mr. Christian's arrival. A daughter? A son? Grandchildren?

"Of course, having recently enjoyed a fine repast," Mr. Christian said, addressing Ellen and Jack directly, but raising his voice just enough to carry to all corners of the caboose, "we'd do well to save all this for a while, wouldn't we?"

"I don't like liver," Jack announced, this time managing to dodge the inevitable elbow from Ellen. "But I wouldn't mind havin' some of that pretty sugar."

Morgan chuckled, but Lizzie saw him glance anxiously in the direction of the windows.

"Later," Mr. Christian promised. "Let us savor the anticipation for a while."

Both children's brows furrowed in puzzlement. The peddler might have been speaking in a foreign language, using words like *repast* and *savor* and *anticipation*. Raised hardscrabble, though, they clearly understood the concept of *later*. Delay was a way of life with them, young as they were.

Lizzie moved closer to Morgan, spoke quietly, while the

music box continued to play. "Whitley," she said, "is an exasperating fool. But we can't let him wander out there. He'll die."

Morgan sighed. "I was just thinking I'd better go and bring him back before he gets lost."

"I'm going, too. It's my fault he's here at all."

"You're needed here," Morgan replied reasonably, with a slight nod of his head toward John Brennan. "I can't be in two places at once, Lizzie."

"I wouldn't know what to do if Mr. Brennan had a medical crisis," Lizzie said. "But I *do* know how to follow railroad tracks."

Morgan rested his hands on Lizzie's shoulders, just lightly, but a confounding sensation rushed through her, almost an ache, stirring things up inside her. "You're too brave for your own good," he said. "Stay here. Get as much water down Brennan as you can. Make sure he stays warm, even if the fever makes him want to throw off his blankets."

"But what if he—?"

"What if he dies, Lizzie? I won't lie to you. He might. But then, so might all the rest of us, if we don't keep our heads."

"You're exhausted," Lizzie protested.

"If there's one thing a doctor learns, it's that exhaustion is a luxury. I can't afford to collapse, Lizzie, and believe me, I won't."

Wanting to cling to him, wanting to make him stay, even if she had to make a histrionic scene to do it, Lizzie forced herself to step back. To let go, not just physically, but emotionally, too. "All right," she said. "But if you're not back within an hour or two, I *will* come looking for you."

Morgan sighed again, but a tiny smile played at the corner of his mouth, and something at once soft and molten moved in his eyes. "I'll keep that in mind," he said. And then, after making only minimal preparations against the cold, he left the caboose.

Lizzie went immediately to the windows, watched him pass alongside the train. *Keep him safe,* she prayed silently. *Please, keep him safe. And Whitley, too.*

John Brennan began to cough. Lizzie fetched one of the cups, dashed outside to fill it with snow, set it on the stove. The chill bit deep into her flesh, gnawed at her bones.

Ellen and Jack whirled like figure skaters to the continuing serenade of the music box, Mr. Christian having demonstrated that it could play many different tunes, by virtue of small brass disks inserted into a tiny slot. Woodrow seemed to dance, inside his cage. Mr. and Mrs. Thaddings took in the scene, smiling fondly.

"I'm burnin' up," Mr. Brennan told Lizzie, when she came to adjust his blankets. "I need to get outside. Roll myself in that snow—"

Lizzie shook her head. She had no medical training, nothing to offer but the soothing presence of a woman. "That's your fever talking, Mr. Brennan," she said. "Dr. Shane said to keep you warm."

"It's like I'm on fire," he said.

How, Lizzie wondered, did people stand being nurses and doctors? It was a sore trial to the spirit to look helplessly upon human suffering, able to do so little to relieve it. "There, now," she told him, near to weeping. "Rest. I'll fetch a cool cloth for your forehead."

"That would be a pure mercy," he rasped.

Lizzie took her favorite silk scarf from her valise, steeled herself to go outside yet again.

Mr. Thaddings stopped her. Took the scarf from her hands and made the journey himself, shivering when he returned.

The snow-dampened scarf proved a comfort to Mr. Brennan, though the heat of his flesh quickly defeated the purpose. Lizzie, on her knees beside the seat where he lay, turned her head and saw that Zebulon Thaddings had brought in a bucketful of snow. Gratefully, she repeated the process.

"It would be a favor if you'd call me by my given name," Mr. Brennan told her. His coughing had turned violent, and he seemed almost delirious, alternately shaking with chills and trying to throw off his covers. "I wouldn't feel so far from home thataways."

Lizzie blinked back another spate of hot tears. "You'll get home, John," she said, fairly choking out the words. "I promise you will."

A small hand came to rest on her shoulder. She looked around, saw Ellen standing beside her. "I could do that," the child said gently, referring to the repeated wetting, wringing and applying of the cloth to John's forehead. "So you could rest a spell. Have some of that tea Mr. Christmas made."

Lizzie's first instinct was to refuse—tending the sick was no task for a small child. On the other hand, the offer was a gift and oughtn't to be spurned. "Mr. Christmas?" she asked, bemused, distracted by worry. "Don't you mean Mr. Christian?"

Ellen smiled, took the cloth. Edged Lizzie aside. "Here, now, Mr. Brennan," the little girl said, sounding like a miniature adult. "You just listen, and I'll talk. Me and my ma and my brother Jack and my little sister, Nellie Anne, we're on our way to the Triple M Ranch—"

Lizzie got to her feet, turned to find Mr. Christian holding out a mug full of spice-fragrant tea, hot and strong and probably laced with the very expensive colored sugar.

Mr. Christmas. Maybe Ellen had gotten the peddler's name right after all.

Chapter Four

The cold was brutal, the snow blinding. Morgan slogged through it, following the rails as best he could. It was in large part a guessing game, and he had to be careful to stay away from the bank on the left. That presented a challenge, since he couldn't be entirely certain where it was.

Carson, the damn fool, had left footprints, but they were filling in fast, and the man was clearly no relation to the famous scout with the same last name. Tracking him was more likely to lead Morgan to the bottom of the ravine than the nearest town.

Cursing under his breath—the wind buffeted it away every time he raised his head—Morgan kept going, ever mindful of the passing of time. If he took too long finding Carson and bringing him back, he knew Lizzie would make good on her threat to mount a one-woman search. John Brennan was too sick to stop her, let alone make the trek in her stead, and the peddler, well, he was a curious fellow, now guarding that sample case of his as if it contained the Holy Grail, now serving up goose-liver pâté and other delicacies on fancy china plates. He might keep Lizzie in the caboose, where she belonged, or send her out into the blizzard with his blessings. Morgan, by necessity an astute observer of the human animal, wasn't sure the man was completely sane.

Lizzie. In spite of his own situation, he smiled. What a hard-headed little firebrand she was—pretty. Smart as hell. Calm in a crisis that would have had many females—and males, too, to be fair—wringing their handkerchiefs and bewailing a cruel fate. He hadn't been joking when he'd said she'd make a good nurse.

Now, in the strange privacy of a high-country blizzard, he could admit something else, too—if only to himself. Lizzie McKettrick would make an even better doctor's wife than she would a nurse.

He felt something grind inside him, both painful and pleasant.

It was sheer idiocy to think of her in such intimate terms. They barely knew each other, after all, and she was set on teaching school, married or single. On top of that, she'd been fond enough of Whitley Carson to bring him home to her family during a sacred season. Her irritation with Carson would most likely fade, once they were all safe again. She'd forget the man's shortcomings soon enough, when the two of them were sipping punch beside a big Christmas tree in some grand McKettrick parlor.

The realization sobered Morgan. He felt something for Lizzie, though it was far too soon to know just what, but opening his time-hardened heart to her would be foolhardy. Rash. Until this trip, Morgan Shane had never done anything rash in his life. A week ago, even a few *days* ago, he wouldn't have considered taking the kind of stupid chance he was in the midst of right now, bumbling into the maw of a storm that might well swallow him whole.

Yes, he was a doctor, and a dedicated one. He was a pragmatist's pragmatist, in a field where the most competent were bone skeptical. He believed that, upon reaching the age of reason, everyone was responsible for their own actions, and the resultant consequences. Therefore, if Whitley Carson was stupid enough to set off looking for help in the middle of a snowstorm, he had that right. From Morgan's perspective, his own duty, as a man and as a physician, lay with John Brennan, Mrs. Halifax and her children, the peddler, the Thaddingses, and Lizzie.

Hell, he even felt responsible for the bird.

So why was he out there in the snowstorm, when he knew better, knew the hopelessness of the task he'd undertaken?

The answer made him flinch inside.

Because of Lizzie. He was doing this for Lizzie. Whatever her present mood, she loved Carson. Bringing the man home to the bosom of her fabled clan was proof of that.

Flesh stinging, Morgan kept walking. His feet were numb, and so were his hands. His ears burned as though someone had laid hot pokers to them, and every breath felt like an inhalation of flame. He fumbled for the flask Nicholas Christian had given him earlier, managed to get the lid off, and took a swig, blessing the bracing warmth that surged through him with the first swallow.

He found Carson sprawled in the snow, just around a bend. Was he dead?

Morgan's heartbeat quickened, and so did his half-frozen brain. He crouched beside the prone body, searched for and found a pulse.

Carson opened his eyes. "My leg," he scratched out. "I

think I've broken my leg...slipped on the tracks...almost went over the side—"

Morgan confirmed the diagnosis with a few practiced motions of his hands, even though his wind-stung eyes had already offered the proof. He opened the flask again, with less difficulty this time, and held it to Carson's lips. "I'll get you back to the train," he said, leaning in close to be heard over the howl of the wind, "but it's going to hurt."

Carson swallowed, nodded. "I know," he rasped. He groaned when Morgan hoisted him to his one good foot, cried out when he tried to take a step.

Morgan sighed inwardly, crouched a little, and slung Carson over his right shoulder like a sack of grain. He remembered little of the walk back to the train—it was a matter of staying upright and putting one foot in front of the other. At some point, Carson must have passed out from the pain—he was limp, a dead weight, and several times Morgan had to fight to keep from going down.

When the train came in sight, Morgan offered a silent prayer of thanks, though it had been a long time since he'd been on speaking terms with God. The peddler, Mr. Christian, met him at the base of the steps leading up to the caboose. Stronger than Morgan would have guessed, the older man helped him get the patient inside.

Lizzie had concocted something on the stove—a soup or broth of some sort, from the savory aroma, but when she saw her unconscious beau, alarm flared in her eyes and she turned from the coffee can serving as an improvised kettle. "Is he... he's not—"

Morgan shook his head to put her mind at ease, but didn't answer verbally until he and the peddler had laid their burden down on the bench seat opposite the place where John Brennan rested.

"His leg is broken," Morgan said grimly, rubbing his hands together in a mostly vain attempt to restore some circulation. He had a small supply of morphine in his bag, along with tincture of laudanum—he'd sent his other supplies ahead to Indian Rock after agreeing to set up a practice there. He could ease Carson's pain, but he dared not give him too much medicine, mainly because the damned fool had been tossing back copious amounts of whiskey since the avalanche. "I have to set the fracture," he added. "For that, I'll need some straight branches and strips of cloth to bind them to the leg."

Lizzie drew nearer, peering between Morgan and the peddler to stare, white-faced, at Carson. "Is he in pain?" she asked, her voice small.

No one answered.

"I'll see what I can find for splints," the peddler said.

Morgan replied with a grateful nod. He'd nearly frozen, hunting down and retrieving Carson. If he went out again too soon, he'd be of no use to anybody. "Stay near the train if you can," he told Christian. "And take care not to slip over the side."

The peddler promised to look out for himself and left. Mrs. Halifax and the children were sleeping, all of them wrapped up together in the quilt. Mr. and Mrs. Thaddings were snoozing, too, the sides of their heads touching, though Woodrow was wide-awake and very interested in the proceedings.

"When your friend regains consciousness, he'll be in considerable pain," Morgan said, in belated answer to Lizzie's question. Her concern was only natural—anyone with a shred of compassion in their soul would be sympathetic to Carson's plight. Still, the intensity of her reaction, unspoken as it was, reconfirmed his previous insight—Lizzie might *think* she no longer loved Whitley Carson, but she was probably fooling herself.

She did something unexpected then—took Morgan's hands into her own, removed the gloves he'd borrowed from Christian earlier, chafed his bare, cold skin between warm palms. The act was simple, patently ordinary and yet sensual in a way that Morgan was quite unprepared to deal with. Heat surged through him, awakening nerves, rousing sensations in widely varying parts of his anatomy.

"I've made soup," Lizzie told him, indicating the coffee can on the stove, its contents bubbling cheerfully away. Morgan recalled the tinned ham from the peddler's crate and the dried beans from the freight car. "You'd better have some," she added. "It will warm you up."

She'd warmed him up plenty, but there was no proper way to explain that. Numb before, Morgan ached all over now, like someone thawing out after a bad case of frostbite. "Best get Mr. Carson ready for the splints," he said. "The more I can do before he wakes up, the better."

She nodded her understanding, but dipped a clean mug into the brew anyway, and brought the soup to Morgan. He took a sip, set the mug aside, shrugged out of his coat. Using scissors from his bag, he cut Carson's snow-soaked pant leg from hem to knee and ripped the fabric open to the man's midthigh. Lizzie neither flinched nor looked away.

Morgan had the brief and disturbing thought that Lizzie might not be unfamiliar with the sight of Carson's bare flesh. He shoved the idea aside—Lizzie McKettrick's private life was patently none of his business. He certainly had no claim on her.

"I've got a petticoat," she said.

The announcement startled Morgan. Meanwhile, Carson had begun to stir, writhing a little, tossing his head from side to side as, with consciousness, the pain returned. Morgan paused to glance at Lizzie.

She went pink. "To bind the splints," she explained.

Morgan nodded, trying not to smile at her embarrassment.

Lizzie stepped back, out of his sight. There followed a poignantly feminine rustle of fabric, and then she returned to present him with a garment of delicate ivory silk, frothing with lace. For one self-indulgent moment, Morgan held the petticoat in a tight fist, savoring the feel of it, the faint scent of lavender caught in its folds, then proceeded to rip the costly fabric into wide strips. In the interim, Lizzie fetched his bag without being asked.

Carson opened his eyes, gazed imploringly up at her. "I meant..." he whispered awkwardly, the words scratching like sandpaper on splintery wood. "I meant to find help, Lizzie.... I'm so sorry...the way I acted before..."

"Shh," she said. She sat down on the bench, carefully placed Carson's head on her lap, stroked his hair. Morgan felt another flash of envy, a deep gouge of emotion, raw and bitter.

Christian returned with the requested tree branches, trimmed them handily with an ivory-handled pocketknife. The scent of pine sap lent the caboose an ironically festive air.

"This is going to hurt," Morgan warned Carson bluntly, gripping the man's ankle in both hands.

Carson bit his lower lip and nodded, preparing himself.

"Can't you give him something for the pain?" Lizzie interceded, looking up into Morgan's face with anxious eyes.

"Afterward," Morgan said. He didn't begrudge Carson a dose of morphine, but it was potent stuff, and the patient was in shock. If he happened to be sensitive to the drug, as many people were, the results could be disastrous. Better to administer a swallow of laudanum later. "It'll be over quickly."

"Do it," Carson said, and went up a little in Morgan's estimation. Perhaps he had some character after all.

Morgan closed his eyes; he had a sixth sense about bones

and internal organs, something he'd never mentioned to a living soul, including his father, because there was no scientific explanation for it. He saw the break in his mind, as clearly as if he'd laid Carson's hide and muscle open with a scalpel. When he felt ready, he gave the leg a swift, practiced wrench.

Carson yelled.

But the fractured femur was back in alignment.

Quickly, deftly, and with all the gentleness he could manage—again, this was more for Lizzie's sake than Carson's—Morgan set the splints in place and bound them firmly with the long strips of petticoat.

Taking a bottle of laudanum from his kit, Morgan pulled the cork and held it to Carson's mouth. "One sip," he said.

Sweating and pale, Carson raised himself up a little from Lizzie's lap and gulped down a mouthful of the bitter compound. The drug began taking effect almost immediately—Carson sighed, settled back, closed his eyes. Lizzie murmured sweet, senseless words to him, still smoothing his hair.

Morgan had set many broken limbs in his time, but this experience left him oddly enervated. He couldn't look at Lizzie as he put the vial of laudanum back in his kit, took out his stethoscope. There was something intensely private about the way she ministered to Carson, as tenderly as a mother with a child.

Or a wife with a husband.

Morgan turned away quickly, the stethoscope dangling from his neck, and crossed the railroad car to check Mr. Thaddings's heart, which thudded away at a blessedly normal rate, then moved on to examine John Brennan again.

"How are you feeling?" he asked the soldier gruffly. The question was a formality; the feverish glint in Brennan's eyes and the intermittent shivers that seemed to rattle his protruding skeleton provided answer enough.

Brennan's voice was a hoarse croak. "I heard that feller yell—"

"Broken leg," Morgan said. "Don't fret over it."

A racking cough tore itself from the man's chest. When he'd recovered, following a series of wheezing gasps, Brennan reached out to clasp at Morgan's hand, pulled. Morgan leaned down.

Brennan rasped out a ragged whisper. "I got to stay alive long enough to see my boy again," he pleaded. "It's almost Christmas. I can't have Tad recalling, all his life, that his pa passed...." The words fell away as another spate of coughing ensued.

Morgan crouched alongside the bench seat, since there were no chairs in the caboose. He was not accustomed to smiling under the best of circumstances, so the gesture came a lot harder that day. Brennan had one foot dangling over an open grave, and unless some angel grabbed him by the coattails and held on tight, he was sure to topple in.

"You'll be all right," he said. "Don't think about dying, John. Think about *living*. Think about fishing with your son— about better times—" Much to his surprise, Morgan choked up. Had to stop talking and work hard at starting again. He couldn't remember the last time he'd lost control of his emotions—maybe he never had. *If you're going to be any damned use at all,* he heard his father say, *you've got to keep your head, no matter what's going on around you.*

"My wife," John said, laboring to utter every word, "makes a fine rum cake, every Christmas—starts it way down in the fall—"

"You suppose she baked one this year?" Morgan asked quietly, when he could speak.

John smiled. Managed a nod. As hard as talking was for him, he seemed comforted by the exchange. Probably he was clutching one end of the conversation for dear life, much as

Lizzie had held on to Morgan's looped belt earlier, when she'd slipped in the snow. "She doubled the receipt," he ground out. "Just 'cause I was going to be home for Christmas."

Morgan noted the old-fashioned word *receipt*—his family's cook, Minerva, had used that term, too, in lieu of the more modern *recipe*—and then registered Brennan's use of the past tense. "You'll be there, John," he said.

Exhausted, John settled back, seemed to relax a little. His gaze drifted, caught on someone, and Morgan realized Lizzie was standing just behind him. She held a mug of steaming ham and bean soup and one of the peddler's fancy spoons.

Morgan straightened, glanced back at Carson, who seemed to be sleeping now, though fitfully. Sweat beaded the man's forehead and upper lip, and Morgan knew the pain was biting deep, despite the laudanum.

"I thought Mr. Brennan might require some sustenance," she said, her eyes big and troubled. She'd paled, and her luscious hair drooped as if it would throw off its pins at any moment and tumble down around her shoulders, falling to her waist.

Morgan nodded, stepped back out of the way.

Lizzie moved past him, her arm brushing his as she went by, and knelt alongside Brennan. "It would be better with onions," she said gamely, holding a spoonful of the brew to the patient's lips. "And salt, too." When he opened his mouth, she fed him.

"Them beans is sure bony," Brennan said. "I guess they ain't had time to cook through."

Lizzie gave a rueful little chuckle of agreement.

And Morgan watched, struck by some stray and nameless emotion.

It was a simple sight, a woman spooning soup into an invalid's mouth, but it stirred Morgan just the same. He wondered if Lizzie would fall apart when this was all over, or if she'd carry on. He was betting on the latter.

Of course, they'd have to be rescued first, and the worse the weather got, the more unlikely that seemed.

The thin soup soothed Brennan's cough. He accepted as much as he could and finally sank into a shallow rest.

Creeping shadows of twilight filled the car; another day was ending.

The peddler had engaged the children in a new game of cards. Carson, like Brennan, slept. Mrs. Halifax and the baby lay on the bench seat, bundled in the quilt, the woman staring trancelike into an uncertain future, the infant gnawing on one grubby little fist.

Madonna and Child, Morgan thought glumly.

He made his way to the far end of the car, sat down on the bench and tipped his head back against the window. Tons of snow pressed cold against it, seeped through flesh and bone to chill his marrow; he might have been sitting in the lap of the mountain itself. He closed his eyes; did not open them when he felt Lizzie take a seat beside him.

"Rest," he told her. "You must be worn-out."

"I can't," she said. He heard the slightest tremor in her voice. "I thought—I thought they'd be here by now."

Morgan opened his eyes, met Lizzie's gaze.

"Do you suppose something's happened to them? My papa and the others?"

He wanted to comfort her, even though he shared her concern for the delayed rescue party. If they'd set out at all, they probably hadn't made much progress. He took her hand, squeezed it, at a loss for something to say.

She smiled sadly, staring into some bright distance he couldn't see. "Tomorrow is Christmas Eve," she said, very quietly. "My brothers, Gabriel and Doss, always want to sleep in the barn on Christmas Eve, because our grandfather says the animals talk at midnight. Every year they carry blankets out there and make beds in the straw, determined to hear the milk cows and the horses chatting with each other. Every year they fall asleep hours before the clock strikes twelve, and Papa carries them back into the house, one by one, and Lorelei tucks them in. And every year, I think this will be the time they manage to stay awake, the year they stop believing."

Morgan longed to put an arm around Lizzie's shoulders and draw her close, but he didn't. Such gestures were Whitley Carson's prerogative, not his. "What about you?" he asked. "Did you sleep in the barn on Christmas Eve when you were little? Hoping to hear the animals talk?"

She started slightly, coming out of her reverie, turning to meet his eyes. Shook her head. "I was twelve when I came to live on the Triple M," she said.

She offered nothing more, and Morgan didn't pry, even though he wanted to know everything about her, things she didn't even know about herself.

"You've been a help, Lizzie," he told her. "With John Brennan and with Carson, too."

"I keep thinking about the conductor and the engineer—their families...."

"Don't," Morgan advised.

She studied him. "I heard what you told John Brennan—that he ought to think about fishing with his son, instead of... instead of dying—"

Morgan nodded, realized he was still holding Lizzie's hand, improper as that was. Drew some satisfaction from the fact that she hadn't pulled away.

"Do you believe it really makes a difference?" she went on, when she'd gathered her composure. "Thinking about good things, I mean?"

"Regardless of how things turn out," he replied, "thinking about good things feels better than worrying, wouldn't you say? So in that respect, yes, I'd say it makes a difference."

She pondered that, then looked so directly, and so deeply, into his eyes that he felt as though she'd found a peephole into the wall he'd constructed around his truest self. "What are *you* thinking about, then?" she wanted to know. "You must be worried, like all the rest of us."

He couldn't tell Lizzie the truth—that despite his best efforts, every few minutes he imagined how it would be, treating patients in Indian Rock, with her at his side. "I can't afford to worry," he said. "It isn't productive."

She wasn't going to let him off the hook; he could see that. Her blue eyes darkened with determination. "What was Christmas like for you, when you were a boy?"

Morgan found the question strangely unsettling. His father had been a doctor, his mother an heiress and a force of nature, especially socially. During the holiday season, they'd gone to, or given, parties every night. "Minerva—she was our cook—always roasted a hen."

Lizzie blinked. Waited. And finally, when certain that nothing more was forthcoming, prodded, "That's all? Your cook roasted a chicken? No tree? No presents? No carols?"

"My mother wouldn't have considered dragging an evergreen into the house," Morgan admitted. "In her opinion, the practice was crass and vulgar—and besides, she didn't want pitch and birds' nests all over the rugs. Every Christmas morning, when I came to the breakfast table, I found a gift waiting on the seat of my chair. It was always a book, wrapped in brown paper and tied with string. As for carols—there was a church at the end of our street, and sometimes I opened a window so I could hear the singing."

"That sounds lonely," Lizzie observed.

His childhood Christmases had indeed been lonely, Morgan reflected. Which made December 25 just like the other 364 days of the year. For a moment he was a boy again, he and Minerva feasting solemnly in the kitchen of the mansion, just the two of them. His dedicated father was out making a house call, his mother sleeping off the effects of a merry evening passed among the strangers she preferred to him.

"If you hadn't mentioned a cook," Lizzie went on, when he didn't speak, "I would have thought you'd grown up in a hovel."

He smiled at that. His mother had regarded him as an inconvenience, albeit an easily overlooked one. She'd often rued the day she'd married a poor country doctor instead of a financier, like her late and sainted sire, and made no secret of her regret. Morgan's father had endured by staying away from home as much as possible, often taking his young son along on his rounds when he, Morgan, wasn't locked away in the third-floor nursery with some tutor. Those excursions had been happy ones for Morgan, and he'd seen enough suffering, visiting Elias Shane's patients, most of them in tenements and charity hospitals, to know there were worse fates than growing up with a spoiled, disinterested and very wealthy mother.

He'd had his father, to an extent.

He'd had Minerva. She'd been born a slave, Minerva had. To her, Lincoln's Emancipation Proclamation was as sacred as Scripture. She'd actually met the man she'd called "Father Abraham," after the fall of Richmond. She'd clutched at the sleeve of his coat, and he'd smiled at her. *Such sorrow in them gray, gray eyes,* she'd told Morgan, who never tired of the much-told tale. *Such sadness as you'd never credit one man could hold.*

Morgan withdrew from the memory. He'd have given a lot to hear that story just one more time.

Lizzie bit her lip. Took fresh notice of his threadbare clothes, then caught herself and flushed a fetching pink. "You're *not* poor," she concluded, then colored up even more.

He laughed, and damn, it felt good. "Oh, but I am, Lizzie McKettrick," he said. "Poor as a church mouse. Mother didn't mind so much when I went to Germany to study. She figured it would pass, and I'd come to my senses. When I came home and took up medicine in earnest, she disinherited me."

Lizzie's marvelous eyes widened again. "She did? But surely your father—"

"She showed him the door, too. She was furious with him for encouraging me to become a doctor instead of overseeing the family fortune. Minerva opened a boardinghouse, and Dad and I moved in as her first tenants. We found a storefront, hung out a shingle and practiced together until Dad died of a heart attack."

Sorrow moved in Lizzie's face at the mention of his father's death. She swallowed. "What became of your mother?" she asked, sounding meek now, in the face of such drama.

"She sold the mansion and moved to Europe, to escape the shame."

"What shame?"

God bless her, Morgan thought, she was actually confused. "In Mother's circles," he said, "the practice of medicine— especially when most of the patients can't pay—is not a noble pursuit. She could have forgiven herself for marrying a doctor—youthful passions, lapses of judgment, all that—but when I decided to become a physician instead of taking over my grandfather's several banks, it was too much for her to bear."

"I'm sorry, Morgan," Lizzie said.

"It isn't as if we were close," Morgan said, touched by the sadness in Lizzie McKettrick's eyes as he had never been by Eliza Stanton Shane's indifference. "Mother and I, I mean."

"But, still—"

"I had my father. And Minerva."

Lizzie nodded, but she didn't look convinced. "My mother died when I was young. And even though I'm close to Lorelei—that's my stepmother—I still miss her a lot."

He couldn't help asking the question. It was out of his mouth before he could stop it. "Is money important to you, Lizzie?" He'd told her he was poor, and suddenly he needed to know if that mattered.

She glanced in Carson's direction, then looked straight into Morgan's eyes. "No," she said, with such alacrity that he believed her instantly. There was no guile in Lizzie McKettrick—only courage and sweetness, intelligence and, unless he missed his guess, a fiery temper.

He wanted to ask if Whitley Carson would be able to support her in the manner to which she was clearly accustomed, considering the fineness of her clothes and her recently acquired education, but he'd recovered his manners by then.

"Miss McKettrick?"

Both Lizzie and Morgan turned to see Ellen standing nearby, looking shy.

"Yes, Ellen?" Lizzie responded, smiling.

"I can't find a spittoon," Ellen said.

Lizzie chuckled at that. "We'll go outside," she replied.

"A spittoon?" Morgan echoed, puzzled.

"Never mind," Lizzie told him.

"I believe I'll go, too," Mrs. Halifax put in, rising awkwardly from her bed on the bench because of her injured arm, wrapping her shawl more closely around her shoulders.

Lizzie bundled Ellen up in the peddler's coat, readily volunteered, and the trio of females braved the snow and the freezing wind. The baby girl stayed behind, kicking her feet, waving small fists in the air, and cooing with sudden happiness. She'd spotted the cockatiel with the ridiculous name. What was it?

Oh, yes. Woodrow.

"I reckon we ought to be sparing with the kerosene," the peddler told Morgan, nodding toward the single lantern bravely pushing back the darkness. "Far as I could see when we checked the freight car, there isn't a whole lot left."

Morgan nodded, finding the prospect of the coming night a grim one. When the limited supply of firewood was gone, they could use coal from the bin in the locomotive, but even that wouldn't last more than a day or two.

The little boy, Jack, like Brennan and Carson, had fallen asleep.

The peddler spoke in a low voice, after making sure he wouldn't be overheard. "You think they'll find us in time?"

Morgan shoved a hand through his hair. "I don't know," he said honestly.

"You know anything about Miss Lizzie's people?"

Morgan frowned. "Not much. I met her uncle, Kade, down in Tucson."

"I've heard of Angus McKettrick," Christian confided, his gaze drifting briefly to Whitley Carson's prone and senseless form before swinging back to Morgan. "That's Miss Lizzie's grandpa. Tough as an army mule on spare rations, that old man. The McKettricks have money. They have land and cattle, too. But there's one thing that's more important to them than all that, from what I've been told, and that's kinfolks. They'll come, just like Miss Lizzie says they will. They'll come because she's here—you can be sure of that. I'm just hoping we'll all be alive and kicking when they show up."

Morgan had no answer for that. There were no guarantees, and plenty of dangers—starvation, for one. Exposure, for another. And the strong likelihood of a second, much more devastating, avalanche.

"You figure one of us ought to try hiking out of here?"

Morgan looked at Carson. "*He* didn't fare so well," he said.

"He's a greenhorn and we both know it," the peddler replied.

"How far do you think we are from Indian Rock?"

"We're closer to Stone Creek than Indian Rock," Christian said. "Tracks turn toward it about five miles back. It's another ten miles into Stone Creek from there. Probably twenty or more to Indian Rock from where we sit."

Morgan nodded. "If they're not here by morning," he said, "I'll try to get to Stone Creek."

"You're needed here, Doc," the peddler said. "I'm not as young as I used to be, but I've still got some grit and a good pair of legs. Know this country pretty well, too—and you don't."

Lizzie, Mrs. Halifax and Ellen returned, shivering. Lizzie struggled to shut the caboose door against a rising wind.

Morgan and the peddler let the subject drop.

They extinguished the lamp soon after that, ate ham and "bony" bean soup in the dark.

Everyone found a place to sleep.

And when Morgan opened his eyes the next morning, at first light, he knew the snow had stopped. He sat up, looked around, found Lizzie first. She was still sleeping, sitting upright on the bench seat, bundled in a blanket. John Brennan hadn't wakened, and neither had Mrs. Halifax and her children. Whitley Carson, a book in his hands, stared across the car at him with an unreadable expression in his eyes.

"The peddler's gone," he told Morgan. "He left before dawn."

Chapter Five

Lizzie dreamed she was home, waking up in her own room, hearing the dear, familiar sounds of a ranch house morning: stove lids clattering downstairs in the kitchen; the murmur of familiar voices, planning the day. She smelled strong coffee brewing, and wood smoke, and the beeswax Lorelei used to polish the furniture.

Christmas Eve was special in the McKettrick household, but the chores still had to be done. The cattle and horses needed hay and water, the cows required milking, the wood waited to be chopped and carried in, and there were always eggs to be gathered from the henhouse. Behind the tightly closed doors of Papa's study, she knew, a giant evergreen tree stood in secret, shimmering with tinsel strands and happy secrets. The luscious scent of pine rose through the very floorboards to perfume the second floor.

Throughout the day, the uncles and aunts and cousins would come, by sleigh or, if the roads happened to be clear, by team and wagon and on horseback. There would be exchanges of food, small gifts, laughter and stories. In the evening, after attending church services in town, they would all gather at the main house, where Lizzie's grandfather Angus would read aloud, his voice deep and resonant, from the Gospel of Luke.

And there were in the same fields, shepherds, guarding their flocks by night...

Tears moistened Lizzie's lashes, because she knew she was dreaming. Knew she wasn't on the Triple M, where she belonged, but trapped in a stranded train on a high, treacherous ridge.

The smell of coffee was real, though. That heartened her. Gave her the strength to open her eyes.

Her hair must have looked a sight, that was her immediate thought, and she needed to go outside. Her gaze found Morgan first, like a compass needle swinging north. He stood near the stove, looking rumpled from sleep, pouring coffee into a mug.

He crossed to her, handed her the cup.

The small courtesy seemed profound to Lizzie, rather than mundane.

"Today," she said, "is Christmas Eve."

"So it is," Morgan agreed, smiling wanly.

Whitley, resting with his broken leg propped on the bench seat, caught her eye. "Good morning, Lizzie-bet," he said.

She gave a little nod of acknowledgment, embarrassed by the nickname, and sipped at her coffee. Evidently, Whitley's apology the day before had been a sincere one. He was on his best behavior. She discovered that she did not have an opinion on that, one way or the other.

"Where is Mr. Christian?" she asked Morgan, having scanned the company and noticed he was missing. The caboose was chilly, despite the efforts of the little stove. "Has he gone looking for firewood?"

A glance passed between Morgan and Whitley. Whitley raised both eyebrows, but didn't speak.

"He's on his way to Stone Creek," Morgan said, sounding resigned.

Lizzie sat up straighter, nearly spilling her coffee. "*Stone Creek?* That's miles from here—" She paused, confounded. "And you just *let him go?*"

Whitley finally deigned to contribute to the conversation. "He left before Dr. Shane woke up, Lizzie. And his mind was made up. Nobody could have stopped him."

Lizzie absorbed that. She thought of the tinkling music box and the tins of goose liver pâté and wondered if any of them would ever see Mr. Christian again.

"I'm going forward to the engine, for coal," Morgan said, taking up a bucket.

Lizzie thought of the conductor and engineer, lying frozen where they'd died. She thought of Mr. Christian, bravely making his way through snow that would be up to his waist in some places, over his head in others. The last, tattered joy of her Christmas dream faded away.

She simply nodded, and concentrated on drinking her coffee.

"Lizzie," Whitley said, when Morgan had gone, "come and sit here beside me."

The others were still sleeping. After a moment's hesitation, Lizzie crossed the caboose to join Whitley.

"Have you forgiven me?" Whitley asked, very quietly. His hazel eyes glowed with earnest affection; he really *was* a good person, Lizzie knew.

"I guess you were just scared," she said.

"I acted like a fool," Whitley told her.

Lizzie said nothing.

Shyly he took her hand. Squeezed it. "Now I've got to

start the courtship all over again, don't I? I've botched things that badly."

"C-courtship?" Lizzie had looked forward to Whitley's proposal for months, dreamed of it, rehearsed the experience in her imagination, practiced her response. How many, many ways there were to say "yes." Now, something had changed, forever, and she knew it had far more to do with meeting Dr. Morgan Shane than anything Whitley had said or done since the avalanche. It wouldn't be fair, or kind, to pretend otherwise.

"Tell me I haven't lost you for good, Lizzie," Whitley said, tightening his grip on her hand as he read her face. "Please."

Just then, John Brennan began to cough so violently that Lizzie bolted off the seat and rushed across the caboose to help him sit up. The fit eased a little, but Lizzie felt desperately helpless, standing there patting the man's back while he struggled to breathe.

Whitley, meanwhile, got to his feet and stumped over to offer his flask. "It's just water," he said, when Lizzie looked at it askance, recalling all the whiskey he'd consumed from the vessel earlier.

She took the flask, opened it, held it to John's gray lips until he'd taken a few sips. After several tense moments, he seemed nominally better. Lizzie tested his forehead for fever, using the back of her hand as she'd seen Lorelei do so many times, and found it blazing hot.

Despair threatened Lizzie again. She swayed slightly on her feet, and Whitley caught hold of her arm just as Morgan returned, on a rush of cold wind, lugging a scuttle full of coal.

Time seemed to stop, just for a moment, as abruptly as the train had stopped when the avalanche struck.

Morgan carried the coal to the stove, crouched and tossed a few handfuls in on top of the last of the dry firewood.

Then the children woke up, and baby Nellie Anne began to wail for her breakfast. Whitley made his slow way back to the other side of the caboose, lowered himself onto the seat. Lizzie performed what ablutions she could, brushing her hair and pinning it up again, then grooming Ellen's hair, too. Mrs. Thaddings took Woodrow out of his cage so he could perch on her shoulder, ruffling his feathers and muttering bird prattle.

"Where's Mr. Christmas?" Jack asked, very seriously, as they all made a breakfast of leftover soup, crackers and goose liver pâté. Mrs. Halifax, clearly regaining her strength, had melted snow to wash her children's hands and faces, and they looked scrubbed and damp. "He said he'd teach me and Ellen to play five-card stud."

"He'll do no such thing," Mrs. Halifax said, but she smiled. Then she turned questioningly to Morgan. "Where *is* Mr. Christian?" she asked.

"He's making for Stone Creek," Whitley said, before Morgan could reply. "He should have stayed here."

Both Lizzie and Morgan gave him ironic looks—he'd broken his leg on a similar errand, after all—and he subsided, at least briefly.

Lizzie glanced at the windows overlooking the broad valley, hundreds of feet below the train's precarious perch on the mountainside. "At least the snow has stopped," she mused. "The traveling won't be any easier, but he'll be able to see where he's going."

Once the improvised meal was over, time seemed to crawl.

Mrs. Thaddings introduced Ellen and Jack to Woodrow, and they stared at him in fascination.

"If he was a homing pigeon," Ellen observed, bright child that she was, "he could go for help."

"We might have to eat him," Jack said solemnly, "if we run out of food."

Mr. Thaddings, who hadn't said much up until then, chuckled and shook his head. "He'd be pretty stringy," he told the boy.

"Stringy," Woodrow affirmed, spreading his wings and squawking once for emphasis.

Amused, Lizzie busied herself tending to John Brennan, while Morgan paced the center of the car and Mrs. Halifax discreetly nursed the baby, her back to everyone. Presently, when Woodrow retired to his cage for a nap, Jack and Ellen shyly approached Whitley, and sat themselves on either side of him.

He sighed, met Lizzie's gaze for a long moment, then flipped back to the front of the book he'd nearly finished, and began reading aloud. "'It was the best of times—'"

And so the morning passed.

At midafternoon, a knock sounded at the door of the caboose.

Hope surged in Lizzie's heart—her father and uncles had come at last—but even before she opened the door, she knew they wouldn't have bothered to knock. They'd have busted down the door to get in.

Mr. Christian stood on the small platform, frost in his eyebrows, his whiskers, his lashes. He clutched a very small pine tree in one hand and gazed into Lizzie's face without apparent recognition, more statue than man.

Morgan immediately moved her aside, took hold of the peddler by the arms, and pulled him in out of the cold.

"Tracks are blocked," Mr. Christian said woodenly, as Morgan took the tree from him and set it aside. "I had to turn back—"

Morgan began peeling off the man's coat, which appeared to be frozen and made a crackling sound as the fabric bent. Mr. Thaddings helped with the task, while Mrs. Thaddings rushed to fill a mug with coffee. Mr. Christian still seemed baffled, as though surprised to find himself where he was.

Perhaps he wondered if he was in the caboose at all, or in the midst of some cold-induced reverie.

"Frostbite," Morgan said, examining the peddler's hands. "Lizzie, get me snow. Lots of snow."

Confounded, Lizzie obeyed just the same. She hurried out, filled the front of her skirt with as much snow as she could carry, returned to find that Morgan had settled Mr. Christian on the bench seat, as far from the stove as possible. She watched as Morgan took the snow she'd brought in, packed it around the peddler's hands and feet.

The process was repeated several more times, though when Mr. Thaddings saw that Lizzie's dress was wet, he took over the task, using the coal scuttle.

Mr. Christian lay on the train seat, shivering, wearing only his long johns by then, staring mutely up at the roof of the car. He still did not seem precisely certain where he was, or what was happening to him, and Lizzie counted that as a mercy. She was relieved when Morgan finally gave the poor man an injection of morphine and stopped packing his extremities in snow.

"The children," Mr. Christian murmured once. "The children ought to have some kind of Christmas."

Tears scalded Lizzie's eyes. She had to turn away, and while Morgan was monitoring the patient's heartbeat, she sneaked out of the car, unnoticed by everyone but Whitley.

He started to raise an alarm, but at one pleading glance from Lizzie, he changed his mind.

She made her way to the baggage car and, after some lugging and maneuvering, began opening trunks until she'd found what she sought. Her fine woolen coat, the paint set she'd brought all this way to give to John Henry, shawls and stockings. A pipe she'd bought for her father. A book for her grandfather. A pocket watch she'd intended to give to Whitley. Next, she looted Whitley's trunk, helped herself to his heavy overcoat, more stockings and warm underwear. When a tiny velvet box toppled from the pocket of the coat, Lizzie's heart nearly stopped.

She bent, picked up the box, opened it slowly. A shining diamond ring winked inside. More tears came; so Whitley *had* intended to propose marriage over the holidays. Lizzie tucked her old dreams inside that box with the ring, closed it, set it carefully back in Whitley's trunk.

When she'd taken a few moments to recover, she bundled the things she'd gathered into Whitley's coat and made her way outside again, along the side of the train, into the caboose.

Her return, like her departure, caused no particular stir.

She set her burden aside and went to stand in front of the stove, trying to dry the front of her dress. John Brennan was already down with pneumonia, Whitley's leg was in splints, Mrs. Halifax sported a sling, and now poor Mr. Christian was nearly dead of frostbite. It wouldn't do if she added to their problems by taking sick herself.

Everyone settled into sort of a stupor after that.

Lizzie, now dry, turned to gaze out the windows. The sun was setting, and there was no sign of an approaching rescue party. She drew a deep breath.

It was still Christmas Eve, whatever the circumstances, and Lizzie was determined to celebrate in some way.

Soon the sky was peppered with stars, each one shining as brightly as the diamond ring Whitley had meant to place on her finger. The snow glittered, deep and pristine, under those spilling stars, and the scent of the little pine tree Mr. Christian had somehow cut and brought back spiced the air.

Morgan looted the freight car again, and returned with a stack of new blankets and the spectacular Christmas ham they'd all agreed not to eat, just the day before. He fetched more coal and built up the fire, and they feasted—even John Brennan and Mr. Christian managed a few bites.

As the moon rose, spilling shimmering silver over the snow, Morgan stuck the trunk of the tiny tree between the slats of Mr. Christian's empty crate, and Whitley donated his watch chain for a decoration. Lizzie contributed several hair ribbons from her handbag, along with a small mirror that seemed to catch the starlight. Mrs. Thaddings contributed her ear bobs.

They sang, Lizzie starting first, Mrs. Halifax picking up the words next, her voice faltering, then John and Whitley and the children. Even Woodrow joined in.

"'O little town of Bethlehem, how still we see thee lie...'"

"We ain't gettin' our oranges," Jack announced stoically, as his mother tucked him and Ellen into the quilt bed, after many more carols had been sung. "There's no stockings to hang, and St. Nicholas won't find us way out here."

Ellen gazed at the little tree as though it were the most splendid thing she'd ever set eyes on. "It's Christmas, just the same," she said. "And that tree is right pretty. Mr. Christmas went to a lot of trouble to bring it back for us, too."

Jack sighed and closed his eyes.

Ellen gazed at the tree until she fell asleep.

Morgan moved back and forth between John Brennan and Mr. Christian. He'd given Whitley more laudanum after supper, when the pain in his injured leg had contorted his face and brought out a sheen of sweat across his forehead. Mr. and Mrs. Thaddings, having settled Woodrow down for the night, read from a worn Bible.

Watching them, Lizzie marveled at their calm acceptance. It seemed that, as long as they were together, they could face anything. She knew so little about the couple, and yet it would be obvious to anyone who looked that the marriage was a refuge for them both.

She wanted to be like them. To get old with someone, to live out an unfurling ribbon of years, as they had.

Presently, she turned to Morgan.

"I thought they'd come," Lizzie confided, very quietly. She was kneeling in front of the tree by then, breathing in the scent of it, remembering so many things. "I thought my family would come."

Morgan moved to sit cross-legged beside her. He said nothing at all, but simply listened.

A tear slipped down Lizzie's cheek. She dashed it away with the back of one hand. Straightened her spine.

"Maybe in the morning," she said.

"Maybe," Morgan agreed, gently gruff.

She got to her feet, retrieved the bundle she'd brought from the baggage car earlier. She folded Whitley's expensive overcoat neatly, placed it beneath the tree. John Henry's paint set went next, and then the pocket watch. Her beautiful velvet-collared coat found its way under the tree, too, and so did the pipe and the book and a few other things, as well.

She sat back on her heels when she'd finished arranging the gifts. Was surprised when Morgan reached out and took her hand.

"Lizzie McKettrick," he said, "you are something."

She bit her lower lip. Glanced in Whitley's direction to make certain he was asleep. He seemed to be, but he might have been "playing possum," to use one of her grandfather's favorite terms.

"He's going to ask me to marry him," she said, without intending to speak at all.

Morgan was silent for a long moment. Then he replied, "And you'll say yes."

She shook her head, unable to look directly at Morgan.

"Why not?" Morgan asked, his voice pitched low. It seemed

intimate, their talking in the semidarkness, now that the lamp had been extinguished, the way her papa and Lorelei so often did, late at night, when they were alone in the kitchen, with the stove-fire banked low and the savory smell of supper still lingering in the air.

"Because it wouldn't be right," Lizzie said. "For Whitley or for me. He's a good man, Morgan. He really is. He deserves a wife who loves him."

Morgan didn't answer. Not right away, at least. "These are trying circumstances, Lizzie—for all of us. Don't make any hasty decisions. You'll have a long time to regret it if you make the wrong ones."

Again, Lizzie glanced in Whitley's direction, then down at her hands, knotted atop the fabric of her ruined skirts. "Maybe I'm not cut out to be married anyhow," she ventured. "Some people aren't, you know."

She felt his smile, rather than saw it. "It would be a waste, Lizzie, if you didn't marry. But I agree that you're better off single than tied to the wrong man."

"My pupils," Lizzie mused. "They'll be my children." Even as she said the words, a soft sorrow tugged at her heart. She so wanted babies of her own, sons and daughters, bringing the kind of rowdy, chaotic joy swelling the walls of the houses on the Triple M.

"Will they be enough, Lizzie?" Morgan asked, after a lengthy silence. "Your pupils, I mean?"

"I don't know," she answered sadly.

Morgan squeezed her hand again. "You have time, Lizzie. You're a beautiful woman. If you and Whitley can't come to terms, you'll surely meet someone else."

Lizzie feared she'd already met that "someone else," and he was Morgan. Normally a confident person, she suddenly felt out of her depth. The McKettricks were certainly prominent, and they were wealthy, but they lived in ranch houses, not mansions. Nobody dressed for dinner, or employed servants, or rode in fancy carriages, as Morgan's people surely had. She'd attended Miss Ridgley's, where she'd learned which fork to use with which course of a meal, how to embroider and entertain, and after that she'd gone to San Francisco Normal School. Morgan had studied medicine abroad. Estranged from his mother or not, he would be at home in high society, while Lizzie would be considered a frontier bumpkin at worst, one of the nouveaux riches at best.

"Lizzie?" Morgan prompted, when she didn't reply to his comment.

"I was just wondering why you'd want to live and work in a place like Indian Rock, instead of Chicago or New York or Philadelphia or Boston," she said. "Don't you miss...well... all the things there are to *do* in places like that?"

"Such as?"

"Concerts. Art museums. Stores so big you have to climb stairs to see everything they sell."

Morgan chuckled. "Do *you* miss concerts and museums and shopping, Lizzie?"

"No," she said. "San Francisco is beautiful—I really enjoyed being there. I made a lot of friends at school. But there were times when I was so homesick, I wasn't sure I could stand it."

Morgan caressed her cheek with the backs of his knuckles, his touch so gentle that a hot shiver went through her. "I guess I'm homesick, too," he said, "but in a different way. The home I want is the one I never had—the one I'm hoping to find in Indian Rock."

Lizzie's throat thickened. It was only too easy to picture Morgan as a small child, having Christmas dinner in the kitchen of some yawning mausoleum of a house, with only the family cook for company. On the other hand, things would be different in Indian Rock—once word got around town that the new doctor didn't have a wife, the scheming and flirtations would begin. Meals would be cooked and brought to his door in baskets. He'd be invited to Sunday suppers, and unmarried women for miles around would suddenly develop delicate ailments requiring the immediate attention of the attractive new physician.

Thinking of it made Lizzie give a very unladylike snort.

In the moonlight, she saw Morgan's right eyebrow rise slightly, and a smile played at one corner of his mouth. "Now, what accounts for *that* reaction, Lizzie McKettrick?" he asked.

She loved it when he called her by her full name, though she could not have said why. But she was mightily embarrassed that she'd snorted in front of him, like an old horse nickering for oats. "You won't be single long," she said. "Once you get to Indian Rock, I mean."

She regretted the statement instantly; it revealed too much. Like a contentious colt, it had bolted from the place she contained such things and kicked up a fuss inside Lizzie.

Again, that crooked little smile from Morgan. "I think I'd like to be married," he mused, surprising her yet again; she'd *thought* she was getting used to his blunt way of speaking. "A lovely wife. A passel of children. It all sounds very good to me right now, but maybe I'm just being sentimental."

For some reason she could not define, Lizzie wanted to cry. And it wasn't because she was far from home on Christmas Eve, or because she knew she would have to turn down Whitley's proposal and he would be hurt and disappointed, or even because all their lives were in danger.

Not trusting herself to speak, or govern what she said if she made the attempt, Lizzie remained silent.

Morgan brushed her cheek with the tips of his fingers. "Get some sleep," he counseled. "Tomorrow's Christmas."

Tomorrow's Christmas. Lizzie found that hard to credit, even with the little tree and the presents so carefully arranged beneath it. She nodded, and she was about to get to her feet when, with no warning at all, Morgan suddenly caught her face between his hands and placed the lightest, sweetest kiss imaginable on her mouth.

A jolt shot through Lizzie; she might have captured liquid lightning in a metal cup, like fresh spring rain, and swigged it down. She knew Morgan felt her trembling before he lowered his hands from her face to take hers and help her to her feet.

"Good night, Lizzie McKettrick," he said gruffly. "And a happy Christmas."

She found a place to lie down on one of the long bench seats, never dreaming that she'd sleep. Her heart leaped and frolicked like a circus performer on a trampoline, and she could still feel Morgan's brief, innocent kiss tingling on her lips.

To distract herself from all the contradictory feelings Morgan had aroused in her, she imagined herself at home on the Triple M. She stood for a few moments in the familiar kitchen, lamp-lit and warm from the stove, and saw her papa and Lorelei sitting in their usual places at the table, though they did not seem to see her.

Mentally, she climbed the back stairway, made her way first to the room John Henry, Gabriel and Doss shared. They were all sound asleep in their beds, fair hair tousled on the pillows and flecked with hay from the customary Christmas Eve visit to the barn, and each one had hung a stocking from a hook on the wall, in anticipation of St. Nicholas's arrival. The stockings were still limp and empty—Lorelei would fill them later, when she was sure they wouldn't awaken. Rock candy. Toy whistles. Perhaps small wooden animals, hand carved by Papa, out in the wood shop.

The scene was achingly real to Lizzie—it made her eyes sting and her throat ache so fiercely that she put a hand to it. As she stared down at her brothers, drinking in the sight of them, John Henry opened his eyes, looked directly at her.

"Where are you?" he asked, using his hands to sign the words he couldn't speak.

Lizzie signed back. "I'll be home soon."

John Henry's small hands flew. "Promise?"

"Promise," Lizzie confirmed.

And then the vision faded, leaving Lizzie longing to find it again.

As she settled her nerves, she was aware of Morgan moving about the caboose, probably checking his various patients: Mrs. Halifax with her injured arm, Whitley with his broken leg, the peddler, Mr. Christian, who'd nearly gotten himself frozen to death, and last of all poor John Brennan, struggling with pneumonia.

And over them all loomed the mountain, ominously silent. Finally Lizzie slept.

Christmas.

It had never meant so much to Morgan as it did that night. He wanted to give Lizzie everything—trinkets, the finest silks and laces, and beyond those things…his heart. For a brief fraction of a moment, he actually wished he'd granted his mother's wishes and become a banker, instead of a doctor.

Annoyed with himself, he shoved both hands through his hair, as he always did when he was frustrated—and that was often.

He concentrated on what he knew, taking care of the sick and injured, knowing full well that sleep would elude him.

John Brennan seemed marginally better.

Mrs. Halifax would be fine, once she'd gotten some real rest.

Mr. Thaddings was resting quietly, the bluish color gone from his lips.

Even Christian, the peddler, who had come dangerously close to dying, appeared to be rallying somewhat. He might lose a few toes, but otherwise, he'd probably be his old self soon.

Whitley Carson's leg would mend; he was young, healthy and strong. Unless he was the biggest fool who ever lived, he'd pursue Lizzie until she accepted his proposal, married him and bore his children. Maybe he was smart enough to know that a woman like Lizzie McKettrick came along about as often as the proverbial blue moon, and maybe he wasn't.

Morgan hoped devoutly for the latter.

If they got out of this situation alive, Morgan decided, and if Lizzie *didn't* change her mind about marrying Whitley, by some miracle, he would court her himself.

Did he love her?

He didn't know. He certainly admired her, respected her and, God knew, *wanted* her, and not just physically. She'd opened some whole new region in his soul, an actual landscape, golden with light. Should Lizzie refuse his suit, as she well might, he'd have that magical place to retreat into, for the rest of his life, and he'd find some sad solace there.

He shook his head. Such thoughts were utterly foreign to his nature. He was a realist; did not have a fanciful bone in his body. He was a doctor, not a poet. And yet Lizzie had changed him, and he knew the alteration was permanent.

The coffee was cold, and full of grounds, but he poured some anyway, and lifted it to his lips. Moved to the window side of the car to look out over the blue-white night. He sipped, pondering the irony of meeting Lizzie in this peculiar time and place.

And before he'd swallowed a second sip of coffee, he heard the deep, growling rumble overhead.

Chapter Six

The caboose shook violently, rousing Lizzie instantly from a shallow sleep. She sat bolt upright, the startled shouts of the others echoing in her ears, her heart in her throat, and waited for the railroad car to go tumbling over the side of the cliff.

It didn't.

There was a second great shudder, and then...stillness.

Was this what it was like to die?

She looked around, but the darkness was as densely black as India ink. She might have been at the bottom of a coal mine at midnight, for all she could see.

"Morgan?" she called softly.

"I'm here," he assured her, from somewhere close by.

"What happened?" asked one of the children.

"How come it's so dark?" inquired the other, the words scrambling over those of the other child.

"Dark!" Woodrow fretted loudly. "Dark!"

"There's been another avalanche," Morgan said matter-of-factly, over Woodrow's continuing rant. "The snow must be blocking the windows, but we're still on the tracks, I think."

"Did the Christmas tree get ruint?" Lizzie identified the voice as Ellen's.

"Never mind the Christmas tree," Whitley said, sounding testy and shaken. "And will somebody shut that bird up?"

"Will somebody shut that bird up?" Woodrow repeated.

"How long will the air last?" John Brennan asked.

"I don't know," Morgan asked. "Everybody stay put. I'll see if I can get the door open to have a look. Maybe we can dig our way out."

"We could smother in here," Whitley said.

"Hush," Lizzie snapped. "We're not going to smother!"

"Stringy bird!" Woodrow prattled on. "Don't eat the bird!"

The baby began to cry, first tentatively, then with a full-lunged wail.

Mrs. Halifax sang to the infant, her soft voice quavering.

Mrs. Thaddings spoke tenderly to Woodrow.

A match was struck, lamplight flared, feeble against the terrible darkness. Morgan stood holding the lantern, a man woven of shadows. The incongruous thought came to Lizzie that he needed a shave.

Snow covered the windows on both sides of the car now, and it was clear that Morgan had been unable to force the door open. They were effectively buried alive.

Remarkably, the forlorn little Christmas tree still stood, the gifts undisturbed beneath it.

"Look!" Ellen cried, nudging a blinking Jack and pointing to the spectacle. "St. Nicholas came!"

Lizzie's gaze locked with Morgan's. Something unspoken passed between them, and Morgan nodded.

Lizzie worked up a cheerful smile. "And there are presents for everyone," she said, making her way to the tree. She took her prized coat up first, handed it to Mrs. Halifax. "For you," she said. She gave John Henry's paint set to Ellen and Jack, and Whitley's hand-tailored overcoat went to John Brennan, the pipe she'd bought for her father to Mr. Christian. Whitley got the book, and Morgan the pocket watch. She gave Mr. and Mrs. Thaddings a small box of hand-dipped chocolates from a shop in San Francisco, specially chosen for Lorelei.

"What about you?" Ellen asked, staring first at the paint set and then at Lizzie. "Isn't there something for you, Miss Lizzie?"

For the first time since he'd returned to the railroad car, clutching that little tree, Mr. Christian spoke a coherent sentence. "Why, St. Nicholas meant the music box for Lizzie," he said weakly.

Ellen relaxed, much to Lizzie's relief, and set to examining the paints and brushes and special paper she and Jack were to share. She wouldn't accept the music box, of course, as generous as Mr. Christian was to offer it—it had belonged to his late wife, after all. It was an heirloom.

They couldn't build a fire, for fear the chimney was covered by a deep layer of snow, and the chill set in pretty quickly. If they were going to die, Lizzie decided, they would die in good spirits.

She squared her shoulders and lifted her chin, but before she could speak, she heard the first, faint clank, and then another.

"Listen!" she said, shushing everyone.

Another clank, and then another—metal, striking metal. Shovels? Distant and faint, perhaps up the line of cars a ways, toward the engine.

"They're here," Lizzie whispered. "They're here!"

Everyone looked up, as though expecting their rescuers to descend through the roof.

Time seemed to stop.

Clank, clank, clank.

And then—some minutes later—footsteps on the metal roof of the caboose, a muffled voice.

Her papa's voice.

"Lizzie!" Holt McKettrick called.

"In here, Papa!" Lizzie cried, on a joyous sob. "In the caboose!"

She heard him speak to the others—her uncles and perhaps even her grandfather. The clanking commenced in earnest then, and the voices became clearer.

"Lizzie?" Her papa again. "Hold on, sweetheart."

The door Morgan had been unable to open earlier jostled on its hinges, then creaked with an ear-splitting squeal. Holt McKettrick gave a wrench from outside, and then he was there, filling the chasm.

Big. Strong. So handsome he made Lizzie's heart swell with pride and gladness. Holt McKettrick would have moved heaven and earth, if he had to, for his daughter, for a train full of strangers.

Lizzie flew to him.

He scooped her up into his arms, clean off her feet, and kissed her hard on top of the head. She felt the warmth of his tears in her hair. "Thank God," he murmured. *"Thank God."*

She clung, crying freely now, not even trying to hold back the sobs of joy rising from the very core of her being. "Papa… Papa!"

"Hush," Holt said gruffly. "You're all right now, girl."

Behind him, she saw her uncles enter—Rafe then Kade then Jeb. Then another man, someone Lizzie didn't recognize.

"Pa!" Ellen and Jack screamed in unison, rushing to be enfolded in the tall, lean cowboy's waiting arms. Over their heads he exchanged a look of reverent gratitude with Mrs. Halifax, who was holding the baby so tightly that it struggled in her embrace. Tears slipped down her face.

Lizzie finally recovered a modicum of composure when Holt set her back on her feet. She gulped, looking up at him. "I knew you'd come," she said.

Holt grinned. "Of course we came," he replied. "We couldn't have had Christmas without our Lizzie."

"S-some of the others are hurt," Lizzie said, remembering suddenly, feeling some chagrin that, in her excitement, she'd forgotten them.

Her uncles were already assessing the situation.

"We'd better get out of here quick, Holt," Rafe said, with an upward glance. He was a big man, burly and dark-haired, his eyes the intense blue of a chambray work shirt.

Kade, meanwhile, greeted Morgan with a handshake. "Hell of a welcome to Indian Rock," he said, as Lizzie drank in the sight of him—well built, with chestnut hair and a quiet manner. He gave her a wink.

Morgan looked solemn—and completely exhausted. "The engineer and the conductor didn't make it," he told Kade. "They're in the locomotive."

Kade nodded grimly. "We'll have to come back for them later," he said. "Along with any trunks or the like. Rafe's right. We'd best get while the getting is good."

After that, things happened fast, and Lizzie experienced it all through a numbing haze, shimmering silvery at the edges. They'd brought a large, flat-bed sleigh, as Lizzie had expected they would, piled with loose straw and drawn by four gigantic plow horses. There were blankets and bear hides, too, to keep the travelers warm, and flasks filled with strong spirits. Farther along the tracks, her father told her, half the hands from the Triple M waited, having set up camp the night before, when they'd all had to stop because of the darkness and the weather.

Lizzie was bundled, like a child, in quilts she recognized from home, and her uncle Jeb, the youngest McKettrick brother, fair-haired and agile, carried her to the sleigh. She settled into a sort of dizzy stupor, the sweet scent of the fresh straw lulling her further.

"You're safe now, Lizzie-bet," Jeb told her, his azure eyes glistening suspiciously. "Pa kicked up some kind of fuss when we wouldn't let him come along to find you. Too hard on his heart, Concepcion said. We had to hogtie him and throw him in jail, and we could still hear him bellowing five miles out of town."

Lizzie smiled at the image of her proud grandfather behind bars. He'd be prowling like a caged mountain lion, furious that they'd left him behind. "There'll be the devil to pay when you let him out," she warned.

Jeb chuckled, ran the sleeve of his wool-lined leather coat across his eyes. "We're counting on you to put in a good word for us," he said, tucking straw in around her before turning to go back and help bring out the others.

When they had all been rescued, and placed securely on the back of the heavy sled, Holt took the reins and shouted to the team. Kade and Jeb rode mules, as did Mr. Halifax.

The going was slow, the snow being so deep, and it was precarious. Lizzie drifted in and out of her hazy reverie, aware of Whitley nearby, and Morgan at a little distance.

Considerable time passed before they reached the camp Holt had mentioned. Cowboys greeted them with hot coffee and good cheer, and they lingered awhile, in a broad, snowy clearing under a copse of bare-limbed oak trees, safe from the possibility of another avalanche.

It was past nightfall when they reached Indian Rock.

A soft snow was falling, church bells rang, and it seemed the whole town had turned out to greet the Christmas travelers. Lorelei rushed to Lizzie, knelt on the bed of the sleigh, and pulled her into her arms.

"Lizzie," she whispered, over and over again. "Oh, Lizzie!"

Next, Lizzie saw her grandfather, tall and fierce-faced, his thick white hair askew because he'd been thrusting his fingers through it. His gaze swept over his sons, daring any one of them to interfere, then he gathered Lizzie right up and carried her inside the Arizona Hotel.

The lobby was blessedly warm, and alight with glowing lamps.

There were people everywhere.

"Lizzie-bet," Angus McKettrick said, "you like to scared me to death when your train didn't turn up on time."

Lizzie rested her head against his strong shoulder. "I'm sorry, Grampa," she said. Then she looked up into his face. "I reckon you're pretty mad at Papa and Kade and Rafe and Jeb," she ventured. "For locking you up, I mean."

"I'll have their hides for it," Angus vowed, and though his voice was rough as sandpaper, Lizzie heard the tenderness in it. He loved his four sons deeply, and probably understood that they'd only been trying to protect him by throwing him in the hoosegow. "Right now, Lizzie-girl, all I care about is that you're safe. Soon as you've rested up, we'll all head home to the Triple M."

"I guess I missed Christmas," Lizzie said.

Angus carried her up the stairs and into a waiting room. He laid her gently on the bed, and stepped back to let Lorelei attend to her. Only then did he reply, "You didn't miss Christmas. We held it for you."

"Leave us alone, Angus," Lorelei said quietly. "I need to get Lizzie out of these wet, cold clothes and into something warm and dry."

Angus clenched his jaw, then inclined his head to Lizzie in reluctant farewell before leaving the room and closing the door softly behind him.

"What happened out there?" Lorelei asked, as she deftly undid the buttons on Lizzie's shoes.

"There was an avalanche," Lizzie said. The warmth of the room made her skin burn, and she wondered, briefly, if she'd been frostbitten. If she'd lose fingers and toes or maybe an ear. Tears scalded her eyes. She was *alive,* that was what mattered. And she was home—or almost home. "I didn't let myself think for one moment that Papa and the others wouldn't come for us." Her conscience stirred. "Well," she added, "maybe there were a *few* moments—"

Lorelei smiled gently, continuing to peel away Lizzie's clothes, then dressing her again in a long flannel nightgown. "You were McKettrick tough," Lorelei said, when she'd pulled the bedcovers up to Lizzie's chin. "We're all very proud of you, Lizzie."

"The others—Morgan, Whitley...the children...?"

"They're all being taken care of, sweetheart. Don't worry."

Lizzie closed her eyes, sighed. "I hope I'm not dreaming," she said "You're really here, aren't you, Lorelei? You and Papa and Grampa—?"

"Rest, Lizzie," Lorelei said, with tears in her voice. "It's not a dream. You're back home in Indian Rock, with your family around you."

She recalled the Thaddingses and how they expected to find Miss Clarinda Adams running a dressmaker's shop, not a high-toned brothel. Would Miss Adams take them in, Mr. and Mrs. Thaddings and Woodrow? Or would they refuse, in their inevitable shock, to accept hospitality from the town madam?

Where would they go, either way? Lizzie knew very little about them, but she had discerned that they weren't rich.

"There's an older couple—they have a bird—they think Clarinda Adams makes dresses for a living—"

Lorelei smiled, patting Lizzie's hand. "Clarinda's moved

on," she said. "Married one of her clients and high-tailed it back east three months ago."

"But Mr. and Mrs. Thaddings—they expected to stay with her...."

"Everyone will be taken care of, Lizzie, so stop worrying. Right now, you need to rest."

"There's a bird—"

"Hush," Lorelei said, kissing Lizzie's forehead. "I'll make sure the Thaddingses *and* their bird find lodging."

Lizzie sighed again and slept.

Morgan assessed his new quarters. The town had built on to the hotel, providing him with a small office and examination room and living space behind that. The place was well furnished and well supplied. He found coffee on the shelf above the small stove and put some on to brew.

His bed was within kicking distance, narrow and made up with clean blankets, obviously secondhand. There was a bathtub, too, a great, incongruous thing served by a complicated system of exposed pipes, equally close, and with a copper hot water tank attached to the wall above it.

He smiled to himself. If only his mother could see him now.

Morgan lit the gas jet under the boiler on the hot water tank—it would take a while to heat—and put coffee on to brew while he waited. Finally he filled the tub with water, steaming gloriously. His clothes and other belongings were still on the train, out there on the mountainside, but thanks to the McKettricks, he'd been provided with a change of clothes, shaving gear, soap and a tall bottle of whiskey.

After he poured coffee into a chipped cup, also donated no doubt, and then added a generous dollop of whiskey for good measure, he stripped and lowered himself into the tub.

The bath was bliss, and so was the whiskey-laced coffee.

But the best thing was knowing Lizzie was all right, safe upstairs, being cared for by her stepmother.

John Brennan's family had been right there to greet him as soon as they arrived, and two of the townsmen had carried him, blanket-wrapped and half-delirious, toward the mercantile. If John made it through the night, Morgan figured he'd have a good chance of surviving.

Whitley Carson was resting in one of the hotel rooms, as were the Halifaxes, the Thaddingses and Woodrow.

Morgan hadn't seen where the peddler was taken, but he assumed he'd been gathered up, too, by kinfolks or friends. For the time being, Morgan could allow himself to simply be a very relieved, very tired man, not a doctor.

He finished the coffee and soaked until the water began to cool, then hastily shaved, scrubbed and got out of the tub. Dressed in his borrowed clothes, he headed for the lobby. The place was so crowded he'd have sworn somebody was throwing a party.

After a few moments, he realized his first impression had been right. The entire town seemed to be present, hoisting a glass, celebrating that the lost had been found. Kade caught his eye and beckoned, and Morgan followed him through the cheerful throng into the hotel dining room.

"Figured you'd be hungry for hot food," McKettrick said.

Morgan *was* hungry, though he hadn't realized it until that moment. His stomach grumbled loudly, and he sat down at one of the tables next to the window, looking out at the Christmas-card snowfall.

A waitress appeared, and Kade, seated across from him, ordered for them both. There was no one else in the dining room.

"Thanks," Morgan said.

McKettrick raised one eyebrow, but didn't speak.

"For coming for us," Morgan clarified. "Lizzie said you would. I don't think she ever doubted it—but I wasn't so sure."

Kade smiled fondly at the mention of Lizzie's name. "If there's one of us missing from the supper table," he said, "the rest will turn the whole countryside on its top to find them."

"It must be nice to be part of a family like that," Morgan said, without really meaning to. He didn't feel sorry for himself, and he didn't want to give the impression that he did.

"It has its finer moments," Kade answered mildly. "I take it you don't come from a big outfit like ours?"

"There's just me," Morgan replied. "That peddler—Mr. Christian—did somebody come to meet him?"

Kade frowned. "Who?"

The waitress returned with hot bread, a butter dish and two cups of coffee, all balanced on a tray.

Morgan didn't answer until she'd gone again.

"Mr. Christian. An older man, a peddler with a sample case."

Kade shook his head. "I don't recall anybody fitting that description," he said. "There was you and Lizzie, the Halifaxes, the soldier, an elderly pair with a bird and the yahoo with the broken leg."

Morgan started to rise from his chair, certain the old peddler must have been left behind by mistake. Or maybe he'd fallen off the sleigh, somewhere along the way, and nobody had noticed—

"Sit down," Kade said. "We got everybody off that train. Everybody who was still alive, anyway."

Morgan sank back into his chair, befuddled. "But there has to be some kind of mistake. There was an old man—ask Lizzie—ask any of the others—"

"I'll do that, if it makes you happy," Kade allowed. "But we got everybody there was to get."

The food came. Fried chicken, mashed potatoes swimming in gravy, green beans cooked with onions and bacon. It was a feast, and Morgan was so desperately hungry that he practically dove into his plate. He was done-in, he told himself. Not thinking straight. In the morning, after a good night's sleep, he'd make sense of the matter of Mr. Christmas, as the children had called him.

They'd lighted the candles on the tree for him, and made him up a nice bed on the settee, there in the fine apartments above the mercantile, and his wife and boy were staying close, while the in-laws hovered in the distance. There was good food cooking, and a fire blazing on the hearth, and John Brennan figured he'd died for sure and gone straight to heaven.

"St. Nicholas *did too* come," Jack told his smilingly skeptical father. "He brought a paint set for Ellen and me."

"Did he now?" Ben Halifax asked his son. Mama, Ellen and the baby were all sleeping, cozied up in the same hotel bed. Ben and Jack would share the other, and, in the morning, if the weather was good and everybody was up to the trip, they'd all head out to the Triple M, where they'd be staying on, not just passing through. "I guess he must have been in two places at once, then, because he filled some stockings out at the ranch, too."

Jack widened his eyes. He'd had supper, and he knew he ought to be in bed asleep, like his mama and sisters, but he was just plain too excited. "But me and Ellen wasn't there to hang any stockings," he argued.

"I hung them up for you," his father said. "And darned if I didn't wake up this morning and find those old work socks just a-bulging with presents."

Jack blinked, wonderstruck. "I guess if anybody could be

in two places at once," he said with certainty, "it would be St. Nicholas who done it."

Ben laughed, ruffled the boy's hair. His eyes glistened, and if Jack hadn't known better, he'd have bet his pa was crying. "It's Christmas," Ben said, his voice sounding all scrapey and rough. "The time when miracles happen."

"What's a miracle?" Jack asked, puzzled.

"It's having you and your ma and your sisters right here with me, where you belong," Ben answered. Then he did something Jack couldn't remember him ever doing before. He lifted Jack onto his lap, held him real tight, and kissed him on top of the head. "Yesiree, that's all the miracle I need."

Zebulon Thaddings bent to strike a match to the fire laid in the hearth of the sumptuously decorated parlor. The lamps all had painted globes, the rugs were foreign, the furniture plentiful and fussy, and there were naked people cavorting in the paintings on the walls.

"Your sister has done well, for a dressmaker," he told Marietta, who was gazing about with an expression of troubled wonder on her dear face. In point of fact, he hadn't wanted to make this journey in the first place, since he'd known all along, even if his wife hadn't, how Clarinda had been able to afford the fine jewelry and exquisite clothing she'd worn when she visited them in Phoenix. There simply hadn't been any other possible explanation.

Zebulon had lost his job running an Indian school, and with it, of course, the minuscule salary and the tiny house provided for the headmaster and his wife. They were destitute. The plain and difficult truth was that they had hoped Clarinda would take them in, along with Woodrow, not just welcome them for a holiday visit.

They'd had nowhere else to go, and Zebulon had used

the last few dollars he had to pay for their train fare to Indian Rock.

Now they were basically squatting in Clarinda's grand house. God only knew where they would go next, but for the time being, at least, they had a roof over their heads, a bed to sleep in, and a pantry stocked with foodstuffs.

Woodrow, provided with a fresh supply of birdseed by a kindly shopkeeper, sat in his shiny cage, looking around.

"Why are all these people...naked?" Marietta fretted, wringing her hands a little as she took in the large and scandalous painting above the fireplace. Bare-fleshed men and women lay about a forest, some of them intertwined, eating grapes, sipping from elaborate chalices and generally looking swoony.

"Naked!" Woodrow exclaimed. "Naked as a jaybird!"

Woodrow mostly repeated the words of others, but occasionally, like now, he added commentary of his own from his past repertoire. Zebulon had to smile.

Crossing to Marietta, the Turkish rug soft beneath the thin soles of his shoes, he embraced his wife. She'd been a true helpmeet over the years, never complaining about their near penury, never voicing her great disappointment that they hadn't been blessed with children of their own.

"Dearest," he said, after clearing his throat. "About Clarinda—"

Marietta looked up at him, tears gleaming in her gentle eyes. "She isn't a dressmaker, is she?"

Zebulon shook his head. "No," he answered.

"What are we going to do, Zebulon?"

Zebulon's own eyes burned. He blinked rapidly. "I don't know," he said.

"Perhaps Clarinda intends to return soon," Marietta speculated hopefully, brightening a little.

"Perhaps," Zebulon agreed, though doubtful.

"Hadn't we better send her a wire or write a letter? Some-one in Indian Rock must have her address."

The scent of cigar smoke lingered in the air. Clarinda's pos-sessions were all around, giving the strange impression that she'd merely left the room, not the territory.

"You ought to lie down and rest awhile, dear," Zebulon told Marietta. "I'll brew a nice pot of tea."

Marietta hesitated, then nodded. Gently raised, and a preacher's daughter into the bargain, she hadn't quite accepted the obvious—that her spirited younger sister ran a house of ill repute. She settled herself on the long, plush sofa facing the fireplace, and Zebulon covered her tenderly with a knit-ted afghan.

"Tea!" Woodrow chirped, as Zebulon left the room, headed for the massive kitchen. "Tea for two!"

When Lizzie opened her eyes, the room was full of snow-gleam, and her young brothers were standing next to her bed. Well, at least, John Henry was standing—Doss and Gabriel were jumping up and down on the foot of the mattress, shout-ing, "Wake up! Wake up!"

Lizzie laughed, used her elbows to push herself upright. After fluffing her pillows, she leaned back against them.

Lorelei appeared and whisked the younger boys away, both of them protesting vigorously. Was Lizzie going to sleep all day long? Wouldn't they *ever* get to go home and open their Christmas presents?

John Henry stayed behind, regarding Lizzie with solemn, thoughtful eyes.

She ruffled his hair.

"I saw you in our room," John Henry signed. "On Christmas Eve."

A shock went through Lizzie as she remembered her imagined visit home. "I was still on the train on Christmas Eve," she signed back.

John Henry shook his head, repeated, the motions of his small, deft hands insistent, "I *saw* you, Lizzie," he reiterated. "You were wearing a man's coat and your hair was all mussed up. You said not to worry, because you were coming home soon."

Lizzie blinked. Something tightened in her throat, making it impossible to speak.

The door of the hotel room opened, and her father came in. He sent John Henry downstairs to have breakfast with his brothers, and the child scampered to obey, but not before he cast one last, knowing look back at Lizzie.

Holt dragged a chair up alongside the bed. "Feeling better?" he asked.

Lizzie nodded.

"Lorelei's bringing up a tray. All your favorites. Sausage, hotcakes with lots of syrup, and tea."

He offered Lizzie his hand, and she took it. After swallowing, she managed to speak. "Morgan," she said. "Is he... is he all right?"

"He's fine," Holt answered with a slight frown. "I guess I figured you'd be more interested in the other one. According to young Mr. Carson, he means to set about claiming your hand in marriage, first chance he gets. Already asked for my permission to propose."

Lizzie's emotions must have shown clearly on her face, because her father's frown deepened. "What did you say?" she asked, almost in a whisper.

"I told him you were nineteen years old, and if you want to marry him, that's all right by me." Holt shifted in the hotel chair, which seemed almost too spindly to support his powerful frame. "Should I have said something different, Lizzie?"

A tear slipped down Lizzie's cheek. "I don't love Whitley, Papa. I thought I did—oh, I *really* thought I did—but when everything happened up there on the mountain—"

Holt leaned forward, folded his arms, rested them on his knees as he regarded his daughter. "It's the doctor you love, then," he said. "Morgan Shane."

"I wouldn't say I love him," Lizzie replied slowly, after some thought. "I don't know *what* I feel. He's strong and he's good and when people were hurt and sick, he forgot about himself and did what had to be done. On the other hand, he makes me so angry sometimes—"

Holt smiled. "I see. I assume Mr. Carson didn't comport himself in the same way?"

"No," Lizzie said. "But I suppose I could overlook that, if I wanted to. It's just that, when I met Morgan, everything changed."

"Well then, when the proposal comes, you'll have to turn it down."

"Couldn't you just—withdraw your permission? Tell Whitley you've changed your mind and he can't propose to me after all?"

Her father chuckled, shook his head. "It isn't like you to take the coward's way out," he said. "You brought that young fella all the way up here from California, intending to show him off to all of us and, I suspect, hoping he'd give you an engagement ring. You'll have to tell him the truth, Lizzie. However he might have behaved on that train, he deserves that much."

Lizzie sighed heavily and sank back onto her pillows. "You're right," she said dolefully.

Holt laughed. "It's nice to hear you admit that," he said, as Lorelei came in with the promised tray, and despite the prospect of refusing Whitley Carson's suit, Lizzie ate with a good appetite. She expected to remember that particular meal for the rest of her natural life, it was so delicious.

When her father had gone—there had been a thaw, and he, Rafe, Kade and Jeb were heading out to the ranch to feed livestock—Lorelei had a bathtub brought to the room and filled bucket by bucket with gloriously hot water. After breakfast, a bath and a shampoo, Lizzie felt fully recovered from her ordeal. She dressed in clothes Lorelei had purchased for her at the mercantile, a green woollen dress with lace at the collar, lovely sheer stockings and fashionable high-button shoes.

"You mustn't overdo," Lorelei fretted. Usually a practical person, today Lizzie's stepmother seemed almost fragile. The shadows under her eyes indicated that she'd worried a great deal over the past few days, and gotten little or no sleep.

"Lorelei," Lizzie said, placing her hands on her stepmother's pale cheeks, "I'm home. I'm *fine*. You said it yourself—I'm McKettrick tough."

"I was so frightened," Lorelei confessed, with an uncharacteristic sniffle.

The two women embraced, clung tightly.

"I want to look in on the others," Lizzie said, when they'd drawn apart. "Morgan—Dr. Shane—first. Then Whitley and Mr. and Mrs. Thaddings and the Halifaxes and John Brennan and Mr. Christian—"

Lorelei frowned. "Mr. Christian? I recall the other names— and I met Dr. Shane last night. But no one mentioned a Mr. Christian."

"You must have seen him," Lizzie insisted. "He was very ill—with frostbite—and he would have needed tending. I'll ask Morgan."

Lorelei still seemed puzzled. "Perhaps I'm mistaken," she said doubtfully. Lorelei McKettrick was rarely mistaken about anything, and everyone knew it. She paused, rallied a little.

"I'd better round up your brothers. They must have finished breakfast by now, and my guess is, they'll be up to mischief pretty soon."

Lizzie and Lorelei went down the stairs together and parted in the lobby. Lizzie immediately noticed Whitley sitting alone in a leather chair, his injured leg propped on an ottoman, gazing out at the snowy street beyond the window. He looked almost forlorn.

Procrastinating, Lizzie decided resolutely, would only make matters worse. She approached, cleared her throat softly when Whitley didn't notice her right away.

When he did, his face lit up and he started to rise.

"Please," Lizzie said. "Don't get up."

He sank back into his chair, gestured goodnaturedly at the plaster cast replacing the improvised splint Morgan had applied onboard the stranded train. "Modern medicine," he said. "I'll be walking properly within six weeks."

"That's wonderful," Lizzie said, wringing her hands a little, then quickly tucking them behind her back. "I'm... I'm so sorry, Whitley."

"For what?" he asked.

"Getting you into all this," Lizzie answered, flustered. "Inviting you here— You wouldn't have broken your leg if I hadn't, or nearly perished in an avalanche—"

Whitley's smile faded, and he tried to stand again.

To keep him in his chair, Lizzie drew up a second ottoman and perched on it, facing him.

"Lizzie?" he prompted when she didn't say anything right away. She, affectionately known on the Triple M as "chatterbox," couldn't seem to find words.

"I saw the ring," she said. "When I took your good overcoat out of your trunk to put under the Christmas tree for John Brennan."

"Ah," Whitley said, still unsmiling. "The ring. It belonged to my grandmother, you know. I had it reset, before we left San Francisco."

Pain flashed through Lizzie. For a moment, she actually considered accepting Whitley's ring, going through with the wedding, just to keep from dashing his hopes. Reason soon prevailed—she'd do him far greater harm if she trapped him in a loveless marriage. "It's very beautiful," she said sadly.

Whitley's face filled with eagerness and hope. "Will you marry me, Lizzie? I know this isn't the most romantic proposal, and I don't even have the ring to put on your finger, since it's still in my trunk and none of our things have been recovered from the train yet, but I've already spoken to your father—"

"Whitley," Lizzie said, almost moaning the name, *"stop."*

"Lizzie—"

"No," she whispered raggedly. "Please. I can't marry you, Whitley. I don't… I don't love you."

"You'll *learn* to love me—"

Lizzie shook her head.

Whitley reddened. "It's Shane, isn't it? He's stolen you away from me, turned your head, acting like a hero on the train—"

Again Lizzie shook her head. Then she couldn't bear it any longer, and she got to her feet and turned to flee, only to collide hard with Morgan.

Chapter Seven

Morgan gripped Lizzie's shoulders gently and steadied her. Spoke her name in a worried rasp. Behind her, Lizzie heard Whitley shoving to his feet, and his anger struck her back like a flood of something hot and dark.

"What can he give you?" Whitley demanded furiously. "Tell me what *Dr.* Morgan Shane can give you that I can't!"

Mortified, Lizzie gazed helplessly up into Morgan's concerned face. She saw a muscle twitch in his strong jawline, and his gaze sliced past her to Whitley.

His expression strained—he was clearly trying to rein in his temper—Morgan pressed Lizzie into a nearby chair and turned on Whitley.

"What the *hell* is going on here?" he growled.

Awash in misery and abject humiliation, Lizzie sat up very straight and breathed deeply. She had not turned down Whitley's proposal precisely because of her feelings for Morgan, though they had certainly been part of her reasoning. Now Morgan would think she'd set her cap for him, refused Whitley so she could pursue Indian Rock's handsome new doctor instead.

In fact, she hadn't decided anything of the kind. Yes, she was drawn to Morgan, profoundly so, but it was far too soon to know if the attraction would last. And how in the *world* was she going to look him directly in the eye, after a scene like this?

"You took advantage!" Whitley shouted at Morgan, every word ricocheting off Lizzie's most tender places like a stone flung hard and true to its mark.

"Sit down, before you fall over," Morgan replied, his voice ominously calm. "And may I remind you that this is a public place?"

Lizzie couldn't look at either of them. Indeed, it was all she could do not to cover her face with both hands in absolute mortification.

"What can you give her, Shane?" Whitley persisted, sputtering now. "Tell me that! A name? A respectable home? Money?" He paused, gathering his forces to go on. "*My* family has a mansion on Nob Hill and a place in San Francisco society. Our name—"

Out of the corner of her eye, Lizzie saw her grandfather striding toward them, from the direction of the hotel dining room. "Lizzie *has* a name—a fine one," Angus boomed. "It's McKettrick. And she'll never lack for money or a 'respectable home,' either!"

Lizzie risked a glance at Morgan and saw that he looked confounded and not a little angry. He must have felt her gaze, because he returned it, though only briefly, a sharp, cutting edge.

"It is my understanding," he said coolly, ignoring Angus and Lizzie, too, "that Miss McKettrick intends to teach school, rather than marry. If she's spurned you, Carson, you have my sympathies, but her decision has nothing to do with me. And if you want your nose broken as well as your leg, just keep raving like a lunatic. I'll be happy to oblige."

At last, drawing some quiet strength from her grandfather's presence, Lizzie managed to look directly, and steadily, at Whitley and Morgan. They were standing dangerously close to each other, their hands clenched into fists at their sides, their eyes blazing.

"Reminds me of a couple of bucks facing off in rutting season," Angus observed, looking and sounding amused, now that he knew what the ruckus was about, and that his granddaughter was in no physical danger.

Lizzie blushed so hard her cheeks ached. "Whitley misunderstood," she told Morgan, after swallowing hard. "When I told him I couldn't accept his proposal, he jumped to the conclusion that…that something was happening between you and me."

"Imagine that," Morgan said, his tone scathing.

Inside, where no one could see, Lizzie flinched. Outside, she wore her fierce McKettrick pride like an inflexible garment. "Imagine that indeed," she retorted, as a frown took shape on Angus's face. "It just so happens that I'm not the least bit interested in *either* of you."

With that, she made for the doorway leading onto the street.

As she left, she heard mutters from both Whitley and Morgan, and a low burst of laughter from her grandfather.

At least Lizzie wasn't going to marry Carson, Morgan reflected, while he willed himself to simmer down. His pride stung, he'd retreated to his office, and once there, he took a fresh look around.

Carson was right. Morgan couldn't offer Lizzie a mansion, or a name more prominent than the one she already had. God knew, he didn't have money, either.

Saddened, Morgan went on through the office and into his living quarters—the stove, the bulky bathtub, the too-narrow bed. He couldn't imagine Lizzie living happily in such a place—though the bed had a certain delicious potential—when she was used to big ranch houses, fancy schools, the best of everything.

He heard the office door open, shoved a hand through his hair and went to see if he had a patient. He found Angus McKettrick looming in the examining room, which must have seemed hardly larger than a tobacco tin to a man of his size and stature. White-haired and wise-eyed, McKettrick studied Morgan.

"Where there's smoke," he said, in that portentous voice of his, "there's bound to be fire."

Morgan studied him, at a loss for a response.

"Our Lizzie-bet," Angus went on, after indulging in a crooked little smile and folding arms the size of tree trunks, "is too much woman for most men."

Morgan felt his neck heat up. "Lizzie's independent-minded, all right," he agreed evenly. "But if you're here because you think I wrecked her marriage plans with Mr. Nob Hill out there, I didn't."

"Oh, I believe you did," Angus said complacently. "You just don't seem to *know* it."

Something inside Morgan soared, then dived straight back to hard ground, landing with shattering impact. "You heard Lizzie," he said, when he was fairly certain he could speak rationally. "She's not interested in Carson *or* me."

"So she says," Angus drawled. "I don't think Lizzie knows what's going on here any more than you do."

"Look around you," Morgan bit out, waving one hand for emphasis. "This is what I have to offer your granddaughter."

"Not much to it," Angus agreed, his tone dry, his eyes

twinkling. "But I think there's something to *you,* Dr. Shane. You've got some gumption and grit, the way I hear it, and Lizzie's cut from the same kind of cloth. She'd climb straight up the velvet draperies, penned up in some fancy house in San Francisco. She's a country girl, and something of a tomboy. She sits a horse as well as any of us, and she can shoot, too. Before you go deciding you don't have what she needs, you might want to spend a little time finding out just what that is."

The old man's words nettled Morgan and, at the same time, gave him hope. "What makes you think I'm interested in Lizzie?" he asked.

Angus merely chuckled. Shook his head.

And, having said his piece, he turned and left Morgan's office, the door standing wide open behind him.

Lizzie stormed toward nothing in particular, delighting in the bracing chill of the winter air as she left the Arizona Hotel, the familiar sights and sounds surrounding her, the hustle and bustle of wagons, buckboards and buggies weaving through the snowy street. Furious tears scalded her cheeks, and she wiped them away with a dash of one hand, walking faster and then faster still.

When she found herself in front of the mercantile, its wide display window cheerfully festooned with bright ribbon and evergreen boughs, she stopped, drew a deep breath and went inside.

The scent of Christmas assailed her—a tall pine stood in the center of the general store, bedecked with costly German ornaments, shining and new. Brightly wrapped gifts, probably empty, encircled the base of the tree.

A woman in her early thirties rounded the counter, smiling. She wore a practical dress of lightweight gray woolen, and her blond hair, pinned into a loose chignon at her nape, escaped in wisps around her delicate face. Her eyes were a shining blue, and they smiled at Lizzie a fraction of a moment before her bow-shaped mouth followed suit.

"Aren't they lovely?" the woman asked, apparently referring to the blown-glass balls and angels and St. Nicholases shimmering on the fragrant tree.

Lizzie nodded. She had not come into the mercantile to admire the merchandise, but to inquire after John Brennan. When she'd last seen him, he'd been desperately ill. "Mrs. Brennan?" she asked.

The woman nodded. Approached Lizzie and put out a hand. "Call me Alice," she said. "You must be Lizzie McKettrick. John told me how kind you were to him."

Lizzie swallowed. "Is he—is he better?"

Alice Brennan smiled. She was as pretty, and as fragile, as the most delicate of the tree ornaments. "He's holding on," she said, worry flickering in her eyes. "Would you like to see him?"

"I wouldn't want to disturb his rest," Lizzie said.

"I think he'd welcome a visit from you," Alice replied, turning slightly, beckoning for Lizzie to follow her.

Lizzie did follow, at once reluctant to impose on the Brennans and eager to see John and measure his progress with her own eyes.

There were stairs at the back of the large store, behind cloth curtains. Alice led the way up, with Lizzie a few steps behind.

The family living quarters above were spare, by comparison to downstairs, where every shelf and surface was stuffed with merchandise of various kinds, but a large iron cookstove chortled out heat in one corner, and there was a smaller Christmas tree on a table in front of the windows overlooking the street.

John Brennan lay, cosseted in blankets, on a settee. He smiled wanly when he saw Alice.

"I've brought you a visitor," Alice told her husband.

A little boy, undoubtedly Tad, sat on the floor near the settee, playing with a carved wooden horse. He looked up at Lizzie with benign curiosity, then went back to galloping the toy horse across a plain of pillows.

John beamed when he saw Lizzie; he'd been lying prone when she came in, and now he tried to sit up, but he was weak, and failed in the effort. Alice bent to kiss his forehead, smooth his hair back, murmur something to him. Then she stepped back and, with a gesture of one hand, offered Lizzie a seat in a sturdy wing-back chair nearby.

Lizzie sat, feeling like an intruder.

"You said I'd get home to Alice and the boy," John said, his eyes shining, "and here I am."

Lizzie only smiled, blinked back tears. John Brennan was home, but he was still a very sick man, obviously, and hardly out of danger. Had he survived the ordeal on the train, and the rigorous journey to Indian Rock by horse-drawn sleigh, only to succumb to pneumonia after all?

"I reckon if you say I'll get well," John labored to add, "that will happen, too. There's something real special about you, Lizzie McKettrick."

Lizzie's throat ached. "You'll get well," she said, more because she *wanted* to believe than because she did. Alas, there was no magic in her, as John seemed to think. She was an ordinary woman. "You've got little Tad to raise, and Alice and her folks will need your help running the store."

John nodded, relaxed a little, as though Lizzie had given him some vital gift by saying what he needed to hear. "You seem to be holding up all right," he said, the words rattling up out of his thin chest.

"I'll be fine," she said, and she knew that was true, at least. She'd hurt Whitley, and alienated Morgan in the process, but she still had her family, her friends, her teaching certificate, her future. John Brennan might not be that lucky.

"The others?" John asked.

She told him what she could about their fellow passengers—Whitley, the Halifaxes, Morgan. Mr. and Mrs. Thaddings, who were staying, according to Lorelei, in Clarinda Adams's house. She spoke of everyone except Mr. Christian; for some reason, she was hesitant to mention him.

"That's good," he said, and Lizzie saw that he could barely keep his eyes open. She'd stayed too long—it was past time for her to be on her way.

"Is there anything I can do to help?" she asked Alice, at the top of the stairs.

"Just pray," Alice said. "And come back to visit when you can. It heartens John, receiving company."

Lizzie nodded.

There had been no sign of Alice's parents, who actually owned the mercantile, according to what John had told her on the train. She'd meet them later, she was sure, since Indian Rock was a small town and she'd be trading at the store regularly, once she moved into the little room behind the schoolhouse.

Outside again, Lizzie decided she wasn't ready to go back to the hotel. Lorelei would insist that she lie down again, and even if she managed to avoid Morgan and Whitley as she passed through the lobby, she would still be painfully aware of their presence.

She pulled her cloak, provided by Lorelei, more tightly around her, raised the hood to protect her ears from the clear but bitter cold and proceeded along the sidewalk, again with no particular destination in mind. She wasn't headed *toward* anything, she realized uncomfortably, but *away* from Whitley's anger and Morgan's terse dismissal.

She went to the schoolhouse, a red-painted framework building with a tiny bell tower and quarters in back, for the teacher. Her aunt Chloe, Jeb's wife, had once taught here, and made her home in the little room behind the classroom.

All the doors were locked, but she stood on tiptoe to peer in a window at what would be her home directly after New Year's, when she took up her duties. There was a little stove, an iron bedstead, a table and chair and not much else. She'd looked so forward to teaching school, earning her own money, paltry though her salary was, shaping the lives of children in small but important ways.

Now it seemed a lonely prospect, as empty as those cheery packages under the Christmas tree in the mercantile.

She sighed and turned from the window and was startled to find Mr. Christian standing directly behind her. He looked particularly hearty, showing no signs of frostbite or exhaustion. In fact, there seemed to be a faint glow to his skin, and his eyes shone with well-being.

He touched the brim of his bowler hat. Smiled.

Lizzie felt something warm inside her, despite the unrelenting cold. "I'm so glad to see you," she said. "No one seems to remember—"

"No one seems to remember what?" Christian asked kindly. He wore a very fine overcoat, one Lizzie hadn't seen before, and his hands bulged in the deep pockets.

"Well," Lizzie said, groping a little, *"you."*

Mr. Christian smiled again. "Dr. Shane remembers," he said. "And the children will, too. Little Ellen and Jack will remember—always."

The oddness of the remark struck Lizzie, but she was so pleased to see that her friend had recovered that she paid little mind to it. "I've just been to visit John Brennan," she said. "I'm afraid—"

Mr. Christian cut her off with a kindly shake of his head. "He'll recover," he said with certainty.

Lizzie frowned, puzzled. "How can you be so sure?"

"Call it a Christmas miracle," Mr. Christian said.

A little thrill tripped down Lizzie's spine. The freezing air seemed charged somehow, as though electricity had gathered around the two of them, silent, a small, invisible tornado. "I'd like to introduce you to my stepmother, Lorelei," she said, after a moment in which her heart seemed to snag on something sharp.

"Because she doesn't believe I exist?" Mr. Christian asked, his smile muted now, and full of quiet amusement.

Lizzie sighed. "Not *only* that," she protested. "Lorelei probably knows your family and—"

"I have no family, Lizzie. Not the kind you mean, anyway."

"But you said—"

Again, the faint and mysterious smile came. The glow Lizzie had noticed before intensified a little. And it came to her that Mr. Christian simply could not have recovered so completely in such a short time. Had he…died? Was she seeing his ghost? She'd heard of things like that, of course, but never given them serious consideration before that moment.

"Who are you?" she heard herself ask, in a near whisper.

He didn't answer.

Lizzie reached out, meaning to clutch at his sleeve, a way of insisting that he reply, but grab though she might, she couldn't seem to catch hold of him. It was the strangest sensation—he was *there,* not transparent as she imagined a spirit might be, but a real person, one of reality and substance. Without moving at all, he still managed to evade her touch.

"Who are you?" she repeated, more forcefully this time.

"That's not important," he said quietly. Then he pointed to someone or something just past Lizzie's left shoulder. "Look there," he added. "There's your young man, coming to make things up. Give him every opportunity, Lizzie. He's the one."

Lizzie turned to look, saw Morgan vaulting over the school-yard fence, starting toward her. She turned again, with another question for Mr. Christian teetering on the tip of her tongue, but he was gone.

Simply *gone.*

Startled, her heart pounding, Lizzie swept the large yard, but there was no sign of Mr. Christian. She hurried to look behind the building, but he wasn't there, either. Nor was he behind the outhouse or the little shed meant to house a horse or a milk cow.

"Lizzie?"

She whirled.

Morgan stood at her side. "What's the matter?" he asked, frowning.

"Mr. Christian," she sputtered. "He was just here—surely you must have seen him—"

Morgan frowned. "I didn't see anybody but you," he said, taking her arm. "Are you all right?"

She was shaking. She felt like laughing—and like crying. Like dancing, and like collapsing in a heap in the powdery snow.

The snow.

She searched the ground—Mr. Christian would have left footprints in the snow, just as she had. But there were no tracks, other than her own and Morgan's.

She sagged against Morgan, stunned, and his arms tightened around her. "Lizzie!" There was a plea in his voice. *Be all right,* it said.

"I… I must be seeing things—" She gulped in a breath, shook her head. "No. I *did* see Mr. Christmas— *Mr. Christian*— he was right here. We spoke…he told me—"

"Lizzie," Morgan repeated, gripping her upper arms now, looking deep into her eyes. "Stop chattering and *breathe*."

"He was here!"

Morgan led her around to the front of the schoolhouse, sat her down on the side of the porch, where the snow had melted away, took a seat beside her. "I believe you," he said, holding her hand. She felt his innate strength, strength of mind and spirit and body, flowing into her, buoying her up. Sustaining her. "Lizzie, *I believe you*."

She let her head rest against his shoulder, not caring who saw her and Morgan, sitting close together on the schoolhouse porch, holding hands, even though it was highly improper.

For a long while, neither of them spoke. Lizzie was willing her heartbeat to return to normal, and Morgan seemed content just to be there with her.

Finally, though, he broke the silence. "You're really not going to marry Carson?" he asked, looking as sheepish as he sounded.

"I'm really not going to marry Whitley," Lizzie confirmed. Her heart started beating fast again.

"He was right," Morgan went on, after heaving a resigned sigh. He gazed off toward the distant mountain, where they'd been stranded together, nearly buried under tons of snow. "About all the things he said earlier, back at the hotel, I mean. I can't offer you what he can. No position in society. No mansion. No money to speak of."

Lizzie blinked, studied him. "Morgan Shane," she said, "*look* at me."

He obeyed, grinned sadly.

"What are you saying?" she asked.

He hesitated for what seemed to Lizzie an excruciatingly long time. Then, with another sigh, he answered her question with one of his own. "Can you imagine yourself being courted by a penniless country doctor with no prospects to speak of?"

Lizzie's breath caught. She considered the matter for all of two seconds. "Yes," she said. "I can imagine that very well."

He enclosed the hand he'd been holding in both his own, looked straight into Lizzie's soul. "I know it will take time. There's a lot we don't know about each other. You've got classes to teach, and I'll be building a medical practice. But if you'll have me, Lizzie McKettrick, I'll be your husband by this time next year."

"D-do you love me?" Lizzie asked, color flaring in her cheeks at the audacity of her question.

"I'm pretty sure I do," Morgan replied, with a saucy grin. "Do you love me?"

"I certainly feel *something*," Lizzie said, blissfully bewildered. "But I'm not sure I trust myself. After all, I thought I loved Whitley. All I could think about, before we left San Francisco—" *before I met you* "—was whether he'd propose to me over Christmas or not."

Morgan chuckled.

"I guess it proves something my grandfather always says," Lizzie went on. "Be careful what you wish for, because you might damn well get it."

This time Morgan laughed out loud. "Amen," he said.

Lizzie turned thoughtful. "I'd want to go right on teaching school, even if we got married," she warned.

"And I'll want children," Morgan said.

A great joy swelled inside Lizzie, one she could barely contain. "At least four," she agreed. "Two girls and two boys."

Morgan's eyes gleamed. "The room behind my office might get a little crowded," he told her.

"We'll think of something," Lizzie said.

"The hardest part will be waiting," Morgan told her, leaning in a little, lowering his voice. "To get those babies started, I mean."

Lizzie blushed, well aware of his meaning. She'd never been intimate with a man, not even Whitley, though she'd allowed him to kiss her a few times, but she craved *this* man, this "penniless country doctor," with her entire being. She wondered if she could endure a whole year of such wanting.

Reading her expression, Morgan chuckled again, rested his forehead against hers. "I'm about to kiss you, Lizzie McKettrick," he said. "Like I've wanted to kiss you from the moment I first laid eyes on you. And if the whole town of Indian Rock sees me do that, so be it."

Lizzie swallowed, tilted her head upward, ready for his kiss. Longing for it. And feeling utterly scandalized by the ferocity of her own desire.

He laid his mouth to hers, gently at first, then with a hunger to match and even exceed her own. His lips felt deliciously warm, despite the frigid weather, and wonderfully soft. She trembled as the kiss deepened, caught fire inside when his tongue found hers. It was a foretaste of things to come, things that could only happen when they were married, but she felt it in her most feminine parts, as surely as if he'd laid her down on that schoolhouse porch and taken her outright, made her his own.

She moaned.

Morgan's soft laugh echoed in her mouth.

He knew. He *knew* what she was thinking, what she was feeling.

Lizzie's face felt as hot as the blood singing through her veins.

"Oh, my goodness," she gasped, when the kiss was over.

"Only the beginning," Morgan promised gruffly, twisting a loose tendril of her hair gently around one finger.

"Hush," she said helplessly.

He let go of her face, which he'd been holding between his hands while he kissed her, while he *possessed* her, and put a slight but eloquent distance between them. "I'd better get back to the hotel," he said. "I'm expecting some patients, now that I've figuratively hung out my shingle."

"I'll go with you," Lizzie said, not because she particularly wanted to return to the hotel, where she would be treated like an invalid, albeit a cherished one, but because she couldn't be parted from Morgan.

Not yet. Not after what had just happened between them—whatever it was.

As Lizzie had expected, word had gotten around that the new doctor was young, handsome and eligible. Three women, all of them known to Lizzie and notoriously single, awaited him, in varying stages of feigned illness.

She had the silliest urge to shoo them away, like so many hens fluttering around a rooster. Fortunately, she recovered her good sense in time, and simply smiled.

Whitley had left the lobby, perhaps retreating to his nearby room, and Lizzie was relieved by that. She'd be glad when he left Indian Rock, but she knew it might be a while before the train ran again, and the roads were all but impassable.

Suddenly hungry, she made her way through the empty dining room to the kitchen, and found Lorelei there, chatting with the Chinese cook.

"There you are," Lorelei said, in a tone of goodnatured scolding. "Your cheeks are flushed. Have you taken a chill?"

Lizzie still felt the tingle of Morgan's kiss on her mouth, and things had melted inside her, so that she was a little unsteady on her feet. She sank into a rocking chair near the stove, smiling foolishly. "No," she said. "I haven't taken a chill. But I'm famished."

The cook dished up a bowl of beef stew dolloped with dumplings and handed it to Lizzie where she sat, along with a spoon, then left.

Lorelei drew up a second chair.

"Something very strange happened to me today," Lizzie confided, without really intending to, between bites of savory stew.

"I saw you come in with Dr. Shane," Lorelei said, with a gentle but knowing smile. "Lizzie McKettrick, I do believe you've fallen in love."

Perhaps she *had* fallen in love, Lizzie thought. Time would tell.

"Lizzie?" Lorelei prompted, when Lizzie didn't confirm or deny her stepmother's assertion.

"He's going to court me," she said. "Do you think Papa will object?"

"No," Lorelei responded, watching Lizzie very closely. "Would it matter if he did?"

Lizzie laughed. "No," she said. "I don't think it would."

Lorelei smiled, her eyes glistening with happy tears. "It's love, all right. When I met your father, I figured we were all wrong for each other, and I wanted to be with him so badly that I couldn't think straight."

"Something else happened," Lizzie went on, because there was very little she didn't share with her stepmother. Quietly, carefully, she told Lorelei about her encounter with Mr. Christian, at the schoolyard, leaving nothing out.

"Good heavens," Lorelei said, when the tale was told. Then she reached out and tested Lizzie's forehead for fever. Finding her flesh cool, she frowned and managed to look relieved at one and the same time.

"You believe me, don't you?" Lizzie asked shyly.

"If you say you saw this Mr. Christian," Lorelei said, without hesitation, "then you saw him. You are no flibbertigibbet, Lizzie McKettrick."

"But how could he have just—just *disappeared* that way?"

"I don't have the faintest idea," Lorelei answered. Then she rose from her chair. "Finish your stew. I'll be back in a few minutes, and we'll have tea."

Lizzie nodded and her stepmother hurried out of the kitchen, only to be replaced by Angus. He helped himself to a cup of coffee from the pot on the stove and stood watching Lizzie curiously, as though she'd changed in some fundamental way.

And perhaps she had.

"You did a fine job after that avalanche," he told her. "Looking after folks. Trying to keep their spirits up."

"Thank you," Lizzie said. Hers was an independent spirit, but she valued her grandfather's opinion of her, along with those of Lorelei and, of course, her papa.

He sipped his coffee. "You're all right, aren't you, Lizzie-girl? You seem—well—different."

"It's possible I'm in love," she said.

Angus smiled, lifted his coffee cup as if in a toast. "I'll drink to that," he replied, just as Lorelei returned to the kitchen, carrying a Bible.

Lizzie set aside her bowl of stew, and Lorelei practically shoved the Good Book under her nose.

"Read this," she ordered, pointing to a passage in Hebrews, thirteenth chapter, second verse:

"Be not forgetful to entertain strangers; for thereby some have entertained angels unawares."

Chapter Eight

"Mr. Christian makes an unlikely angel," Lizzie told Morgan, standing in his examining room, several hours after Lorelei had shown her the Bible verse in the hotel kitchen. "Don't you think?"

Morgan pulled his stethoscope from around his neck and set it aside. "Not having made the acquaintance of all that many angels," he replied, "I couldn't say."

"He played cards with the children," Lizzie said, groping for reasons why Mr. Christian could not be a part of the heavenly host. "He pulled a gun on Whitley once, and he gave you *whiskey* when you went out into the blizzard—"

"Positively demonic," Morgan teased. "I guess I missed the part where he drew a gun."

"You were outside," Lizzie answered.

"Why would a peddler feel compelled to threaten Carson with a gun, annoying though he is?"

Lizzie shook off the question. "I'm *trying* to make some

sense of what happened, Morgan," Lizzie protested, "and you are not helping."

He grinned. "Some things just don't make sense, Lizzie McKettrick," he said. "Like why every unmarried woman in Indian Rock seems to have developed some fetching and very melodramatic malady."

Lizzie laughed, though she wasn't amused. "No mystery to that," she answered. "You're an eligible bachelor, after all."

He moved closer to her, rested his hands on her shoulders. "Oh, but I'm *not* eligible," he said, his low voice setting things aquiver inside Lizzie. "I'm definitely taken."

He was about to kiss her again, but the office door crashed open with a terrible bang, and both of them turned to see Doss, Lizzie's seven-year-old brother, standing on the threshold.

"Pa's back!" he shouted exuberantly. "The roads are clear, and after church, we can go home and have Christmas!" He paused, his small face screwed into a puzzled frown. "Were you *smooching?*" he demanded, looking suspicious.

Lizzie laughed, and so did Morgan.

"No," Lizzie said.

"Yes," Morgan replied, at the same moment.

"You'd better get married, then," Doss decided. "You're not supposed to kiss people if you're not married to them."

"Is that right?" Morgan asked, approaching Doss and ruffling his thick blond hair.

"I bet it says so in the Bible," Doss insisted solemnly.

"Do we have a budding preacher in our midst?" Morgan asked Lizzie, his eyes full of warm laughter.

Lizzie giggled. "Doss? Perish the thought. He's more imp than angel."

At the word *angel,* a little silence fell. Lizzie thought of Mr. Christian, of course, and the insoluble mystery he represented.

"We had to wait to have Christmas," Doss complained. "There are a whole *bunch* of packages under our tree at home, and some of them are mine. And now we have to sit through *church,* too."

Lizzie's attention was on Morgan. "Will you come with us?" she asked. "To celebrate a McKettrick Christmas, I mean?"

Morgan looked reluctant. "I'd be intruding," he said.

"That man with the broken leg is going," Doss put in, relentlessly helpful.

Morgan merely spread his hands to Lizzie, as if to say *I told you so.*

"You belong with us," Lizzie said, not to be put off. It would be awkward, celebrating their delayed Christmas with both Whitley and Morgan present, but that was unavoidable. To leave Whitley alone at the hotel while everyone else enjoyed roast goose and eggnog was simply not the McKettrick way.

In the end Morgan relented.

Pastor Reynolds held a Christmas Eve service at sunset, and the whole town attended. Candles were lit, carols were sung, a gentle sermon was preached. After the closing prayer, gifts were given out to all the children, and Lizzie recognized her father's handiwork, made in his woodshop, and the cloth dolls and animals Lorelei and the aunts had sewn. Every child received a present.

Mr. and Mrs. Thaddings watched fondly, and somewhat wistfully, Lizzie thought, as Ellen Halifax showed off the doll she'd wanted so much. Jack received a stick horse with a yarn mane, and galloped up and down the aisle, despite his mother's protests. John and Alice Brennan were there, too, with Alice's parents and little Tad, who seemed fascinated with his toy buckboard.

Lizzie approached the Thaddingses. She knew Pastor Reynolds had wired Clarinda Adams on their behalf, hoping she'd allow them to stay on until she either returned or sold the house, but there hadn't been time for an answer.

Mrs. Thaddings embraced her. "You look well, Lizzie," she said.

"I'm happy to be home," Lizzie replied. Whitley, standing nearby, letting his crutches support his weight, looked despondent. She wondered if he'd ever considered staying on in Indian Rock, or if he'd always intended to insist they live in San Francisco, after they were married.

She would probably never know, she decided. And it didn't matter.

"We'd better get back and see to Woodrow, dear," Mr. Thaddings told his wife, taking a gentle hold on her elbow. "Before this snow gets too deep."

Lizzie wasn't about to let the Thaddingses walk home, and quickly conscripted her goodnatured uncle Jeb to drive them in his buggy.

Later, when the McKettrick clan left Indian Rock for the Triple M, Morgan was with them, seated next to Lizzie in the back of her father's wagon. Whitley, alternately scowling and looking bleak, rode in the other. The snow, so threatening on the mountain, fell like a blessed benediction all around them, soothing and soft, almost magical.

The first sight of the main ranch house brought tears to Lizzie's eyes. She'd thought, before the rescue, that she might never see the home place again, never warm herself before one of the fires, dream in a rocking chair while a summer rain pattered at the roof. But there it was, sturdy and dearly familiar, its roof laced with snow, its windows alight with a golden glow.

Dogs barked a merry greeting, and small cousins, as well as

aunts and uncles, poured from wagons and buckboards, their voices a happy buzz in the wintry darkness.

Lizzie stood still, after Morgan helped her down from the wagon, taking it all in. Hiding things in her heart.

Inside her grandfather's house, a giant tree winked with tinsel. Piles of packages stood beneath it, some simply wrapped in brown paper or newsprint, others bedecked in pretty cloth and tied with shimmering ribbons.

Concepcion, her grandfather's wife, must have been cooking for days. The house was redolent with the aromas Lizzie had yearned for on the stranded train—freshly baked bread, savory roast goose, spices like cinnamon and nutmeg. Lizzie breathed deeply of the love and happiness surrounding her on all sides.

The children were excited, of course, all the more so because, for them, Christmas was just plain late. At Holt's suggestion, they were allowed to empty their bulging St. Nicholas stockings and open their packages.

Chaos reigned while dolls and games and brightly colored shirts and dresses were unwrapped. Lizzie watched the whole scene in a daze of gratitude and love for her large, boisterous family. Morgan stood nearby, enjoying the melee, while Whitley slumped in a leather chair next to the fireplace, wearing an expression that said, "Bah, humbug."

If she hadn't known it before, Lizzie would have known then that Whitley simply didn't belong with this rowdy crew. Morgan, on the other hand, had soon taken off his coat, pushed up his sleeves and knelt on the floor to help Doss assemble a miniature ranch house from a toy set of interlocking logs.

A nudge from her father distracted Lizzie, and she started when she saw what he was holding in his hands—Mr. Christian's music box, the one he'd given her on Christmas Eve, aboard the train.

She blinked. Surely they'd left it behind, along with most of their other possessions, to be collected later.

"The tag says it's for you," Holt said, looking puzzled. Clearly, he didn't recall seeing the music box before.

Lizzie's hands trembled as she accepted the box. A strain of "O Little Town of Bethlehem" tinkled from its depths, so ethereal that she was sure, in the moment after, that she'd imagined it.

She found a chair—not easy since the house was bulging with McKettricks—and sank into it, stricken speechless.

Whitley, as it happened, already occupied the chair next to hers. He frowned, eyeing the music box resting in Lizzie's lap like some sacred object to be guarded at all costs.

"That's pretty," he said, with a grudging note to his voice. "Did Shane give it to you?"

Lizzie shook her head, made herself meet Whitley's gaze. "Don't you remember, Whitley?" she asked, referring to Christmas Eve on the train, when they'd *all* seen the music box, listened with sad delight to its chiming tunes.

"Remember what?" Whitley asked. He wasn't pretending, Lizzie knew. He honestly didn't recall either the music box *or* Mr. Christian.

"Never mind," Lizzie said.

Dinner was announced, and Whitley got up, reaching for his crutches, and stumped off toward the dining room. Most of the children had fallen asleep on piles of crumpled wrapping paper, and the adults had all gone to eat.

All except Morgan, and Lizzie herself, that is.

"Hungry?" Morgan asked, extending a hand to Lizzie.

She set the music box aside, on the sturdy table next to her chair, and took Morgan's hand. "Starved," she said.

Instead of escorting her into the dining room, where everyone else had gathered—their voices were like a muted symphony of laughter and happy conversation, sweet to Lizzie's ears—Morgan drew her close. Held her as though they were about to swirl into the flow of a waltz.

"If what I'm feeling right now isn't love," Morgan said, his lips nearly touching Lizzie's, "then there's something even *better* than love."

Lizzie's throat constricted. She whispered his name, and he would have kissed her, she supposed, if a third party hadn't made his presence known with a clearing of the throat.

"Time for that later," Angus said, grinning. "Supper's on the table."

By New Year's, the tracks had been cleared and the trains were running again. Lizzie waited on the platform, alongside Whitley, the sole traveler leaving Indian Rock that day.

A cold, dry wind blew, stinging Lizzie's ears, and she felt as miserable as Whitley looked.

You'll meet someone else.

That was what she wanted to say, but it seemed presumptuous, under the circumstances. Whitley's feelings were private ones, and she had no real way of knowing what they were.

"You're sure about this?" he asked quietly, as the train rounded the bend in the near distance, whistle blowing, white steam chuffing from the smokestack against a brittle blue sky. "We could have a good life together, Lizzie."

Lizzie blinked back tears. Yes, she supposed they *could* have a good life together, she and Whitley, good enough, anyway. But she wanted more than "good enough," for herself and Morgan—and for Whitley. "You belong in San Francisco," she told him gently. "And I belong right here, in Indian Rock."

Whitley surprised her with a sad, tender smile. "I hate to admit it," he said, "but you're probably right. Be happy, Lizzie."

The train was nearly at the platform now, and so loud that Lizzie would have had to shout to be heard over the din. So she stood on tiptoe and planted a brief, chaste kiss on Whitley's mouth.

Metal brakes squealed as the train came to a full stop.

Whitley stared into Lizzie's eyes for a long moment, saying a silent fare-thee-well, then he turned, deft on his crutches, to leave. She watched until he'd boarded the train, then turned and walked slowly away.

In the morning, her first day of teaching would commence. She headed for the schoolhouse, where her father and her uncle Jeb were unloading some of her things from the back of a buckboard.

Jeb nodded to her and smiled before lugging her rocking chair inside, but Holt came to Lizzie and slipped an arm around her shoulders. Kissed her lightly on the forehead.

"Goodbyes can be hard," he said, knowing she'd just come from the train depot, "even when it's for the best."

Lizzie nodded, choked up. "I was so sure—"

Holt chuckled. "Of course you were sure," he said. "You're a McKettrick, and McKettricks are sure of everything."

"What if I'm wrong about Morgan?" she asked, looking up into her father's face. "I don't think I could stand to say goodbye to him."

"Don't borrow trouble, Lizzie-bet," Holt smiled. "You've got a year of courting ahead of you. And my guess is, at the end of that time, you'll know for sure, one way or the other."

She nodded, swallowed, and rested her forehead against Holt's shoulder.

Later, when she'd explored her classroom, with its blackboard and potbellied stove and long, low-slung tables, for what must have been the hundredth time, she went into her living quarters.

Her father and uncle had gone, and her personal belongings were all around, in boxes and crates and travel trunks. Her books, her most serviceable dresses, a pretty china lamp from her bedroom at the ranch, the little writing desk her grandfather had given her as a Christmas gift.

Lorelei had packed quilts and sheets and fluffy pillows, meant to make the stark little room more homelike, and before they'd gone, her father and uncle had built a nice fire in the stove.

Lizzie searched until she found the music box, set it in the middle of the table, and sat down to admire it. And to wonder.

Truly, as the bard had so famously said, there *were* more things in heaven and earth than this world dreams of.

A light knock at her door brought Lizzie out of her musings, and she went to open it, found Morgan standing on the small porch facing the side yard. His hands stuffed into the pockets of his worn coat, he favored her with a shy smile.

"I know it isn't proper, but—"

"Come in," Lizzie said, catching him by the sleeve and literally pulling him over the threshold.

Inside, Morgan made such a comical effort not to notice the bed, which dominated the tiny room, that Lizzie laughed.

"I can't stay," Morgan said, making no move to leave.

"People will talk," Lizzie agreed, still amused.

His gaze strayed past her, to the music box. "This was quite a Christmas, wasn't it?" he asked.

"Quite a Christmas indeed," Lizzie said, watching as he approached the table, sorted through the stack of little brass disks containing various tunes, and slid one into the side of the music box. He wound the key, and the strains of a waltz tinkled in the air, delicate as tiny icicles dropping from the eaves of a house.

Morgan turned to Lizzie, holding out his arms, and she moved into his embrace, and they danced.

They danced until the music stopped, and then they went on dancing, in the tremulous silence that followed, around the table, past the rocking chair and the bed. Around and around and around they went, the doctor and the schoolmarm, waltzing to the beat of each other's hearts.

Chapter Nine

December 20, 1897

"Miss McKettrick?" lisped a small voice.

Lizzie looked up from the papers she'd been grading at her desk and smiled to see Tad Brennan standing there. Barely five, he was still too young to attend school, but he often showed up when classes were over for the day, to show Lizzie his "homework."

"Tad," she greeted him, cheered by his exuberant desire to learn. In the year Lizzie had been teaching, he'd mastered his alphabet and elementary arithmetic, with a lot of help from his father. By the time he officially enrolled in the fall, he'd probably be ready to skip the first grade.

"Mama says you're getting married to Dr. Shane soon," Tad said miserably.

"Well, yes," Lizzie said, resisting an urge to ruffle his hair. She knew her little brothers hated that gesture. "Dr. Shane and

I *are* getting married, the day before Christmas. You're invited to the ceremony, and so are your parents and grandparents."

Tad's eyes were suddenly brilliant with tears. "That means we'll have a new teacher," he said. "And I wanted *you*."

Lizzie pushed her chair back from her desk and held out her arms to Tad. Reluctantly he allowed her to take him onto her lap. Like her brothers, he regarded himself as a big boy now, and lap sitting was suspect. "I'll be your teacher, Tad," she said gently. "The only difference will be, you'll call me Mrs. Shane instead of Miss McKettrick."

The child looked at her with mingled confusion and hope. "But aren't you going to have babies?"

Lizzie felt her cheeks warm a little. She and Morgan had done their best to wait, but one balmy night last June, the waiting had proved to be too much for both of them. They'd made love, in the deep grass of a pasture on the Triple M, and since then, they'd been together every chance they got.

"I'm sure I'll have babies," she said. "Eventually."

"Mama says women with babies have to stay home and take care of them," Tad told her solemnly.

"Does she?" Lizzie asked gently.

Tad nodded.

"Tell you what," Lizzie said, after giving him a little hug. "I promise, baby or no baby, to be here when you start first grade. Fair enough?"

Tad beamed. Nodded. Scrambled down off Lizzie's lap just as the door of the schoolhouse sprang open.

The scent of fresh evergreen filled the small room, and then Morgan was there, in the chasm, lugging a tree so large that Lizzie could only see his boots. The school's Christmas party was scheduled for the next afternoon; Lizzie and her students, fourteen children of widely varying ages, would spend the morning decorating with paper chains and bits of shiny paper garnered for the purpose.

"Miss McKettrick promised to be my teacher in first grade," Tad told Morgan seriously, "*even* if she's got a baby."

Morgan's dark eyes glinted with humor and no little passion. Late the night before, he'd knocked on Lizzie's door, and she'd let him in. He'd stayed until just before dawn, leaving Lizzie melting in the schoolteacher's bed.

"I just saw your pa," he told the child, letting the baby remark pass. "He's wanting you to help him carry in wood."

Tad said a hasty goodbye to Lizzie and hurried out. John Brennan had come a long way in the year since they'd all been stranded together in a train on the mountainside, but his health was still somewhat fragile and he counted on his son to assist him with the chores.

"Did you really meet up with John?" Lizzie asked, suspicious.

Morgan grinned, leaned the tree against the far wall and crossed the room to bend over her chair and kiss her soundly. Electricity raced along her veins and danced in her nerve endings. "I could have," he said. "Walked right past the mercantile on my way here."

Lizzie laughed, though the kiss had set her afire, as Morgan Shane's kisses always did. "You're a shameless scoundrel," she said, giving his chest a little push with both palms precisely because she wanted to pull him close instead.

"We're invited to supper at the Thaddingses'," Morgan replied, still grinning. He could turn her from a schoolmarm to a hussy within five minutes if he wanted to, and he was making sure she understood that. "They have news."

Lizzie stood up, once Morgan gave her room to do so, and began neatening the things on her desk. "News? What kind of news?"

Morgan stood behind her, pulled her back against him. She felt his desire and wondered if he'd step inside with her, after walking her back from supper at the Thaddingses', and seduce her in the little room in back. "I don't know," he murmured, his breath warm against her temple. "I guess that's why it will come as—well—*news*."

His hands cupped her breasts, warm and strong and infinitely gentle.

"Dr. Morgan Shane," Lizzie sputtered, "this is a *schoolroom*."

He chuckled. "So it is. I'd take you to bed and have you thoroughly, Miss McKettrick, but I saw your father and one of your uncles coming out of the Cattleman's Bank a little while ago, and my guess is, they're on their way here right now."

With a little cry, Lizzie jumped away from Morgan. Smoothed her hair and her skirts.

Sure enough, a wagon rolled clamorously up outside in the very next moment. She heard her father call out a greeting to someone passing by.

Lizzie put her hands to her cheeks, hoping to cool them. One look at her, in her present state of arousal, and her father would know what she'd been up to with Morgan. If he hadn't guessed already.

Morgan perched on the edge of her desk, folded his arms and grinned at her discomfort. "Damn," he said, "you're almost as beautiful when you want to make love as just afterward, when you make those little sighing sounds."

"Morgan!"

He laughed.

The schoolhouse door opened, and Holt McKettrick came in, dressed for winter in woolen trousers, a heavy shirt and a long coat lined in sheep's wool. His gaze moving from Morgan to Lizzie, he grinned a little.

"Lorelei sent some things in for the new house," he said.

"Rafe and I will unload them over there, unless you'd rather keep them here until after the wedding."

"There would be better," Lizzie said.

Over Morgan's protests, when their engagement had become official on Lizzie's twentieth birthday in early August, her grandfather had purchased a little plot of land at the edge of town, and now a small white cottage with green-shuttered windows awaited their occupancy. Angus, Holt, the uncles and Morgan had built the place with their own hands and, little by little, it had been furnished, with one notable exception: a bed.

When Lizzie had commented on the oversight the week before, while they sat in the ranch house kitchen sewing dolls to be given away at church on Christmas Eve, her stepmother had smiled and said only, "I was your age once."

Morgan, whistling merrily under his breath, gave the evergreen a little shake, causing its scent to perfume the schoolhouse, and nodded a greeting to Holt.

"We'll be going, then," Holt said, with a note of bemused humor in his voice. His McKettrick-blue eyes twinkled. "Lorelei and the other womenfolk are wanting to fuss with your wedding dress a little more, so you'd best pay a visit to the ranch in the next day or two."

Lizzie nodded. "I'll be there," she promised.

Her papa kissed her cheek, glanced Morgan's way again and left.

As soon as Holt had gone, Morgan kissed Lizzie, too, though in an entirely different way, asked her to meet him at Clarinda Adams's place at six, and took his leave as well.

"Company!" Woodrow squawked, from inside the oncenotorious Clarinda Adams house. "Company!"

Morgan smiled down at Lizzie, who stood with her cloak

pulled close around her, shivering a little. The ground was blanketed with pristine white snow, and it glittered in the glow from the gas-powered streetlight on the corner. Curlicues of frost adorned the front windows. "That bird takes himself pretty seriously," Morgan observed.

"Hurry up!" Woodrow crowed. "Hurry up! No time like the present! Hurry up!"

Lizzie chuckled. The Thaddingses had become dear friends to her and to Morgan—and so had Woodrow. Once, Mr. Thaddings had even brought the bird to the schoolhouse, and the children had been fascinated by his ability to repeat everything they said to him.

The door opened, and Zebulon stood on the threshold. He wore a red silk smoking jacket, probably left behind by one of Clarinda's clients, and held a pipe in one hand. "Come in," he said. "Come in."

"Come in!" Woodrow echoed.

Gratefully, Lizzie preceded Morgan into the warm house. Once, according to local legend, there had been paintings of naked people on the walls, but they were long gone.

Woodrow hopped on his perch. "Lizzie's here!" he cried jubilantly. "Lizzie's here!"

She laughed and, as Morgan closed the front door behind them, Woodrow flew across the entry way to land on Lizzie's shoulder.

"Lizzie's pretty," the bird went on. "Lizzie's pretty!"

"Smart bird," Morgan said, amused.

Woodrow tugged at one of the tiny combs holding Lizzie's abundance of hair in a schoolmarmish do.

"Flatterer," Zebulon scolded Woodrow affectionately. Then, to Lizzie and Morgan, he confided, "He's been after that comb all along."

Lizzie laughed again. Stroked Woodrow's top feathers with

a light finger. "When are you coming back to school?" she asked him.

"Woodrow to school!" he crowed. "See the pretty birdie!"

"He'll keep this up for hours if we let him," Zebulon said, turning to lead the way into the main parlor.

Just as they reached that resplendent room, Mrs. Thaddings—Marietta, to Lizzie—entered from the dining room, carrying a tray in both hands. She was gray and frail, but Lizzie had long since stopped thinking of Marietta Thaddings as elderly. She was an active member of Indian Rock society, such as it was, hosting card clubs and giving recitations from her vast store of memorized poetry. She was the soul of kindness, and Lizzie loved her like a grandmother.

"Come, sit down by the fire," Marietta said. "I've brewed a nice pot of tea, and supper is almost ready."

Lizzie sat.

Morgan took the tray from Marietta's hands and placed it on the low table between the settee and several chairs drawn up close to the fire. Although Morgan was always polite, his solicitude worried Lizzie a little. He was, after all, Marietta's doctor as well as her friend. Was her health failing?

Marietta's eager smile belied the idea. She sat, and Woodrow flew to perch in the back of her chair.

"We've heard from Clarinda," she announced.

Lizzie braced herself. Was the legendary Miss Adams about to return to Indian Rock, and upset the proverbial apple cart? During her absence, the Thaddingses had served as caretakers of sorts. If Clarinda returned, she would almost certainly reestablish her business.

Morgan's hand landed lightly on Lizzie's shoulder, steadying her. There was so little she could hide from him; he sensed every change of mood.

"Lizzie's been a little nervous lately," he said. "What with the wedding coming up in a few days and all."

Zebulon and Marietta beamed. "So it is," Zebulon said. "Christmas Eve, after the church service the two of you will be married."

"It's so romantic," Marietta sighed sweetly.

"Let's tell them our news," Zebulon said, after giving his wife a long, adoring look.

"Clarinda has decided not to come back to Indian Rock," Marietta told them. "She hired us as permanent caretakers, and we can do what we want with the place. Turn it into a hospital or a boardinghouse." She paused, and she and Zebulon exchanged a glance. "Or a sort of school."

Lizzie's eyes stung with happy tears.

"We'll need to do something," Zebulon hurried to contribute. "To make ends meet, I mean, and the Territory is willing to pay us a stipend if we'll take in Indian children. The ones with no place else to go."

"You wouldn't feel we were—infringing or anything, would you, Lizzie?" Marietta asked, gently anxious.

"Infringing?" Lizzie repeated, confused. "I think it's wonderful."

Both Zebulon and Marietta sighed with relief.

"Are you up to it?" Morgan asked them, ever the practical one. "Kids are a lot of work."

Zebulon's eyes shone. "We never had children of our own, as you know, and we love them so. We'll be fine." He turned to Lizzie, looking worried again. "It will mean more pupils for you," he said. "The schoolhouse will probably have to be expanded. Usually, these little ones have been shuffled from place to place, and they're the ones without a family to take them in. They might get up to some mischief."

"After the wedding," Morgan said diplomatically, "Lizzie

won't need the teacher's quarters anymore. If the town council agrees, it would be easy enough to knock out a wall and add a few desks."

Both Zebulon and Marietta looked relieved.

When it came time to serve supper, Lizzie followed Marietta back to the kitchen to help in whatever way she could.

"What's it like to live here?" she asked, because curiosity was her besetting sin and she hadn't stopped herself in time.

Marietta looked gently scandalized. "Early on, several confused gentlemen came to the door," she admitted, cheeks pink. "For a while, there, we got at least one caller every time the train stopped at the depot."

"I shouldn't have asked," Lizzie said.

"It's natural to wonder," Marietta assured her. "And Lord knows, I've done *my* share of wondering. Clarinda and I were raised in a decent, God-fearing home. My sister was always spirited, that's true, but I certainly never *dreamed* she'd grow up to run a...a *brothel*."

Marietta took a roast from the oven and placed it carefully on a platter. Lizzie picked up a bowl brimming with fluffy mashed potatoes, answering, "People are full of surprises."

"Whatever she's done in the past, it's kind of Clarinda to let Zebulon and me live here. Heaven only knows what we'd have done if she hadn't given us shelter. Why, she even wired the people at the mercantile, instructing them to let us buy whatever we needed on her account."

When the four of them were seated in the massive dining room, huddled together at one end, Zebulon offered grace. After the amen, they all ate in earnest. Woodrow remained in the parlor, squawking away.

"It hardly seems possible," Zebulon said, "that a whole year has gone by since we all met."

Morgan gave Lizzie a sidelong glance. "It seems like a long time to some of us," he said.

Lizzie elbowed him and smiled at Zebulon. "When will the children arrive?"

It was Marietta who answered. "Right after New Year's," she said. "We'll have a lot to do, Zebulon and I, to get ready."

"I can promise a whole crowd of McKettrick women to help out," Lizzie told her, with absolute confidence that it was so.

After supper, Lizzie and Marietta attended to the dishes while Zebulon, Morgan and Woodrow talked politics in the parlor.

A fresh snowfall had begun when Lizzie and Morgan left the Thaddingses' house. Instead of heading for the school-house, Morgan steered Lizzie toward their cottage on the outskirts of town.

To Lizzie's surprise, lights glowed in the windows, and the tiny front room was warm when they stepped inside. They visited the house often, separately and together—Lizzie liked to imagine what it would be like, living there with Morgan, and she suspected the reverse was true, too.

The plank floors gleamed with varnish, the scent of it still sharp in the air. Two wing-backed chairs faced the small brick fireplace, and lace curtains, sewn by her stepmother and aunts, graced the many-paned windows. A hooked rug, Concepcion's handiwork, added a splash of cheery color to the room.

Dreaming, Lizzie moved on to the kitchen, with its brand-new cookstove, its stocked shelves. There was a table with four chairs; her father had built it himself, in his wood shop on the ranch.

In addition to the parlor and kitchen, there was a little bath-room with all the latest in plumbing. A bedroom stood on ei-ther side—the smaller one empty, the larger one furnished with

a bureau and a wardrobe, donated by Lizzie's grandfather, but
no bed.

"Where are we going to sleep?" Lizzie asked.

Morgan laughed and drew her into his arms. Kissed the tip
of her nose. "I'm not planning on doing all that much sleeping," he said. "Not on our wedding night, at least."

Lizzie's cheeks burned with both anticipation and embarrassment. "Be practical," she said. "We need a bed. Shouldn't
we order one at the mercantile?"

Morgan held her close, and then closer still. "Stop worrying," he said. "Things always turn out for the best, don't they?
Look at Zebulon and Marietta—at John Brennan—and us."

Lizzie rested her forehead against Morgan's shoulder, content to be there, wrapped in his strong embrace. Things *had*
turned out for the best—the Halifaxes were living happily on
the Triple M, Ellen and Jack attending Chloe's school, rather
than her own, because the ranch was a long way out of town.
Whitley had written recently to say that he'd met the woman
he wanted to marry; they'd met at a party following a polo
match. Morgan's practice was thriving, though he earned next
to nothing, and Lizzie loved teaching school.

"Do you ever think about Mr. Christian?" she asked.

Morgan stroked her hair. "Sometimes," he said. "Especially
with Christmas coming on. Mostly, though, Lizzie McKettrick,
I think about you."

She tilted her head back to look up into his face. "I love
you, Dr. Morgan Shane," she said.

He kissed her, with a hungry tenderness, then forced himself to step back. They had been intimate, but never in the
cottage. They were saving that.

"And I love you," he said, after catching his breath. "Does
it bother you, Lizzie, to take my name? You won't be a Mc-
Kettrick anymore, after we're married."

"I'll *always* be a McKettrick," Lizzie told him. "No matter what name I go by. I'll also be your wife, Morgan. I'll be Lizzie Shane."

He grinned, his hands resting lightly on her shoulders. His eyes glistened, and when he spoke, his voice came out sounding hoarse. "You're the best thing that ever happened to me," he said. "I never once thought—"

Lizzie stroked his cheek with gentle fingers still chilled from being outside in the snowy cold. "Hush," she told him. "Stop talking and kiss me again."

The main ranch house seemed about to burst at the corners, the morning of Christmas Eve, as Lizzie stood obediently on a milk stool in Angus and Concepcion's bedroom upstairs, feeling resplendent in her lacy wedding dress, while Lorelei and the aunts, Emmeline, Mandy and Chloe, pinned and stitched and chattered.

Katie, the child born late in life to Angus and Concepcion, now eleven-going-on-forty, as Lorelei liked to say, sat on the side of her parents' bed, watching the proceedings. With her dark hair and deep-blue eyes, Katie was exquisitely beautiful, although she hadn't realized it yet.

"When I get married," she said, her gaze sweeping over Lizzie's dress, "*I'm* not going to change my name. I'm still going to be Katie McKettrick, forever and ever, no matter what."

"You won't be getting married for a while yet," Chloe told her. Married to Lizzie's uncle Jeb, Chloe was a beauty herself, with copper-colored hair and bright, intelligent eyes. She taught all the children on and around the ranch in the little schoolhouse Jeb had built for her as a wedding present. "By then, you might have changed your mind about taking your husband's name."

Stubbornly, Katie folded her arms. "No, I won't," she said.

"You're just like your father," Concepcion told her daughter, entering the room and closing the door quickly behind her, so none of the men would get a glimpse of Lizzie in her dress. "Katie, Katie, quite contrary."

Lizzie smiled. "You'll make a very lovely bride," she told the little girl.

Katie beamed. "You look so pretty," she told Lizzie. "Like a fairy queen."

Lizzie thanked her, and the pinning and stitching went on. Finally, though, the sewing was done, and she was able to step behind the changing screen, shed the sumptuous dress and get back into her everyday garb. That day, it was a light-blue woolen frock with prim black piping and a high collar that tickled her under the chin.

Ducking around the screen again, she was surprised to see that though Concepcion, Lorelei and the aunts had gone, Katie remained.

Lizzie sat down on the bed beside her and draped an arm around Katie's shoulders. Although Katie was much younger, she was actually Lizzie's aunt, a half sister to Holt, Rafe, Jeb and Kade.

"All right," Lizzie said gently, "what's bothering you, Katie-did?"

Tears brimmed in Katie's eyes. "You're getting married," she said. "Everything is going to be different now."

"Not so different," Lizzie replied. "I'll still be your niece."

Katie giggled at that, and sniffled. "I missed you so much when you went away to San Francisco," she whispered.

Lizzie hugged her. "And I missed you. But I'm home now, and I'm staying."

"You're getting *married*," Katie repeated insistently. "You're going to be Lizzie Shane, not Lizzie McKettrick. What if

Morgan decides he doesn't like living in Indian Rock and takes you somewhere far away?"

"That isn't going to happen," Lizzie said.

"How can you be so sure? When a woman gets married, the man's the boss from then on. You have to do what he says."

Lizzie smiled. "Now, where would you have gotten such an idea, Katie McKettrick?" she teased. "Does your mama do what your papa tells her? Do any of your sisters-in-law take orders from your brothers?"

Katie brightened. "No," she said.

"Morgan and I have talked all this through, Katie. We're staying right in Indian Rock, for good. He'll do his doctoring, and I'll teach school."

"Will you have babies?"

The question made Lizzie squirm a little. She'd checked the calendar that morning, for a perfectly ordinary reason, and realized something important. "I certainly hope so," she said carefully.

Katie wrapped both arms around Lizzie and squeezed hard. "The little kids think St. Nicholas is coming on Christmas Eve," she confided. "But I'm big now, and I know it's Papa and Mama who fill my stocking and put presents under the tree."

"Do you, now?" Lizzie countered mysteriously, thinking of Nicholas Christian—Mr. Christmas, as the Halifax children had called him.

"You're all grown up," Katie said. "You don't believe in St. Nicholas."

"Maybe not precisely," Lizzie replied, "but I certainly believe in miracles."

"What kind of miracles?" Katie wanted to know. Young as she was, she had a tenaciously skeptical mind.

"I think angels visit earth, disguised as ordinary human beings, for one thing."

"Why would they do that?"

"Maybe to help us be strong and keep going when we're discouraged."

"Have you ever been discouraged, Lizzie?"

"Yes," Lizzie answered. "Last Christmas, when Morgan and I and all the rest of us were trapped aboard that train, up in the high country, I wondered if we'd make it home. I kept my chin up, but I was worried."

"You knew Papa and Holt and Rafe and Kade and Jeb would come get you," Katie insisted.

Lizzie nodded.

"Then why were you scared?"

"It was cold, and folks were sick and injured, and I was far away from all of you. There had been an avalanche, and one avalanche often leads to another."

"And an angel came? Did it have wings?"

Lizzie laughed. "No wings," she said. "Just a sample case and a flask of whiskey. He went out into the blizzard, though, and came back with a Christmas tree."

Katie wrinkled her nose, clearly disappointed. "That doesn't sound like any angel I've ever heard of," she replied. "They're supposed to fly, and have wings and halos—"

"Sometimes they have bowler hats and overcoats instead," Lizzie said. "I know I met an angel, Katie McKettrick, a real, live angel, and you're not going to change my mind."

"How did you *know?*" Katie wondered, intrigued in spite of herself. "That he was an angel, I mean?"

Lizzie glanced from side to side, even though they were alone in the room. "He disappeared," she said. "I was talking to him last year, around this time, in the schoolyard in town. I turned away for a moment, and when I looked back, he was gone."

Katie's wondrous eyes widened. "Are you joshing me,

Lizzie?" she demanded. "I'm not a little kid anymore, you know."

Lizzie chuckled. "I'm telling you the truth," she said, holding up one hand, oath-giving style. "And you know what else? He didn't leave any footprints in the snow. Mine were there, and so were Morgan's, but it was as if Mr. Christmas hadn't been there at all."

Katie let out a long breath.

Lizzie gave her young aunt another squeeze. "The point of all this, Katie-did," she said, "is that it's important to believe in things, even when you're all grown up."

"I still don't believe in St. Nicholas," Katie said staunchly.

A knock sounded at the bedroom door, and Concepcion stuck her head in. "We're all leaving for town early," she announced. "Angus says the way this snow is coming down, we might be in for another Christmas blizzard."

Chapter Ten

The wind rattled the walls and windows of that sturdy little church, and as Holt McKettrick waited to walk his daughter up the aisle, following the Christmas Eve service, he thought about miracles. A year before, he'd come closer to losing Lizzie for good than he was willing to admit, even to himself. Now, here she stood, at his side, almost unbearably lovely in her wedding dress.

His little girl. About to be married.

Married.

She'd been twelve when she'd come to live with him—before that, he hadn't even known she existed. For a brief, poignant moment, he yearned for those lost years—Lizzie, learning to walk and talk. Wearing bows in her hair. Coming to him with skinned knees, disappointments and little-girl secrets.

But if there was one thing he'd learned in his life, it was that there was no sense in regretting the past. The *present,* that was what was important. It was all any of them really had.

The children in the congregation were restless, having sat through the service—it was Christmas Eve, after all—and the adults were eager. A low murmur rose from the crowd, and then a small voice rang out like a bell.

"Is it over yet?"

Doss, his and Lorelei's youngest.

The wedding guests laughed, and Holt joined in. Relaxed a little when his gaze connected with Lorelei's. She favored him with a smile and nodded slightly.

Holt nodded back. *I love you,* he told her silently.

And she nodded again.

Holt shifted his attention to the bridegroom.

The man standing up there at the altar, straight-backed and bright-eyed, was the *right* man for Lizzie, Holt was convinced of that. He suspected they'd jumped the gun a little, Lizzie and Morgan, and if Morgan hadn't been exactly who he was, Holt would have horsewhipped him for it.

They were young, as Lorelei had reminded him, when he'd told her he thought the bride and groom had been practicing up for the wedding night ahead of time, and they were in love.

He warmed at the memory of Lorelei's smile. "Remember how it was with us?" she'd asked. In truth, that part of their relationship hadn't changed. They had children and a home together now, so they couldn't be quite as spontaneous as they'd once been, but the passion between them was as fiery as ever.

The organist struck the first note of the wedding march.

"Ready?" Holt asked his daughter, his voice coming out gruff since there was a lump the size of Texas in his throat.

"Ready," Lizzie assured him gently, squeezing his arm. "I love you, Papa."

Tears scalded Holt's eyes. "I love you right back, Lizzie-bet," he replied.

And they started toward the front of the church, where

Morgan and Preacher Reynolds waited. The crowd blurred around Holt, and he wondered if Lizzie sensed that they were stepping out of an old world and into a brand-new one. Things would be different after tonight.

She was so beautiful, Morgan thought, as he watched Lizzie gliding toward him on her father's arm, a vision in her spectacular home-sewn dress. There was love in every stitch and fold of that gown and in every tiny crystal bead glittering on the bodice. Though he wasn't a fanciful man, Morgan knew in that moment that one day he and Lizzie would have a daughter, and she, too, would wear this dress. He'd know how Holt felt, when that day came. At the moment, he could only guess.

Finally Lizzie stood beside him.

His head felt light, and he braced his knees. Damn, but he was lucky. Luckier than he'd ever dreamed he could be.

"Who giveth this woman in marriage?" the preacher asked, raising his voice to be heard over the blizzard raging outside.

"Lorelei and I do," Holt answered gravely. He kissed the top of Lizzie's head and went to sit beside Lorelei in the front pew, along with Angus and Concepcion.

Morgan smiled to himself. Earlier in the evening, Angus had informed him, in no uncertain terms, that if he ever did anything to hurt Lizzie, he'd get a hiding for it.

The holy words were said, the vows exchanged.

And then the preacher pronounced Lizzie and Morgan man and wife.

"You may kiss the bride," Reynolds said.

His hands shaking a little—the hands that were so steady holding a scalpel or binding a wound—Morgan raised Lizzie's veil and gazed down into her upturned face, wonderstruck. She glowed, as though a light were burning inside her.

He kissed her, not hungrily, as he would later that night,

when they were alone in the cottage, but reverently. A sacred charge passed between them, as though they had not only been joined on earth, but in heaven, too, and for all of time and eternity.

The organ thundered again, a joyous, triumphant sound, bouncing off the walls of that frontier church, and again a child's voice piped above the joyous chaos.

"It's over!"

Morgan laughed along with everybody else, but he was thinking, *It isn't over. Oh, no. This is only the start.*

The reception was held in the lobby of the Arizona Hotel, where a giant Christmas tree loomed over the proceedings, glittering with tinsel and blown-glass balls, presents piled high beneath it. Knowing the family wouldn't be able to get back to the ranch after the wedding, because of the storm, Lizzie's grandfather had had everything loaded onto hay sleds and brought to town. Most of the McKettricks would be staying at the hotel, while the overflow spent the night with the Thaddingses.

Lizzie, dazed with happiness, ate cake and posed for the photographer, with Morgan beside her. There were piles of wedding gifts: homemade quilts, preserves, embroidered dish towels and pillowcases. She was hugged, kissed, congratulated and teased.

A band played, and she danced with her father first, then her grandfather, then each of her uncles in turn. By the time Morgan claimed *his* dance, Lizzie was winded.

When the time finally came for her and Morgan to take their leave, Lizzie was both relieved and quivery with nervous anticipation. She was Morgan's *wife,* now. And she had a gift for him that couldn't be wrapped in pretty paper and tied with a shimmery ribbon.

How would he respond when she told him?

A horse-drawn sleigh awaited the bride and groom in the snowy street outside. Lizzie left her veil in Lorelei's care, and they hastened toward the sleigh, Morgan bundling Lizzie quickly in thick blankets before huddling in beside her. Looking through the blinding flurries of white, she saw a figure hunched at the reins and wondered which of her uncles was driving.

The sleigh carried them swiftly through the night.

Lamps burned in the cottage windows when they arrived, glowing golden through the storm.

Morgan helped Lizzie down from the sleigh, swept her up into his arms, and carried her up the path to the front door. Looking back over her new husband's shoulder, Lizzie caught the briefest glimpse of the driver as he lifted his hat, and recognized Mr. Christmas. She started to call out to him, but the blizzard intensified and horse, sleigh and driver disappeared in a great, glittering swirl of snow.

And then they were inside, over the threshold.

Someone had decorated a small Christmas tree, and placed it on a table in front of the window. Lizzie nearly knocked it over, rushing to look outside, hoping to see her unlikely angel again.

The wind had stopped, and the snow fell softly now, slowly, big, fluffy flakes of it, blanketing the street in peace.

"Lizzie, what is it?" Morgan asked, standing behind her, wrapping his arms around her waist and drawing her back against him.

"I thought I saw—"

"What?"

She sighed, turned to Morgan, smiled up at him. "I thought I saw an angel," she said.

Morgan smiled, kissed her forehead. "It's Christmas Eve. There might be an angel or two around."

Lizzie swallowed, thinking that if she loved this man even a little bit more, she'd burst with the pure, elemental force of it. She paused, smiled. "I have a Christmas gift for you, Morgan," she told him, very quietly.

He glanced down at the packages under the little tree, raised an eyebrow in question.

She took his hand, pressed it lightly to her lower abdomen. "A baby," she said. "We're going to have a baby."

Morgan's face was a study in startled delight. "When, Lizzie?"

"July, I think," she replied, feeling shy. And much relieved. A part of her hadn't been sure Morgan would be pleased, since they were so newly married and had yet to establish a home together.

Gently, Morgan untied the laces of her cloak, slid it off her shoulders, laid it aside. "July," he repeated.

"There'll be some gossip," she warned. "I'm the school-marm, after all."

Morgan chuckled, his eyes alight with love. "You know what they say. The first baby can come anytime, the rest take nine months."

Lizzie was too happy to worry about gossip. She wasn't the first pregnant bride in Indian Rock, or in the McKettrick family, and she wouldn't be the last. "You're really glad, then?" She had to ask. "You don't wish we'd had more time?"

"I wouldn't change anything, Lizzie. Not anything at all."

She sniffled. "I love you so much it scares me, Dr. Morgan Shane."

He kissed her, lightly, the way he'd done in front of the altar earlier that night, when the preacher pronounced them man and wife. "And I love you, Mrs. Shane."

She laughed, and they drew apart, and Lizzie glanced at the little tree and the packages beneath it. "Did you do this?" she asked.

Morgan shook his head. "I thought you did," he replied.

"It must have been Lorelei, or the aunts," Lizzie said, pleasantly puzzled. She picked up one of the packages and recognized her stepmother's handwriting. "To Morgan," the tag read. "Open it," she urged.

Morgan's expression showed clearly that he had other things in mind than opening Christmas presents, but he took the parcel and unwrapped it just the same. Inside was an exquisitely made toy locomotive, of shining black metal—a reminder of how he and Lizzie had met.

He smiled, admiring it. "Open yours," he said.

Lizzie reached for the second parcel, gently tore away the ribbon and brightly colored paper. Lorelei had given her a baby's christening gown, frothy with lace, and a tiny bonnet to match.

"They *knew*," she marveled.

Morgan's grin was mischievous. "Maybe we were too obvious," he said.

Lizzie's cheeks warmed.

Morgan laughed and curved a finger under her chin. "Lizzie," he said, "Holt and Lorelei aren't exactly doddering old folks. They're in love, too, remember?"

She smiled. Nodded. "I'd like to change out of this dress," she said.

Morgan's eyes smoldered. "You do that," he replied gruffly. "I'll build up the fire a little."

Lizzie nodded and headed for the bedroom, stopping on the threshold to gasp. "Morgan!" she called.

He joined her.

A beautiful bed stood in the place that had been so noticeably vacant before, the headboard intricately carved with the image of a great, leafy oak, spreading its branches alongside a flowing creek. Birds soared against a cloud-strewn sky, and both their names had been carved into the trunk of the tree, inside a heart. Lizzie + Morgan.

Lizzie drew in her breath. This was her father's wedding gift, to her and to Morgan. It was more than a piece of furniture, more than an heirloom that would be passed down for generations. It was his *blessing,* on them and on their marriage.

"Lizzie McKettrick Shane," Morgan said, leaning to kiss the side of her neck, "you come from quite a family."

She nodded, moved closer to the bed, stroked the fine woodwork with the tips of her fingers, marveling at the time, thought and love that had gone into such a creation. "And now you're part of it," she told Morgan. "You and our baby and all the other babies that will come along later."

Morgan lingered in the doorway, framed there, looking so handsome in his new suit, specially bought for the wedding, that Lizzie etched the moment into her memory, to keep forever. *Her husband.* Even when she was an old, old lady, creaky-boned and wrinkled, she knew she would recall every detail of the way he looked that night.

"I'll see to the fire," he said, after a long, long time.

Lizzie nodded, shyly now. Waited until Morgan had stepped away from the door before taking a lacy nightgown from the trunk containing her trousseau and changing into it. She folded her wedding gown carefully, placed it in a box set aside for the purpose. She took down her hair and brushed it in front of the vanity mirror until it shone.

Morgan had never seen her with her hair down.

Warmth filled the cottage and, one by one, the lamps in the parlor went out. Lizzie waited, her heart racing a little.

Morgan filled the bedroom doorway again, a man-shaped

shadow, rimmed in faint, wintry light. The sweet silence of the snow outside seemed to muffle all sound. They might have been alone in the world that Christmas Eve, she and Morgan, two wanderers who'd somehow found their way to each other after long and difficult journeys.

Morgan whispered her name, came toward her.

She slipped into his arms.

They'd looked forward to making love on their wedding night, both of them. Now, by tacit agreement, they waited, savoring every nuance of being together.

Morgan threaded his hands through Lizzie's hair.

She felt beautiful.

"To think," Morgan said quietly, "that I almost didn't get on that train last Christmas."

"Don't think," Lizzie teased. He'd said the same thing to her, once, while they were stranded on the mountainside.

He chuckled, and kissed her with restrained passion. Eagerness and wanting sang through Lizzie, but she was willing to wait. There was no hurry: she and Morgan were married now, after all. They would make love countless times in the days, weeks, months and years ahead.

They'd already conceived a child, and Lizzie knew something of the pleasures awaiting her, but tonight was special. It was their first time as husband and wife.

Her breath caught, and her heartbeat quickened as Morgan caressed her, touching her lightly in all the places she loved to be touched, all the places she *needed* to be touched.

She gave herself up to him, completely, joyously, with little gasps and sighs as he pleasured her, slowly. Ever so slowly, and with such expertise that Lizzie wished that night would never end.

She was transported, in the bed with the tree carved into the headboard. She died there, and was reborn, a new woman, even stronger than before. She gasped and whimpered and sobbed out Morgan's name, clinging to him with everything she had, riding wave after wave of sacred satisfaction.

Hours passed before they slept, sated and spent, arms and legs entwined.

Lizzie awakened first, to the cold, snowy light of a clear Christmas morning. The fire had gone out during the night, but she was warm, through and through, snuggled close to Morgan under a heavy layer of quilts.

He stirred beside her, opened his eyes. "I'd better get the fire going," he said, his voice sleepy.

"Not yet," Lizzie whispered, burrowing closer to him.

"We'll freeze," he said.

Lizzie laughed and shook her head. "I don't think so," she answered, nibbling mischievously at his neck.

He rolled on top of her, his elbows pressed into the mattress on either side. "Have I married a hussy?" he asked.

"Most definitely," Lizzie answered, beaming. "And you thought I was only a schoolmarm."

Morgan laughed, and the sound was beautiful to Lizzie, and in the distance the church bells pealed, ringing in Christmas.

★ ★ ★ ★ ★

AN OUTLAW'S CHRISTMAS

In loving memory of Dale Macomber.
Knowing you was a gift I'll always be grateful for.

Chapter One

December, 1915

All but hidden behind a rapidly thickening veil of snow that cold afternoon, Blue River, Texas, looked more like a faint pencil sketch against a gray-and-white background than a real town, constructed of beams and mortar and weathered wood and occupied by flesh-and-blood folks. Squinting against the dense flurries, Sawyer McKettrick could just make out the pitch of a roof or two, the mounded lines of hitching rails and horse troughs, the crooked jut of the occasional chimney. Here and there, the light of a lamp or lantern glowed through the gloom, but as far as Sawyer could tell, nobody was stirring along the sidewalks or traveling the single wide street curving away from the tiny railroad depot.

Beside him, his buckskin gelding, Cherokee, nickered and tossed his big head, no doubt relieved to finally plant four sturdy hooves on solid ground after long hours spent rattling over the rails in a livestock car. Sawyer's own journey, sitting

bolt upright on a hard and sooty seat in the near-empty passenger section, had been so dull and so uncomfortable that
he probably would have been happier riding with the horse.

Naturally, Cherokee didn't hold up his end of a conversation, but he was a fine listener and a trustworthy companion.

Now, the engineer's whistle sounded a long, plaintive hoot
of fare-thee-well behind them, and the train clanked slowly
out of the station, iron screeching against iron, steam hissing
into the freezing air.

They waited, man and horse, until the sounds grew muffled
and distant, though for what, Sawyer couldn't have said. He
hadn't expected to be met at the depot—Clay McKettrick, his
cousin and closest friend, lived on a ranch several miles outside of Blue River and, given the weather, the trail winding
between there and town must be nigh on impassable—but just
the same, a momentary sense of loneliness howled through
him like a wind scouring the walls of a canyon.

With a glance back at the station, where he'd left his trunk
of belongings behind, meaning to fetch it later, Sawyer swung
up into the saddle and spoke a gruff, soothing word of encouragement to the horse.

There was a hotel in Blue River—he'd stayed there on his
last visit—but he wanted to let Cherokee walk off some stiff-
ness before settling him in over at the livery stable with plenty
of hay and a ration of grain, and then making his way back to
rent a room. Once he'd secured a bed for the night, he'd send
somebody for his trunk, consume a steak dinner in the hotel
dining room, and, later on, take a bath and shave.

In the meantime, though, he wanted to attend to his horse.
Sawyer gave the animal his head, let him forge his own way,
at his own pace, through the deep snow and the unnerving
silence.

The buildings on either side of the street were visible as

they passed, though only partially, dark at the windows, with their doors shut tight. Most folks were where they ought to be, Sawyer supposed, gathered around stoves and fireplaces in their various homes, with coffee brewed and supper smells all around them.

Again, that bleak feeling of aloneness rose up inside him, but he quelled it quickly. He did not subscribe to melancholy moods—it wasn't the McKettrick way. In his family, a man— or a woman, for that matter—played the cards they were dealt, kept on going no matter what, and tended, to the best of their ability, to whatever task was presently at hand.

Still, there was a prickle at his nape, and Cherokee, rarely skittish, pranced sideways in agitation, tossing his head and neighing.

Sawyer had barely pushed back his long coat to uncover his Colt .45, just in case, when he heard the gunshot, swaddled in the snowy silence to a muted pop, saw the flash of orange fire and felt the bullet sear its way into his left shoulder. All of this transpired in the course of a second or so, but even as he slumped forward over Cherokee's neck, dazed by the hot- poker thrust of the pain, spaces wedged themselves between moments, stretching time, distorting it. Sawyer was at once a wounded man, alone on a snow-blind street except for his panicked horse, and a dispassionate observer, nearby but oddly detached from the scene.

He didn't see the shooter or his horse, but the calm, watch- ing part of him sized up the situation, sensed there had been a rider. If anybody had seen anything, or heard the muffled gun- shot, they weren't fixing to rush to his rescue, and he didn't have the strength to draw his .45, even if he could have seen beyond Cherokee's laid-back ears.

Fortunately, the horse knew that—in cases like this any- way—discretion was the better part of valor. Cherokee bolted for safer territory, leapfrogging through the powdery snow, and Sawyer, hurting bad and only half-conscious, simply lay over the pommel, with the saddle horn jabbing into his middle like a fist, and held on to reins and mane for all he was worth.

Maybe the gunman lost sight of them in the storm, or maybe he just slipped back through the edges of Sawyer's awareness, into the pulsing darkness that surrounded him, but the second shot, the one that would have finished him off for sure, never came.

His mind slowed, and then slowed some more. He was aware of the *thud-thud-thud* of his heart, the raspy scratch of his breath, clawing its way into his lungs and then out again, and the familiar smell of wet horsehide, but his vision dimmed to a gray haze.

Cherokee kept moving. Sawyer's consciousness seemed to retreat into the far corners of his mind, but growing up on the Triple M Ranch in Arizona, he'd practically been raised on the back of a horse, and the muscles in his arms and legs must have drawn on some capacity for recollection beyond the grasp of the waking mind, because he managed to stay in the saddle.

It was only when the horse came to a sudden stop in a spill of buttery light on glistening snow that Sawyer pitched sideways with a sickening lurch, jarred his wounded shoulder when he struck the snow-padded ground, and passed out from the pain.

Piper St. James, seated at the desk in her empty schoolroom and glumly surveying the scrawny, undecorated pine tree leaning against the far wall, wished heartily, and not for the first time, that she'd never left Maine to strike out for a life of adventure in the still-wild West.

Her cousin Dara Rose, in love with her handsome rancher

husband, had painted a fine picture of Blue River in her letters, telling Piper what a wonderful place it was, full of good
people and wide-open to newcomers.

Piper sighed. Of course Dara Rose would see things that
way—she was so happy in her new marriage and, being a
generous soul, she wanted Piper to be happy, too. Life had
been hard for her cousin and her two little girls, but Clay Mc-
Kettrick had changed all that.

Piper's pupils—all thirteen of them—were safe at home,
where they belonged, and that was a considerable comfort
to her. She'd spent the entire day alone, though, shut up in
the schoolhouse, feeding the potbellied stove from an ever-
dwindling store of firewood, keeping herself occupied as best
she could. Tomorrow was likely to bring more of the same,
since the storm showed no signs of letting up—it might even
get worse.

Piper shuddered at the thought. She had plenty of food,
thanks to the good people of Blue River, but her supply of
well water was running out fast, like the wood. Soon, she'd
have no choice but to pull on a pair of oversize boots, bundle
up in both her everyday shawls *and* her heavy woolen cloak,
raise the hood to protect her ears from the stinging chill, and
slog her way across the school yard, once to the woodshed, and
once to the well. To make matters worse, she was getting low
on kerosene for the one lamp she'd allowed herself to light.

She told herself that Clay, Dara Rose's husband, would come
by to check on her soon, but there was no telling when or if
he'd be able to get there, given the distance and the state of
the roads. For now, Piper had to do for herself.

The wind howled around the clapboard walls of that small,
unpainted schoolhouse, sorrowful as a whole band of banshees
searching for a way in, making her want to burrow under the
quilts on her bed, which took up most of the tiny room in

back set aside for teacher's quarters, and hide there until the weather turned.

She might freeze if she did that, of course, and that was if she didn't die of thirst beforehand.

So she put on the ungainly boots, left behind by Miss Krenshaw, the last teacher, wrapped herself in wool, drew a deep breath and opened the schoolhouse door to step out onto the little porch.

The cold buffeted her, hard as a slap, trapping the breath in her lungs and nearly knocking her backward, over the threshold.

Resolute, she drew the shawls and the cloak more tightly around her and tried again. The sooner she went out, the sooner she could come back *in,* she reasoned.

She stopped on the schoolhouse porch, peering through the goose-feather flakes coming down solid as a wall in front of her. Was that a horse, there in the thin light her one lamp cast through the front window?

Piper caught her breath, her heart thudding with sudden hope. There *was* a horse, and a horse meant a rider, and a rider meant company, if not practical help. Perhaps Clay *had* braved the tempest to pay her a visit—

She trudged down the steps and across the yard, every step an effort, and got a clearer look at the horse. A sturdy buckskin, the animal was real, all right. The creature was saddled, reins dangling, and she saw its eyes roll upward, glaring white.

But there was no rider on its back.

Although Piper had little experience with horses, she felt an instant affinity for the poor thing, evidently lost in the storm. It must have wandered off from somewhere nearby.

She moved toward it slowly, carefully, partly because of the bitter wind and partly because of her own rising trepidation. She didn't recognize the horse, which meant that Clay *hadn't* come to look in on her, nor had any of the other men—fathers, brothers or uncles of her students—who might have been concerned about the schoolmarm's welfare.

The buckskin whinnied wildly as she approached, backing up awkwardly, nearly falling onto its great, heaving haunches, lathered despite the chill.

"There, now," Piper said, reaching for the critter's bridle strap. There was a shed behind the schoolhouse—some of the students rode in from the country when class was in session and tethered their mounts there for the day, so there was some hay, and the plank walls offered a modicum of shelter—but just then, that shack seemed as far away as darkest Africa.

Before she could take hold of the horse's bridle, Piper tripped over something solid, half buried in the snow, fell to her hands and knees, and felt the sticky warmth of blood seeping through her mittens.

She saw him then, the rider, sprawled on his back, hat lying a few feet away, staining the snow to crimson.

Sitting on her haunches, Piper stared down at the unfortunate wayfarer for a few long moments, snowflakes slicing at her face like razors, confounded and afraid.

Bile surged into the back of her throat, scalding there, and she willed herself not to turn aside and retch. Something had to be done—and quickly.

"Mister?" she called, gripping the lapels of his long gunslinger's coat and bending close to his face. "Mister, are you alive?"

He groaned, and she saw one of his eyelids twitch.

The horse, close enough to step on one or both of them, whinnied again, a desperate sound.

"You'll be all right," Piper told both the horse and the man, on her knees in the snow, her mittens and cloak damp with blood, but she wasn't at all sure that was the truth.

The man was around six feet tall—there was no way she could lift him, and it was clear that he couldn't stand, let alone walk.

Piper deliberated briefly, then stumbled and struggled back into the schoolhouse, through to her room, and wrenched the patchwork quilt—she'd done the piecework herself and the task had been arduous—off the bed.

Warmer now, from the exertions of the past few minutes, Piper rushed outside again and somehow managed to get the quilt underneath the bleeding stranger. He opened his eyes once—even in the dim light she could see that they were a startling shade of greenish azure—and a little smile crooked the corner of his mouth before he passed into unconsciousness again.

In a frenzy of strength, she dragged man and quilt as far as the steps, but there was no getting him up them. She had no way of knowing how long he'd been lying in the school yard, injured, and frostbite was a serious possibility, as was hypothermia.

She gripped him by his shoulders—they were broad under her hands, and hard with muscle—and shook him firmly. "Mister!" she yelled, through the raging wind. "You've got to rally yourself enough to get up these steps—I can't do this without some assistance, and there's no one else around!"

Miraculously, the stranger came to and gathered enough strength to half crawl up the steps, with a lot of help from Piper. From there, she was able to pull him over the threshold onto the rough-plank floor, where he lay facedown, bleeding copiously and only semiconscious.

"My horse," he rasped.

"Bother your horse," Piper replied, but she didn't mean it. The stranger, being a human being, was her first concern, but she was almost as worried about that frightened animal standing outside in the weather, and she knew she wouldn't be able to ignore it.

"Horse," the man repeated.

"I'll see to him," Piper promised, having no real choice in the matter. She collected another blanket from her quarters, covered the man, and steeled herself to hurry back outside.

Ever after, she'd wonder how she'd managed such an impossible feat, but at the time, Piper worked from a sense of expediency. She got ahold the horse's reins and somehow led him around back, through what seemed like miles of snow, and into the dark shed. There, she removed his saddle, the blanket beneath it, and the bridle. She spread out some hay for him and found a bucket, which she filled with snow—that being the best she could do for now. When the snow melted, the creature would have drinking water.

The horse was jumpy at first, and Piper took a few precious moments to speak softly to him, rubbing him down as best she could with an old burlap sack and making the same promise as before—he *would* be all right, and so would his master, because she wouldn't have it any other way.

On the way back to the schoolhouse, she fought her way into the woodshed and filled her arms with sticks of pitch-scented pine.

The stranger was still on the floor, upon her return, lying just over the threshold, either dead or sleeping.

Hastily, murmuring a prayer under her breath, Piper dumped the firewood into the box beside the stove, went back to the man, pulled off one ruined mitten and felt for a pulse at the base of his throat. His skin was cold, a shade of grayish-blue, but there was a heartbeat, thank heaven, faint but steady.

There was still water to fetch—why hadn't she done this chore earlier, in the daylight, as she'd intended, instead of starting a pot of pinto beans and reading one of Sir Walter Scott's novels?—and Piper didn't allow herself to think beyond getting to the well, filling a couple of buckets, and bringing them inside.

She marched outside again, moving like a woman floundering in a bad dream, taking the water buckets with her. Just getting to the well took most of her strength and, once there, she had to lower the vessels, one by one, by a length of rope.

She'd discarded her mittens by then, and the rough hemp burned like fire against her palms and the undersides of her fingers, but she lowered and filled one bucket, and then the other. Her hands ached ferociously as she carried those heavy pails toward the schoolhouse, up the steps, and once inside, she set them both down an instant before she would surely have spilled them all over the man lying in a swoon on her floor.

There was no time to spare—if there had been, Piper might have had the luxury of succumbing to helplessness and giving herself up to a fit of useless weeping—so she filled a kettle and put it on the stove to heat, right next to the simmering beans.

With one eye on the inert visitor the whole time, she peeled off her bloody cloak and shawls and stepped out of the boots. Her hands were numb, and she shook them hard, hoping to restore the circulation, which only made them hurt again. When the water was warm enough, she poured some into a basin and scrubbed sticky streaks of crimson from her skin.

The stranger didn't stir, even once, and he might very well be dead, but Piper talked to him anyway, in the same brisk, take-charge tone she used when her students balked at staying behind their desks, where they belonged. "You can stop fretting over your horse," she said. "He's safe in the shed, with hay and water aplenty."

There was no response, and Piper made herself walk over to the man, stoop, and, once again, feel for a pulse.

It was there, and it seemed the bleeding had slowed, if not stopped altogether.

She was thankful for small favors.

Noticing the ominous-looking gun jutting from a holster on his right hip, she shivered, extracted the thing gingerly, by two fingers. It was heavy, and the handle was intricately carved, as well as blood-speckled. She made out the initials *S.M.* as she held the dreadful weapon in shaking hands, carried it into the cloakroom and set it carefully on a high shelf.

Heat surged audibly into the water kettle, causing it to rattle cheerfully on the stove top. Piper moved, with quiet diligence, from one effort to another, emptying the basin in which she'd washed her hands through a wide crack in the floorboards, wiping it out with a rag, settling it aside. She had cloth strips to use as bandages, since one or the other of her pupils were always getting hurt during recess, and there was a bottle of iodine, too, so she fetched these from their customary places in the cabinet behind her desk.

Her mind kept going back to that dreadful pistol. No one carried guns these days—it was the twentieth century, after all—except for lawmen, like Clay, who was the marshal of Blue River, and, well, *outlaws.*

Had the stranger used that long-barreled weapon to hold up banks, rob trains, accost law-abiding citizens on the road? She'd seen no sign of a badge, so he probably wasn't a constable of any sort, but he might have identification of some kind, in his pockets, perhaps, or the saddlebags, left behind in the shed with the horse and its attendant gear.

Put it out of your mind, she ordered herself. There was no sense in pandering to her imagination.

Since she couldn't quite face searching the fellow's pockets—it seemed too intimate an undertaking—she turned her thoughts to other things. After collecting a pair of scissors from the drawer of her battered oak desk, Piper undertook the task she would rather have avoided, kneeling beside the man's prone form and gently rolling him onto his back.

The singular odors of gunpowder and blood rose like smoke, one acrid, one metallic, to fill her nostrils, then her lungs, then her fretful stomach. She gagged again, swallowed hard, and forced her trembling hands to pick up the scissors and begin snipping away at the front of the man's once-fine coat.

The bullet had torn its way through the dark, costly fabric, through the shirt—probably white once—and the flesh beneath.

When Piper finally uncovered the wound, she was horrified all over again. She slapped one hand over her mouth, though whether to hold back a scream or a spate of sickness she couldn't have said.

The deep, jagged hole in the flesh of the stranger's shoulder began to seep again.

Piper shifted her gaze to the supplies she'd gathered, now resting beside her on the floor—a basin full of steaming water, strands of clean cloth, iodine—and was struck by their inadequacy, and her own.

This man needed a surgeon, not the bumbling first aid of a schoolmarm.

She raised her eyes to the night-darkened window and the huge flakes of falling snow beyond, and mentally calculated the distance to Dr. Howard's house, on the far side of Blue River.

At most a ten-minute walk away, in daylight and decent weather, Doc's place might as well have been on another continent, for all the chance she had of reaching it safely. Furthermore, the man wasn't a physician, but a dentist, albeit a very competent one who would definitely know what do to in such an emergency.

Since she had no means of summoning him, she would have to do what she could, and hope the Good Lord would lend a hand.

Piper spent the next half hour or so cleaning that wound, treating it with iodine, binding it closed with the strips of cloth. Stitches were needed, she knew, but threading a needle and sewing flesh together, the way she might stitch up a patchwork quilt, was entirely beyond her. If she made the attempt, she'd get sick, faint dead away, or both, thereby making bad matters considerably worse.

Mercifully, the stranger did not wake during the long, careful process of applying the bandages. When she'd finished, Piper covered him again, brought a pillow and eased it under his head, and, rising to her feet, looked down at the front of her dress.

Like the cloak and the mittens, it was badly stained.

Piper rinsed the basin, filled it with clean water, and retreated into the little room at the back of the schoolhouse. She stripped to her petticoat and camisole, shivering all the while, and gave herself a quick sponge bath. After that, she donned a calico dress—a little scant for the season, but she'd need her gray woolen one for some time yet and wanted to keep it clean. Once properly clad again, she took her dark hair down from its pins and combs, brushed it vigorously, and secured it into a loose chignon at her nape.

Needing to keep herself occupied, Piper burned her knitted mittens in the stove—there was no use trying to get them clean—and then assessed the damage to her cloak. It was dire.

Resigned, and keeping one eye on the unmoving victim, Piper took up her scissors again and cut away the stained parts of her only cloak, consigned the pieces to the stove, and folded what remained to be used for other purposes.

Waste not, want not. She and Dara Rose, growing up together in a household of genteel poverty, had learned that lesson early and well.

She ate supper at her desk—a bowl of the beans she'd been simmering on the stove all afternoon—and wondered what to do next.

She was exhausted, and every muscle ached from the strain of dragging a full-grown man halfway across the school yard and inside, tending to the horse as well as its master, fetching the wood and the water. She didn't dare close her eyes to sleep, though—the stranger might be incapacitated, but he was *still* a stranger, and he was accustomed to carrying a gun. Suppose he came to and did—well—*something?*

From a safe distance, Piper assessed him again, cataloging his features in her mind. Caramel-colored hair, a lean, muscular frame, expensive clothes and boots. And then there was the horse, obviously a sturdy creature, well-bred. This man was probably a person of means, she concluded, but that certainly didn't mean he wasn't a rascal and a rounder, too.

He might actually be dangerous, a drifter or an unscrupulous opportunist.

Again, she considered braving the weather once more, making her way to the nearest house to ask for help, since Doc's place was too distant, but she knew she'd never make it even that far. She had no cloak, and in that blizzard, she didn't dare trust her sense of direction. She might head the wrong way, wander off into the countryside somewhere and perish from exposure.

She shuddered again, rose from her chair, and carried her empty bowl and soup spoon back to the washstand in her quarters, where she left them to be dealt with later.

Still giving the stranger a fairly wide berth, she perched on one of the students' benches and watched him, thinking hard. She supposed she could peel that overcoat off him, put it on, and tramp to the neighbors' house, nearly a quarter of a mile away, but the effort might do him further injury and, besides, the mere thought of wearing that bloody garment made her ill.

Even if she'd been able to bear *that,* the problem of the weather remained.

She was stuck.

She retrieved her knitting—a scarf she'd intended to give to Dara Rose as a Christmas gift—and sat working stitches and waiting for the man to move, or speak.

Or die.

"Water," he said, after a long time. "I need—water."

New energy rushed through Piper's small body; she filled a ladle from one of the buckets she'd hauled in earlier, carried it carefully to his side, and knelt to slip one hand under his head and raise him up high enough to drink.

He took a few sips and his eyes searched her face as she lowered him back to the floor.

"Where—? Who—?" he muttered, the words as rough as sandpaper.

"You're in the Blue River schoolhouse," she answered. "I'm Miss St. James, the teacher. Who are you?"

"Is…my horse—?"

Piper managed a thin smile. She didn't know whether to be glad because he'd regained consciousness or worried by the problems that might present. "Your horse is fine. In out of the storm, fed and watered."

A corner of his mouth quirked upward, ever so slightly, and his eyes seemed clearer than when he'd opened them before, as though he were more present somehow, and centered squarely within the confines of his own skin and bones. "That's…good," he said, with effort.

"Who are you?" Piper asked. She still hadn't searched his pockets, since just binding up his wound had taken all the courage and fortitude she could muster.

He didn't answer, but gestured for more water, lifting his head without her help this time, and when he'd swallowed most of the ladle's contents, he lapsed into another faint. His skin was ghastly pale, and his lips had a bluish tinge.

He belonged in a bed, not on the floor, but moving him any farther was out of the question, given their difference in size. All she could do was cover him, keep the fire going— and pray for a miraculous recovery.

The night passed slowly, with the man groaning hoarsely in his sleep now and then, and muttering a woman's name— Josie—often. At times, he seemed almost desperate for a response.

Oddly stricken by these murmured cries, Piper left her chair several times to kneel beside him, holding his hand.

"I'm here," she'd say, hoping he'd think she was this Josie person.

Whoever she was.

He'd smile in his sleep then, and rest peacefully for a while, and Piper would go back to her chair and her knitting. At some point, she unraveled the scarf and cast on new stitches; she'd make mittens instead, she decided, to replace the ones she'd had to burn. With so much of the winter still to come, she'd need them, and heaven only knew what she'd do for a cloak; since her salary was barely enough to keep body and soul together. Such a purchase was close to impossible.

She wasn't normally the fretful sort—like Dara Rose, she was hardworking and practical and used to squeezing pennies—but, then, this was hardly a normal situation.

Was this man an outlaw? Perhaps even a murderer?

He was well dressed and he owned a horse of obvious quality, even to her untrained eyes, but, then, maybe he was highly skilled at thievery, and his belongings were ill-gotten gains.

Piper nodded off in her chair, awakened with a start, saw that it was morning and the snow had relented a little, still heavy but no longer an impenetrable curtain of white.

The stranger was either asleep or unconscious, and the thin sunlight struck his toast-colored hair with glints of gold.

He was handsome, Piper decided. All the more reason to keep her distance.

She set aside her knitting and proceeded to build up the fire and then put a pot of coffee on to brew, hoping the stuff would restore her waning strength, and finally wrapped herself in her two remaining shawls, drew a deep breath, and left the schoolhouse to trudge around back, to the shed.

The trees were starkly beautiful, every branch defined, as if etched in glimmering frost.

To her relief, the buckskin was fine, though the water bucket she'd filled with snow was empty.

Piper patted the horse, picked up the bucket, and made her way back to the well to fill it. When she got back, the big gelding greeted her with a friendly nicker and drank thirstily from the pail.

As she was returning to the shelter of the schoolhouse, holding her skirts up so she wouldn't trip over the hem, she spotted a rider just approaching the gate at the top of the road and recognized him immediately, even through the falling snow.

Clay McKettrick.

Piper's whole being swelled with relief.

She waited, saw Clay's grin flash from beneath the round brim of his hat. His horse high-stepped toward her, across the field of snow, steam puffing from its flared nostrils, its mane and tail spangled with tiny icicles.

"I told Dara Rose you'd be fine here on your own," Clay remarked cordially, dismounting a few feet from where Piper stood, all but overwhelmed with gratitude, "but she insisted on finding out for sure." A pause, a troubled frown as he took in her rumpled calico dress. "Where's your coat? You'll catch your death traipsing around without it."

She ignored the question, wide-eyed and winded from the hard march through the snow.

Clay was a tall, lean man, muscular in all the right places, and it wasn't hard to see why her cousin loved him so much. He was pleasing to look at, certainly, but his best feature, in Piper's opinion, was his rock-solid character. He exuded quiet strength and confidence in all situations.

He would know what to do in this crisis, and he would *do* it.

"There's a man inside," Piper blurted, finding her voice at last and gesturing toward the schoolhouse. By then, the cold was indeed penetrating her thin dress. "He's been shot. His horse is in the shed and—"

Clay's expression turned serious, and he brushed past her, leaving his own mount to stand patiently in the yard.

Piper hurried into the schoolhouse behind Clay.

He crouched, laying one hand to the man's unhurt shoulder. "Sawyer?" he rasped. "Damn it, Sawyer—*what happened to you?*"

Chapter Two

Sawyer, Piper thought distractedly—Sawyer *McKettrick,* Clay's cousin, the man he'd been expecting for weeks now. That explained the initials on the man's holster, if not much else.

Down on one knee beside the other man now, Clay took off his snowy hat and tossed it aside. Piper caught the glint of his nickel-plated badge, a star pinned to the front of his heavy coat. Clay was still Blue River's town marshal, but it was a job he was ready to hand over to someone else, so he could concentrate on ranching and his growing family.

"Sawyer!" Clay repeated, his tone brusque with concern.

Sawyer's eyes rolled open, and a grin played briefly on his mouth. "I must have died and gone to hell," he said in a slow, raspy drawl, "because I'd swear I've come face-to-face with the devil himself."

Clay gave a raucous chuckle at that. "You must be better off than you look," he commented. "Can you get to your feet?"

Solemnly amused, Sawyer considered the question for a few moments, moistened his lips, which were dry and cracked despite Piper's repeated efforts to give him water during the night, and struggled to reply, "I don't think so."

"That's all right," Clay said, gruffly gentle, while Piper's weary mind raced. She'd heard a few things about Sawyer, and some of it was worrisome—for instance, no one, including Clay, seemed to know which side of the law he was on—though Dara Rose had liked him. "I'll help you." With that, Clay raised Sawyer to a sitting position, causing him to moan again and his bandages to seep with patches of bright red, draped his cousin's good arm over his shoulders, and stood, bringing the other man up with him.

"I'll put Sawyer on your bed, if that's all right," Clay said to Piper, already headed toward her quarters in the back. The schoolhouse was small, and everybody knew how it was laid out, since the building of it had been a community effort.

When word got around that she'd harbored a man under this roof, bleeding and insensible with pain or not, her reputation would be tarnished, at best.

At worst? Completely ruined.

The injustice of that was galling to Piper, but nonetheless binding. Lady teachers in particular were scrutinized for the slightest inclination toward wanton behavior, though their male counterparts sometimes courted and then married one of their students, with impunity. A practice Piper considered reprehensible.

"Certainly," she said now, well aware that Clay hadn't been asking her permission but feeling compelled to offer some kind of response.

She hovered in the doorway of her room—little more than a lean-to, really—with one tiny window, high up, while Clay wrestled Sawyer out of his coat then eased him down carefully onto the bed, pulled off his boots.

The effort of going even that far must have been too much

for Sawyer, strong as he looked, because he shut his eyes again, and didn't respond when Clay spoke to him.

"I'll get the doc," Clay said to Piper, as she stepped out of the doorway to let him pass. "Do you have any more blankets? It's important to keep him warm."

Piper thought with a heavy heart of the fine, colorful quilts lying neatly folded in her hope chest. She'd always envisioned them gracing the beds of some lovely house, once she was married, like Dara Rose, with a proper home.

"Yes," she said bravely, and though she didn't begrudge Sawyer McKettrick those quilts, she couldn't help lamenting their fate. She'd worked hard to assemble them from tiny scraps of fabric, carefully saved, and many of the pieces were all she had to remember friends she'd left behind in Maine.

She swept over to her bulky cedar chest, raised the lid, and rummaged through the treasured contents—doilies and pot holders, tablecloths and dish towels and the like—until she'd found what she was looking for.

As she spread the first of those exquisitely stitched coverlets over Mr. McKettrick, he stirred again, opened his eyes briefly, and smiled. "Thanks, Josie," he said, and there was a caress in the way he said the name.

Briskly, because she was a little hurt, though she couldn't have pinpointed the reason why such an emotion should afflict her, Piper put another quilt on top of her patient, and then another.

Then, because it was nearly eight o'clock, she went to the other end of the building, where the bell rope dangled, and gave it a tug. Surely none of her pupils would make it to school on such a day, but Piper believed in maintaining routine, especially during trying times. There was something reassuring about it.

The silvery bell, high overhead in its little belfry, chimed once, twice, three times, summoning students who would not come.

Piper's hands, rope-burned from hauling up well water the night before, stung fiercely, and she was almost glad, because the pain gave her something to think about besides the man sprawled on her spinster's bed, probably bleeding all over her quilts.

She retrieved a tin of Wildflower Salve from her bureau, careful not to make too much noise and disturb Mr. McKettrick. Carrying the salve back to her schoolroom, she sat down at her desk and smiled a little as she twisted off the pretty little lid to treat her sore palms.

There was an abundance of the stuff, since Dara Rose, impoverished after the scandalous death of her first husband, upstairs at the Bitter Gulch Saloon, had once planned to sell the product door-to-door in hopes of making enough money to support herself and her two small daughters, Edrina and Harriet. Instead, Dara Rose had fallen in love with Clay McKettrick, married him, and thus retained what amounted to a lifetime supply of medicinal salve, which she generously shared.

A half hour passed before Clay returned, with Dr. Jim Howard, the local dentist, riding stalwartly along beside him on the mule that usually pulled his buggy.

Everybody in Blue River liked Dr. Howard, whose young daughter, Madeline, was one of Piper's best students. At eight, the little girl could read and cipher with the acuity of an adult. *Mrs.* Howard, however, was not so easy to like as her husband and daughter. Eloise wore nothing but velvet or silk, dismissed the town as a "bump in the road" and told anyone who would listen that she'd "married down."

"Miss St. James," Dr. Howard greeted her, with a friendly smile and a tug at the brim of his Eastern-style hat, as he stomped the snow off his boots on the schoolhouse porch, the way Clay had done a moment before. Doc was a large man, good-natured, older than his wife by some twenty years, and his eyes were a kindly shade of blue. He carried a battered leather bag in one gloved hand.

Piper barely stopped herself from rushing over and embracing the man, she was so glad to see him. The responsibility of keeping Mr. McKettrick alive had, she realized, weighed more heavily upon her than she'd thought it did.

She merely nodded in acknowledgment, though, as he closed the door against the cold daylight wind, and she hung back when Clay led the way through the schoolroom and into the chamber behind it.

Of course she couldn't help overhearing most of the conversation between Clay and Dr. Howard, given that the whole place was hardly larger than Dara Rose's chicken coop out on the ranch, classroom, teacher's quarters and all.

Clay was asking how bad the injury was, and Dr. Howard replied that it was serious enough, but with luck and a lot of rest, the patient would probably recover.

Probably recover? Piper thought, sipping from the mug of coffee she'd poured for herself. When Clay and the doctor—more commonly referred to as "Doc"—came out of the back room, she'd offer them some, too. She owned three cups, not including the bone china tea service for six nestled in her hope chest, which would remain precisely where it was, unlike her once pristine quilts.

"I'd like to take Sawyer out to my place," she heard Clay say.

"Better wait a few days," came Doc's response. "He's lost a lot of blood. The bullet went clear through him, though, which saves me having to dig it out, and Miss St. James did a creditable job of binding him up. He'll have scars, but the wound looks clean, thanks to her." A pause followed. "There's a bottle of carbolic acid in my bag there—hand it to me, will you?"

There was another short silence, during which Clay must have done as Doc asked, soon followed by a hoarse shout of angry protest from the patient. He swore colorfully, and Piper winced. She believed that cursing revealed a poor vocabulary, among other personal shortcomings.

"Can't take a chance on infection setting in," the dentist said peaceably, evidently unruffled by the outburst. "The burning will stop after a while."

Sawyer muttered something unintelligible.

Piper's hands trembled as she set her coffee mug down on her desk. Doc's reply to Clay's statement about taking his cousin out to the ranch echoed in her mind. *Better wait a few days.*

All well and good, she thought fretfully, but what was *she* supposed to do in the meantime? There was only one bed, after all, and she couldn't sleep in a chair until the man was well enough to be moved, could she?

Mr. McKettrick was indeed badly injured, but this was a *schoolhouse,* frequented by children five days a week—children who would go home after dismissal and tell their parents there was a strange man recuperating in Miss St. James's room. She wouldn't be able to hide him from them any more than she could hide that enormous gelding of his, quartered in the shed out back. Even unconscious, Sawyer filled the place with his presence, breathed up all the air.

Clay emerged from her room just then, took a second mug from the shelf near the stove and poured himself some coffee. He was probably cold, Piper realized with some chagrin, having ridden in from the ranch, proceeded to Doc Howard's, and then made his way back to the schoolhouse again.

"I guess we've got a problem," he said now. Was there a

twinkle in those very blue eyes of his as he studied her expression?

"Yes," Piper agreed, somewhat stiffly. Maybe Clay found the situation amusing, but *she* certainly didn't.

Clay took another sip, thoughtful and slow, from his mug. He'd shed his long coat soon after he and Doc arrived, and his collarless shirt was open at the throat, showing the ridged fabric of his undergarment. Like Sawyer, he wore a gun belt, but he'd set the pistol aside earlier, an indication of his good manners. "You probably heard what Doc Howard said," he told her, after a few moments of pensive consideration. "I could stay here with Sawyer and send you on out to the ranch to stay with Dara Rose and the girls, but it's hard going, with the snow still so deep."

Jim Howard came out of Piper's room, wiping his hands clean on a cloth that smelled of carbolic acid. "I gave him some laudanum," he told Clay. "He'll sleep for a while."

Piper propped her own hands on her hips. She'd spent a mostly sleepless night hoping and praying that someone would come to help, and she'd gotten her wish, but for all that, the problem was only partially solved.

Perhaps she should have been more specific, she reflected, rueful.

"Must I point out to you gentlemen," she began, with dignity, "that this arrangement is highly improper?"

Clay's grin was slight, but it was, nonetheless, a grin, and it infuriated her. She was an unmarried woman, a schoolmarm, and there was *a man in her bed,* likely to remain there for the foreseeable future. All her dreams for the future—a good husband, a home, and children of her own—could be compromised, and through no fault of her own.

"I understand your dilemma, Piper," he said, sounding like

an indulgent older brother, "but you heard the doc. Sawyer can't be moved until that wound of his mends a little."

"Surely you could take him as far as the hotel without doing harm," Piper reasoned, quietly frantic. She kept her hands at her sides, but the urge to wring them was strong.

Dr. Howard shook his head. Helped himself to the last mug and some coffee. "That could kill him," he said bluntly, but his expression was sympathetic. "I'm sure Eloise wouldn't mind coming over and helping with his care, though. She's had some nursing experience, and it would temper any gossip that might arise."

As far as Piper was concerned, being shut up with Eloise Howard for any length of time would be worse than attending to the needs of a helpless stranger by herself. *Much* worse.

"I couldn't ask her to do that," Piper said quickly. "Mrs. Howard has you and little Madeline to look after." She turned a mild glare on Clay. "Your cousin needs *male* assistance," she added. She'd dragged Sawyer McKettrick in out of the cold, cleaned his wound, even taken care of his horse, but she wasn't *about* to help him use the chamber pot, and that was final.

"I'll do what I can," Clay said, "but Dara Rose is due to have our baby any day now. I can't leave her out there alone, with just the girls and a few ranch hands. Once the weather lets up, though..."

His words fell away as Piper's cheeks flared with the heat of frustration. She could demand to be put up in the hotel herself, of course, until Sawyer McKettrick was well enough to leave the schoolhouse, but that would mean he'd be alone here. And he was in serious condition, despite Doc's cheerful prognosis.

What if something went wrong?

Besides, staying in hotels cost money, and even there in the untamed West, many of them had policies against admitting single women—unless, of course, they were ladies of the evening, and thus permitted to slip in through an alley door, under cover of darkness, and climb the back stairs to ply their wretched trade.

"You do realize," Piper persisted, "that I have nowhere to sleep?" *And no good man will ever marry me because my morals will forever be in question, even though I've done nothing wrong.*

Dr. Howard walked over and laid a fatherly hand on her shoulder. "I'll bring over anything you need," he assured her. "And stop in as often as I can. I'm sure Clay will do the same."

Clay nodded, but he was looking out the window, at the ceaseless snow, and his expression was troubled. "I've got to get back to Dara Rose," he said.

Piper's heart went out to him. As untenable as *her* situation was, Dara Rose needed Clay right now, and so did the children. Edrina and Harriet, though uncommonly precocious, were still quite small, and they couldn't be expected to know what to do if their mother went into labor.

"Go home, Clay," she said gently. "Give Dara Rose my best regards. Edrina and Harriet, too."

Clay's expression was even more serious now, and he looked at her for a long time before giving a reluctant nod and promising, "I'll come back for Sawyer as soon as Doc decides he can travel. I appreciate this, Piper. I wouldn't ask it of you, but—"

"I understand," she said, when words failed him again. And she *did* understand. Clay and Sawyer, like Piper and Dara Rose, were first cousins, the next best thing to siblings, and the bond was strong between them.

The snow came down harder and then harder still, and Doc Howard finished his coffee, collected his bag and took one more look at Sawyer, then headed out, after assuring Piper that he'd return before day's end and asking what he ought to bring back.

Blankets, she'd said, flustered, and kerosene, and whatever medicine the patient might need.

Clay attended to Sawyer's horse, said goodbye, and left for the ranch.

Watching him disappear into a spinning vortex of white, Piper felt a lump rise in her throat.

Once again, she was alone, except for Sawyer McKettrick and he, of course, was a hindrance, not a help.

True to his word, Doc was back within the hour, despite the increasingly bad weather, bringing a fresh supply of laudanum, a jug of kerosene, more carbolic acid and several warm blankets, wrapped in oilcloth so they'd stay dry.

He examined Sawyer again—reporting that he was still sleeping but that his heartbeat was stronger than before and he seemed to be breathing more easily—gave Piper a few instructions, and quickly left again, because nightfall would be coming on soon, making the ordinarily short journey home even more difficult than it already was.

Piper thanked him, asked him to give Eloise and Madeline her best, and watched through the front window until he and his mule were gone from sight.

Then, feeling more alone than she ever had, she got busy.

She washed down the already clean blackboard.

She dusted every surface in the schoolroom and refilled the kerosene lamp.

She drank more coffee and fed more wood into the stove.

Before he'd gone, Clay had assured her that Sawyer's horse would be fine until morning, which meant she could stay inside, where it was comparatively warm, so that was *one* less worry, anyhow. Gaps between the floorboards let in some of the cold, but that couldn't be helped. Using the spare blankets Doc had brought, she made a bed on the floor, close to the stove and hoped all the mice were hibernating.

She lit the kerosene lamp as the room darkened, and tried to cheer herself up by imagining the Christmas tree, still in its pail of water and leaning against the far wall, glowing with bright decorations. She took comfort in its green branches and faintly piney scent and thought, with a smile, of the recitations her students were memorizing for the school program.

Christmas Eve, just ten days away, fell on a Friday that year, so school would be in session until noon—weather permitting—and the recital would be presented soon after. After the poems and skits, everyone would sing carols. The owner of the mercantile had promised to donate oranges and peppermint sticks for the children, and the parents would bring pies and cookies and cakes.

This gathering represented all the Christmas some of the children would have, and all thirteen of them were looking forward to the celebration.

She moved, quiet as a wraith, to the window, and glumness settled over her spirit as she looked out.

And still the snow fell in abundance, unrelenting.

It was the pain that finally roused him.

Sawyer came to the surface of consciousness with a fierce jolt, feeling as though he'd been speared through his left shoulder.

His stomach lurched, and for a moment he was out there on that snowy street again, unable to see his assailant, reaching in vain for his .45.

He went deliberately still—not only was there no Colt at his hip, but he'd been stripped to his birthday suit—and tried to orient himself to reality.

The room was dark and a little chilly, and it smelled faintly of some flowery cologne, which probably meant there was a woman around somewhere.

The thought made him smile, despite the lingering pain, which had transmuted itself from a stabbing sensation to a burning ache in the few minutes since he'd opened his eyes. There weren't many situations that couldn't be improved by the presence of a lady.

He squinted, managed to raise himself a little, with the pillows behind him providing support. Snow-speckled moonlight entered through the one window, set high in the wall, and spilled onto the intricate patterns of the several quilts that covered him to the waist.

"Hullo?" he called into the darkness.

She appeared in the doorway then, carrying a flickering kerosene lamp, a small but well-made woman with dark hair and a wary way of carrying herself.

She looked familiar, but Sawyer couldn't quite place her.

"You're awake, then," she said rhetorically, staying well away from the bed, as if she thought he might grab hold of her. The impression left him vaguely indignant. "Are you hungry?"

"No," he said, because his stomach, though empty, was still reacting to the rush of pain that had awakened him. "How's my horse?"

In the light of the lantern, he saw her smile slightly. Decided she was pretty, if a mite on the scrawny side. Her waist looked no bigger around than a fence post, and she wasn't very tall, either.

"Your horse is quite comfortable," she said. "Are you in pain? The doctor left laudanum in case you needed it."

Sawyer guessed, from the bitter taste in his mouth, that he'd already had at least one dose, and he was reluctant to take another. Basically distilled opium, the stuff caused horrendous nightmares and fogged up his brain.

"I'm all right," he said.

She didn't move.

He had fuzzy memories of being shot and falling off his horse, but he wasn't sure if he'd actually seen his cousin Clay or just dreamed he was there. He did recollect the doctor, though—that sawbones had poured liquid fire into the gaping hole in his shoulder, made him yell because it hurt so bad.

"Do you have a name?" he asked.

She bristled, and he guessed at the color of her eyes—dark blue, maybe, or brown. It was hard to tell, in the glare of that lantern she was holding. "Of course I do," she replied primly. "Do you?"

Sawyer gave a raw chuckle at that. She was an impertinent little dickens, he thought, probably able to hold her own in an argument. "Sawyer McKettrick," he conceded, with a slight nod of his head. "I'm Clay's cousin, here to take over as town marshal."

"Well," she said, remaining in the doorway, "you're off to a wonderful start, aren't you?"

He chuckled again, though it took more energy than he felt he could spare. "Yes, ma'am," he said. "I reckon I am."

"Piper St. James," she said then, without laying any groundwork beforehand.

"What?"

"You asked for my name." A pause, during which she raised the lantern a little higher, saw that he was bare-chested, and quickly lowered it again. "You can call me 'Miss James.'"

"Thanks for that, anyhow," he said, enjoying the exchange, however feeble it was on his end. "Thanks for looking after my horse, too, and, unless I miss my guess, saving my life."

Miss St. James's spine lengthened; she must have been all of five foot two, and probably weighed less than his saddlebags. "I couldn't just leave you lying out there in the snow," she said, with a sort of puckish modesty.

From her tone, Sawyer concluded that she'd considered

doing just that, though, fortunately for him, her conscience must have overruled the idea.

"You'd have had to step over me every time you went out," he teased, "and that would have been awkward."

He thought she smiled then, though he couldn't be sure because the light fell forward from the lantern and left her mostly in shadow.

"What is this place?" he asked presently, when she didn't speak.

"You're in the Blue River schoolhouse," Miss St. James informed him. "I teach here."

"I see," Sawyer said, wearying, though he was almost as much in the dark, literally and figuratively, as before he'd asked the question. "Was Clay here?" he threw out. "Or did I imagine that part?"

"He was here," Miss St. James confirmed. "He's gone home now—his wife is expecting a baby soon, and he didn't like leaving her alone—but he'll be back as soon as the weather allows."

Sawyer was quiet for a while, gathering scraps of strength, trying to breathe his way past a sudden swell of pain. "You don't have to be scared of me," he told her, after a long time.

"I'm not," she lied, still cautious. Still keeping her distance.

"I reckon I can't blame you," Sawyer said, closing his eyes to regain his equilibrium. The pain rose to a new crescendo, and the room had begun to pitch and sway.

"The laudanum is there on the nightstand," she informed him helpfully, evidently seeing more than he'd wanted her to. "And the chamber pot is under the bed."

He felt his lips twitch. "I'll keep that in mind," he said.

"You're certain you don't want something to eat?"

"Maybe later," he managed to reply.

He thought she'd go away then, but she hesitated. "You

were asking for someone named Josie," she said. "Perhaps when the weather is better, we could send word to her, that you've been hurt, I mean."

Sawyer opened his eyes again, swiftly enough to set the little room to spinning again. "That won't be necessary," he bit out, but he felt a certain bitter amusement imagining what would happen if word of his misfortune were to reach her. Josie was his last employer's very fetching wife, and she'd made it clear that she wanted more from Sawyer than protection and cordial conversation. He'd had the same problem before, with other wives of men he worked for, along with their sisters and daughters in some instances, and he'd always managed to sidestep any romantic entanglements, be they physical or emotional—until Josie.

He'd *wanted* Josie, and that was why he'd agreed to come to Blue River and fill in for Clay, as temporary marshal—to put some distance between himself and the sweet temptation to bed his boss's wife, to burn in her fire, let lust consume him.

He'd left in the nick of time.

Or had he?

Had the shooter been one of Henry Vandenburg's hirelings, one of his own former colleagues, sent to make sure Sawyer stayed away from the old man's wife—forever?

It was possible, of course. Vandenburg was rich, and he was powerful, and he probably wasn't above having a rival dispensed with, but even for him, ordering the murder of one of Angus McKettrick's grandsons would have been pretty risky. His and Clay's granddad, even at his advanced age, was a force of nature in his own right, owning half of Arizona as he did, and so were his four sons. Holt, Rafe, Kade—Sawyer's father—and Jeb, who'd sired Clay, were all law-abiding citizens, happily married men with children and even a few grandchildren, money in the bank and a prosperous ranch to run. Still, the untimely death of any member of the clan would rouse them to Earp-like fury, and Vandenburg surely knew that. In fact, it was that dogged quality that had caused the old reprobate to hire Sawyer as a bodyguard in the first place.

"Mr. McKettrick?" Miss Piper St. James was standing right beside the bed now, holding the lantern high. There was concern in her voice—enough to draw her to his bedside, thereby risking some nefarious assault on her virtue. "Are you all right? For a moment, you looked—I thought…"

She lapsed awkwardly into silence.

He might have reminded her, if he'd had the strength, that, *no,* actually, he *wasn't* "all right," because he'd been *shot.* Instead, he asked slowly, measuring out each word like a storekeeper dispensing sugar or flour, "Do you happen to have any whiskey on hand?"

Chapter Three

"Of course I don't have any whiskey," Piper replied, with a little more sharpness in her tone than she'd intended to exercise. "This is a *school,* not a roadhouse."

"Well, damn," Sawyer said, affably gruff and clearly still in pain. "I could sure use a shot of good old-fashioned rotgut right about now. Might take the edge off."

Having set the kerosene lantern on the nightstand so she wouldn't drop it and set the whole place on fire, Piper took a step back. Rotgut, indeed. "Then I guess it's too bad you fell off your horse here instead of in front of the Bitter Gulch Saloon."

He favored her with a squinty frown at this, and she wondered distractedly what he'd look like in the daylight, cleaned up and wearing something besides bandages, her quilts and the dish-towel sling Dr. Howard had put on his left arm. "Are you one of those hatchet-swinging types?" he asked, with a note of benign disapproval. "The kind who go around hacking perfectly good bars to splinters, shattering mirrors and breaking every bottle on the shelves?"

Piper stiffened slightly, offended, though she couldn't think why she ought to give a pin about this man's—this *stranger's*—opinion of her. "No," she said tersely. "If some people choose to pollute their systems with poison, to the detriment of their wives and children and society in general, it's none of my concern."

He laughed then, a hoarse bark of a sound, brittle with pain. "If you say so," he said, leaving his meaning ambiguous.

Annoyed, Piper was anxious to be gone from that too-small room. She wished she hadn't approached the bed, if only because she could see so much of his bare chest. It was disturbing—though it did remind her of the gods and heroes she'd read about in Greek mythology.

She gathered her dignity, an effort of unsettling significance, reached out to reclaim the lantern. "If you don't need anything, I'll leave you to get some rest," she said, speaking as charitably as she could.

"I do need something," he told her quietly.

Piper took another step back. The lantern light wavered slightly, and she renewed her grip on the handle. "What?" she asked cautiously.

"Company," Sawyer replied. "Somebody to talk to while I wait for this bullet hole in my shoulder to settle down a little—it feels like somebody dropped a hot coal into it. Why don't you take a chair—if there is one—and tell me what brings a proper lady like you to a rough town like Blue River."

Was he making fun of her, using the term "a proper lady" ironically?

Or was she being not only harsh, but priggish, too?

She set the lantern back on the night table and drew her rocking chair into the faint circle of light, sat down and folded her hands in her lap. For the moment, that was all the concession she could bring herself to make. And it seemed like plenty.

"Well?" Sawyer McKettrick prompted. "I can tell by the way you talk and carry yourself that you're an Easterner. What are you doing way out here in the wilds of Texas?"

"I told you," Piper said distantly, primly. "I teach school."

"They don't have schools back where you came from, in Massachusetts or New Hampshire or wherever you belong?"

"I'm from Maine, if you must know," she allowed, suppressing an urge to argue that she "belonged" wherever she wanted to be. "Dara Rose—Clay's wife—is my cousin. She persuaded me to come out here and take over for the last teacher, Miss Krenshaw."

"Dara Rose," he said, with a fond little smile. "Clay's a lucky man, finding a woman like her."

"I quite agree," Piper said, softening toward him, albeit unwillingly and only to a minimal degree.

He studied her thoughtfully in the flickering light of the lantern. "Does it suit you—life in the Wild West, I mean?" he inquired politely. She saw that a muscle had bunched in his jaw after he spoke, knew he was hurting, and determined to ride it out without complaint. Like Clay, he was tough, though Clay wore the quality with greater grace, being a more reticent sort.

Piper paused, considering her reply. "It's lonely sometimes," she admitted, at last.

"Everyplace is lonely sometimes," he answered.

This was a statement Piper couldn't refute, so she made one of her own. "It sounds as if you speak from experience," she said carefully.

He grinned a wan shadow of a grin, lifted his right hand in a gesture of acquiescence. "Sure," he replied. "Happens to everybody."

Even in his weakened state, Sawyer McKettrick did not

strike Piper as the kind of person who ever lacked for anything. There was something about him, some quality of quiet
sufficiency, of untroubled wholeness, that shone even through
his obvious physical discomfort.

"I do enjoy spending my days with the children," she said,
strangely flustered, sensing that there was far more to this man
than what showed on the surface.

"I reckon that's a good thing, since you're a teacher," he
observed dryly.

A silence fell, and Piper found herself wanting to prattle,
just to fill it. And she was most definitely *not* a prattler, so this
was a matter for concern.

"I might be able to handle some food, after all," Sawyer
ventured presently, unhurriedly. "If the offer is still good,
that is."

Relieved to have an errand to perform, however mundane,
Piper fairly leaped to her feet, took the lamp by its handle.
"There's bean soup," she said. "I'll get you some."

When she returned with a bowl and spoon in one hand and
the lantern in the other, she saw that her visitor had bunched
up the pillows behind him so he could sit up straighter.

She placed the lantern on the night table again and extended
the bowl and spoon.

He looked at the food with an expression of amused wist-
fulness. "I've only got one good arm," he reminded her. "I
can feed myself, but you'll have to hold the bowl."

Piper should have anticipated this development, but she
hadn't. Gingerly, knowing she wouldn't be able to reach far
enough from the rocking chair, she sat down on the edge of
the mattress, the bowl cupped in both hands.

The sure impropriety of the act sent a little thrill through her.

Deep down, she was something of a rebel, though she managed to hide that truth from most people.

Sawyer smiled and took hold of the spoon, tasted the soup. Since the fire in the stove had burned low while they were talking earlier, the stuff was only lukewarm, but he didn't seem to mind. He ate slowly, and not very much, and finally sank back against the pillows, looking exhausted by the effort of feeding himself.

"Would you like more?" Piper ventured, drawing back the bowl. "I could—"

Sawyer grimaced, shook his head no. His skin was a waxy shade of gray, even in the thin light, and he seemed to be bleeding from his wound again, though not so heavily as before. "That'll do for now," he said. "I might take some laudanum, after all, though."

Piper nodded, put the spoon and the bowl down, and reached for the brown bottle Dr. Howard had left, pulled out the cork. "I'll just wipe off the spoon and—"

Before she could finish her sentence, though, he grabbed the bottle from her hand and took a great draught from it. The muscles in his neck corded visibly as he swallowed.

Piper blinked and snatched the vessel from him. "Mr. *McKettrick,*" she scolded, in her most teacherly voice. "That is *medicine,* not water, and it's very potent."

"I hope so," he said with a sigh, closing his eyes and gritting his teeth. Waiting for the opium to reach his bloodstream. "I'd have preferred whiskey," he added, moments later.

Soon, he was fast asleep.

Piper made sure the bottle of laudanum was out of his reach and rose to carry the lantern and the bowl and spoon out of the room, walking softly so she wouldn't wake him—not that there seemed to be much danger of that, from the steady rasp of his breathing.

Once she'd set the bowl and spoon aside, along with the lantern, she wrapped one of the extra blankets Dr. Howard had brought around her shoulders, in lieu of a cloak, and marched herself outside, into the snowy cold, carrying the lantern again now, lighting her way to the outhouse. Normally, she would have used the enamel chamber pot tucked beneath her bed, but not this time.

The going was hard, though not quite as arduous as when she'd gone out for wood and water before, and to take care of Mr. McKettrick's horse. She heard a reassuring dripping sound—snow melting off the eaves of the schoolhouse roof, probably—and the sky was clear and moonlit and speckled with stars.

For the time being at least, the storm was over, and that heartened Piper so much that, after using the outhouse, she went on to the shed, where the big buckskin gelding stood, quietly munching hay.

She spoke to him companionably, stroked his sturdy neck a few times, and made sure he had enough water. Clay had filled the trough earlier, instead of just setting a pail on the dirt floor of the shed, so there was plenty.

Returning to the schoolhouse, Piper set the lantern down, put the covered kettle of boiled beans on the front step, so the cold would keep its contents from spoiling. Then she shut the door, lowered the latch, and went over to bank the fire for the night.

The lamp was starting to burn low by then, so she quickly made herself a bed on the floor, using the borrowed blankets, washed her face and hands in a basin of warm water, and brushed her teeth with baking soda. Donning one of her flannel nightgowns was out of the question, of course, with a man under the same roof.

Resigned to sleeping in her clothes, she put out the lamp and stretched out on the floor, as near to the stove as she could safely get, and bundled herself in the blankets. The planks were hard, and Piper thought with yearning of her thin, lumpy mattress, the one she'd so often complained about, though only to herself and Dara Rose.

She closed her eyes, depending on exhaustion to carry her into the unknowing solace of sleep, but instead she found herself listening, not just with her ears, but with all she was. A few times, she thought she heard small feet skittering and scurrying around her, which didn't help her state of mind.

At some point, however, she finally succumbed to a leaden, dreamless slumber.

When she awakened on that frosty floor, sore and unrested and quite disgruntled, it took her a few moments to remember why she was there, and not in her bed.

The bed was *occupied,* she recalled, with a flare of heat rising to her cheeks. By one Sawyer McKettrick.

But the sun was shining, and that lifted her spirits considerably.

She shambled stiffly to her feet, hurried to build up the fire in the potbellied stove, glanced with mild alarm at the big Regulator Clock ticking on the schoolhouse wall. It was past eight, she saw, and she hadn't rung the schoolhouse bell.

A silly concern, admittedly, since her students weren't likely to show up, even though the snow had stopped falling and cheery daylight filled the frigid little room, absorbing the blue shadows of a wintry yesterday and the night that had followed. At the front window, Piper used the palm of one hand, no longer sore, to wipe a circle in the curlicues of frost to clear the glass. She peered out, encouraged to see that the sky was indeed blue and virtually cloudless.

Moisture dripped steadily from the roof overhead, and the road was taking shape again, a slight but visible dip in the deep, blindingly white field of snow that seemed to stretch on and on.

The voice, coming from behind her, wry and somewhat testy, nearly caused Piper to jump out of her skin. For a few moments, glorying in the change in the weather, she'd forgotten all about her uninvited guest, her night on the floor, and most of her other concerns, as well.

"Is there any coffee in this place, or would that be sinful, like keeping a stock of whiskey?" Sawyer McKettrick asked grumpily.

Piper whirled, saw him standing—*standing,* under his own power—in the doorway to her private quarters. He was still bare-chested, his bandages bulky and his bad arm in the sling Doc had improvised for him the day before, but, thankfully, he'd somehow managed to get into his trousers and even put on his boots.

He looked pale, gaunt, but ready for whatever challenges the day—or the next few minutes—might bring.

She smiled, relieved. If Sawyer was up and around, he'd be leaving soon. Maybe *very* soon. "I'll make some coffee," she said. "Sit down."

He was leaning against the framework of the doorway now, probably conserving his strength, and he looked around, taking in the small desks, the benches. "Where?" he asked, practically snarling the word.

Piper was determined to be pleasant, no matter how rude Mr. McKettrick chose to be. "There's a chair behind my desk," she pointed out. "Take that."

He groped his way along the wall, proof that he wasn't as recovered as she'd first thought, pulled back the wooden chair and sank into it. "Where's my shirt?" he asked. "And my .45?"

Piper ladled water into the small enamel coffeepot that, like the three drinking mugs, her narrow bed and the rocking chair, came with the schoolhouse. "I burned your shirt," she said cheerfully. "It was quite ruined, between the bullet hole and all the blood. And I put away the pistol, since you won't have use for it here."

Sawyer thrust his free hand through his hair in exasperation. Clearly, the laudanum had worn off, and he hadn't rested well. "I need that shirt," he said. "*And* the .45."

"I'm sorry," Piper answered. "Perhaps Clay will bring you fresh clothes, when he comes to take you out to the ranch." She refused to discuss the gun any further.

Sawyer frowned. His chin was bristly with beard stubble, and he narrowed his blue-green eyes practically to slits. "When will that be?" he growled. "My trunk is over at the train depot. Plenty of clothes in there."

Piper didn't reply right away, since she didn't know precisely when Clay would return, and fetching Sawyer's baggage from the depot was not presently an option. Instead, she put some coffee beans into the grinder and turned the handle, enjoying the rich scent as it rose to entice her. Coffee was normally a treat for Piper, though she'd been drinking more of it lately, being snowed in and everything. Since the stuff wasn't considered a staple, like canned goods and meat, potatoes and butter, the town didn't provide it as a part of her wages. Since she saved practically every penny toward a train ticket home to Maine, Dara Rose bought it for her, along with writing paper, postage stamps and bathing soap.

God bless Dara Rose's generous soul.

Sawyer cleared his throat, a reminder, apparently, that she'd neglected to answer his cranky question. "Clay will be coming back—when?"

"I don't know," Piper said honestly. "Soon, I hope."

His frown deepened as he looked around again. "Where did you sleep last night?"

She measured coffee into the pot and set it on the stove to boil. "You needn't concern yourself with that," she said sunnily.

He gave a gruff chortle at her response, completely void of amusement. Then he pushed back the chair and stood, with an effort he clearly wanted very much to hide. "I suppose the privy is out back?" he asked.

Piper kept her face averted, so he wouldn't see her blush. "Yes," she said. "But the snow is deep and the path hasn't been cleared yet." She paused, mortified. "There's a chamber pot under the bed."

"I'm not using a chamber pot," he informed her, each word separated from the next by a tick of the Regulator clock. Slowly, he crossed the room, snatched up the same blanket she'd used earlier, in lieu of a coat, wrapped it around his mostly naked upper body like an enormous shawl, and left the schoolhouse.

The door slammed behind him.

Piper hoped he wouldn't collapse in the snow again, because she wasn't sure she'd be able to get him back inside the schoolhouse if that happened. She waited tensely, added water to the coffeepot when it bubbled, and resisted the urge to stand at the window and watch for his return.

He did reappear, after a few minutes, and he kept the blanket around him as he made his way back to the desk chair and sat down.

Piper poured coffee for him—the grounds hadn't settled completely, but that couldn't be helped—and set the mug on the surface of the desk.

"Breakfast?" she asked.

He finally smiled, though grudgingly. "More beans?" he countered.

"I have some salt pork and a few eggs," Piper responded. "Would that do, or should I risk life and limb to fetch something more to your liking from the hotel dining room? I could just hitch up the dogsled and be off."

He laughed, and it seemed that his color was a little better, though that could probably be ascribed to the cold weather outside. "You don't lack for sass, do you?" he said.

"And *you* don't lack for rudeness," Piper retorted, but, like before, she was softening toward him a little. There was something about that smile, those intelligent, blue-green eyes, that supple mouth...

Whoa, ordered a voice in her mind, bringing her up short. *Forget his smile, and his mouth, too.* Silently, Piper reminded herself that, to her knowledge, Sawyer McKettrick had just one thing to recommend him—that he was Clay's cousin—which most definitely did *not* mean he was the same kind of man. Families, even ones as illustrious as Clay's, *did* have black sheep.

"Sorry," he said wearily, with no hint of actual remorse.

She fetched the salt pork and the eggs, which were kept in a metal storage box in the cloakroom, that being the coldest part of the building, and proceeded to prepare breakfast for both of them.

"There's a little house for the marshal to live in," she said busily, after a few stiff minutes had passed. "The town provides it."

"I know," Sawyer said. "I was here in Blue River once before." Now that he had coffee to drink, his temperament seemed to be improving. A hot meal might render him tolerable. "Dara Rose lived there at the time, with her daughters."

"Oh," Piper said, apropos of nothing, turning slices of salt pork in the skillet, then cracking three eggs into the same pan, causing them to sizzle in the melted lard.

"These accommodations of yours are pretty rustic," he said, evidently to make conversation, which Piper could have done without just then. "The bed feels like a rock pile, and there's no place to take a bath."

Piper, who yearned for an indoor bathroom like the one

Dara Rose had now, in her lovely new ranch house, and a feather bed, and many other things in the bargain, took umbrage. *These accommodations of hers,* humble as they were, had very probably saved his life. "I manage just fine," she said coolly.

Sawyer sighed wearily. "I didn't mean it as an insult," he said.

Piper plopped the salt pork and two of the eggs onto a tin plate—also provided by the good people of Blue River—and carried it over to him, along with a knife and fork.

She set the works down with an eloquent clatter and rested her hands on her hips.

"Would you like more coffee?" she demanded inhospitably.

He grinned up at her, enjoying her pique. "Yes, ma'am, I would," he said. "If you please."

She stormed back to the stove, took up a pot holder, and brought the coffee to the desk that doubled as a table. There was a heavy clunking sound as the base of it met the splintery oak surface.

"Thank you," the new marshal said sweetly.

"You're welcome," she crabbed.

A knock sounded at the schoolhouse door just then, and hope filled Piper, displacing her irritation and her strangely injured pride. Perhaps Clay had returned, or Doc Howard—

But when she answered the firm rap, she found Bess Turner standing on the step, looking poised to flee if the need arose. Bess ran the brothel above the Bitter Gulch Saloon, and if she'd ever tried to look respectable, she'd given up on it long ago.

Her hair was a brassy shade of yellow, her thin cheeks were heavily rouged, and her mouth was hard, not with anger, Piper had often thought, but with the strain of bearing up under one tribulation and sorrow after another.

"I'm sorry to bother you," Bess said, almost meekly. She

wore a pink satin cloak, completely inadequate for a December day, and her dancing shoes were soaked through.

"Come in," Piper said quickly, stepping back. "There's coffee made—I'll pour you some."

Bess's tired gaze strayed past Piper, dusted over Sawyer, and came back to Piper again. "Thank you," she said, very quietly.

"Stand over here by the stove," Piper urged, with a shiver, hastening to rinse out a coffee cup. "You must be freezing!"

Bess sidled close to the fire, and Piper noticed that the woman's hands were gloveless, and blue with cold. "I can't stay long," she said, stealing another glance at Sawyer. Naturally, she'd be curious about his presence, but she wasn't likely to carry tales, like some of the other townswomen would have done. "My Ginny-Sue is hectoring me something fierce about the Christmas program," she added fretfully. "She's learned the whole second chapter of Luke by heart, that being her piece for the recital, and she's afraid school won't take up again before then, because of the snow."

Piper was touched. Ginny-Sue, a shy ten-year-old, was one of her brightest pupils. Except for Madeline Howard, she was the best-dressed, too, always neatly clad in ready-made dresses, with her face scrubbed and her brown hair plaited. Her shoes were the envy of the other girls, sturdy, but with buttons instead of laces, and always polished to a high shine.

"Christmas is still more than a week away," Piper said gently, handing Bess the coffee. "I'm sure we won't have to cancel the program."

Bess nodded, looking straight at Sawyer now and making no effort to hide her curiosity. "Now, who would you be?" she asked him, straight out.

He'd risen to his feet, abandoning his breakfast for the moment. "Name's Sawyer McKettrick," he answered cordially. "I'm the new town marshal."

"He's Clay's cousin," Piper added hastily, as though that explained what he was doing in the schoolhouse at this hour of the morning, wearing nothing but boots, trousers and a blanket.

"Howdy," said the local madam. "I'm Bess Turner. Miss St. James here teaches my girl, Ginny-Sue."

Sawyer dropped back into his chair. "Good to meet you," he said, and resumed eating, though he continued to take an undisguised interest in the visitor.

"He was shot," Piper went on anxiously. "Clay and Dr. Howard said he couldn't be moved, so he spent the night here—"

Bess smiled, and a twinkle appeared in her faded eyes, just for the briefest moment. "Shot, was he?" she replied, looking Sawyer over again, this time more thoroughly. "You'd never guess it."

Piper thought of Dara Rose's late husband, who had died in Bess's establishment, and wondered if the two of them had been together at the time of his scandalous demise. Not that she'd ever be so forward as to ask, of course. There were some things a body had to be content to wonder about in perpetuity.

Piper looked back at Sawyer, who moved the blanket aside just enough to show the bandage and part of his sling. He'd guessed that she was embarrassed, evidently, and the fact seemed to amuse him.

"Did you see who shot you?" Bess asked. It was a question Piper hadn't thought to ask, and neither, as far as she knew, had Clay or Doc Howard.

"The snow was too thick," Sawyer answered, with a shake of his head.

"Well, I'll be," marveled Bess, finishing her coffee. "Blue River's always been a peaceful town, for the most part. I hope we're not drawing in all sorts of riffraff, like some other places I could name."

The corner of Sawyer's well-made mouth quirked up in a semblance of a grin, probably at the term "riffraff," coming from someone like Bess, but he didn't say anything.

Bess handed over the empty mug and smiled at Piper. "So I can tell my Ginny-Sue there'll still be a Christmas?" she asked.

"I'm sure of it," Piper said, though that was mostly bravado. Inwardly, she wasn't so sure that the warmer weather would hold—but she *hoped* it would, and fiercely.

Bess nodded a farewell to Sawyer and walked purposely toward the door, Piper following.

On the threshold, Bess paused, lowered her voice and said, "If you need any help, Teacher, just send word over to the Bitter Gulch. My girls and me, we'll do whatever we can to lend a hand."

Piper's throat tightened, and the backs of her eyes burned a little. She wondered how many of the other women of Blue River, besides Dara Rose, of course, would have made such an offer. "Thank you, Mrs. Turner," she said warmly.

"Bess," the other woman corrected, patting Piper's hand before taking her leave. "I never was nobody's missus, and I won't pretend I was."

With that, she started down the slippery steps of the school-house porch, drawing her tawdry cloak more closely around her. The sun glinted in her dandelion-colored hair, and she looked back at Piper, smiled once more, and waved.

Piper waved back, and closed the door slowly.

When she turned around, she saw that Sawyer had finished his breakfast. Still seated at her desk, he watched her over the rim of his coffee mug.

"Christmas," he said, in a musing tone, his gaze skimming over the undecorated tree leaning forlornly against the far wall, slowly but surely dropping its needles. Piper had sent the bigger boys out to find it the previous week, thinking they'd all be able to enjoy it longer that way, though now she wished she'd waited. "I forgot all about it."

"You'll be at Clay and Dara Rose's place by then," Piper said, holding on to blind faith that it would be so, "probably much mended."

"I'll need to round up some presents for those little girls," Sawyer mused.

"I wouldn't worry," Piper counseled, liking him again. Sort of. "They're well provided for, Edrina and Harriet."

He smiled. "Yes," he said. "They would be, with Clay for a father."

The remark stung Piper a little, on Dara Rose's behalf, dampening her kindly inclination toward Mr. McKettrick, even though she sensed no rancor in the remark. Her cousin had had a difficult life, almost from the first, but Dara Rose was and always had been a devoted mother. "If Clay were here," she said moderately, "he'd tell you that he's the fortunate one."

Sawyer sighed. He looked paler than before, though breakfast and the coffee must have braced him up. "I've managed to get on the wrong side of you again," he said. "I *know* Clay loves his wife, and he considers those girls his own, as much as he does the baby he and Dara Rose are expecting."

Piper bit her lower lip for a moment. "I apologize," she said. "I didn't sleep very well last night, and I confess that I'm worried that I might have spoken out of turn to Bess Turner—" She paused, swallowed. "If there's another storm, Christmas will have to be canceled and the children will be so disappointed."

His grin flashed again, brief but bright as the sunlight on

the snow outside. "Christmas happens in the heart," he said. *"Especially* the heart of a child."

She regarded him for a long moment. "That's a lovely sentiment," she said, taken by surprise, "and I'm sure it's true, for fortunate children like Edrina and Harriet, and Doc Howard's little girl, Madeline, but there are others, like Ginny-Sue Turner, who need more." She inclined her head toward the forlorn little tree, leaning against the schoolhouse wall. "They need the sparkle and the carols, the excitement and, yes, the oranges and the peppermint sticks, because the other three-hundred-sixty-four days of the year can be bleak for them."

Sawyer, clearly tiring, leaned against the framework of the bedroom doorway again, and smiled sadly. "You really care about these kids," he said.

"Of course I do," Piper replied.

"What do *you* want for Christmas, Miss St. James?" he asked quietly.

She hadn't thought of her own secret wishes for a long time, and the question unsettled her. "You need to rest," she hedged. "Go in and lie down."

"Not until I get an answer," he replied, folding his good arm across the sling that held his injured one in place.

Piper blushed. "Very well, then," she said, throwing out the first thing that came to mind so he would drop the subject and leave her in peace. "I'd like a new cloak, since you bled all over mine and I had to burn all but a few scraps of it."

Sawyer McKettrick smiled again. "Done," he said. And then he turned around and went back to bed.

Chapter Four

Clay returned shortly after noon, at the reins of a sledge improvised from lengths of lumber, probably left over from the building of his house and barn, with two enormous plow horses hitched to the front. He grinned and waved when Piper stepped out onto the schoolhouse porch, shielding her eyes from the bright sun with one hand.

"How's that ornery cousin of mine faring?" he called, bringing the team to a halt. The back of the sledge was piled high with an assortment of things—crates and boxes, a supply of hay for Sawyer's horse, a few bulging feed bags and, most notably, the parts of an iron bedstead and a mattress secured with rope.

"He was up and around earlier," Piper replied, staring at the bedstead and wondering whether Clay planned to leave it at the schoolhouse for her or use it to transport Sawyer to the ranch, "but he's resting at the moment."

"Up and around?" Clay echoed, pleased. He climbed off the strange conveyance and approached through the knee-deep but already-melting snow. "I guess I shouldn't be surprised. Sawyer always had more gumption than good sense."

"He's wanting his trunk from the depot," Piper said, as Clay reached her and she stepped back so they could both go inside, where it was warmer.

"I figured as much," Clay told her, taking off his hat and hanging it from a peg near the door. He'd stomped most of the snow off his boots out on the porch. "Picked it up before I came here."

Sawyer, who must have heard the commotion, appeared in the doorway to Piper's room, looking rumpled and grim. He obviously needed more laudanum, and Piper made up her mind to fetch it and supervise the dosage this time, make sure he didn't guzzle the stuff down again.

"You ready to make the trip out to our place?" Clay asked his cousin, looking doubtful even as he spoke. "I can haul you out there today if you want to go, and in style, too, like Caesar reclining on Cleopatra's barge."

Piper felt a pang of sadness at the thought of Sawyer's leaving the schoolhouse, which was just plain silly, because she ought to be relieved instead. She *really* ought to be relieved.

Sawyer frowned, puzzlement personified. "Caesar? Cleopatra's barge? What the devil are you yammering on about?"

"Either way, I came prepared," was all the answer Clay gave. He was still grinning, proud of his resourcefulness, and he waxed unusually loquacious, for him. "I brought along a kind of sleigh I rigged up last year, out of some old boards—normally use it to haul feed out to the cattle on the range when the wagons can't get through—even brought a bed along, in case you were ready to head out to the ranch sooner than expected. There's hay and some grain for your gelding, too, if you'd rather stay put a while longer. In that case, I'll set the bedstead up for Piper, so she won't have to sleep on the floor until you're out of her hair."

Piper blinked.

"You slept on the floor?" Sawyer asked, practically glowering at her, as though accusing her of some unconscionable perfidy.

"Where did you *think* she was sleeping?" Clay inquired good-naturedly. "This is a one-room schoolhouse, Sawyer, not a big-city hospital or a grand hotel."

"I cannot have a bed in my schoolroom," Piper put in hastily, though neither man seemed to be listening.

"I'll go back with you," Sawyer said to Clay, though when he took a step, he winced and swayed on his feet so that his cousin immediately stepped forward and took him by the arms, lest he collapse.

Sawyer flinched and his face drained of color.

Chagrined, Clay loosened his grip, though he didn't dare let go completely. "I don't believe you're ready quite yet," he said reasonably.

"My .45," Sawyer said, looking dazed. "She—took it."

"Never mind that," Clay told him. "Right now, we've got to get you back to bed."

Sawyer allowed himself to be turned around and led in the other direction, most likely because he didn't have much choice in the matter. "My *pistol*," he insisted.

Piper glanced toward the cloakroom, where she'd hidden the weapon, climbing onto the food box to push it to the back of a wide, high shelf. She wanted that dreadful thing out of sight *and* out of reach, so none of her students would stumble upon it, once they returned to school, and bring about a tragedy.

For all that, something in Sawyer's tone bothered her. Was

he afraid the man who had shot him would return, make another attempt on his life and, this time, succeed in killing him?

Maybe, she concluded, but the fact remained that Sawyer wasn't in his right mind, given all the blood he'd lost and the pain he'd suffered. By now, the shooter was surely putting as many miles as he could between himself and Blue River, no doubt believing that his quarry was dead.

She shuddered, hugged herself against an inner chill.

What if she was wrong? What if, by hiding the gun, she was putting both Sawyer and herself in danger?

In the next room, Clay murmured something, and then the bedsprings creaked as Sawyer lay down again.

Piper paced. She'd ask Clay what to do with the gun when he came back.

He took his time, though, speaking quietly to Sawyer, probably giving him laudanum from Doc's bottle. By the time he returned to the schoolroom, Piper had reheated the coffee left over from breakfast and poured some into a mug for him.

"Thanks," Clay said, accepting the cup and taking a restorative sip before going on. "Has Doc been back? Sawyer's in bad shape."

Piper shook her head no. "He'll be here," she said, with confidence. Weather or no weather, Doc Howard was not the kind to stay away when he was needed. "Clay—?"

He raised one eyebrow. "If you're worried about me setting up that bedstead in the schoolroom—"

Again, she shook her head. "Sawyer's been asking for his gun," she said. "I put it away, but now I'm wondering if I ought to give it back to him. In case—in case—"

Clay's expression was a solemn one. "Where is it?" he asked.

She led the way into the cloakroom and pointed upward.

Clay was so tall that he didn't need anything to stand on to reach the Colt .45 in its hiding place. He extended one hand, felt around a little, and found the pistol. Bringing it down to eye level, he examined it, expertly checking the cylinder to see that there were bullets inside.

"Better give it back to him," he said. "I know Sawyer, and he won't get any real rest as long as this thing is out of his reach."

Piper's heart pounded. "But—" She paused, swallowed, tried again. "He's not himself. What if he doesn't recognize you or me or Doc and shoots someone?"

To Piper's surprise, Clay chuckled, though it was a raspy sound, not really an expression of amusement. "Sawyer's himself, all right," he assured her. "Always is, no matter what. And he won't shoot anybody who isn't fixing to shoot *him,* no matter how delirious he might be."

"How can you be so sure?" Piper persisted. She hated guns. These were modern times, for heaven's sake, and they were not the Old West but the new one.

"I know my cousin," Clay replied matter-of-factly. "We grew up together, he and I. He's been shooting almost as long as he's been riding horses, and he showed a unique talent for it from the first."

Again, Piper shuddered. "You're saying that he's a—a gunslinger?"

"I'm saying he's good with a gun. There's a difference."

"But what if he's a criminal? You've said it yourself—no one is sure, including you, that Sawyer isn't an outlaw."

Clay held the pistol carefully but competently, keeping the barrel pointed toward the floor as he passed her, leaving the cloakroom. "Even if he *is* an outlaw," he replied easily, "he wouldn't shoot anybody down in cold blood. He's also a *McKettrick,* after all."

Piper was exasperated. The McKettrick family had their own distinct code of ethics, hammered out by the patriarch,

Angus, and handed down to his sons and their sons after them, but it seemed obvious that Sawyer might not subscribe to that honorable philosophy, given his secrecy about his vocation. On the other hand, Clay trusted his cousin enough to hand over his own badge, and that was no small matter.

Clay carried the pistol to Sawyer's bedside and came back, intent on the next task. "I'll see to my cousin's horse," he said, "and unload the supplies."

Doc Howard showed up while Clay was outside, and the two of them carried the bedstead and mattress, still roped together, into the schoolhouse.

The bed wasn't very wide—it probably belonged to either Edrina or Harriet—but there was no room for it in front, so they took it into the teacher's quarters. Piper fussed and hovered like a hen chased away from its nest, but Clay only said, "You can't sleep on the floor," and proceeded to set the thing up in the little space available—crosswise at the foot of the bed where Sawyer lay, sound asleep.

It made a T-shape, and Piper figured that *T* stood for *trouble*.

"You'll be quite safe," Doc added, in fatherly tones, after helping Clay assemble the second bed. Sawyer's eyelids fluttered, but he didn't stir otherwise. The pistol rested, a daunting presence in its own right, on the night table. "Mr. McKettrick here is an invalid, remember."

An invalid? Piper thought. Sawyer had gotten out of bed without help just that morning, visited the shed where his horse was kept as well as the privy, and returned to the schoolhouse with enough strength to drink coffee and eat breakfast.

"Safe?" Piper challenged, folding her arms. "By now, my reputation must be in tatters."

"Nobody knows Sawyer's here," Clay reasoned, unwinding the rope that left a deep dent in the middle of the bed. "I haven't said a word to anybody but Dara Rose. She sent some things for you, by the way, staples, mostly, and a book she ordered from back East. Says she'll read it when you're finished."

Piper thought of her cousin with both gratitude and frustration. If only Dara Rose were here, too. As a respectable married woman, she could have defused any gossip by her mere presence.

Doc wouldn't look at Piper, though it took her a moment to notice, and when she did, she saw that his neck had reddened above his tight celluloid collar. He'd told Eloise, of course—his wife would have demanded an explanation for his leaving the house when everyone else was staying home, close to the fire.

"Doc?" Piper prodded suspiciously.

"I've sworn Mrs. Howard to secrecy," he said, but he still wouldn't meet her gaze.

Some things, like a mysterious man occupying the schoolmarm's bed, able-bodied or not, were simply too deliciously improper to keep silent about, especially for people like Eloise Howard. Bess Turner, by ironic contrast, wouldn't say a word to anyone—Piper was sure of that.

She groaned aloud.

"It's too late anyhow," Clay observed lightly, straightening after he'd crouched to tighten a screw in the framework of the bedstead. "If there's damage to your good name, it's already been done."

Piper flung out her hands. "Well," she sputtered, "thank you very much for *that,* Clay McKettrick. But why should *you* worry? *You're* not the one who'll wind up an old maid and maybe even lose her job!"

He chuckled and shoved a hand through his dark hair. "I reckon it's a certainty that I'll never be an old maid," he conceded. "But you probably won't, either. There aren't so many women way out here that men can afford to be choosy."

Doc Howard closed his eyes, shook his head.

Piper would have shrieked at Clay if it hadn't been for Sawyer, placidly sleeping nearby. She didn't want to startle him awake—he might grab for his pistol then and shoot them all.

"Choosy?" she fired back, in a ferocious whisper.

Doc Howard put a hand to each of their backs and steered both Clay and Piper out into the schoolroom. "Now, Clay," the dentist said, in a diplomatic tone meant to pour oil on troubled waters, "any man would be proud to have a lovely woman like Piper here for a wife. Piper, Clay's going to pull his foot out of his mouth any moment now and apologize for the thoughtless remark he just made."

Clay did look sorry. Deflated, too. "I didn't mean that the way it sounded," he said. "I do ask your pardon." When Piper just glared at him, not saying a word in reply, he sighed miserably, turned and headed outside, ostensibly to bring in Sawyer's trunk and the things Dara Rose had sent in from the ranch.

Doc smiled and touched her upper arm. "There, now," he told her. "Matters are rarely as bad as they seem."

Piper opened her mouth, closed it again, remembering childhood counsel. If she didn't have something nice to say, she shouldn't say anything at all.

"I'm going back in there to check the wound and change the bandages," Doc said, leaving Sawyer himself completely out of the equation, it seemed to Piper.

She busied herself building up the fire. Clay carried in a crate filled with supplies, and she spotted not only the promised book, one she'd been yearning to read, but a bag of coffee beans, tea leaves in a tin canister, several jars of preserves, two loaves of bread, and even part of a ham, with the bone intact, so she could make soup later.

Piper said nothing.

Clay, resigned, went out again, lugged a sizable travel trunk over the threshold and on into the little room that now contained two beds instead of one.

As if she'd consider sleeping in such close proximity to a man, an armed *stranger,* no less, of dubious moral convictions.

Spending another night on the floor wasn't a happy prospect either, though, so she put that out of her mind, along with thoughts of Sawyer McKettrick.

Doc and Clay conferred again, and soon came out of the bedroom, single file. Doc's hands were wet from a recent washing—he must have used the basin on Piper's bureau—and he was rolling down his sleeves, shrugging back into his coat to make his departure.

Most likely, he would go straight home and tell Eloise that the problem of sleeping arrangements over at the schoolhouse had been solved. Now the teacher would have a bed of her very own.

Inwardly, Piper sighed. Doc, having only the best of intentions himself, mistakenly believed that everyone else was the same way.

"I'll tie Cherokee behind the sleigh and lead him out to the ranch," Clay told Piper. "That way, you won't have to worry about feeding and watering him if it snows again."

"Thank you," Piper said crisply. This, it seemed, was Clay's version of appeasement, at least in part. "When will you be back?" The question was addressed to both Clay and Doc Howard.

"I'll get here tomorrow if it's at all possible," Doc promised.

"Soon as I can," Clay said, in his turn. "Dara Rose tells me the baby's dropped a little, says it means we'll have another daughter or a son anytime now, so a lot depends on how she's feeling."

"Maybe Dara Rose would be safer in town," Piper said,

fretful again as she thought of her cousin way out there on that lonely ranch, heavily pregnant. "Closer to Doc."

"I'm a *dentist*," Doc reminded them both.

"You've delivered babies before," Piper said. It was true; she herself knew of two different occasions when he had served as midwife.

"Only because I didn't have a choice," Doc answered.

"I've brought a few colts and calves into the world," Clay put in, affably confident. "It can't be all that different."

Piper had had enough male wisdom for one day. As much as she dreaded their leaving, a part of her couldn't wait for both Clay *and* Doc to make themselves scarce. Naturally, that meant she'd be alone with Sawyer again, but he slept most of the time anyway.

"Tell Dara Rose I'm grateful for the things she sent to town for me," she said moderately. "Especially the book."

Clay smiled. "She wrote you a letter, too. It's in the box somewhere."

The news heartened Piper, and at the same time made her regret that she hadn't anticipated this and prepared a letter of her own, to send back with Clay. "I hope to see all of you at the Christmas program, if not before then," she said.

Clay looked dubious. "I'll do my best to bring the girls in for the party, if the weather allows, but I can't see Dara Rose making the trip."

"No," Piper agreed sadly. "I suppose not. She's well, though?"

Clay smiled. "She's just fine, Piper. Don't you worry." His eyes lit up. "Tell you what. If Sawyer's better by then, I'll bring both of you out to the ranch Christmas Eve, after the program, and we'll all celebrate the big day together. I'll even see that you get back to Blue River before school takes up again after New Year's."

"I'd like that," Piper said, cheered. The prospect of spending time with her cousin and the children, holding the baby if it had arrived by then, and, yes, taking long, luxurious baths in Dara Rose's claw-footed tub, complete with hot and cold running water, renewed her.

A few minutes later, after bringing in more water and firewood, Clay and the doctor left.

Piper watched them go through the schoolhouse window, Sawyer's buckskin gelding plodding along behind the team and sled. The sky had gone from blue to gray, she saw with trepidation, but she kept her thoughts in the present moment, since worrying wouldn't do any good.

Emptying the crate Dara Rose had filled for her took up a happy half hour—there were notes from Edrina and Harriet, as well as a long, chatty letter from their mother—and Piper, feeling rich, made herself a pot of tea, lit the lantern against the gathering gloom of a winter afternoon, and sat down at her desk to read.

Dara Rose gave a comical account of ranch life, especially in her current condition, assured Piper that she had nothing to fear from Sawyer McKettrick, and related funny things the children had said. Between the approach of Christmas and being virtually snowed in, Edrina and Harriet had an excess of energy and bickered constantly, settling down only when Clay reminded them that St. Nicholas paid attention to good behavior and dispensed gifts accordingly.

By the time she'd finished reading the letter through for the first time, Piper was both smiling and crying a little. She'd miss Dara Rose and the children terribly if she went back to Maine, she reminded herself silently. They were all the family she had, after all, here *or* there.

Still, in Maine she wouldn't be the schoolmarm who'd housed a half-naked outlaw, as she would be here in Blue

River. She could get another teaching position and eventually meet a suitable man and get married. Finally have a home and children of her own.

A hoarse shout from the bedroom startled her so much that she nearly upset her cup of tea. Alarmed, she bolted to her feet and hurried in to investigate.

Sawyer sat up in bed, breathing hard, his eyes wild, his flesh glistening with perspiration even though the room was fairly cold, being far from the stove. He was holding the pistol in his right hand, and the hammer was drawn back.

For one hysterical moment, Piper thought the shooter must have returned, maybe crawled in through the high window, but there was no one else in the room.

She kept her gaze on the Colt .45 in Sawyer's hand. The barrel was long, and it glinted evilly in the thin light.

"Don't shoot," she said weakly.

Sawyer came back to himself with a visible jolt, blinked a couple of times, and, much to Piper's relief, set the gun aside on the night table. "Sorry," he said. "Guess I must have been dreaming."

Piper lingered in the doorway, waiting for her flailing heart to slow down to its normal pace. Doc had done a good job of replacing Sawyer's bandages; they looked clean and white against his skin. "Are you hungry?" she asked. "Dara Rose sent a lovely ham, and some preserves, too."

He blinked again, then gave a raw chuckle. "You keep asking if I'm hungry," he said. "Why is that?"

"You haven't eaten since breakfast," Piper said, a little defensively. "It's almost supper time now."

Sawyer looked surprised, and she could tell he was wondering where the day had gone. "It is?" he asked.

"Yes," she said.

"Did Clay bring me any clothes?"

She nodded. "Your trunk is right over there," she said, pointing it out. "Shall I get you something from it?"

He considered the offer. "I'll do it myself," he said. "The way I figure it, the more I move around, the better off I'll be. Besides, I need to go outside again."

"Your horse is at the ranch," Piper told him. "Clay took it with him when he left."

He grinned. "I know that," he said. "This trip isn't about the horse."

She blushed.

Sawyer swung his legs over the side of the bed. Though the quilt covered his private parts, she couldn't help noticing that he wasn't wearing trousers.

She backed quickly out of the bedroom, followed by the sound of his laughter.

She didn't speak to him or even glance in his direction, minutes later, when he came out of the bedroom, but she knew he was dressed this time, instead of wrapping his upper body in a blanket.

She busied herself heating water—she was desperate for a bath, and planned on locking herself in the cloakroom with her small copper tub later on, when she was sure Sawyer had gone back to sleep—and then sliced Dara Rose's fresh-baked bread and some of the ham, placing the food on plates. She opened a jar of peaches and added those, as well.

Sawyer returned and, forgetting, she looked his way. Saw that he'd strapped on a gun belt when he got dressed. The handle of the Colt .45 jutted beneath his coat, which was shorter than the ruined one, and just as well made.

"Supper," she said, gesturing toward his full plate, which she'd already carried over to the desk, along with a knife, fork and spoon.

Sawyer nodded in acknowledgment of the one-word invitation, closing the door behind him. "I see there's another bed in the back room," he said. "I was going to offer to sleep on the floor so you wouldn't have to, but I guess that won't be necessary."

Piper was at once touched and flustered by this statement, and turned her head so he wouldn't see that in her face. She wasn't about to discuss the second bed, because she didn't expect to sleep in it, but she kept that to herself, too.

"Clay insisted it would be safe to let you have your pistol back," she said, recalling the look in his eyes when he'd awakened from whatever nightmare he'd been lost in and immediately grabbed the gun, prepared to fire. "I don't mind telling you that I'm not convinced it was a wise decision."

Sawyer smiled wanly at this, made his way to her desk, and stood there, looking bewildered. He was wondering where she planned to sit, and she hastened, plate and silverware in hand, to one of the students' places and sat on the bench.

Looking relieved, and singularly worn-out from getting dressed and making the long slog to and from the outhouse, he said he'd like to wash up before he ate.

With a nod of her head, she indicated the basin she'd already filled with warm water and set on top of a bookshelf, along with a bar of soap and a towel. While Sawyer cleansed his hands and splashed his face, she began to eat. The ham and bread tasted especially good, after a couple of days of boiled pinto beans, and just the sight of those lovely peaches, picked in the autumn from Clay and Dara Rose's own orchard and put up in their kitchen, made her mouth water in anticipation.

Sawyer dried his face and hands with the towel. "I could use a shave," he said, as he returned to the desk and sat down to have his supper.

"Maybe tomorrow," Piper replied. The stubble on his chin made him look like the rascal he probably was, but she didn't find it unattractive. She probably should have, though, she thought. Particularly since they were shut in together, the pair of them, and almost certainly raising more of a scandal with every passing day.

And night.

"I'll buy you a new cloak," Sawyer said, out of the blue.

Piper stopped eating, delicious though the food was. "I couldn't accept," she said hurriedly. "It would be improper."

He grinned. "We're way past what's proper already, wouldn't you say?"

It was all too true. Piper colored up again. "You needn't remind me," she said.

The grin held. "I ruined your other cloak, didn't I?" Sawyer asked. "The least I can do is replace it, so you don't freeze to death this winter."

"I'll manage," Piper insisted.

He concentrated on consuming his supper after that, even had a second helping of ham, but his gaze found her every few moments, and each time he looked at her, she saw a twinkle in his eyes.

At last he tired, gathered up his plate and silverware, and looked around for a place to put them.

"I'll take those," Piper said, and did. Since there wasn't a sink in the schoolhouse, she'd wash them later in a basin she reserved for the purpose. By then, she was thinking about the bath she'd take in the cloakroom, once Sawyer had retired to his bed.

Presently, he said good-night and left her alone.

Piper immediately put water on the stove to heat, then hurried outside, to the shed, where she kept the washtub she meant to use.

The snow seemed to be melting, but by the time she returned to the schoolhouse, the hem of her dress was soaked and she was shivering with cold.

It would only be slightly warmer in the cloakroom, she knew, than it was outside, but there was nothing for it. She'd worn these same clothes all of yesterday, then slept in them, and then worn them all day *today*. Now, she felt grimy.

She set the washtub in the cloakroom, filled it bucket by bucket, a process that took a very long time. Sneaking into her bedroom, relieved to see that Sawyer was sleeping peacefully, she collected a flannel nightgown, a washcloth, soap and a towel.

Inside the cloakroom, with a kerosene lantern to light her way, Piper moved the food box in front of the door, just in case, and quickly stripped off her clothes.

Goose bumps sprang up on her bare flesh, and her teeth chattered, but she was resolute. She *would* bathe, even if it was agony, because being dirty was far worse.

The lantern flickered—there was a breeze coming up through the cracks between the planks in the floor—and the bathwater, having taken so long to prepare, was lukewarm when she stepped into it.

Piper scrubbed diligently, dried off with the towel, and donned the flannel nightgown.

The prospect of sleeping on the floor again loomed before her and, as she moved the food box aside, took up the lantern and fled the cloakroom with her discarded day garments wadded up under one elbow, she wondered just how much one small, well-meaning and wholly decent person was meant to endure for the sake of propriety. Especially when that particular horse was already out of the barn, so to speak.

She stopped suddenly when she realized Sawyer was seated at her desk again, wearing half a shirt, since he hadn't been able to put his injured arm through the appropriate sleeve.

He looked up from the book he was reading and smiled. "I wondered if you were shut up in there," he said, with a nod toward the gaping door of the cloakroom. "Even considered coming to your rescue."

"I thought you were asleep," Piper said, still shivering even though—or perhaps *because*—she was wearing her warmest nightgown.

Sawyer's blue-green gaze moved over her like a caress, came back to her face. "Yes," he agreed. "I suppose you did think that. As it happens, though, I woke up and that was that. So I came out here, expecting to find you asleep on the floor, since you're probably too stubborn to use that bed even after all the trouble Clay went to to bring it here."

Piper shifted yesterday's clothes, petticoat, bloomers and camisole included, from her side to her front, like a rumpled shield. "Don't look at me," she said.

He chuckled, averted his eyes. "That's a tall order," he replied, "but whatever else I am, I'm a gentleman, so I'll comply with your request."

"Good," Piper said, not moving.

Sawyer seemed to be reading again, but Piper didn't trust appearances. Nor was she convinced that he was a gentleman.

"Go ahead and take the bedroom," he said. "I'll sleep out here."

Chapter Five

"Don't be silly," Piper immediately countered, still clutching her clothes against her bosom. Her nightgown was warm enough, but her bare feet felt icy against the planks, where she seemed to be rooted. "You're in no condition to sleep on a hard floor."

Sawyer, remaining at her desk with a book open in front of him, smiled and carefully kept his gaze averted. Or so she hoped—desperately.

"Neither are you, I'll wager," he said dryly. "Anyhow, I saw a mouse run through here a few minutes ago. Bold little critter, too—scampered right through the middle of the room."

Piper shuddered, and not just from the cold. She had a horror of things that crawled, slithered or scurried, though she'd kept that information to herself in case any of the rambunctious boys in her class got ideas about scaring Teacher with a garter snake or any other objectionable creature.

"What kind of name is Piper, anyhow?" Sawyer asked,

turning the pages of the book so rapidly that he couldn't possibly be reading from them.

"What kind of name is Sawyer?" she countered, edging toward the stove. If she'd stayed put, she was convinced the soles of her feet would attach themselves to the icy floor. And where, at this precise moment, was that mouse he'd mentioned seeing?

He chuckled. "I'm named after a great-uncle on my mother's side of the family," he confessed. His lashes were long, she noticed, the same shade of toasty gold as his hair. "My folks— Kade and Mandy McKettrick—had three girls before me, so I reckon they were prepared to call me Mary Ellen."

In spite of herself, Piper laughed. She was warmer now, standing so near the stove, but no less embarrassed to be wearing nothing but a nightgown. Oddly, the sensation was not completely unpleasant. "You have three sisters?"

Sawyer nodded. "How about you? Do you have sisters or brothers?"

"I'm an only child," Piper said. *And an orphan,* added a voice in her mind. "Dara Rose and I were raised together, though, so we're as close as sisters."

"That's good," Sawyer responded. He cleared his throat. "Aren't you cold?" he asked.

Piper *was* cold, though the proximity of the stove helped a little. Suddenly, no matter what the shameful implications, she realized she couldn't bear the idea of sleeping on the floor again. "Do you promise to conduct yourself like a gentleman if I agree to spend the night in the spare bed?" she asked, horrified to hear herself uttering such a thing.

Sawyer lifted his good arm, palm out, as if swearing an oath in a court of law. "You have my word," he said.

Piper started for the bedroom doorway, giving him as wide

a berth as she could in such a small, cramped space. "Wait until I say it's all right before you come in," she said.

Suppressing a grin, he nodded his agreement.

And Piper dashed past him, into the room that had been hers and hers alone, until night before last. Using sheets and blankets provided by Dara Rose, along with the bed itself and the lovely supper she and Sawyer had shared that evening, Piper quickly made up a cozy nest. Then, driven by the continuing cold and the shock of her own brazen boldness, she scrambled under the covers and lay there shivering until she'd adjusted to the chill of the sheets.

"I'm—ready," she sang out, after a long time.

She saw the light from the lanterns, the one she'd used in the cloakroom and the one Sawyer had been reading by, blink out. He appeared in the doorway, a shadow etched against the darkness, and Piper's heart began to pound so that she dared not speak, lest her voice tremble and betray the nervous excitement she felt.

Sawyer moved through the room, with only a slant of moonlight to see by, and, with an effort Piper could hear from beneath her blankets, took off his clothes. She heard the springs creak as he sat down on the other bed.

"Good night, Miss St. James," he said, with a smile in his voice. "And sleep well."

Piper didn't answer. She was hoping he'd think she was already asleep.

Closing her eyes, she pretended as hard as she could.

Lying there in the darkness, Sawyer cupped his right hand behind his head and smiled up at the ceiling, recalling the delicious look of surprise on Piper St. James's very pretty face a little while before, when she came bursting out of the cloakroom in her nightdress and found him reading at her desk. Her mouth had been blue with cold at the time, and he'd wanted to wrap her up in a blanket—or better yet, his arms—to warm her.

Given her schoolmarm-skittishness, he reckoned that would have been about the worst thing he could do, but knowing that didn't stop him from imagining the way she'd fit against him, curvy and soft against his own hard lines and angles.

The sensual image tightened his groin painfully, a reaction he wasn't going to be able to do a damn thing about and therefore had better ignore as best he could. Sawyer set his back teeth, so great was the effort it took to change the course of his thoughts. Altering the path of a river probably would have been easier, he soon concluded.

He willed himself to relax, one muscle group at a time, starting with the part of his anatomy in the most need of quieting, and when he'd finished, still taut and achy in too many places, he resorted to counting in his head, by odd numbers. After a while, as the imagined digits mounted to astronomical totals, he found he could breathe normally again. Some people prayed, and some people counted sheep, but Sawyer always took refuge in arithmetic.

He closed his eyes, hoping to sleep.

It was no use, though. He was too aware of Piper, lying close by, in her spinsterish nightgown, with her glowing, just-bathed skin, and her dark hair clinging to her cheeks and forehead in moist tendrils. The scent of her was like perfume, faintly flowery, subtle.

"Mr. McKettrick?" Her voice was tentative. Soft. "Are you awake?"

He smiled again, having suspected she was playing possum. She'd called him by his given name once or twice that day, but now that they were both bedded down in the same room,

"Mr. McKettrick" probably seemed a more prudent way to address him. "I'm awake," he confirmed.

He heard her draw in a breath. "I was just wondering if— well, if you think the man who shot you might come back?"

Bless her prim little heart, she was scared.

"Not likely," Sawyer said.

"Why not?"

"Because he probably thinks he's already killed me. Anyway, Blue River is small and a stranger would stand out."

"That didn't stop him before," she reasoned. "He just rode right up and shot you, bold as you please."

Sawyer grinned harder. His shoulder hurt, and he was lying a few feet from a woman he wanted and couldn't have, but he was enjoying this exchange. Maybe, he speculated, Miss Piper St. James was scared enough to leave her bed and share his.

"Yep," he said. "That's what happened."

"Suppose he didn't leave Blue River at all? Because of the storm, I mean. He could be holed up around here somewhere, couldn't he? Just waiting for his chance to strike again?"

"Maybe," Sawyer allowed, relishing her concern. If it hadn't meant Piper and her charges could be caught in the cross fire, he might have welcomed such a confrontation, since he'd be able to return the favor and put a bullet in the bastard, thereby evening the score. "It's not likely, though."

"What makes you so sure?"

"I've had some experience with these things," he replied.

"*That* isn't much comfort," Piper said. "Are you saying that you've been shot before?"

He had to chuckle. "No," he said. "I was referring to the nature of my work, that's all."

"What kind of 'work' involves getting shot?"

Sawyer said nothing.

"Are you an outlaw, Mr. McKettrick?" Piper persisted.

"Would you believe me if I said I wasn't?"

She made a muffled sound, like a scream of anger, held captive in her throat. It made him smile again. "I think you owe me an answer," she said, after a few moments.

"You do, do you?" he teased.

"Are you an outlaw?"

He thought it over. He'd killed a man once, though he'd been defending Henry Vandenburg, his former employer, at the time. Vandenburg's attacker, one of those wild-eyed anarchist types, had shoved his way through a crowd, in a busy railway station, and thrust the business end of a gun barrel into the boss's ample belly. Sawyer had stepped in, there was a struggle, and the pistol went off. The would-be killer bled out on the floor before the municipal police arrived in their paddy wagons.

"No," he answered, feigning offense at the question. "Would Clay have asked me to serve as town marshal if I were?"

"Possibly," she replied, after some thought. "You're his cousin, and the two of you grew up together. It might be that he's just giving you the benefit of the doubt by assuming that you are still the person he knew as a boy."

"Could be," Sawyer said, amused. She hadn't been this talkative before, and he wondered if that meant anything. Then he decided she felt safer speaking her mind because they were under cover of darkness, and she couldn't see him, or he her.

In a way, it reminded him of the old days on the Triple M, when he and Clay used to spend the night at their grandparents' house sometimes. The room they'd shared had two beds in it, and the dark of a country night had been like a curtain between them, making it possible to tell each other things they'd have choked on in the daylight.

"That," Piper said, "is a most unsatisfactory answer."

"Clay trusts me because I've never given him any reason not to," Sawyer said, relenting. Now that he wasn't in Vandenburg's employ any longer, he figured he didn't have to be so secretive, but he still wasn't inclined to spill his whole history. "I'm not an outlaw," he added.

"Then what are you? Only outlaws carry guns."

"Clay carries one. Is he an outlaw?"

"Well, *no*," Piper admitted. "But he's the marshal."

There was a silence.

He waited.

"Are you a lawman?" she asked.

"Not exactly," Sawyer replied. He wondered if she'd warmed up yet, and if she was still scared—in need of a little manly protection. Being nobody's fool, he didn't ask. "How did you become acquainted with a lady of the evening?" he inquired instead, recalling that morning's visit from Bess Turner.

Piper sounded impatient. "You heard what she said—her daughter, Ginny-Sue, is one of my pupils. And if you're 'not exactly' a lawman, what are you?"

"I was paid to protect a man and his family," Sawyer said. "And that's all you need to know." He barely paused before giving her a dose of her own medicine by barging right into her private business. "Generally, respectable women don't befriend people like Ginny-Sue's mother, no matter what the circumstances."

Her tone was huffy. "Maybe I'm not a respectable woman. Did you ever think of that?"

Sawyer laughed. "Oh, you're respectable, all right. You wouldn't be so worried about my seeing you in a nightgown, not to mention our sharing a bedroom, if you weren't."

Piper was quiet for so long that Sawyer began to think she'd fallen asleep. Finally, though, she spoke again, and there was a note of gentle sorrow in her voice. "Bess loves her child, just like anybody else, and besides, however misguided she might be, she's a human being. I see no earthly reason to shun her."

Something thickened in Sawyer's throat, which was odd. He wasn't usually sentimental, especially not over prostitutes like Bess Turner, but something about Piper's offhand compassion touched him in a deep place, and caused a shift in the way he thought of her.

The realization caused him considerable consternation.

"Sawyer?"

He smiled at Piper's use of his first name. That was more like it. "What?"

"I'm—afraid."

"Don't be. I won't hurt you."

"It's not you I'm scared of. It's the man who shot you."

"In that case," he said, only half joking, "maybe you'd better crawl in with me."

"I couldn't do that!"

"Where's the harm in it? Your reputation is probably ruined anyhow."

There was a snap of irritation in her reply. "Be that as it may, I don't want to give you the wrong impression. I am *not* the sort of woman who gets into bed with a man she isn't married to." She swallowed so hard that he heard it. "I'm—unbesmirched."

Unbesmirched.

In other words, a virgin. No real surprise there.

"I won't lay a hand on you, Miss St. James," he assured her. That much was certainly true. He might *want* to do plenty, once Piper was lying beside him in that narrow bed, but he'd never tried to persuade an unwilling woman to share her favors before and he wasn't going to start now.

To his amazement, he heard her get out of the other bed, hurry over, and slip in beside him. The mattress was more suited to one than two; they collided, and Piper almost sprang out of bed again when she realized he wasn't wearing anything but the bandages and the sling on his left arm.

He knew this by the gasp she gave.

"It's *all right,* Piper," he said.

She gave a comical little wail. "You might have told me you were—well—*indisposed!*"

"You didn't ask," he pointed out.

"This is horrible," she lamented. But she was still there, under the covers. With him.

"Hardly," he said. "We're just two people keeping each other warm on a cold winter's night, that's all."

"Maybe that's all it is to *you,*" Piper retorted. "I had hopes of getting married someday, and having a home and a family, before you came along and spoiled everything."

He smiled in the darkness. "If that's so, then I'm sorry," he told her.

"You don't *sound* sorry," Piper accused.

He yawned expansively. "Would you be convinced if I rounded up a preacher and the two of us got hitched?"

She gasped again.

He laughed, but the idea of taking a wife—*this* wife—was already starting to grow on him. He'd have preferred to court Piper St. James properly before he put a ring on her finger and took her home to the Triple M and the rest of the McKettrick family, but she had a point. Whether it was fair or not, she was probably compromised, all right, simply because they'd been alone together for a couple of days and nights. Some folks were just hypocritical enough to assume she'd thrown caution to the winds and succumbed to rampant lust at the first opportunity.

It was downright ridiculous, Sawyer knew, to assume a conscientious schoolmarm would turn into a raving wanton overnight, since she'd given shelter to a wounded stranger of the opposite sex, and never mind the kindness and courage she'd shown by dragging him inside and looking after him as best she knew how. After this, Piper would be no better than Bess Turner, as far as a lot of the locals were concerned.

Piper hadn't answered his question and now, judging by the moisture he felt against the upper part of his right arm, she was in tears.

"Hey," he said hoarsely, "don't cry."

"I can't help it," she sobbed. Since he reckoned she wasn't the kind who cried easily, this was even worse. "Isn't it enough that you *ruined my life?* Do you have to add insult to injury by *mocking* me, too?"

Sawyer was honestly confused. "Mocking you?" he rasped. God, he hated it when women cried, especially when it was his fault. Like now. "When did I do that?"

"When you m-made that r-remark about getting—hitched!"

"Piper," he said, surprising himself as he much as he had her, "I was serious. I'll marry you, if it'll make you feel better."

She struggled to a sitting position, and moonlight turned her tears silvery on her cheeks. Her hair fell loose around her shoulders and down her back, nearly reaching her waist. "But we don't *love* each other!" she cried, in obvious despair.

Gently, he drew Piper back down beside him, holding her with his good arm. She rested her head on his bare shoulder, sniffling. "That's true," he said carefully, "but we certainly wouldn't be the first couple who ever got married for practical reasons. Clay and Dara Rose tied the knot so she and the girls would have a place to live, and that arrangement worked out."

Instead of comforting her, Sawyer's words made her cry harder.

He was confounded, figuring he'd made a good case for holy matrimony.

He patted the back of her head ineffectually, afraid to say anything more in case he got it wrong. Again.

"That's different!" Piper wailed out, after some shuddering and sniffling.

"What's different?" Sawyer asked carefully.

"Clay and Dara Rose are different!"

"Why?"

"Because they were in love with each other from the very first," Piper sobbed. "It just took them a while to notice!"

Against his better judgment, Sawyer laughed. He couldn't help it. "People get married for all sorts of reasons," he reiterated, when he'd caught his breath. "Love isn't always one of them."

"Well, it should be!"

"Lots of things 'should be,' but they aren't." It was the wrong thing to say, but Sawyer didn't realize that until after he'd said it, when she slammed the side of one small fist into his belly. The blow didn't hurt, but it sure startled him, and it knocked the wind out of him for a moment, too.

Piper might be small, but she packed a punch. Raised by and around strong women, Sawyer considered that a good thing.

"I don't even know what kind of man you are," she lamented, though she seemed to be regaining some control of her runaway emotions. "You could be a scoundrel, or worse."

He smiled. "What's worse?" he teased. A strand of her hair tickled his mouth, and he decided he liked the feeling.

"Murder," she said. "Highway robbery. *Bigamy*."

"Bigamy?"

"Dara Rose thought she was married to Edrina and Harriet's father," Piper blurted out, on one long breath, "and it turned out he already had a wife and children, that stinker!"

Sawyer remembered Clay telling him the story, the year

before. He hadn't thought about it since, though. "I'm not married," he said quietly. "Never have been."

She sat up again, looking down at him. "How do I know you're telling the truth?"

Was she considering saying yes?

"You don't," he said solemnly. "You'll just have to trust me."

She ruminated on that for a while, still sitting up. "You didn't—you couldn't have—*meant* what you said? About us getting married?"

"I meant it, all right," Sawyer replied. He actually *liked* the idea, and that was a bit unsettling.

"If we go through with this, it would be a marriage in name only."

Up until now, Sawyer couldn't have imagined himself agreeing to such terms, but he did. "All right," he said. "But I reserve the right to try to change your mind."

Piper mulled that over. He reckoned she was going to come to her senses and pull out of the deal. "Not until *after* we're married," she negotiated.

"Fair enough," Sawyer said, and something inside him soared, as proud and free as a lone eagle against a wide blue sky. "Can I at least kiss you?"

More consideration on her part followed.

He sat up, careful to keep the quilts in place, just above his waist.

They stared at each other for a while, in the light of a waning moon filtering through a weather-grimed window.

Then she closed her eyes, puckered up, and waited.

Sawyer bit the inside of his lower lip, so he wouldn't laugh. Then he placed his hand on the back of her head, very gently, and pressed her face toward his. He kissed her, worked her lips with his own until Piper sighed and opened to him.

He used his tongue. Carefully.

She moaned and slipped her arms around his neck.

He deepened the kiss slowly, because she was so obviously an innocent.

Piper whimpered, but she didn't try to pull away.

It was Sawyer who did that. "Piper," he said, his voice ragged from the strain of giving up what the rest of his body was demanding, "no more. I'm trying to do the right thing here."

"I'd better go back to the other bed," she said shyly.

"That might be a good idea," Sawyer replied. He was hard as tamarack by then, and he didn't want Piper to know it.

She left him, got back into the bed Clay had brought in from the ranch. The small distance between them seemed like miles to Sawyer, who fell back onto his pillows with a heavy sigh.

"Sawyer?" Piper said.

He probably sounded abrupt when he replied. "What?"

"I've never—" She fell silent, embarrassed again.

"I know," he said more gently.

And after that, by some miracle, they both went to sleep.

Piper's eyes flew open when she realized it was morning, and she'd not only let Sawyer kiss her in the night, but she'd kissed him *back*. She sat up in her borrowed bed, pulling the covers up to her chin, and looked in his direction, but he wasn't there.

She scrambled out from under the blankets, landed both feet on the icy floor, and made a dash for her bureau, where she rummaged for bloomers and a camisole. Clutching them in one hand, she grabbed her woolen dress, the one she'd planned on saving for really cold days, and stuck her head out the bedroom door.

Sawyer wasn't in the schoolroom—he must have gone outside, to the privy.

Piper dressed in seconds, fumbling, hopping about, nearly tripping over her hem in the process, and then did what she could with her hair, winding it into a single plait and twisting it around the back of her head, where she secured it with hairpins.

The schoolroom was warm—Sawyer must have built up the fire—and the delicious aroma of fresh coffee filled the air. She went to the window, looked out. The snow was nearly gone, but she barely took note of that because she spotted Sawyer, dressed and talking amiably with Doc Howard, who didn't get down off his mule. The poor animal was muddy to its knees.

Piper saw Doc smile and nod his head, and she ducked back from the window quickly, hoping he hadn't seen her.

What was Sawyer *saying* out there?

Her cheeks flamed so hot that she pressed her palms to her face, trying to cool them down. *Surely* Sawyer wasn't asking Doc Howard to fetch a preacher, so he and the schoolmarm could "get hitched," she thought frantically. Yes, they'd talked about marriage, and it had seemed like a viable idea at the time, but in the bright light of day it was—well, it was insane, that's what it was. It was *out of the question.*

She remembered the kiss, felt the heat and pressure on her mouth as surely as if Sawyer's mouth was on hers right then.

Her heart pounded, and bolts of fiery lightning shot through her, weakening her knees, melting parts of her that were too personal even to *think about.*

She *was* wanton, she concluded, horrified. She'd not only *gotten into bed* with Sawyer McKettrick the night before, she'd let him kiss her. *Let* him? She'd as good as thrown herself at the man, and then she'd *carried on.* In fact, if Sawyer hadn't sent her back to her own bed, she might have been swept away.

Things, she decided, could not possibly get worse.

Except that they did, and almost immediately.

Sawyer opened the door, came inside, spotted her sitting on one of her students' desks with her hands pressed to her burning face.

He smiled. "There are some kids coming down the road," he informed her. "Your students, I presume."

Piper cried out, bolted to her feet. "No!"

"Yes," Sawyer said. "Doc will be back at three-thirty, with a license and a preacher." With that, he headed for the bedroom, pausing to pour himself a mug full of coffee along the way. From the inside doorway, he looked back at her over his right shoulder. "Better step lively, Teacher," he said. "School's about to be in session."

He was barely out of sight when Ginny-Sue Turner burst in, cheeks pink, eyes eager. "I know the whole second chapter of Luke!" she blurted joyfully. "By heart!"

Piper's smile might have been a little shaky, but Ginny-Sue was too young, and too excited, to notice. "That's wonderful," she said, resting a hand on the child's shoulder.

"And Christmas is going to happen, after all!" Ginny-Sue enthused, glowing as she got out of her coat and mittens and warm woolen hat. "Mama said it would, because you told her so."

Piper's throat tightened, and she managed a little nod. She had no power to keep another snowstorm away, of course, but this child clearly believed she did.

It was a weighty responsibility.

Madeline Howard arrived next, small and blonde and very pretty, like her mother, followed by half a dozen other children.

"May I ring the bell, Miss St. James?" Madeline asked, beaming.

Piper assented, and the other students arrived by twos and threes. Even Edrina and Harriet made it into town for class—Clay had driven them in a wagon drawn by those same two plow horses he'd hitched to the sledge the day before, and he waved and smiled from the seat, reins in hand.

"Has the baby arrived?" Piper asked breathlessly, after picking her way through the mud to stand beside Clay's wagon, looking up at him.

He shook his head. "Not yet," he said, "but Dara Rose was mighty eager to get the girls out of the house this morning, so I figure she's about ready."

"You'd better get back there, quick," Piper said, worried, but thrilled, too. In her excitement, she forgot about Sawyer McKettrick, hiding out in her bedroom behind the schoolhouse.

He'd be discovered, of course, if only because Edrina and Harriet surely knew he was there, and would want to greet him.

Clay nodded, lifted the reins and released the brake lever with his left hand. "Sawyer doing all right?" he asked, in parting.

Piper colored up, quite against her will, but held Clay's gaze. "Yes," she said.

Clay touched the brim of his hat in farewell, brought down the reins on the horses' backs, setting them in noisy motion, and drove away.

If it hadn't been so cold outside, sunny sky or none, Piper might have lingered in the school yard, putting off the moment when she'd have to face her pupils, but she didn't have a cloak and she'd forgotten to wrap the blanket around her before coming to greet Clay.

So she marched inside, clapping her hands to get the children's attention.

They were gathered around the undecorated Christmas tree, examining it for bird's nests and chatting among themselves. Edrina and Harriet, as she'd expected, were out of sight, and she could hear them talking with Sawyer in the back room.

She closed her eyes for a moment.

"Can we fix up the Christmas tree today, Miss St. James?" one of the boys asked. "Jack and me, we could fix up a stand for it in no time, out in the woodshed."

Piper set her hands on her hips and considered the suggestion in a teacherly way. "That would be fine," she said, at long last.

The children cheered.

Two of the boys rushed outside, followed by several more.

"Edrina, Harriet!" Piper called pleasantly. "Come out here, please. We're going to decorate the tree."

Dara Rose's children, both beautiful, with heads full of shining curls and cherubic faces, appeared in the bedroom doorway.

Harriet opened her little bow-shaped mouth, most likely on the verge of making some remark about her kinsman's presence, but Piper quickly pressed an index finger to her own lips, shushing her.

Though she was very young, only in the first grade, Harriet read Piper's signal and bit back whatever she'd planned to say.

For the next hour, the children kept busy, cutting strips of colorful paper, saved especially for the purpose, and pasting them together in loops, so they turned into long chains.

The boys returned from the shed, triumphant, with several pieces of wood cobbled together to serve as a stand for the tree.

After much ado, the stem of the tree was wedged into the simple stand. Piper found the box of handmade ornaments on the cloakroom shelf and brought it into the schoolroom, where the lid was ceremoniously raised.

Inside were other chains, made by other students and other teachers, along with a few carefully wrapped glass balls, tiny rag-doll angels, and stars cut from tin. Some of the stars had rusted, which only added to their charm, and the children were as enthralled as if they'd just found a pirate's treasure.

Soon, the tree stood glittering, ready for Christmas.

By midday, the weather was turning gloomy again, the sky dark and heavy with snow, and fathers and uncles arrived in wagons and on horseback, to collect their offspring and see them safely home. Two of the mothers came as well, and peered curiously at Piper, as though they weren't sure they recognized her.

When the first fat snowflakes drifted down, Ginny-Sue took her leave, squeezing Piper's hand before she hurried outside. "Don't worry, Teacher," she said.

"Christmas will still come—you'll see!"

Chapter Six

Of all Piper's pupils, only Edrina and Harriet remained at the schoolhouse, waiting for Clay to come for them. Heedless of the continuing snow, they laughed with Sawyer, who had hauled Piper's rocking chair out of the bedroom and now sat with one of the little girls on each knee, telling stories about himself and Clay as boys.

The fire in the stove warmed the room and steamed up the windows in a cozy way, and the Christmas tree lent a definite air of festivity, but Piper was nervous, just the same.

From a practical standpoint, she knew that Clay wasn't late—it was not quite three o'clock and he had farther to travel than most of the other parents—and even if he'd gotten off to an early start, the weather would surely slow him down.

No, it was Dara Rose she was concerned about.

Hadn't Clay said, that very morning, that Dara Rose had seemed anxious to get her daughters out of the house? Wasn't that an indication that the baby might be coming?

Piper bit her lower lip and busied herself at her desk, pretending to study her attendance records. Dara Rose was healthy, she reminded herself, and strong. She'd had two other children with no problem at all, hadn't she?

But Edrina and Harriet had been born in a large *city,* with a real doctor present at each of their births, and Dara Rose had been younger then.

Was she giving birth right now, this minute, way out there on that isolated ranch?

Had she run into some kind of trouble with the delivery, the kind Clay didn't have the knowledge or skill to handle?

At three-fifteen Piper heard the squeal of wagon wheels being braked, the snorting and tromping of horses, and rushed to the front window to wipe away some of the mist and look outside.

Clay, wearing a heavy coat, with the brim of his hat pulled low over his eyes to shield his face from the blustery weather, jumped down from the wagon box and left the team standing, their nostrils puffing out white clouds of breath.

Piper looked harder, trying to discern something from Clay's bearing or manner—his face was still hidden from view by the angle of his hat—but he revealed nothing as he made his way toward the schoolhouse with long, even strides.

Edrina and Harriet must have heard the team and wagon, too, because they were beside Piper in a matter of moments, standing on tiptoe, fingers gripping the windowsill, trying to see out. Perhaps they'd been more anxious than they'd let on.

Clay finally reached the porch, paused to stomp the snow and mud from his boots.

Piper wrenched open the door, but stepped aside when Edrina and Harriet scrambled past her.

Clay stepped over the threshold, shut the door, and crouched, putting out an arm for each of the girls. His hat fell backward and the beaming smile on his face was revealed.

"Girls," he told his stepdaughters, his eyes misting over like the windows, "you've got a brand-new baby brother waiting for you out at the ranch. Your mama's just fine, and she's hankering to show the little fellow off to you."

Edrina and Harriet jumped up and down with happiness as Clay straightened, nodded a brief greeting to Sawyer, then shifted his gaze to Piper.

"It was an easy birth," he told her quietly. "Dara Rose is well, if a mite worn-out, and the baby is big enough to fight bear with a switch."

Piper wept tears of joyful relief and gave Clay a quick, sisterly hug.

"Congratulations," she said, stepping back and smiling up at him.

That was when she felt Sawyer standing behind her. He rested his good hand on her shoulder briefly before reaching past her to extend it to Clay.

The two men shook hands.

"Another McKettrick," Sawyer said. "I'm not sure the world is ready for that."

Clay laughed. His face and ears were red with cold, but his eyes gleamed with love and pride. "We're going to call him Jeb," he said, "after my pa."

"Will you stay for coffee?" Piper asked, out of practicality. "It'll help keep you warm on the way back home."

But Clay shook his head in refusal, nodded to the girls to get their things together so the three of them could get going. "If we hurry, we can make it before dark," he said, more to Piper and Sawyer than the children, who were busy bundling up for the long, chilly ride ahead. "Dara Rose will fret if we're not back in time for supper."

Piper felt tearful again, full of longing. Oh, to go with Clay and Edrina and Harriet, to make supper for the family and fuss over Dara Rose and the new baby.

Clay seemed to read her mind. "It'll be Christmas soon," he said, gruffly gentle. "You'll see Dara Rose and make Jeb's acquaintance then."

She swallowed, nodded, and hastened to help Edrina and Harriet with their coats and hats and mittens and scarves. She kissed each one of them goodbye—when the other pupils were around she tried hard not to show favoritism—and said she'd see them in the morning, if the weather allowed.

"You need anything?" Clay asked as an afterthought, glancing at Piper but mainly addressing Sawyer, after he'd put on his hat and sent the girls racing for the wagon out front.

"No," Sawyer said, with warmth and amusement in his voice. "You go on home and look after your family, cousin. We'll be just fine on our own."

Inwardly, Piper stiffened. In all the excitement over the new baby, she'd forgotten all about Doc's imminent return, with the preacher in tow.

No sense bringing that up in front of Clay, though. It would take too much explaining, and he might feel torn between going home to Dara Rose and the baby and staying for the wedding.

Not that there was going to *be* a wedding.

Piper meant to make that abundantly clear as soon as she and Sawyer were alone. She'd made a rash decision, she'd tell him, but now she'd changed her mind.

Only when Clay and the girls drove away did she turn around to face Sawyer.

He was standing so close that his injured arm, still in its sling, bumped against her breast. A slow, sultry smile lit his eyes and touched his mouth. *That* mouth. Piper could almost feel it against her own, seeking, exploring, and finally, commanding.

She caught her own breath. "About last night—"

Sawyer grinned, easy in his skin and damnably sure of himself, and curled his right index finger under her chin. "A deal's a deal, Miss St. James," he told her huskily. "Besides, the word's surely out by now. There's a man over at the schoolhouse, that's what folks are saying, and something unseemly is going on for sure."

Piper pressed her back teeth together. He was right, of course. She'd seen the way those mothers, those *hens,* had looked at her, when they came to gather their chicks under their figurative wings. They'd known, even before their children got a chance to give an account. Eloise Howard must have spread the word, just as Piper had feared she would.

Besides, the Blue River schoolhouse was too small to contain such a secret; even though Sawyer had been courteous enough to stay out of sight while the students were there, they would have guessed that Edrina and Harriet weren't addressing empty space when they'd hurried into the back room that morning, chattering like happy little magpies. Why, they hadn't even paused to take off their coats.

Piper gave a little groan of frustration. "What if we're making a terrible mistake?" she whispered hoarsely.

Sawyer smiled, placed a brief, feather-soft kiss on her mouth, instantly awakening every wanton tendency she possessed— and the number of those tendencies was alarming.

"Most of your questions start with 'what if' or 'how do I know,'" he observed. "There aren't any guarantees in this life, Piper. The whole proposition is risky from the get-go right up to the end." He paused, wound a finger idly in a tendril of her hair, a gesture almost as intimate as last night's kiss. "I can promise you this much, though—I'll provide for you, I'll protect you, and I'll never lay a hand on you except to give you pleasure."

Pleasure? She blinked at the word. She'd always considered that the province of men and, perhaps, women like Bess Turner.

But, wait, she reflected, avoiding Sawyer's eyes by looking down and to the side. Dara Rose wasn't a loose woman, and she certainly seemed to enjoy married life. She hadn't said so outright, but Piper *had* wondered, a time or two, about the way her cousin and Clay smiled secrets at each other. The way they touched when they thought no one was looking.

Sawyer touched the tip of her nose just then, and her gaze swung straight to his, connected with a jolt, like a metal latch. "You're blushing," he said, in a low, pleased drawl. "Was it the word *pleasure?*"

"Of course not," Piper lied. She'd been raised, like most women of her generation, to believe that "pleasure" and "wickedness" were one and the same thing. Luckily, she was saved from having to make a case for propriety by a knock at the door.

She jumped at the sound, startled because she hadn't heard a wagon or a horse approaching the schoolhouse.

Sawyer merely smiled.

She whirled away from him, in a billow of gray skirts, and opened the door, thinking Clay and the girls must have found the going too hard and turned back. Nothing would have stopped Clay from returning to Dara Rose and the baby, she knew, but that didn't mean he'd put Edrina and Harriet's safety at risk in the doing of it. He'd leave them with her, if he thought they were in any danger.

Instead of Clay and the girls, though, she found herself face-to-face with Doc Howard, his smugly disapproving wife, Eloise, and the Methodist circuit preacher, a towering, bearded man of dour countenance, fearsome as an Old Testament prophet bringing word of impending doom. He looked ready for battle, too, as though he'd come to that little schoolhouse to fight the devil himself, hand to hand, standing there with snow dusting the shoulders of his tattered coat and the brim of his once-fine hat.

"C-come in," Piper said, stepping back to admit them all. She was only too aware of Sawyer standing nearby, looking on with amusement.

Blast him, he was *enjoying* this, she just knew it.

"You've made a wise decision," Mrs. Howard said loftily, pulling off her elbow-length kid gloves and narrowing her eyes at Piper as she spoke. She wore a dark blue woolen cloak over a dress almost the same color, and her hat was huge. With the snow, it looked as though the woman was carrying a miniature landscape on her head.

Dislike welled up in Piper, but she held it in check. She was, regrettably, in no position to make her opinions known, especially since Mrs. Howard was on the school board and could have her dismissed without any difficulty at all.

"Have I?" Piper countered, with false sweetness.

Eloise Howard narrowed her china-blue eyes even farther, to little lash-trimmed slits. Doc Howard, the preacher, and even Sawyer seemed to recede into the now-fuzzy surroundings. "I'm sure you'll agree, *Miss* St. James," Eloise said, through her tiny, perfect teeth, "that the moral well-being of our children must be the paramount consideration here."

Piper was mad enough to spit. She was a good teacher and, besides, it wasn't as if she'd been teaching her pupils to dance the hurdy-gurdy. This situation, meaning Sawyer's presence at the schoolhouse, had *befallen* her—she'd done nothing to bring it about, nothing at all.

Except for trying to do the right thing.

She was to be held accountable, nonetheless, and that, in her opinion, was a travesty.

"Now, Eloise," Doc interceded, after clearing his throat, "leave the preaching to Brother Carson, here."

Nobody laughed at the paltry joke, if it was intended as one, or even smiled.

No one besides Sawyer, that is. Out of the corner of her eye, Piper saw the corner of his mouth twitch.

"Morality is a serious matter," Brother Carson pontificated, in a thundering voice. He held a huge Bible in the crook of one arm, as though poised to use it as a weapon if the need presented itself. His gaze sliced, lethal and dark with condemnation, between Sawyer and Piper. "God is not mocked," he added. "We must root out sin wherever we find it!"

Piper didn't know how to respond to that, except to flinch slightly and take half a step backward, which caused her to collide with Sawyer.

Determinedly jovial, Doc Howard chose that moment to shove a parcel at Sawyer—it was wrapped in brown paper and tied with string. "Here are the things you asked me to fetch from the general store," he said, a little too loudly. Then, spotting the Christmas tree, he went on, "Now isn't that a merry sight!"

"We can thank the Germans for that bit of frippery," the preacher boomed, without appreciation. "A fire hazard at best, idolatry at worst."

"What's this world coming to?" Sawyer mused lightly.

Piper resisted the temptation to elbow him, hard. She couldn't take a chance on doing further injury to his bad shoulder.

Eloise was still watching her, with a sort of curious abhorrence, the way she might watch some poor soul traveling with a freak show, but she directed her words to her husband when she spoke. "What about the marriage license, James?"

she asked, in a condescending tone. "Did you 'fetch' one of those, too?"

Doc Howard blushed slightly, and Piper felt sorry for him.

Her own dealings with Eloise Howard were intermittent ones. His were constant.

He patted the front of his suit coat, then reached into the inside pocket and drew out a folded document. "It's right here," he said. "Judge Reynolds agreed that this is an emergency, so he issued the license without the usual waiting period."

Brother Carson opened his Bible, flipped through the pages until he found a sheet of paper tucked away in the Psalms, and cleared his throat. "Dearly beloved," he growled out, squinting down at the words scrawled in black ink, "we are gathered here—in the sight of God—"

"Wait," Piper interrupted, but after that, words deserted her.

Brother Carson looked up, his black eyebrows bushy as caterpillars.

Eloise Howard blinked once.

"I know this must seem hasty," Doc put in bravely, after an anxious glance at his wife, "but there's nothing for it. Marriage is the only solution."

"But—" Piper protested.

Sawyer cupped a hand under her elbow just then, and, somehow, that gave her strength. They were being railroaded into this, both she and Sawyer, but she supposed the situation could have been worse.

He might have been old and ugly, for instance.

And she might have been repulsed, rather than excited, by his kisses.

She sighed. "Go ahead," she said wearily.

And so it happened that Piper St. James was married—*married*—to a man she barely knew. Instead of a wedding gown, she wore her gray woolen schoolmarm's dress. There were no real guests, no family members present; she didn't even have a bridal bouquet.

The whole ceremony was over in under ten minutes, in fact.

Piper was in such a daze that she barely registered Sawyer's perfunctory wedding kiss.

They each signed the marriage license, and Doc snatched it up like it was a Spanish land grant or something, saying he'd file it with Judge Reynolds and bring back a copy when he could.

The preacher slammed his Bible shut on his handwritten wedding vows, nodded abruptly, and turned to leave without so much as a goodbye.

Doc, too, seemed anxious to escape, and he all but dragged Eloise out of the schoolhouse. Mrs. Howard, Piper suspected, with rancor, would have preferred to stay and gloat for a few minutes.

In what seemed like a blink of an eye, the others were gone, leaving Piper alone with her new husband.

She squeezed her eyes shut, willing herself not to cry.

The rustle of paper caught her attention, and she looked sideways to see that Sawyer was opening the parcel Doc had given him earlier. He'd set it aside, without comment, in order to make his marriage vows.

A garment made of rich, russet-colored wool lay folded inside, along with a narrow gold wedding band, perched atop one of the folds.

Smiling, Sawyer slipped the band onto her finger.

Amazingly, it was a perfect fit, like Cinderella's glass slipper in the fairy tale.

Piper couldn't speak. Moments before, she'd been on the verge of tears, and now she wanted to laugh like a madwoman. She was hysterical, that was it.

And, furthermore, she was *Mrs. McKettrick*.

Who *was* that, exactly? How was she to proceed?

Using his right hand, Sawyer caressed her cheek. "I'll keep my word, Piper," he said. "For now, we're only married on paper."

Her eyes widened. "For now?" she echoed. Surely this was all a dream—a terrible, wonderful dream—and she'd awaken at any moment.

Again, that wicked tilt appeared at the corner of his mouth. "I have every intention of seducing you," he said, his voice at once quiet and forthright, "sooner or later. In the meantime, you're a respectable woman again."

Piper might have taken umbrage at that, if he hadn't chosen that moment to unfurl the beautiful russet-colored cape he'd bought for her. It had a deep, elegant hood and was trimmed in black silk piping.

She'd seen the garment on display over at the mercantile, not once but many times, but it cost the earth and she'd never given a single thought to owning it. Neither had most of the other women in town, she'd bet, since it was the sort of thing a grand lady would wear to the opera.

Needless to say, there was no opera in Blue River, Texas.

Spellbound, she accepted the cloak, draping it around her shoulders, marveling at the weight of it, and the supple softness of the fabric, almost like velvet, and the way it seemed to wrap her in grace.

"Do you like it?" Sawyer asked. He sounded almost shy. "I guess it wouldn't have been a proper gift before, but now that we're married—"

She raised shining eyes to him. "Oh, Sawyer," she said, in a rapt whisper. "I've never seen anything so beautiful."

"Neither have I," he said then, very gravely.

And he was looking at her as he spoke, not at the cloak.

Piper's native practicality reasserted itself a few moments later, and she took the cape to the cloakroom and hung it up there, out of the way, where it wouldn't be stained, or get snagged on something.

"Thank you," she said, with crisp dignity, when she came out again.

Sawyer was feeding wood into the stove by then. "You're welcome," he said.

Shyness overwhelmed Piper in that moment. She didn't know how to be this new person, this Mrs. McKettrick she'd become with almost no warning at all. "You were forced into this," she murmured. "Just as I was. It isn't fair."

"I guess we're victims of circumstance," Sawyer replied philosophically. "Nothing to do now but make the best of things."

"I'll start supper," Piper said quickly, maintaining a safe distance. It wasn't that she didn't trust Sawyer, exactly; if he were a masher, she'd have known it by now. Even with one arm bound up in a sling, he could have taken advantage of her at almost any point in their brief acquaintance.

No, she realized, it was *herself* she didn't completely trust. She'd gotten into bed with this man the night before.

She'd allowed him to kiss her—not only allowed it, but *reveled* in it.

It made her blush to think what she might have let Sawyer do after that, if he hadn't had the decency to send her away.

The truth struck her, hard.

Even the forced marriage hadn't been entirely beyond her control—she could have packed a satchel, boarded a train and left Blue River forever, started over somewhere else, maybe even changed her name. Or she could have put her foot down, that very afternoon, when the Howards and Brother Carson showed up, and flatly refused to go through with the ceremony.

There would have been repercussions, of course. But wasn't being married to a man she barely *knew* a repercussion?

There was no getting around it. Some part of her had *wanted* this, had seen the chance and reached out to grab hold.

Piper was baffled by all this, even stricken, and yet— excited, even thrilled. Her life had always been so proper, so predictable, so *ordinary.*

Now, all of a sudden, some other, unknown Piper had come to the fore and quite handily taken matters into her own hands. This was a bold and brazen Piper, a person she'd never imagined she could be.

Leaving her to her confusion, probably blithely unaware of it, being a man, Sawyer went outside for wood and water, managing these chores ably with one arm, and it struck Piper that he was recovering rapidly. He still needed a shave, but his hair was combed and his color was good, and he seemed to have significantly more stamina than one might have expected, after such a severe and recent injury.

Soon, he'd be well enough to leave the schoolhouse.

Maybe he'd even change his mind about accepting the marshal's job, and go back to his former occupation, whatever that was. He'd said he'd been paid to "protect a man and his family." Was that just a polite way of saying he was a common *henchman?* An outlaw, for all practical intents and purposes?

As for the marriage, well, that might have been some sort of ruse on his part. Men walked out on wives and families all the time, didn't they?

Piper gave herself a mental shake as she sliced more of Dara Rose's ham and laid it in the skillet waiting on the stove. She was letting her imagination run away with her. If Sawyer already had a wife tucked away somewhere, *someone* in that sprawling McKettrick clan would know about her, wouldn't they? According to Dara Rose, Clay exchanged letters with half the family. Surely, he'd have heard the news from one of his many relations, if not Sawyer himself. And honor would have demanded that he step in and prevent an illegal marriage.

Except that Clay hadn't *known* she and Sawyer were about to get married. She hadn't had a chance to tell him, wouldn't have known what to say if she had, and it was a good bet that Sawyer hadn't said anything to his cousin, either.

Sawyer came in, bringing the scent of snow and pine pitch along with him, and dropped wood into the box next to the stove.

"I don't think this weather is going to last," he said. "The snow's melting as soon as it hits the ground."

Piper nodded, biting her lower lip and spearing at the slices of ham with a fork as though the task required all her concentration. This was her wedding night, she thought, with glum amazement, catching sight of the golden band shimmering on her finger.

How had this *happened?*

Just a few days ago, she'd been an ordinary schoolteacher, a little discontented with her lot in life, perhaps, but certainly not unhappy. Now, she was legally Mrs. Sawyer McKettrick— but what did that mean, exactly? Would she even be able to keep her job?

Married women rarely taught school—it was considered improper and a poor reflection on the husband's ability to provide—even if said husband was a worthless layabout, drinking his way to the grave. The wife and any children unfortunate enough to be born of such a union were expected to politely starve to death, without so much as a whimper of complaint, if only for the sake of appearances.

Appearances!

Piper forgot herself and swore aloud. "Thunderation!" she blurted out.

Sawyer reminded her of his presence with a question. "Did you burn yourself?" he asked, from somewhere behind her. He sounded calmly concerned.

"No," Piper said. "I was just thinking about—things."

"Things?"

"Men. Women. Marriage."

He eased her aside, took over the fork she'd been wielding, repeatedly turning the meat in the skillet, whether it needed turning or not. "I'll do this," he said. "And what about men, women and marriage?"

She flounced to her desk chair and plunked down in it, glad to have something to think about besides what might happen when the lamps went out later in the evening. She had no confidence whatsoever in her own ability to conduct herself like a lady.

"Women get a raw deal," she said. "We can't even *vote,* for pity's sake."

"I agree with you there," Sawyer replied, surprising her. "It isn't right."

Piper was picking up steam, like a locomotive chugging out of the station. "Men can go right ahead and beat women, if they want to, wives *and* children. If they're no-accounts, their wives can't go out and earn a living, even to put food on the table or keep a roof over their heads. They wind up like Bess Turner if they try."

"Whoa," Sawyer said affably, forking the meat onto two plates and bringing one to her, along with a slice of the bread she'd already sliced and buttered and a spoonful from the jar of peaches she'd opened the night before. "If that's what you think marriage is going to be like, it's no wonder you're jumpy."

Piper drew in a deep breath. "I might have gotten a little carried away," she admitted, touched that he'd brought her supper to her. Except for Clay, who doted on Dara Rose even though he was unquestionably the head of their family, she'd never seen a married man do that.

He went back for his own plate and sat on the edge of the desk to eat. "I wouldn't beat you," he said, after a long time. "Or any kids we might be lucky enough to have. For that matter, I wouldn't beat a dog or a horse or any other living creature."

She looked up at him. "Not even a man?" she asked.

"That's different," he said, his gaze level as he studied her. "Is it?"

"Yes," Sawyer replied, after a few moments of thought. "I don't go around looking for fights, Piper, but if one comes my way, I mean to hold my own. And if I run into the yahoo who shot me, I'll shoot him without missing a breath."

"You are a very complicated man," she observed presently, having mulled over what he'd said.

He cocked a grin at her. "I reckon I am," he said. "Keeps things interesting, wouldn't you say?"

She sighed, let the question go unanswered, since she knew it didn't need a reply, and presented one of her own. "What happens when you're well, Sawyer?" she asked, with a glance at his sling and bandages, bulging under one side of his half-buttoned shirt. "Will you stay here in Blue River, and serve as marshal?" *Or will you retrieve your fancy horse from Clay's barn and ride out, leaving me behind?*

"I'll be here long enough to track down the son-of-a— the man who shot me, and make sure justice is served. Come spring, though, I expect to head north, home to the Triple M. Build a house and settle down."

In all that, there was no mention of bringing a wife along, but Piper didn't point out the omission. For one thing, she was much more concerned by Sawyer's implacability, and his plan to bring in his assailant.

He could get killed doing that.

Or become a killer.

Both possibilities terrified Piper.

They finished their suppers in silence, and Piper did the dishes—Sawyer tried to help, but she elbowed him aside.

Darkness gathered, thick, at the windows, and the little stove labored hard to keep out the evening chill, though the snow had stopped coming down, at least.

Sawyer rummaged around and found the battered checkerboard and chunky wooden game pieces Miss Krenshaw or one of her predecessors had left behind. Piper sometimes allowed the children to hold tournaments, on days when they'd behaved particularly well and completed their lessons to her satisfaction.

He set the board up on her desk. "Black or red?" he asked.

Piper, drying her hands, turned away from the dish basin, the task complete. "What?" she asked.

Sawyer grinned. "Do you want the red pieces, or the black ones?"

She frowned. "You want to play checkers?"

His grin widened. "There are things I'd rather do," he admitted, "this being our wedding night. But I'm a man of my word, Mrs. McKettrick. A virgin bride you are, and a virgin bride you will remain. For the time being, that is."

She blushed. "Red," she said.

He gestured toward her chair, and she sat down. He rested one hip on the other side of her desk, as he'd done before, when they were having supper.

"Your move," he said.

Chapter Seven

This wasn't how she'd envisioned her wedding night, Piper reflected, as she and Sawyer played game after game of checkers on the surface of her desk—which wasn't to say she'd ever had a clear idea of what was *supposed* to happen. Oh, she knew the fundamentals, of course, the strictly anatomical part, but the rest belonged to the realm of speculation—mostly. She *had* felt some very interesting sensations when Sawyer kissed her the night before, ones that made her want more of the same, but her fear equaled her curiosity, perhaps even exceeded it.

The congress between a man and a woman, she had been taught, mostly by inference and whispers, was mainly a nasty and painful business, something to be tolerated, endured, with the husband's happiness as a reward and, of course, the possible conception of a baby.

To Piper, the bearing, raising and cherishing of a child of her own—and preferably several—was a sacred calling indeed. Although she loved teaching, she knew the vocation was, at least for her, a prelude to mothering.

As for the husband...well, a good one, like Clay, was a blessing. A *bad* one, on the other hand, would be a curse. Which kind *she'd* gotten remained to be seen.

Keeping her gaze focused on her game pieces—she was losing, badly, *again*—Piper considered Dara Rose, and the way she lit up from the inside whenever Clay was around. She hummed a great deal, Piper had noticed on visits to the ranch, and even sang under her breath while she went about her household tasks. And even though there was never any overt sign of their intentions, Dara Rose didn't seem to dread being alone with her husband at night, behind a closed bedroom door.

The whole thing was downright confusing, and Piper wished she'd been bold enough to ask Dara Rose what marital relations were really like, in their most elemental form.

Sawyer knit his brow, and while his eyes smiled, his mouth played at a frown. "What's going on in your mind right about now, Mrs. McKettrick?" he asked.

She didn't protest the "Mrs. McKettrick" part, even though she thought it contained a trace of benign mockery. "Nothing I want to discuss with *you*, Mr. McKettrick," she replied pertly. He'd blocked her few remaining game pieces into a corner of the board, and any move she made would result in sweeping defeat.

"Who, then?" he asked mildly.

"Dara Rose, if you must know," Piper said, and then wished she hadn't.

"Ah," he said, as though that explained a great deal. Resigned, she moved her checker piece and he picked up one of his own and leapfrogged over her little band of huddled checkers, one by one. "Let me hazard a guess," he went on, at his leisure, watching her with a smile in his eyes. "You're wondering what to expect when a man and a woman go to bed together, not like we did, but in earnest."

Piper's cheeks flamed, and she knew her eyes were flashing, too. She couldn't bring herself to refute the statement, though she would have liked very much to do just that. "I may be a—a virgin," she sputtered, "but I'm not a complete fool. I *know* what men and women do together."

He began to set up the board for yet another game, concentrating solemnly on the task. "Then why do you want to ask Dara Rose about it?"

"I did not say, at any time, that I wanted to ask my cousin about her very private relationship with her husband," Piper said stiffly. Maybe she *hadn't* said it, but it was very much on her mind, and he'd guessed that, obviously.

"But you do," Sawyer said lightly.

"I do *not*," Piper lied. This was an unsettling aspect of her new self—skirting the truth—and she didn't approve.

Sawyer's glance strayed toward the front window then, and Piper realized he'd done that a couple of times in the past hour or so. She'd paid it no mind then, figuring he must be thinking about the weather, which was a concern to everybody, but now she sensed that there was another reason. Was he expecting someone? Waiting for something?

He wasn't wearing his gun belt, she noticed now, with relief, but his Colt .45 had somehow found its way to the top of a nearby bookshelf.

"Last game," he said, when the board was ready. He yawned then, but it looked and sounded contrived to Piper.

She studied him suspiciously, decided to call his bluff. "I've had enough of checkers for one night," she told him, rising from her chair and smoothing her skirts, "and this has been a long and trying day." Leaving the nearest lantern for him, she found a second one, struck a match to the wick, wrapped herself in the same old blanket, not wanting to spoil her new cloak, and started for the door.

Sawyer didn't ask where she was going, but he did reach for his .45, shove it under his belt in a disturbingly practiced way, and follow.

"I'm only going to the privy," she whispered, embarrassed.

"Not alone," Sawyer answered. With that, he squired her outside, down the steps, and around to the back of the schoolhouse. The privy loomed ahead, in a faint wash of moonlight.

Much to Piper's relief, he came to a stop at the corner of the school building and stood still, like a guard who took his duty very seriously.

Piper dashed for the outhouse, used it, and hurried out again, holding her breath.

Sawyer remained where he was, looking around, listening.

"What is it?" she demanded, whispering because that seemed to fit the mood of the moment. There was something clandestine about his bearing, and he was so keenly alert she could feel it.

"Nothing," he said, taking her elbow and hustling her around front at such a pace that she nearly stumbled once or twice.

"I don't believe you," Piper said.

He steered her back inside the schoolhouse, shut the door and lowered the latch. "Go to bed," he told her. "I'll be staying up for a while."

"Why?"

Sawyer turned his gaze to her at last, and she saw a worried smile lurking in his blue eyes. "Would you rather I came with you?" he asked.

She reddened. "Well, no, but—"

"Then go," he broke in, distracted. "I'll put out the lanterns and bank the fire in a little while."

Piper opened her mouth, closed it again. Huffed out a sigh of frustrated curiosity.

"Go," Sawyer repeated.

She went, but only after filling a basin with warm water and carrying it into the bedroom with her.

There, she undressed quickly, gave herself a cursory sponge bath, over in moments, and pulled on her nightgown. She hesitated, debating, then got into the spare bed, where she'd slept the night before.

After a while, the lanterns went out, and she expected Sawyer to join her, but he didn't.

She waited, and then waited some more.

Still no Sawyer. Wasn't he coming to bed? *His* bed, that is? It was getting late, and he'd extinguished the lanterns, though she hadn't heard the stove door open and then clang shut, so he hadn't banked the fire.

She got up, finally, and crept to the doorway, peering into the gloom of the schoolroom, faintly tinged with moonlight. Once her eyes had adjusted, she could make Sawyer out. He was next to the front window, but not in front of it, as unmoving as the eternal hills.

Piper saw the gun then—he was holding it in his upraised hand, at the ready.

She stifled a gasp.

"Go back to bed, Piper," he said quietly. Until then, she'd thought he hadn't known she was there.

"I want to know what's happening," she insisted.

"Go to bed," Sawyer repeated.

Piper bristled—he had no business giving her orders, being her husband in name only—but she did as he said.

Wriggling down between the covers, she fumed, but she was afraid, too. Something was definitely wrong.

She closed her eyes, not expecting to sleep, and was immediately swallowed up by a shallow, uneasy slumber.

It was just a feeling, nothing Sawyer could really put a finger on, but over the years, he'd learned to pay attention to the subtler signs. Ever since supper, the fine hairs on his nape had been raised, and there was a familiar sensation, like the touch of an icy fingertip, dead center in the pit of his stomach.

Hell of a wedding night, he thought wryly. First checkers, and now a vigil alongside a darkened window.

He could see part of the school yard from where he stood, being careful not to make a target of himself. The decorated Christmas tree seemed to whisper and sparkle when it captured a stray beam of moonlight, and the desks and stove were nothing but shadows.

Something moved, over by the rope swing dangling from a branch of the oak tree.

A stray dog, probably, or a coyote.

Perspiration tickled his upper lip and his palm felt damp where he gripped the butt of his .45. The wound in his left shoulder throbbed with every heartbeat.

Maybe he was loco—after all, he'd married a woman he'd known for two days, and he'd been delirious part of the time, when he wasn't cotton-headed from the laudanum.

Wasn't that proof that he'd lost his mind?

He swallowed the raspy chuckle that rose to the back of his throat, eased his finger back from the trigger a little. And every instinct urged caution.

There it was again—something moving, more shadow than substance, at least at first. As he watched, holding his breath, silently willing Piper to stay asleep and not come wandering out here to hector him with questions, the shadow took on the shape of a man.

And Sawyer recognized the stance, the way the rifle rested across one forearm with an ease that bespoke long experience.

He'd worked with Chester Duggins, several jobs back, but he hadn't seen him in years, hadn't thought of him, either. If asked, Sawyer would have said Chester was six feet under by now, in some bare-ground-and-thistle cemetery, long forgotten.

"I know you're in there, McKettrick," Duggins called. His voice was quiet, just barely audible, but it carried far enough. "Come on out here, and let's get this over with, so I can collect my money."

Sawyer glanced in the direction of the bedroom, prayed that Piper would stay put. She wouldn't, of course—when she heard the inevitable gunshots, she'd come running. And if Sawyer didn't happen to be the one still standing, Duggins would shoot her, too.

He drew a deep breath, let it out slowly, and moved to the door.

He raised the latch bar, turned the knob as quietly as he could.

Stepped onto the porch, the .45 in his hand, with the hammer drawn back.

"Duggins," he said companionably. "I thought you were dead."

Duggins chuckled in the darkness. He was just a form, with a hat and a rifle, and Sawyer hoped to God that he himself was no more than that to the other man. "Near to it, once or twice," the gunman replied. He hawked and spat. "I thought I'd finished you the other night," he went on, "but darned if I didn't hear otherwise, over at the Bitter Gulch Saloon. I was laying low over there, waiting out the blizzard, and one of the gals hid me in her room. She told me you were here, living and breathing, getting cozy with the schoolmarm."

Sawyer didn't move. He knew Duggins's friendly chatter was meant to lull him, draw him farther out into the open. Knew there was no way out of this particular confrontation without killing or being killed.

And he was damned if he was going to leave Piper at

Duggins's mercy. That, if he recalled correctly, was nonex-
istent.

"I never figured you for a coward, Chester," Sawyer said
easily. They might have been dickering over the price of a
horse or a piece of land, from their tone.

Duggins stiffened, raised the rifle slightly. "I was tired of
tracking you, McKettrick. Plumb worn to a nubbin. Why, I
barely managed to get to this burg before your train came in
as it was, and then there was all that snow. Vandenburg had
been on me for a good week before that, like stink on a ma-
nure pile, wanting you dead." He paused, spat again. "If your
death don't turn up in newspapers all over Texas, and right
soon, I don't get paid."

Sawyer wasn't surprised to learn that Vandenburg was behind the attack; he'd figured as much. "That," he replied,
"would be a real pity."

"Now, don't be thataway!" Duggins whined. "None of this
would even be happening if you'd just left the boss man's missus be. Why, if we'd met up in any other circumstances but
these, you and me, we'd probably have had a drink together
and talked about old times."

"I still think you're a miserable, two-bit coward," Sawyer said cheerfully. He'd heard a sound behind him, in the
schoolhouse, and he knew he was almost out of time. Piper
was awake, and she'd walk right into this in another few seconds. His tone was easy as he went on. "You bushwhacked
me, Chester. In a snowstorm. And you did it that way because you knew you wouldn't have a chance in a fair fight."
He stepped down off the porch and moved slowly to one side,
so if Duggins fired at him and missed, the bullet wouldn't go
right through the schoolhouse door—and Piper's heart.

"I done told you I was fed up with trying to run you to

ground," Duggins complained. "Now, you stand still, and we'll have this out."

"I've already drawn," Sawyer told the other man calmly. "Even if you hit me, which you might not, given how dark it is, I'll still get off at least one shot—more likely, two or three. And you know I'll make them count. So why don't you just lay that rifle down on the ground and step away from it with your hands up, before somebody gets hurt?"

Duggins gave a low, rough bark of laughter, like he was fixing to spit again. "Hell," he said. "You're just trying to talk your way out of this. And you're wasting my time and your breath, because I mean to kill you proper this time."

The whole world seemed to slow down then. Sawyer saw Duggins swing the rifle barrel in his direction, and he'd begun to pull the trigger back on the .45, but before either of them managed to fire, the night ripped apart, rent by a crimson flash of gunpowder and a boom so loud that it rattled the schoolhouse windows.

Duggins folded to the ground, with the gruesome grace of a dancer dying in midpirouette. His rifle struck the ground and went off, the bullet making a *whing* sound as it tore away a chunk of the schoolhouse roof.

Sawyer gaped, stunned, his .45 still unfired in his hand, as Bess Turner stepped out of the darkness and into a thin spill of moonlight, lowering a shotgun, both barrels still smoking, and prodding at Duggins's unmoving form with one foot.

"Reckon he's dead?" she asked calmly.

Sawyer approached, crouched to get a better look. She'd blown the back of Duggins's head off. "Reckon so," he replied.

"Good," said Bess Turner, with a sigh of resignation.

Meanwhile, Piper flew toward them on a run, her feet bare, her hair loose. "What—?" she began, but her words fell away when she looked down and saw old Chester lying there.

Sawyer wanted to send her back inside, but she wouldn't go and he knew it, so he saved himself the aggravation and stood, wrapping his good arm around her, holding her against his side.

"Varmint," Bess said, and gave the body another poke with her toe, harder this time. The woman's yellow hair was down, and she seemed to be wearing some kind of silky going-to-bed getup, though Sawyer couldn't be sure because the moon had slipped behind a cloud and the stars weren't shining all that brightly.

"Let's go inside," Sawyer said. "Half the town will be here in the next few minutes."

Bess nodded and favored Piper with a thin smile. "You all right, Teacher? This varmint here, he didn't hurt you none?"

"Er—no—I'm—" Piper choked on whatever it was she'd meant to say after that, and fell silent.

Sawyer steered both women toward the gaping door of the schoolhouse. The puny light of a single lantern spilled through it, a kind of faltering welcome, it seemed to him.

Inside, Piper rallied a little, lit several more lamps, and got busy making a pot of tea.

Bess leaned her shotgun against the wall, near the door, and sat down on top of one of the smaller desks, looking as though the events of the past few minutes might be catching up with her at last.

Sawyer took a blanket from Piper's bed, went outside, and draped it over the dead man. It wasn't much—just a gesture, really—but he couldn't leave the damn fool uncovered, staring blindly up at the night sky.

As he'd expected, folks had heard the shots, and some of them were already gathering at the top of the schoolhouse road, a cluster of moving lantern light and muffled noise.

Sawyer sighed and went back inside, where he found Piper

still fussing with tea and Bess Turner still sitting on that desk, her gaze fixed on something far away.

"What brought you here tonight?" he asked Bess, very quietly.

Piper paused in her tea-brewing to turn around. Her hair fell around her shoulders, a waterfall of dark curls, and she wore a flannel nightgown. There was mud on her feet, though she didn't seem to care.

"That feller yonder," Bess said, with a toss of her head toward the front of the schoolhouse. "He got one of my girls to hide him, the night of the big snowstorm. She didn't know it was him that shot you—didn't even know it had happened, there at the first—but then, well, these things get around—and Sally Mae, she finally figured out why that galoot was hiding out. She was scared to tell for a while—guess he must have threatened her—but tonight when he got his rifle and lit out on foot, she came and told me. I got my shotgun and followed him, but I was sure wishing Clay McKettrick didn't live way the heck and gone out in the country." Bess paused to draw a shaky breath. "I was here, when that feller called you out, but I wasn't sure what to do. I reckoned if I yelled at him to put the rifle down, he'd probably turn right around and kill me where I stood, so when I saw that he meant to gun you down for sure, I shot him."

Piper's mouth was open. Out of the corner of his eye, Sawyer saw her close it, very slowly.

"You think they'll put me in jail?" Bess fretted, looking over one shoulder as the voices drew nearer. "My Ginny-Sue can't do without a mama—"

"No," Sawyer said. "Nobody's going to put you in jail."

Piper moved to Bess's side, without a word, and slipped an arm around her shoulders.

A vigorous pounding sounded at the door.

Exclamations were raised when somebody evidently stumbled over the blanket-covered body in the school yard.

"Hold your horses," Sawyer said, crossing to open the door.

Doc Howard spilled into the room, closely followed by several other men.

"Great Scot," Howard nearly shouted, "there's a dead man out there!"

"Yep," Sawyer said.

Attention shifted to Bess, and to Piper, standing stalwartly beside her, chin raised.

Sawyer would forever remember that that was when he realized he was in love with Piper St. James McKettrick, though he supposed it would be a while before he got around to saying so.

"What happened?" Doc demanded.

Sawyer explained, and Piper's eyes seemed to widen with every word he said.

"He's the one that shot you?" Doc said, with a shake of his head. Sawyer had already told them as much, but these were peaceable men, and they had trouble taking it in.

"Well, where the devil are we going to put him?" another man asked. "We don't have an undertaker here in Blue River."

"The jailhouse will have to do, for the time being," Sawyer said.

"Better get him buried first thing tomorrow," Doc put in. "Can't have Christmas spoiled. Do we have to report this to somebody?"

Sawyer nodded. Since he hadn't been sworn in yet, Clay was the logical choice, and he said so. A certificate would have to be drawn up, signed by Judge Reynolds and probably Doc Howard, too.

One of the men agreed to ride out to Clay's place and tell him what had happened.

Sawyer would have preferred to make the visit himself, but

he didn't have his horse and, improved though his condition was, he wasn't sure he could make it all that way, anyhow. All this activity had riled up the wound in his shoulder, and it was raising three kinds of hell. Besides, he couldn't leave Piper alone, especially after all that had happened.

When the men went back outside, Sawyer went with them.

Somebody ran to the livery stable, hitched up a buckboard and drove it back to the schoolhouse, and Chester Duggins's mortal remains were hoisted into the back and hauled away.

Doc agreed to make sure Bess Turner got back to the Bitter Gulch Saloon all right, though he seemed nervous about it. Little wonder, Sawyer concluded—that wife of his would kick up some dust if she caught wind of the courtesy.

Inside the schoolhouse, Bess and Piper were sitting there in their nightclothes, calmly sipping tea like two spinsters at a garden club meeting.

The sight touched Sawyer—he thought of how differently this night could have ended. What if Duggins had been startled, and swung that rifle in Piper's direction when she came running out of the schoolhouse door? He might have panicked, pulled the trigger, and killed her.

A headache pounded between Sawyer's temples, and his stomach did a slow, backward roll.

"Let's get you on home now," Doc said to Bess, blinking at the way she was dressed. Evidently, he hadn't noticed until then.

She set aside her cup, smiled graciously, and stood up. "I'll just fetch my shotgun," she said, turning to Piper. "Thank you very kindly for the tea, Miss St. James. I do appreciate your hospitality."

"You're—you're sure you're not hurt?" Piper asked the other woman.

Bess nodded again, looked briefly at Sawyer. "I'm sure," she told Piper.

Doc had averted his gaze to Piper, but it immediately bounced away again, landing square on Sawyer's face. "I'll stop by in the morning," the dentist said. "Have another look at that shoulder. You in any pain right now?"

"No," Sawyer lied. He wanted to be alone with Piper, that was all, and reflect on the glorious fact that they were both still alive.

Doc looked skeptical, but he escorted Bess and her shotgun out into the night, resigned to walking her home.

Sawyer latched the door behind them, turned, leaning against it, and closed his eyes for a moment, willing himself to stay upright.

"Sawyer?" Piper said, very softly. "You look terrible. I'm going to call Doc Howard back."

But Sawyer shook his head. "I'm just—tired."

She slipped an arm around Sawyer, as if to hold him up, which might have been laughable, given her small stature, if the act itself hadn't eased so many things rioting inside him.

"I'm going to require a lot of answers in the morning," she warned, as they made their slow but steady way across the schoolroom.

Sawyer chuckled at that. "And I'll give them to you," he promised. "In the morning."

Sawyer landed heavily on the bed, and barely objected when Piper pulled his boots off his feet and covered him, fully dressed, with the quilts she'd once prized so greatly. She smoothed his hair back from his forehead and bent to kiss his eyelids, first one, and then the other.

He fell asleep so quickly that she worried he'd lost consciousness again, but his breathing was steady and deep, and when she laid her head against his chest, she heard his heart beating with a rhythmic *thud-thud-thud*.

She left him just long enough to put out the lanterns still burning in the schoolroom and bank the fire for the night. He'd set his pistol on one of the desks when he came in earlier, after the shooting, and she picked it up carefully, carried it into the bedroom, and set it on the night table.

For a long time, she sat on the side of the bed, watching him sleep, periodically checking his bandages to make sure he hadn't reopened the wound in his shoulder, but there was no bleeding.

The little room grew colder, and then colder still, and Piper knew she ought to get some sleep herself, but she found she couldn't leave Sawyer, even for the other bed, near as it was.

Finally, shivering, she crawled in beside him, on his right side, snuggling up close for warmth, resting one hand on his strong chest. Again, she felt the thump of his heart against her palm, matched her breathing with his.

And after a while, lulled, she drifted off into sleep, a sound one this time.

The next thing she knew, morning light flooded the room.

Remembering the events of her wedding night, Piper sat bolt upright.

She'd thought Sawyer was still asleep, but she knew by the slow curve of his lips and the way he eased an arm around her that he was very much awake.

"Good morning, Mrs. McKettrick," he said.

"Who was that man and why did he want to kill you?" Piper replied.

Sawyer chuckled and opened his eyes. His chin was stubbly with gold. "I can't say you didn't warn me you'd have questions," he said, "but I *did* expect we'd both be dressed at the time."

Piper clutched at the quilts, drew them up to her chin in a belated effort at modesty, but did not relent. "Tell me," she said.

Sawyer sighed. "His name was Chester Duggins," he said. "He and I worked together once."

"Why did he want to kill you?" Piper reiterated.

"He was sent by a man named Henry Vandenburg—my former employer." He paused, sighed again, but, to his credit, he held her gaze. "Vandenburg believes—mistakenly, as it happens—that I'd enjoyed a dalliance with his wife."

"Josie," Piper breathed, troubled. She couldn't help recalling the way Sawyer had said the other woman's name, like a plea, in the hours after he was hurt.

"Josie," Sawyer confirmed.

"You cared about her," Piper said.

"I was beginning to," Sawyer replied. "That's why I decided to accept Clay's invitation and come to Blue River."

The admission caused Piper a distinct pang, but she found comfort in one thing: Sawyer was telling her the blunt, unembroidered truth. "Do you still care for Josie?" she asked bravely. "Because, if you do, we can have our marriage annulled. Since we haven't—consummated it yet."

He reached up, stroked the line of her cheek very gently with the back of his right hand. "Is that what you want?" he asked quietly. "An annulment?"

Piper considered that. "I don't know," she said, when a few moments had passed. Then, primly, she added, "Answer my original question, please."

Sawyer grinned, like a choirboy caught being wicked. "I do not hold any tender feelings for Josie," he replied.

"But you were *beginning* to—"

He sighed again. As he lowered his hand from her cheek, it brushed briefly over her flannel-covered breast, causing the nipple to turn button-hard and bringing a flush to her cheeks. "There have been other women in my life, Piper," he said. "I don't deny that. But you're the only one I've ever married."

She blinked. Was that supposed to be reassuring? *Was* it reassuring?

"How do I know—?" she began.

He laughed. "'*What if*?" he teased.

"Are there other jealous husbands out there who want to have you killed?" Piper persisted.

"A few rejected suitors, maybe," Sawyer conceded. "But no husbands, at least as far as I know."

"That isn't funny," Piper objected, flustered.

"If they'd wanted to call me out," he said reasonably, "they would have done it by now."

"What happens next?"

Sawyer's mischievous expression turned more serious. "I get well, and then I deal with Vandenburg," he said.

"Let Clay do that," Piper said quickly, though she knew even as she spoke that it was a futile request.

"It's not Clay's responsibility," he answered, regretful but earnest. "It's mine."

"No," Piper argued, in the face of certain defeat. "It isn't. This is why there are laws, Sawyer, and men sworn to enforce them—"

"This is my problem," Sawyer said, "and I'll be the one to set it right."

Piper was almost breathless with panic. She'd thought this waking nightmare was over, now that Duggins was dead, but it clearly wasn't. "By doing what?"

"Never mind that," Sawyer told her, drawing her down beside him, holding her close. She resisted at first, but he felt so warm and strong and solid, and she lost herself in that.

They lay together for a long while, both of them engulfed in a kind of sad silence, thinking their own thoughts.

Chapter Eight

Clay showed up at the schoolhouse soon after the morning fire was built up and the coffee was brewing on the stove, aghast at the news of last night's shooting. Piper and Sawyer were both fully clothed when he finally arrived, she in another inadequate calico, he in trousers and a shirt from his travel trunk.

Having ridden to town on his own gelding, Sawyer's horse, Cherokee, trotting alongside on a lead rope, the erstwhile marshal of Blue River, Texas, left both animals standing in the muddy yard, among ragged patches of dirty snow. A vivid blotch of red remained on the ground where Mr. Duggins had been felled by Bess Turner, making Piper wish for more snow to cover it up.

Sawyer's cousin barely paused to knock, bursting through the front door before Piper could call out a "Come in."

"I'm sorry I couldn't get here before now," Clay announced, passing right on over "good-morning" or even just a "howdy" in his hurry to get Sawyer's report on the events just past. His gaze moved over both of them, probably in search of fresh injury. "It was late when Pete brought word of what happened, and I was tending a sick calf—"

Sawyer, standing near the stove, interrupted with a chuckle. "You might want to hire Bess Turner as marshal, instead of me," he said. "She's mighty good with a shotgun." With that, he poured coffee into a mug and extended it to Clay, who accepted it gratefully.

Piper, wearing an apron to protect her dress, blurted, "Sawyer's got his mind set on going after the man who hired that killer."

"Hold on, now," Clay said, lowering the coffee to look from one of them to the other in plain consternation. "We're getting ahead of ourselves, here. Tell me what happened, and don't leave anything out."

Sawyer, after slicing a mildly reproving glance at Piper, gave a brief but complete account of all that had happened the previous night.

When he'd heard the whole story, Clay gave a long, low whistle of exclamation, and took a thirsty sip from his coffee mug before saying, "*Damn.* And here it is, almost Christmas."

Piper wasn't sure what the approach of the holiday had to do with anything, but she wasn't clearheaded enough to pursue the matter at the moment.

Sawyer stood calmly, his own coffee in hand, the mug raised almost to his mouth but not quite there. "It was an eventful day," he said. "Piper and I got married."

Clay fairly choked on a mouthful of coffee, but he was grinning when he caught his breath. *"What?"* he said.

"I believe you heard me the first time," Sawyer replied. "Given what my staying here has done to the lady's reputation, there didn't seem to be any other course of action."

Clay peered at Piper, who blushed. "You agreed to this?"

Glumly, twisting her wedding band round and round with the fingers of her right hand, Piper nodded. "Yes," she murmured.

Clay gave a burst of delighted laughter but just as quickly sobered again, his expression turning watchful and wary. "Is this marriage real, or just some kind of ruse to keep the townspeople from gossiping for the rest of the school term?"

There was no need to say that Piper wouldn't be teaching at Blue River again in the fall. For all the good it seemed to be doing her, she *was* married. The school board would probably hire a man to replace her, if they could find one. Failing that, they'd settle for a single woman but, either way, she was as good as out.

"It's real," Sawyer said.

"Sort of," Piper clarified.

"Which is it?" Clay asked, somewhat impatiently, once again looking from one of them to the other. "Real, or 'sort of' real?"

Piper couldn't have answered to save her life. Her throat had closed off and her face felt like it was on fire.

"My wife," Sawyer explained, "is probably referring to the fact that we've yet to consummate the marriage."

Piper's blush deepened. How could the man speak so casually of something so intimately personal? She wanted to throttle him, then and there.

"Oh," said Clay, blushing a little himself. "Well, anyhow, congratulations. Of course Dara Rose will have a thing or two to say about missing out on the wedding, but she'll be pleased, too."

All of them were quiet for a while.

Piper, desperate for something to do, proceeded to walk over and ring the schoolhouse bell, pulling vigorously on the rope, though she knew no one would come to class that day despite the fact that the weather had turned and the trails, if muddy, were passable. There had, after all, been a death, right out there in the front yard, and while the danger was past, folks would probably need a day or two to get used to the idea before they sent their children back.

Clay and Sawyer talked quietly all the while, though the bell drowned them out, which was fine with Piper.

"You brought Cherokee," Sawyer said to Clay, after the last peal died away. He was standing at the front window then, looking out, and there was no mistaking the relief in his voice. This only underscored Piper's fears—Sawyer would be leaving Blue River, and her, soon.

"I was thinking you might be ready to come out to the ranch with me," Clay admitted to Sawyer, looking a little sheepish when Piper caught his eye. "That was before I knew about the wedding, you understand."

Sawyer smiled. "I'll be staying here until after the Christmas program," he said. "Then, if it's feasible, Piper and I will both head out to your place."

Clay nodded, but he still seemed befuddled. "Shall I take the horse back with me, then?" he asked.

But Sawyer shook his head, turning again to admire the magnificent animal through the grubby glass in the window. "I can't ride much, but I ought to be able to handle a few minutes in the saddle, now and then, just so I don't forget how."

Clay smiled at that, but when he looked Piper's way again, she saw concern in his handsome face. "Well, then," he said, just a little too heartily, "I guess it's a good thing I brought that hay and grain in the other day, on the sledge. One question, though, cousin—how are you going to manage that saddle with only one usable arm?"

"I'll find a way," Sawyer said, without a trace of doubt.

Clay finished his coffee, set his cup down alongside the

basin, on the small table near the stove. "You say this Duggins yahoo's carcass is laid out over at the jailhouse?"

Sawyer nodded. "Doc Howard wants him buried right away," he said dryly. "Figures a funeral might put a damper on Christmas."

Clay nodded, rubbing his chin. Unlike Sawyer, he'd shaved recently, and there was no visible stubble. "That wouldn't do," he murmured thoughtfully. "Wouldn't do at all." He crossed to the door, took his hat from the peg where he'd hung it up coming in. "I'll send a wire to the federal marshal in Austin," he said. "Just a formality, really." He paused, cleared his throat. "Of course I'll be mentioning Henry Vandenburg's part in this."

Piper saw a muscle bunch in Sawyer's jaw, even under his thickening beard. "Nobody can be arrested on mere hearsay, Clay. You know that."

"The federal marshal still has to be told," Clay said. Although his manner was cordial, there was steel in his tone. "What he does with the information is his concern, not ours."

"I want to handle this," Sawyer said, glaring at his cousin.

"Fine," Clay retorted, on his way out. "If there's anything left to *handle* by the time you're fit to travel, you just have at it with my blessing. In the meantime, I'm still marshal and I'll do what needs doing."

Sawyer started to argue, Piper saw, but he ended up giving an exasperated sigh and shoving the splayed fingers of his good hand through his hair in frustration. "All right, then," he said, "but I'm going to the jailhouse with you."

Evidently, Clay was willing to concede that much, if nothing more. "You say Bess Turner shot this fella?" he asked, refraining from helping as his cousin struggled halfway into his coat. Sawyer had a harder time buckling on his gun belt but, somehow, he managed it, and slipped the .45 deftly into the holster.

Chilled, and not by the weather, Piper hurried to the window when the men went outside, watched as Sawyer put a foot in the stirrup of Cherokee's saddle, gripped the horn, and hauled himself up onto the horse's back. She saw him clench his jaw again, once he was in place, and close his eyes briefly, but other than that, he seemed steady.

Clay and Sawyer were gone upward of an hour, during which time Piper hoped in vain for a pupil or two to wander in, hungry for learning. Because she believed with her whole heart and mind that idle hands were the devil's workshop, she polished all the desks, swept the floors, made up the two beds and fussed with the straggly Christmas tree, with its burden of unassuming decorations.

When the men returned, Doc Howard was with them, on his mule. All three of them looked grimly introspective, and little wonder.

A man was dead.

In the school yard, Sawyer dismounted on his own, but he leaned against Cherokee's side for an extra second or so before stepping back and surrendering the reins to Clay, who led the animal around back to the shed.

Doc walked up to the patch of bloody ground and scuffed at it with one foot, as though to kick dirt over the place where death had left its distinctive mark. He conferred with Sawyer for a few moments, then followed Clay to the shed, returning with a rusted shovel in one hand.

While Sawyer watched, his feet planted a little wider apart than usual as if in an effort to maintain his balance, Doc used the shovel to turn up enough ground to hide the blood spot.

Piper stepped back from the window just as Sawyer turned and started for the door. She tried to look surprised when he came inside, closely followed by Doc, but she knew by Sawyer's wry expression that she hadn't fooled him. He'd never glanced in her direction even once, but he'd known she was at the window, watching, just the same.

"I made more coffee," she said, noting the pallor in Sawyer's face.

He merely nodded, and went on into the bedroom. She heard the bedsprings creak as he lay down.

"He might have overdone things a little," Doc remarked quietly, taking off his hat and coat and hanging them both in the cloakroom.

Piper didn't comment on the understatement. "Coffee?" she said instead.

Doc nodded. "Please," he said, looking around for a place to sit down. He was a sturdy man, so none of the students' desks would have held him.

Piper pointed to the chair behind her desk, and he took it gratefully. "I'm a dentist," he said, as though to remind himself and the world at large of his true calling.

She poured his coffee and took it to him, with a slight, sympathetic smile, barely resisting the temptation to pat his shoulder reassuringly and say, "There, there."

Clay came in, having tended to Sawyer's horse, and looked around for his cousin.

"Sawyer's resting," Piper said. "Coffee?"

"Got any whiskey?" Clay asked.

"Sorry," Piper replied, with a little shake of her head.

Clay sighed and said, "I'll take the coffee, then, please."

While Piper poured the brew, he went into the bedroom, stayed a few moments, and came back with the rocking chair. He offered it to Piper and, when she refused with a shake of her head, sank into it with an exhalation of breath.

Piper gave him the mug. "Did you send that wire?" she

asked Clay, keeping her voice down even though she was fairly sure Sawyer wouldn't overhear her anyway. "To the federal marshal in Austin, I mean?"

"Yes," Clay said, after taking a sip of his coffee. "And I told him Duggins claimed he'd been hired by a fellow named Vandenburg."

"Well, then," Piper said, unable to hide her relief, "no doubt someone will investigate." And, thus, she deduced, Sawyer would not go riding off, the moment he was physically able, to confront the man who'd wanted him dead.

Clay pondered that for a while, then said ruefully, "Sawyer was right. It's mainly hearsay. The marshal might question Vandenburg, but unless he admits to hiring Duggins, the man's not likely to be arrested."

Piper felt something curl up tight in the bottom of her stomach. How did Dara Rose bear it, being married to a lawman? Was she afraid for Clay every time he pinned on his badge, strapped on a gun belt, and left home to do his job?

"Then *Sawyer* won't be able to get him to admit anything, either," she reasoned, her tone bordering on pettish, though what she really felt was fear.

"Vandenburg hired a killer," Clay reminded her flatly, "and Sawyer was shot. Something has to be done, Piper."

"Maybe Mr. Duggins committed the crime all on his own," Piper argued, more than a little frantic now. "He was a *criminal*. It could be that Mr. Vandenburg knew nothing about the plan."

"Yes," Clay said dryly, "and St. Nicholas might join us for Christmas Eve supper at the ranch. Men like Duggins don't act on their own, Piper. They take orders from somebody else."

Doc Howard cleared his throat just then, reminding both Clay and Piper of his presence. It was strange how such a large personage could take up so little thought-space that he went unnoticed.

Piper glowered at Clay and then at Doc, for good measure, and marched into the bedroom to check on Sawyer.

He lay sprawled atop the covers, with his muddy boots on the bed, further staining the already ruined quilt, but Piper's ire ebbed like an outgoing tide at the sight of him.

She approached Sawyer's bedside, smoothed his hair back from his forehead, and smiled a little. The future was full of uncertainty, but, for this moment at least, he was alive and safe, where she could see him, touch him.

She loved Sawyer McKettrick, she realized. What else could this feeling of sweet desolation mean?

Sawyer didn't open his eyes, but he took her hand in his, gave her fingers a brief squeeze, as if he'd read her mind.

Tears brimmed along her lower lashes as she bent and placed the lightest of kisses on his forehead. *I love you,* she told him silently, and then slipped out of the room because Doc had come in again, his sleeves rolled up and his hands still wet from washing, a basin of clean water in his hands and a roll of bandage cloth under one elbow.

Clay was still in the rocking chair when she returned, looking at the Christmas tree, and he stood up quickly when he realized she was there.

"Sit down, Clay," she said quietly.

But Clay shook his head. "I'd best be heading for home, anyway," he said. "There's not much I can do here, and Dara Rose will be watching the road for me."

Piper nodded, thick-throated again. One of these days, she reckoned, she might be "watching the road," too—for Sawyer. Only, unlike Clay, he might never come back to her.

She brought herself up short. She wasn't a real wife to Sawyer, after all, and the schoolhouse wasn't their home. When he was well enough, her "husband" would go his way, and she would go hers.

Clay had read her expression before she realized he was looking at her, guessing her thoughts, and he laid a brotherly hand to one side of her face.

"Give Sawyer a little time," he said. "He'll get things straight in his head pretty soon."

"He's leaving," she said, not meaning to but unable to hold back the certainty that it was so.

"I reckon if Sawyer goes anywhere, he means to take you right along with him," Clay replied, very quietly. "I know you have your doubts, Piper, but Sawyer didn't marry you just to save your reputation. He's a fine man, but he's no martyr, and he could have handled this situation a dozen different ways without standing up with you in front of a preacher."

"Name one," Piper challenged, too proud to cry but wanting to, wanting to very, very much.

Clay chuckled. "Well, he could have sent you to Dara Rose and me, for one thing. There would have been a scandal, sure, but once folks had a chance to jaw about the particulars for a while, they'd have gone on to something else, and you'd be right back here in this schoolhouse, like nothing ever happened. For one thing, teachers aren't that easy to come by, way out here. The pay's pitiful, and it's a hard, lonely life."

Piper gave a small, strangled laugh. "How comforting," she said. "What was I worried about, when I have a 'pitiful' stipend and a hard, lonely life to look forward to?"

Clay grinned, shook his head. "I've never been good with words," he allowed. "What I'm trying to say is that everything will be all right in the end."

"I can't imagine what makes you so sure of that," Piper observed.

"Just the same," Clay countered good-naturedly, "I *am* sure. Besides, it's almost Christmas. Have a little faith, will you?"

Have a little faith, will you?

Clay's offhand injunction played in Piper's mind long after Doc and Clay had both left the schoolhouse.

Easy enough for him to say, she concluded, as she built up the fire and rummaged through the food box in the cloakroom for the makings of a simple meal.

Upon awakening, Sawyer still looked like hell-warmed-over, but he insisted on joining her in the schoolroom for supper. She gave him the desk chair again, and refrained from conversation since he looked a mite grumpy. His fresh bandages were bulky under his sling, and perhaps a little too tight.

"Clay's gone home?" he asked, finally.

Piper refrained from pointing out the obvious. "Yes," she said mildly. "He fed and watered Cherokee before he left, and brushed him down, too."

Sawyer nodded, thanked her when she put a plate in front of him, containing scrambled eggs, some fried ham, and two thick slices of bread toasted on top of the stove. Ate slowly and awkwardly, and with a dignity that pinched Piper's heart.

"In a few days, it will be Christmas," she said, finding the silence unbearable.

"Yes," Sawyer said dully. She knew without asking what was bothering him, or part of it, at least. The aftermath of a death was always sobering, and on top of that, he'd found riding a horse, something he'd probably done almost every day of his life, with unthinking ease, to be suddenly difficult.

"I wonder how Bess is holding up," Piper said. She'd nibbled on some toasted bread earlier, while cooking, but she really wasn't very hungry, so she hadn't filled a plate for herself.

"To hear Doc tell it," Sawyer answered, his eyes bleak,

"she's got other concerns. Her little girl's come down with something."

"Ginny-Sue is sick?" Piper asked, immediately concerned.

Sawyer nodded. "Doc wanted to go and see her, but his wife put her foot down. Said she'd leave him, and take their daughter with her, if he showed his face in a brothel, no matter what the reason."

Piper thought of Ginny-Sue's beaming delight over memorizing the second chapter of Luke, her parting assurance that Christmas would happen for certain now, with the big snowstorm over.

And she put one trembling hand to her mouth.

Sawyer, seeing her face, looked regretful. "Doc said it was probably nothing serious," he said. "Sure, Bess is worried, but you know how mothers are."

Piper was already on her feet, hurrying into the cloakroom, taking the lovely russet cape from its hook and swinging it around her shoulders. She was raising the hood to keep the wind from stinging her ears as she emerged into the schoolroom.

Sawyer was standing by then. "Hold on a second," he said, frowning. "Where are you going? It's dark out, Piper, and it's cold."

"Drat that Eloise Howard," Piper muttered, and that had to suffice for an answer. "I'll be back as soon as I can."

With that, she left the schoolhouse.

It *was* dark, and the wind was brisk, but her cape protected her.

As she crossed the yard, Sawyer called to her from the doorway of the school. "Piper, wait! I'll come with you—"

She turned, still walking, but backward. "You'll be nothing but a hindrance," she called in response. "Stay here, please."

"Piper!" Sawyer yelled, when she turned her back on him again and marched onward.

Thinking only of Ginny-Sue, Piper picked up her pace.

Passing the churchyard, she saw the new grave, where Mr. Duggins had been laid to rest, God forgive him. She wondered if he'd had family somewhere, parents or a wife and children, say, and if anybody would shed tears of sorrow when word of his passing reached them.

On the main street of town, the businesses and shops were all closed up and dark. Except, of course, for the Bitter Gulch Saloon, which seemed to be doing a rousing trade, as usual.

Piper stopped on the plank sidewalk, eyeing the swinging doors with trepidation. Light spilled over and under them, like some smoky liquid, and the tinny clinkity-clink of an out-of-tune piano, badly played, tinkled in the cold air.

Deciding, after much personal deliberation, that she wasn't quite bold enough to walk through those rickety doors into the sawdust heart of a saloon, Piper bustled around back, moving between the buildings, and approached the much less daunting rear entrance.

Standing on a small porch with her chin high and her shoulders squared, she knocked purposefully.

A rotund black woman answered, wide-eyed at the sight of Piper. She laid one hand to her substantial bosom and sucked in a shocked breath. "Lord, have mercy," she said. "It's the schoolmarm!"

Piper drew a deep breath. "Let me in, please," she said. She'd seen the woman once or twice, over at the mercantile, but they'd never exchanged more than a few words. "I've come to look in on Ginny-Sue."

"But, ma'am," the woman argued, "this here's a *bawdy* house!"

As if she hadn't known. Piper looked over one shoulder,

half expecting to see Sawyer in pursuit, but he hadn't caught up to her yet. She met the cook's horrified gaze again and whispered, "Hurry. There's no time to lose."

The woman stepped back, admitting Piper to a large and amazingly ordinary kitchen, well-equipped, with a big cast-iron cookstove, bins for sugar and flour, a table surrounded by matching chairs, and a cabinet filled with lovely china. There was even a sink.

"You really shouldn't be here," insisted Bess Turner's cook, in an anxious whisper. "Anybody sees you, there'll be hell to pay!"

Piper put out a hand and introduced herself as Mrs. McKettrick, rather than Miss St. James. It was a small indulgence, she thought. No harm in pretending for a little while.

"Cleopatra Brown," the cook responded. Her eyes looked enormous in her round ebony face. "You wait here, and I'll fetch Miss Bess."

Piper had spotted the rear stairway by then, and she wanted to climb it, open doors until she found Ginny-Sue, see the child for herself. If Ginny-Sue was seriously ill, she meant to get Doc Howard by the collar and *drag* him over here, and to the devil with any objections *Mrs.* Howard might raise.

She paced while Cleopatra was out of the room, went once or twice to peek through the misted-over window in the back door, in case Sawyer had tracked her this far.

Of course, he, being a man, would probably enter by the *front* way.

The rush of annoyance at the idea sustained Piper in the face of her already waning courage.

After a few minutes—very *long* minutes—Bess descended the rear stairway, be-feathered and bejeweled, with her face painted like a garish mask. Cleopatra hovered close behind.

"You shouldn't have come," Bess fretted, pausing halfway

down, but there was a spark of something that might have been hope in her jaded eyes.

"Nevertheless, I have," Piper replied briskly. "I must know about Ginny-Sue. How is she?"

"She's poorly," Bess admitted, coming the rest of the way down the stairs. "She's real poorly. It came on sudden-like—she was playing outside without her hat and mittens—said she'd found a cat hiding in the woodpile and she was trying to get it to come inside for some warm milk—"

Piper took both Bess's hands, found them colder than her own, even after the walk from the schoolhouse. "I'll get Doc Howard," she said.

"He won't come," Bess said, with sad certainty.

"He *will*," Piper replied, "if I have to drag him!"

Bess smiled tentatively. "If you'd just say howdy to Ginny-Sue, I'm sure that would bring her right around," she said. "She thinks you hung the moon right up there in the sky, you know."

Piper's eyes burned. "Take me to her," she said. "Please."

Bess nodded once, turned, and led the way back up the staircase to the second floor, her thin shoulders stooped and mostly bared by the scantiness of her dress. Cleopatra moved aside to let both women pass, but she didn't look at all congenial, no doubt thinking that nothing good could come of the schoolmarm's highly improper visit to the upper reaches of a brothel.

Piper might have conceded the point, if challenged, but she didn't hesitate, let alone turn back.

The upstairs hallway was lined with gilt-framed mirrors, and there was a costly runner, probably Turkish, on the floor. The air smelled of talcum powder, stale sweat, and quiet depravity.

To know that little Ginny-Sue was growing up in this place

was almost more than Piper could endure. Given her druthers, she'd have bundled the child up in a blanket and physically carried her out of here, never to return.

Bess stopped in front of a door and rapped lightly at the framework. "Let me in, Emmie," she called out softly.

Piper heard a key turn in the lock, and the door creaked open, revealing a scrawny, bare-faced woman clad in a red silk wrapper. Emmie, presumably.

Relieved to learn that someone had been sitting with Ginny-Sue, and that there was a locked door to protect her from unwanted visitors, Piper smiled at Emmie, though only slightly.

Emmie, stepping back to admit them, widened her eyes. Piper concluded that she probably looked as exotic to the other woman as Emmie did to her.

"She's no better," Emmie said to Bess.

The inside of that room was a revelation to Piper, at complete odds with the structure that surrounded and upheld it, but at the moment she was concerned only with Ginny-Sue.

The little girl lay in a huge and elegant bed, with gilt posts and a painting of sheep and shepherdesses on the headboard. She opened her eyes, smiled a tiny smile when she saw Piper.

"I know the whole second chapter of Luke," Ginny-Sue said.

"Shhh," Piper said, smoothing back the child's hair. Her forehead was hot and dry, though the front of her finely embroidered nightgown clung damply to her small chest. "How do you feel?"

"My throat hurts," Ginny-Sue confided, and her hand fluttered up to rest there, fragile as a hatchling bird.

Piper blinked back tears. Smiled. "Maybe you've been practicing your piece too much—for the Christmas program, I mean."

Ginny-Sue smiled back, but the effort seemed to exhaust her. "Is it Christmas yet?" she asked. "Did I miss the program?"

Piper shook her head quickly. "No, sweetheart. Christmas is still a few days away."

Emmie and Bess slipped out, leaving teacher and pupil alone.

Ginny-Sue closed her eyes, but the smile lingered, faint, on her lips.

Piper looked around then, noticed the fireplace, with a lovely blaze burning on the hearth, the velvet draperies on the windows, the carpets on the floor. Paintings of flowers, delicately wrought in watercolor, graced the walls. There were easy chairs, upholstered in cheery prints, and a door opened onto a bathroom. She could see the side of a long porcelain tub. And there was electricity, at least here, if nowhere else in the Bitter Gulch Saloon.

This, then, was the haven Bess Turner had made for her child, a place apart, a world that belonged only to the two of them.

Piper turned back to Ginny-Sue, gently took her hand, and seated herself on the edge of the fancy bed.

Then she closed her eyes and she prayed.

Ginny-Sue slept on.

Cleopatra came back into the room, bringing a tray laden with tea things. "There's a man downstairs," she said solemnly. "Says you'd better come and talk to him." China rattled as she set the tray down, poured fragrant, steaming orange pekoe into a translucent cup. "What do you want me to tell him?"

"Does he have one arm in a sling?" Piper asked calmly.

"Yes, ma'am, he do," Cleopatra answered.

Sawyer, of course. "Tell him to fetch Doc, or send somebody else if he's not strong enough. Whoever goes is to say that if Mrs. Howard objects, I'll come over there myself and see to the matter personally, and she does not want that to happen."

Cleopatra's eyes widened again, and a smile rested lightly on her full mouth. "Sounds like a bluff to me," she said, but there was respect in her tone.

"Sometimes," Piper answered, "a bluff has to do."

Chapter Nine

Half an hour passed, during which Piper sipped tea, listened to the tick of the elegant clock on the mantelpiece, and watched Ginny-Sue toss and turn in her sleep.

Don't let this be diphtheria, Piper prayed, over and over again. *Please.*

She'd seen that disease too many times, in the few years she'd been teaching school. Among the symptoms were fever and a sore throat, and Ginny-Sue had both. Diphtheria was rampantly contagious, and in most instances it was fatal, as well.

Not Ginny-Sue, she pleaded silently, *or any of the others.*

When a tentative knock sounded at the door of that incongruously grand bedchamber, Piper leaped up, crossed the floor, but then hesitated to turn the shining brass key protruding from the lock, remembering that there was a saloon directly downstairs, and that ladies of the evening and their customers surely frequented the other rooms along the corridor.

"Who's there?" she asked.

"Doc and me," Sawyer answered. "Open up."

Almost breathless with relief, Piper unlocked and opened the door to see a disgruntled Doc Howard standing nervously in the hall, with Sawyer right beside him. Doc looked as though he might bolt at any moment, while *Sawyer* looked as though he'd stop him if he did.

"You came," Piper cried, barely restraining herself from throwing both arms around Doc and hugging him in a fit of gratitude.

"Of course I did," Doc replied, stepping past her and striding over to the bed. He'd brought his bag and hopefully there was something inside that would cure Ginny-Sue. "Why is it that nobody around here seems to remember that I'm a dentist?" he muttered to himself, as he leaned over the child, stethoscope in place.

Did dentists use stethoscopes? she wondered. Evidently so. Perhaps some of their patients suffered palpitations at the prospect of an extraction, or having a cavity filled.

Sawyer smiled at Piper, touched her chin. His fingers were icy-cold, and yet, somehow, he warmed her. Had he walked to Doc's place, in his condition, after following Piper to the saloon earlier? If so, he was probably coming to the end of his strength, considerable as it was.

"I'm all right," he told her quietly. It was unsettling, the way he seemed to be able to read her every expression, as if she'd been thinking aloud. "How's the little girl?"

"I don't know," Piper responded, worried again. "She's feverish, and she told me her throat was hurting."

"Doc will do everything he can," Sawyer promised. He indicated his bandaged shoulder with a motion of his head and then added, "He must be hell on a toothache, if he's this good with a bullet wound."

Piper nodded anxiously but offered no reply, since none seemed called-for.

Bess appeared, letting herself in, since Piper hadn't bothered to relock the door. With Sawyer and Doc both there, she knew Ginny-Sue would be safe.

After nodding a greeting to Sawyer, Bess hurried over to stand on the opposite side of the bed from Doc. She wrung her hands, and the expression in her eyes was an eloquent plea for good news.

Doc opened his bag, took out a packet, and held it up. "Headache powders," he said. "Stir a teaspoonful into a cup of water, and we'll see if we can't get her to take it."

Bess rounded the bed, took the packet from Doc's hand, and vanished into the bathroom. She was back in a trice with the water, and Piper handed her a spoon from the tea tray Cleopatra had brought up earlier.

The rattle of the spoon against the glass roused Ginny-Sue enough to open her eyes. They glistened, too bright, and seemed to grope and struggle from one face to the next.

"Mama?" Ginny-Sue said.

"I'm right here, baby," Bess said, moving close to the child, sliding an arm around her to help her sit up, forcing cheer into every word and motion, "you've got to drink this whole glass of water right down. Doc brought you some medicine, and it's going to make you feel a lot better, real soon."

Ginny-Sue's confusion was heartrending for Piper, and she was thankful when Sawyer put his good arm around her waist, lending her strength. Almost holding her up, in fact.

The child sipped from the glass, the bitter taste causing her to wince, and it obviously hurt her to swallow. Still, though the process was a long one, she finally emptied the glass.

"What is it?" Piper whispered to Doc, when he walked over to her and Sawyer, looking solemn and thoughtful, though he'd left his bag on the night table and was taking off his coat like a man who meant to stay rather than go. "What's wrong with Ginny-Sue?"

"If we're lucky, she's got a bad cold," Doc answered, keeping his voice low. "If we're not, on the other hand, then this is probably diphtheria, and it works fast. We ought to know by morning."

Piper reached out, took one of Doc's hands in both of hers. Sawyer stood silently beside her.

"Thank you," she said softly, because she knew Doc had made a sacrifice to come here at all.

Doc's smile was genuine, if somewhat feeble. "Don't thank me yet," he replied. "The aspirin powders will bring down the girl's fever if she's just taken a chill, but if that doesn't happen, well, then we're dealing with a much bigger problem."

"Diphtheria," Piper almost whispered.

Doc nodded. "None of us can leave here until we know for sure," he said, with a rueful shake of his head. "If this *is* diphtheria, it'll spread like a fire in dry grass."

Piper looked at Sawyer, whose expression was unreadable, and then Doc. By then, Bess had left Ginny-Sue's side to join them.

"Did you say my girl has diphtheria?" Bess asked tentatively, going pale under all that kohl and rouge and rice powder.

"I said she *might* have it," Doc said, at once stern and compassionate. "How long has Ginny-Sue been sick?" Before Bess could formulate a reply—she seemed to be juggling conflicting thoughts in her mind—he turned to Piper. "Did she come down with this at school?"

"Just since this afternoon," Bess said finally. "Cleopatra said she seemed fine at breakfast."

"And at school, too," Piper added, after reviewing her memory. Even though Ginny-Sue hadn't exhibited symptoms in class, when all the children had been busy decorating the Christmas tree, it was still possible that the illness was already spreading from one end of Blue River to the other. Edrina—Harriet—little Jeb, the new baby—

She wouldn't be able to bear losing a one of them, or any of her pupils, either.

She almost swooned at the enormity of the threat, but Sawyer took a firm grip on her elbow and steadied her, kept her upright.

He guided her to one of the easy chairs near the fireplace and sat her down.

"What about my girls, and the customers?" Bess asked Doc. "Shouldn't they be told?"

"If you say the word *diphtheria*," Doc replied, "there'll be a panic for sure. On the other hand, we can't have those men carrying the sickness home to their own families. I'll put the whole place under quarantine before I let that happen." He paused, grim and brusque. "I just hope it isn't already too late."

From her chair near the fire, Piper watched tears gather in Bess's eyes. "We'll see that the beer and whiskey flow," she said quietly. "And those that don't pass out, well, maybe the girls can keep them here some other way."

Some other way, Piper thought, half-sick. Innocent or not, she knew what that "other way" was, and the ugliness of it nearly overwhelmed her.

But who was she to judge? In Bess's shoes, with Bess's history and lack of choices, she'd probably be no different.

Doc gave a heavy sigh, nodded in agreement with what Bess had said. He had a child to worry about, too, Piper reminded herself, his Madeline. Doc Howard's daughter was probably a large part of the reason he'd finally braved his wife's disapproval, after refusing once, and answered Piper's summons.

Unless, of course, Sawyer had forced the other man to the

Bitter Gulch Saloon, at gunpoint. She didn't think he'd be above that.

The possibility made Piper sit up very straight, stiff-spined. "Did you—persuade Doc to come?" she asked, fixing her tired eyes on Sawyer.

"Now, how would I do that, with just one good arm?" he countered.

Piper raised both eyebrows, thinking of the Colt .45 her husband was wearing on his right hip, even then. "One way comes immediately to mind," she said.

Sawyer grinned. "Fortunately," he said, picking up on her meaning right away, "I didn't have to threaten anybody. I guess Doc just figured if I thought it was important enough to ride bareback to his place with a big hole in my shoulder, he ought to pay attention."

Piper scooted her chair a little closer to Sawyer's, dropped her voice to barely more than a breath while Doc and Bess conferred over by the door. "Didn't *Mrs.* Howard have something to say about it?"

Sawyer's grin broadened. "Oh, she had *plenty* to say. Told Doc she'd get on the train and head East if he set foot outside the house, never mind heading straight for a brothel, where God only knew what he might bring home. Yes, sir, she'd leave him high and dry. He said she oughtn't to make promises she didn't mean to keep, got his bag, and followed me over here. Didn't even take the time to saddle his mule."

Piper was wide-eyed. "You heard all that?"

Sawyer nodded. "I was downright proud of the man," he added.

"If I wasn't so grateful," Piper replied, "I'd have a few things to say *myself,* Mr. McKettrick, about you riding around on a horse in the dark of night in your condition."

"It seemed like a better idea than walking," Sawyer pointed

out. "I couldn't saddle Cherokee—it's practically impossible to tighten a cinch with one arm—but he didn't complain. I put a bridle on him, led him out of the shed and over to the porch, and climbed on from there."

"I don't suppose it ever occurred to you to heed me and stay put at the schoolhouse?" Piper retorted, though she wasn't actually angry, just fearful to think of all the things that could have gone wrong. Might *still* go wrong.

"I'll always hear you out," Sawyer said, quietly reasonable. "You're an intelligent woman and most of the time your opinion will probably make sense. That said, if I'm not swayed by your arguments, I'll go right ahead and do whatever strikes me as the best choice."

Piper had no reply for that. She was almost too tired to think.

Doc disappeared into the bathroom then and closed the door, while Bess stretched out on the bed alongside her feverish daughter, holding the little girl close, murmuring a lullaby to her.

Though she was still worried sick about Ginny-Sue and every other child in and around Blue River, Piper went over the things Sawyer had said, oddly exhilarated by them, even in her weariness. Yes, he was letting her know that, as a husband, he wouldn't bend to the kind of pressure women like Eloise Howard exerted, but it was the word *always* that had really caught her attention. He'd sounded as if he expected to share his life with her—as if they'd be working out problems and disagreements *years* from now.

"I thought you were leaving," she said carefully. "Heading out to find Mr. Vandenburg as soon as you could ride that far."

"I might still do that," Sawyer answered, one corner of his mouth quirking upward ever so slightly. "But I've done some thinking since last night, about how close I came to losing you when it was me Duggins was after. When you bolted from the schoolhouse a little while ago, hell-bent on storming the Bitter Gulch Saloon for the sake of a sick child, and devil take the gossip that was bound to result, I knew you were the one for me."

Piper sat stunned, stricken by hope even in this uncertain and potentially tragic situation. How was it possible for one person to contain so many powerful emotions, especially ones that were at odds with each other?

Doc emerged from the bathroom, drying his hands on a towel and glancing toward Ginny-Sue, and the woman who was holding her.

"That's quite a setup in there," he commented, cocking a thumb over one shoulder to indicate the bathroom. "Running water, hot and cold. Even a flush toilet." Doc paused then to rub his chin and reflect for a moment or two. "If I put in a bathtub over at our place, I reckon Eloise might decide I'm a passable husband, after all."

Sawyer grinned as Doc pulled over an ottoman and sat down close to the fire, rubbing his hands together and staring into the flames.

"And if she doesn't change her mind?" Sawyer asked.

Piper nudged his foot with her own, but he was undaunted and, anyway, it was already too late to stop him from asking such a personal question.

Doc chuckled, the firelight dancing over his face. "Well, then," he answered, "I may be forced to take a pretty fierce stand."

After that, all three of them alternately dozed and talked in quiet voices.

The fire got low, and Doc built it up again.

Once, feeling restless, Piper ventured into the bathroom and inspected the gleaming porcelain bathtub, trying all the while to imagine the sheer luxury of such a convenience. No water to pump or haul up from the well in a bucket, then heat on the stove, then carry and pour, and repeat the whole process all over again. Why, it would be miraculous—even better, at least in her opinion, than a private telephone and electric lights put together.

Around sunrise, pinkish-gold light glowing cold and clear at the windows, Cleopatra returned with another tray, knocking politely at the bedroom door and calling out in a low voice, "Somebody open this door for me. I've got my hands full out here."

This time, she'd brought fresh coffee, along with cups to drink it from, and a heaping plate of cinnamon buns still warm from the oven. The aromas were heavenly.

Concentrating hard, Cleopatra nearly dropped the whole works when a small voice suddenly piped up and said, "Mama? Did I miss Christmas?"

Everyone turned toward the bed to see Ginny-Sue sitting up, pillows at her back, looking a little wan but clear-eyed and alert.

Bess, who had slept beside Ginny-Sue through the night, gathered the child close again and wept for joy. "No, baby," she said, beaming through her tears. "You didn't miss Christmas. You surely didn't!"

Doc went over to touch Ginny-Sue's forehead, and his broad smile told the story. The fever had broken.

"That's one of the finest chest colds I've ever seen," Doc said, in a jocular voice that nonetheless cracked with fatigue. "A few days of bed rest and I'll wager the little lady here is good as new."

Piper turned immediately into Sawyer's embrace, trembling a little, weak with relief. She felt his lips move against her temple. "Go ahead and cry," he told her softly, patting her back. "God knows, you've earned the right."

There would be no school that day, fortunately for Piper, who probably couldn't have kept her eyes open to teach. Doc gave a dime to the local newspaper boy and told him to spread the word, along with the just-printed edition of the weekly *Blue River Gazette.*

He and Sawyer shook hands, and Piper greeted Cherokee, who'd stood patiently at the hitching rail all night long, even though he'd come untied at some point. Stroking the horse's velvety nose, she promised him an extra ration of grain.

Then Doc headed off toward his place, doubtless girding his loins for battle as he went, and Piper and Sawyer made for the schoolhouse, in the other direction, Sawyer leading Cherokee along behind.

Piper couldn't recall when she'd ever been so tuckered out, or so full of happiness. There would be no outbreak of diph-theria, at least for the time being, and Ginny-Sue was going to be all right.

As soon as they'd reached the schoolhouse, Sawyer put Cherokee away in the shed, and Piper went along, partly to help, and partly to keep her word about the grain.

While Sawyer removed Cherokee's bridle and then pro-ceeded to give the animal a quick brushing down, Piper plunged a hand into one of the feed sacks Clay had brought in from the ranch and held out her palm, heaping with grain.

"Watch your fingers," Sawyer warned, but he was smil-ing as he spoke.

Piper just laughed.

Cherokee ate delicately, for a big-jawed creature with enor-mous teeth, and Piper patted his head when he'd finished, and called him a good boy.

"Hey," Sawyer teased. "I'm starting to get jealous."

Piper made a face at him, but then she sobered a little. "Do you think Doc will really stand up to Eloise?" she asked.

Now it was Sawyer who laughed. Having been on the other side of the horse, he ducked under Cherokee's long neck and came up in front of Piper like a swimmer breaking the surface of still waters.

"No," he said. His voice was sleepy and low, and he still needed a shave. "I think he'll bribe her with a fancy bathtub and an indoor toilet, and she'll let him off the hook—until next time, anyway."

She felt incredibly shy, all of a sudden. Maybe it was from lack of sleep. "The poor man *is* a dentist," she said.

Sawyer laughed again. "Come on, Mrs. McKettrick," he said. "Let's get you inside so you can get some shut-eye."

They went into the schoolhouse, and Sawyer headed for the stove to build a fire while Piper hung up her beautiful russet-colored cloak. She'd never owned a finer garment in all her life, but she was too worn out just now to properly appreciate it.

She wandered into the bedroom, taking off everything but her bloomers and camisole in the shadowy cold, and practically dove into bed, anxious to get warm.

It was only when she caught a fleeting glimpse of Sawyer standing in the doorway that she realized she'd gotten into the wrong bed, the one she was in the habit of sleeping in.

And she was not about to risk more goose bumps by getting out again.

There was a fire going in the stove, she could smell the burning wood and hear the popping, but the warmth was still far away.

"A man could misinterpret aspects of this situation," Sawyer remarked, crossing to sit down on the edge of the bed, right next to her.

She realized then that she must have dozed off for a while, because he was clean-shaven, and his skin and hair, which was damp, smelled of soap.

Piper yawned, stretched luxuriously. "Really?" she asked coyly. For some incomprehensible reason, she'd forgotten how to be afraid, how to mistrust another person's motives. If that other person happened to be Sawyer McKettrick, that is.

"Oh, yes," Sawyer replied seriously, kicking off his boots. "That could easily happen."

"What if a *woman* wanted to be held, for example?" Piper's voice was a little shaky now, and her heart was picking up speed with every beat. She'd only had this feeling once before, when she was much younger and speeding down a snowy hillside in Maine on a homemade toboggan.

"That could be arranged," Sawyer said, after pretending to give the prospect due consideration. "But he might be tempted to, well, *persuade* her a little—beyond holding her, that is."

"I guess that would be acceptable," Piper allowed, from beneath the covers.

Sawyer chuckled, and there was some shifting around, and then he was in the bed beside her—her *husband*—resting one hand on the curve of her hip. "It might take days," he said, his voice husky, "but I'm a patient man."

"You are not," Piper argued, as he uncovered her face and quieted her with a kiss.

It was light and soft at first, that kiss, but it soon gathered momentum.

As Sawyer kissed her, he undid the laces at the front of her camisole. "Oh, but I am," he disagreed, when their mouths parted. "Patient, I mean."

Piper slipped her arms around his neck, gasped when he

opened the camisole and bared her breasts. Stroking one, chafing the nipple gently with the side of his thumb, he nibbled his way down over her collarbone.

"How could it—take—days?" she asked, a little out of step with the flow of conversation.

"I like to take my time," Sawyer replied, measuring out the words slowly, so slowly, like a man muttering in his sleep. "Especially when I'm doing this." And then his mouth closed, warm and wet and pulling ever so gently, around her already distended nipple.

She cried out with pleasure, instinctively arched her back in a plea for more and then still more.

"Days," Sawyer said idly, moving to her other breast.

The pleasure—yes, it *was* pleasure, and it was glorious, and it was *hers*—unleashed something inside Piper, some vast, elemental state of derring-do she hadn't known existed.

Over the next few minutes—or was it hours?—Sawyer raised Piper to a fever pitch with his fingers, his lips, his words. She wriggled out of her bloomers with a shameful lack of encouragement, making him laugh.

When he slid his hand between her legs and began to work her with a light, circular motion of the heel of his palm, she was lost. And then he took her nipple into his mouth again, and she was electrified, more completely and powerfully *alive* than ever before.

"Oh—*Sawyer*—" she sobbed out.

He lifted his head from her breast, where he'd been feasting, and said quietly, "Any time you want me to stop, Piper, all you have to do is say the word and I will."

"Ooooooh," she moaned, raising her hips high off the mattress to maintain contact with his hand. *Stop?* Not if she had anything to say about it.

He quickened the pace of his hand, and she went wild

with desire, with a need that would not be refused. "There's more," he told her softly, gruffly, tracing the length of her neck with his lips. "There's a lot more. But before any of that happens, I want you to know how it's supposed to feel when I make love to you."

She cried out again, frenzied, flying. Wanting. She was wanton, wide-open to him, and she felt no shame, only freedom and ferocious instincts.

"Sawyer!" she pleaded raggedly.

"Let go," he murmured. "Just let go."

There was a fierce seizing sensation then, deep inside her, a thing of the spirit as well as the body, followed by a release so keen that it seemed to consume all of Piper in sweet blazes of satisfaction. Her body flexed and flexed again, speaking its own language of joy.

Finally, she shattered completely and, after what seemed like a very long time, fell back into herself, in a slow but still dizzying drop, dazed, crooning and purring with every small aftershock.

"That's how it's supposed to feel," Sawyer told her, with a grin, much later, when her breathing had returned to something approaching normality and her heart had ceased struggling to flail its way out of her chest and fly heavenward like a bird.

She snuggled against Sawyer. "But there's more," she repeated sleepily.

"Yes," Sawyer said, with a smile in his voice. His chin was propped on the top of her head. "We'll have time for that later."

"Mmm," she said, and moved closer still.

Then she felt the hard length of him against her thigh, and she was instantly wide-awake.

"I did say there was more," Sawyer reminded her, his eyes

alight with mischief and—just possibly, no it couldn't be, not so soon—love.

"Now I know why everyone says it hurts," Piper announced, feeling her eyes go wide.

"Everyone?" Sawyer asked, teasing. "Is this something you talk about a lot?"

She shook her head, nervous and, at the same time, wanting him. All of him. "Of course not," she whispered, as though imparting a secret in the midst of a listening crowd. "But, well, it does seem—logistically impossible."

At that, Sawyer threw back his head and gave a shout of laughter.

She thumped his chest with the side of one fist, though not very hard. "What's so funny, Sawyer McKettrick?" she demanded, blushing from her hairline to her toes.

He didn't answer right away, but his amusement subsided a little.

Their gazes locked and the mood turned serious again.

"*Will* it hurt?" she asked meekly.

"Probably," Sawyer answered, smoothing her hair away from her cheek. "But only the first time, and for just a little while."

"Oh," Piper said.

"It's up to you," he reiterated.

"Let's try," Piper decided.

"It's not like that," Sawyer told her. "There's no 'try.' You do it, or you don't do it."

"Will it hurt you?"

He kissed her forehead, then the tip of her nose. "No," he answered, in his forthright way.

"And there's only pain the first time?"

He nodded. "Usually. And I'll be real careful, I promise."

She believed him. Her heart widened somehow, and took

him in, and that was the moment she truly became his wife. "I love you, Sawyer," she said, and she'd never meant anything more than she meant those words. "I know you probably don't—"

He stopped her from finishing the sentence by pressing an index finger to her lips. "I can speak for myself, woman," he said, with mock sternness. "And it just so happens that I love you, too. I realized it when you took off for the Bitter Gulch Saloon—even before that, really—to see to Ginny-Sue, and there was no talking you out of it."

She blinked. "Really? Why?"

He gave another raspy chuckle and shook his head. "I guess I admire spirit in a woman," he replied, "and you've got plenty of that, all right, with some to spare."

His answer pleased her deeply, settled into her, saturated her with a sense of rightness and perfect safety. "Well, Mr. McKettrick, I think it's about time we consummated our marriage, don't you?"

"You're sure?" He looked troubled, but blue-green fire burned in his eyes.

"I'm absolutely positive," she replied.

Dutifully, she situated herself on the mattress, spread her legs a little, and waited for him to get on top of her.

Instead, he gave another chuckle, and then he drove her to near madness again, caressing her, kissing her, whispering things that made her blood rush hot through her veins.

When Sawyer finally took Piper for his own, in a long, swift thrust, she wanted, *needed* him inside her so much that she barely noticed the twinge of pain as her maidenhead gave way.

Her body responded to his, as if drawing on some ancient knowledge, stroke for stroke, giving and then taking, offering and then demanding, and when he finally stiffened upon her, with a hoarse cry, and she felt him spilling himself into her, ecstasy claimed her once again, even more completely than before, and her cry of triumph rose to meet and mingle with his.

Later, they slept, and it seemed to Piper, as she drifted off, exhausted and utterly spent, a vessel deliciously emptied of all she had to give, that even though their bodies were separate and distinctly individual, their souls had somehow fused into one being, a making-right of many wrongs, large and small, a kind of coming home to all they'd ever really been.

They slept for the rest of that day and all of the night, to Piper's amazement, and awoke to a frost-sparkled morning that had drawn exquisite paisley patterns on the glass in the schoolhouse's few windows.

Sawyer was already up—she could hear him rattling the door of the stove, whistling under his breath.

Smiling, purely happy, she snuggled down in the warmth of the bed, every part of her pulsing with the memory of their lovemaking.

"You'd better get up, Teacher," Sawyer called good-naturedly, from the other room. "School starts in an hour."

Reality jolted through Piper, and she bolted out of bed, immediately beginning to shiver as the cold morning air struck her bare skin. She fumbled for her flannel wrapper and put it on quickly. "An *hour?*" she called back, padding in to squeeze up close to the stove while Sawyer dumped ground coffee beans into the pot.

It was only then that she noticed he'd removed his sling, though not his bandages, and even as he finished putting the coffee on to brew, he was slowly flexing and unflexing his left elbow.

"What are you *doing?*" Piper demanded, instantly alarmed.

"What I can," Sawyer responded. "I still have a lot of use for this arm, Mrs. McKettrick, and I don't want the muscles to atrophy."

"They *won't*," she said. "Doc Howard would have warned us, if that were the case. He'd have said—"

"Doc Howard, for all his versatility, is a dentist, not a medical practitioner," Sawyer reminded her, still moving his limb. "We've got a couple of doctors in the McKettrick clan, and any one of them would tell me to start using this arm a little every day."

Piper started to protest, and then stopped herself. Reasoning with a man was one thing, and nagging him was another. Besides, she recognized a lost cause when she saw one.

"These McKettricks seem to be an opinionated bunch," she observed, ladling hot water from a kettle on the stove into a basin so she could wash up before she put on her clothes.

Sawyer's grin flashed. "You'll fit right in," he said.

Chapter Ten

Afternoon, Christmas Eve

There were so many people in the Blue River schoolhouse, Piper thought happily, that even one more wouldn't fit.

And yet, somehow, there was a place for all the latecomers, with their smiles and words of greeting, their homemade fruitcakes and fruit pies.

The evening before, Clay had brought a fresh Christmas tree in from the ranch, deeming the first one a pitiful sight, past its prime, and Piper and Sawyer had spent a festive hour transferring the ornaments from the old to the new.

Now, Ginny-Sue's eyes widened as Clay lifted her up to touch the feathered wings of the angel that had magically appeared on top of the tree sometime during the night. "Where did she come from?" the child wondered, in an awed whisper. "She wasn't on the *other* tree."

"I guess it's a miracle," Clay told the child, his gaze on Dara Rose, who stood nearby, glowing as she showed off the new baby to one and all. The special angel was their gift to the children of Blue River. "There are a lot of those going around these days, it seems to me."

Ginny-Sue, still weak but mostly recovered, had returned to school only the day before, a little subdued but eager to be a part of things. Once Clay set her on her feet, she hurried off with Edrina, Harriet and Madeline to get ready for the program, and Piper, standing next to Dara Rose, smiled and offered a quick, silent prayer of gratitude.

There was so very much to be thankful for.

Indeed, this *was* a season of miracles, just as Clay had said.

Sawyer, neatly dressed in garments from his travel trunk and temporarily without his sling, caught Piper's eye and winked.

She drew a deep breath and went up to the place where her desk normally stood—it had been pushed back against the wall so the raised floor could be used as a sort of stage—clapping her hands smartly to get everyone's attention.

The cheerful talk ceased, but in a scattered, here-and-there way, and every upturned face was friendly—except, of course, for Eloise Howard's.

Piper gave the other woman a warm smile, secretly feeling sorry for her, and addressed the group in general. "The children have worked very hard to prepare for today's program," she said, in a voice trained to carry to every corner of the room without screeching. "We all hope you'll enjoy it."

Bess Turner, standing in a corner with a cluster of her "girls" from the Bitter Gulch Saloon, faded flowers clad in fuss and feathers, beamed with pride as Ginny-Sue took her place and began to recite the second chapter of Luke. Her performance was flawless, delivered in a bell-like voice, and afterward, no one stinted on applause.

Even Eloise clapped, after a fashion, soundlessly touching the gloved fingers of her right hand to the palm of her left, still flushed with the singular pleasure of informing Piper, twenty minutes before, that her teaching services would no longer be required after the school term ended in early June.

Piper hadn't minded, given that she and Sawyer had already made plans to make their home on the Triple M, up in Arizona, starting the journey north as soon as school was out and the new and more permanent town marshal had arrived, but she'd pretended to feel a *little* bit bad, for Eloise's sake. Heaven knew the poor woman was hard up for things to celebrate, which was a sad thing in and of itself, since she had a good husband, a lovely child and a comparatively easy life, far more than many other people could even have hoped for.

Bess Turner, for example, now hugging and congratulating her proud daughter, might have been grateful for the kind of respectability and love Eloise evidently took for granted—as less than her due.

With a sigh, Piper put the whole matter out of her mind. There was no changing other people; one had to accept them as they were and proceed as best one could, making allowances wherever possible.

The boys took the stage next, putting on a little skit of their own composition, in which shepherds and Roman soldiers speculated about the unusually bright star in the sky over Bethlehem. The soldiers had swords fashioned from kindling and the shepherds had staffs and feed-sack headdresses and, though brief, the play met with critical acclaim and much cheering.

Edrina played a lively tune on her ukulele next, with Harriet turning the pages of her sheet music for her, importantly competent throughout.

Recitations followed, mostly poetry, and when the last of those had mercifully ended, all the students assembled to sing "Silent Night," as rehearsed over many, many days. Piper was touched when, one by one, voice by voice, some awkward, some remarkably sweet, the audience joined in.

It was time then for the presents—the owner of the mercantile had, as usual, brought along the promised oranges and peppermint sticks.

The children were delirious with excitement, especially Ginny-Sue, who had confided to Piper earlier, in a brief moment of privacy, that she had a Christmas tree at home, too. There were parcels tucked into the branches, and "the ladies" had lent all sorts of baubles and ribbons and even silk garters for decorations.

Piper had been delighted by the image and kissed Ginny-Sue on top of the head, telling her, "You'll have a happy Christmas for sure."

And Ginny-Sue had nodded vigorously, eyes shining with joy.

Now, with the oranges and peppermint sticks dispersed, the adults chatted and indulged in pie and cake and all manner of country delicacies, each family, even the poorest ones, having contributed something.

Bess made her way to Piper's side and tugged at the sleeve of her new blue dress, a ready-made from the mercantile. She'd splurged on it, now that she wasn't saving her money to go back to Maine, along with small gifts for Sawyer, Dara Rose and Clay, and, of course, the children.

"We'll be going now," Bess said quietly. "I just wanted to say thank you for everything you did, you and your man, and to wish you a happy Christmas."

Piper's eyes burned, and she smiled, her response delayed by a few moments because she was suddenly choked up. "You're welcome," she said, at last. "And a happy Christmas to you, as well."

"It's the best one ever," Bess confirmed, with a fond glance at her daughter.

And then she and her bevy of twittering birds left the schoolhouse, surrounding little Ginny-Sue, in her warm coat, hat, boots and mittens, like a royal guard escorting a princess home to the palace.

Piper watched them go from the front window, knowing she would treasure the recollection forever after, while the party went on behind her. They were a *family,* those fancy women and that sweet child and blustery Cleopatra, as loving and tightly knit as any other. They'd come to the schoolhouse, knowing there would be some who looked askance, resolved to watch Ginny-Sue make her recitation and celebrate with her classmates, and they'd even put up a Christmas tree, festooning the branches with what they had, rather than tinsel and colored glass.

If that wasn't love, what was?

Sawyer stepped up beside her. "What are you thinking right now, Mrs. McKettrick?" he asked quietly.

She loved it when he called her that. "That Christmas comes in many forms," she replied, leaning against him a little, and delighting in the strength of his arm as it encircled her waist. Then she turned her head, looked up into his handsome face. "Do you miss your family? Because it's Christmas, I mean?"

"*You're* my family," he said, smiling into her eyes.

She let her head rest against his shoulder for a long moment. "I love you," she said.

"And I love you," he replied throatily, holding her a little tighter. Then, in a mischievous whisper, he added, "Let's hurry this party along a little. The sooner it's over, the sooner we'll be alone."

Piper smiled. "We're going to the ranch with Dara Rose and Clay and the children, remember? We won't really be alone until after Christmas, when we move into the marshal's house."

Sawyer grinned and gave her a surreptitious pinch on a part of her anatomy he particularly favored. "Clay and Dara Rose have a big house," he reminded her, "and I made sure we got a room well away from everybody else's."

She flushed. "You're a scoundrel," she accused, though she was pleased at the prospect.

"And you wouldn't have me any other way," he answered.

She laughed in agreement.

With that, they rejoined the festivities.

The ride to the ranch in Clay's largest hay wagon was long and cold, and Piper, bundled up in quilts and blankets in back, with Dara Rose holding the well-wrapped baby, Edrina and Harriet all sitting with her in a bed of fragrant straw, wouldn't have changed a thing about the experience.

It was already perfect, just as it was.

Clay and Sawyer sat up front, Clay at the reins of a four-horse team, and as they traveled, the stars started popping out in the blue-black sky, to the delighted fascination of the two little girls. Edrina's and Harriet's cheeks glowed, and their eyes danced with happiness and anticipation.

The trail was rough and rutted, the wagon jostled along, and Piper was lulled into a brief revelry by the steady clomp-clomp-clomp of the horses' hooves.

Conversation, it seemed, would be too much effort, at least for the women—the men were discussing something, up there in the wagon-box, and Edrina and Harriet chattered like eager little swallows in springtime—but Piper, for her part, was content just to be with them all.

It was later in the evening, long after they'd arrived at the ranch house, to which Dara Rose and Clay were already adding rooms, when the women finally got a chance to talk. They'd had a big supper, a boisterous affair replete with all sorts of food, and Edrina and Harriet had hung their stockings on the living room mantel and gone to bed with no fuss or delay. Dara Rose had retreated to nurse the baby and tuck him into his cradle near the kitchen table, where they sat, now that she'd returned. Clay liked to build things, when he had the time, and baby Jeb had several cradles, in various parts of the house.

The men had gone to the barn right after supper, and they weren't back yet.

"You seem happy, Piper," Dara Rose ventured gently. She was a pretty woman, with blond hair, like her daughters', and lively eyes, full of joyful intelligence. "Are you? Truly, I mean?"

Piper blushed slightly, and then nodded. "Yes," she said. "I'm *very* happy. I'll miss you, though. When Sawyer and I move to Arizona, I mean."

"We'll write often," Dara Rose promised, reaching out to pat Piper's hand. "And when the baby is older, we'll come for a long visit." The house was warm, being well-insulated, unlike the schoolhouse, with a wood-burning furnace and intermittent electrical services. There were several fireplaces, and the kitchen stove was a magnificent thing, with a hot-water reservoir that could be accessed by a spigot.

"Sawyer says Arizona is a fine place," Piper remarked. It had been a while since she'd seen Dara Rose, due to distance and pregnancy, and there was so much to say that it was hard to choose a place to start.

Dara Rose nodded. "Finally," she confirmed, smiling. "Clay says his granddad thinks it would have been better if Arizona remained a territory, says there'd be less interference from the federal government that way."

Piper had heard stories about Angus McKettrick, the head of the family, who had originally hailed from Texas. Sawyer clearly idolized the man, though he'd come right out and said his grandfather was three years older than dirt and deaf as a fence post, so she shouldn't be alarmed if he shouted at her to "Speak up so I can hear you, little gal!"

"I think I'm a bit intimidated," she confessed. "By the family, I mean. There are so many of them, and they're all strong-minded and utterly fearless, from what Sawyer's told me. Why, his own mother used to be a sharpshooter, traveling with a Wild West show."

Dara Rose laughed. "And Miss Mandy," she said, "is one of the *tamer* ones."

"Good heavens," Piper fretted. She had Annie Oakley for a mother-in-law.

"Don't worry," Dara Rose counseled. "I was only teasing. I've met Clay's folks—they came to visit not too long after we got married, traveled all that way by train—and I was real nervous before then. I took a powerful liking to them both right away, and so did the girls." She paused. "Here's the thing about the McKettricks, Piper. Once you marry into the family, you're one of them, for life. Jeb and Chloe—Clay's mother and father—they don't seem to see Edrina and Harriet as their son's stepchildren, any more than he does. To them, the girls are as much a part of the clan as anybody born with the name. They're extraordinary people, really."

Growing up, Piper reflected, she and Dara Rose had depended mostly on each other, when it came to family. It would be lovely to be part of a large group of kinfolks.

"I just hope they like me," Piper said.

"Believe me," Dara Rose insisted, just as the men came in from outside, accompanied by Clay's dog, "they will."

"Are the girls asleep?" Clay asked, bending to kiss Dara

Rose's cheek after hanging up his hat and coat and kicking off his boots to walk about in his stocking feet.

"They're probably pretending they are," Dara Rose said in reply, and all the love she felt for Clay McKettrick showed in her eyes as she watched him lean over the cradle to make sure the baby was warm enough.

Sawyer, dispensing with his own coat and hat—he'd put his sling back on for the ride out from town—crossed to Piper and kissed her ear, sending a fiery shiver through her.

The four of them sat around the table for a while after that, talking quietly while the fire burned low in the furnace downstairs, along with the one in the cookstove. The single bulb illuminating the kitchen blinked on and off periodically, and they used a kerosene lantern in between.

Eventually, Clay went down to the cellar to stoke up the furnace, and Dara Rose lifted their sleeping baby from his cradle, holding him tenderly, his face in the curve of her neck.

"I'll say good-night," Dara Rose told Piper and Sawyer, Sawyer having risen from his chair and drawn back Piper's so she could stand, "and a happy Christmas to both of you."

Piper stepped forward, kissed her cousin's cheek. "Sleep well," she told Dara Rose.

The spare room—Piper had stayed in it before, of course—was on the far side of the house, spacious and comfortably, if simply, furnished. It had its own wood-burning stove, which already crackled with a welcoming fire, but her favorite part of it was the bathroom. Like the one near Clay and Dara Rose's room, which they shared with the girls, this one was well appointed with a pedestal sink, a toilet, and a long, narrow tub made of gleaming porcelain.

Water flowed from a copper tank set into the wall, heated by the small boiler beneath.

Someone, probably Clay, had made sure the boiler was

operating properly, and when Piper put the plug in place and turned the spigots, gloriously hot water soon spilled and splashed into the tub.

By the light of the lantern she and Sawyer had brought from the kitchen—there were no electric bulbs in this part of the house—Piper shed her clothes as quickly as she could and climbed in while the water was still running.

She sighed and closed her eyes. "Bliss," she said.

A chuckle from the doorway made her open her eyes again and turn to see Sawyer standing there, watching her. "I'd have to agree," he said huskily.

She didn't think he was referring to the bath, and his words made her blush slightly.

"Join me?" Piper asked. She'd taken regular baths at the schoolhouse, of course, but that had been an awkward proposition to say the least. This was a *real* bath, with plenty of hot water and scented salts in the bargain.

Sawyer remained where he was, giving his head a slight shake. His gaze caressed her as intimately as a touch of his hand. "I'll take a bath later," he replied. "Right now, I'm content to watch you."

She sighed again, a crooning sound of purest contentment, not just with the bath but with the whole of her life, and leaned against the back of the tub, even though the porcelain was chilly where it touched her bare skin, and allowed herself to sink deeper into the rising water. "Nothing," she said, "could be better than this."

Sawyer stepped into the room then, set the lantern on a shelf, and knelt beside the bathtub. "Is that a fact?" he asked, holding out his right arm to her, as he was in the habit of doing when they undressed, and, without replying to his question, she unfastened his cuff link and rolled his sleeve up past his elbow.

He swirled the water around her lightly, splashed some on

her belly and her breasts. She quivered as his fingertips brushed those same places, and others, too.

"*One* thing might be better than a bath," Piper admitted, feeling saucy.

Sawyer traced the circumference of her right nipple, again, with a fingertip.

A tremor went through her, with a promise of sweet tumult to follow. She groaned, already surrendering to his caresses, even as the water rose and rose, so warm and soothing. The very marrow of her bones seemed to melt.

Sawyer chuckled at her response; he loved the sounds Piper made when he pleasured her, and he was very good at that.

The tub was full, and he turned off the spigots, reached for a bar of soap.

And he began to lather Piper, gently but thoroughly, washing every part of her, and she gave herself up to the sultry, luxurious sensations of his touch, and of the things he said to her, quiet and strictly their own, almost a private language.

Presently, he leaned over and caught her mouth with his, kissed her deeply, all the while stroking the place between her legs, which had opened for him readily, like always.

His lovemaking always seemed new, and exquisitely daring. He'd taken her standing up in the schoolhouse one moonless night, and even now the memory aroused her almost as much as what he was doing now. She'd taken him into her greedily, crying out in welcome as he took her.

"There's more," he always said to her, after each ecstatic surprise.

"There's more," he said now, getting to his feet and reaching for one of the towels Dara Rose had so thoughtfully provided, along with the fancy soap and the ample supply of hot water.

Wobbly-kneed, Piper stood, let him wrap her in the towel.

Stepped over the side of the tub and onto the rug to stand very close to him.

He led her into the warm bedroom, lit only by the light escaping from the edges of the door in the little stove, dried her off, and settled her sideways on the mattress. Easing her onto her back, he kissed her and caressed her for a long time.

She waited, dazed with comfort and anticipation, because when Sawyer said there was more, there always was.

Always.

When he slipped away from her, she tried to pull him back, already wanting him on top of her, inside her, but he eluded her grasp.

And then he knelt again, and parted her knees.

When he took her into his mouth, the most sensitive, intimate part of her, she had to stifle a ragged shout of delight. It was scandalous—it was—

"*Sawyer,*" she whimpered, tangling her fingers into his hair, holding him close to her, pressed hard against her.

His mouth. Dear heaven, *his mouth*. What magic was this? What wild, sweet magic was he working on her?

Without withdrawing from her, he eased both her legs up, setting her heels against the mattress. Her bent knees widened and still he feasted on her, nibbling and tasting, teasing her with just the tip of his tongue until she begged for completion.

One of his hands found her mouth and covered it gently, and that was a good thing, because when satisfaction finally, *finally* overtook her, she was making a primitive sound, part sob and part growl, that would have carried clear to town, never mind to the rest of the house.

Before rising from his knees, Sawyer kissed the insides of Piper's still trembling thighs. Several small, sharp after-releases followed, each one causing her to moan softly and arch her back, as though to find his mouth again.

He arranged her properly in the bed and covered her up. "If Clay hears you yelling like that," he joked quietly, "he'll think I'm killing you and storm the room with a shotgun."

Piper couldn't speak. She was still trying to find her way back to herself, still lost on the outskirts of heaven.

She slept a sweetly shallow sleep, rising to the surface now and then, like some exotic fish. She heard Sawyer running a bath in the next room and, later, felt his weight on the mattress when he climbed into bed beside her. She stirred as, unbelievably, desire reawakened within her, blossoming like some soft-petaled flower.

"Sawyer," she whispered, reaching for him.

He moved on top of her, and she widened her legs for him.

He took her slowly, so slowly, and so deeply that her body instantly responded, even though she was still half-asleep. She began to buckle beneath him, as the first climax seized her, followed by another and then another. They were soft, these releases, and she soared with them as surely as if she'd had wings.

Finally, Sawyer too reached the pinnacle, and gave himself up to her with a long, low groan that seemed to rise from the depths of his soul.

"Get up!" a little voice crowed. "Get up, get up, get up!"

Sawyer opened one eye, spotted Harriet standing beside the bed, holding up a stocking—one of Clay's, probably—bulging with loot.

"It's *Christmas!*" Edrina piped up, from the other side of the bed.

Piper, buried deep under the covers, murmured something.

"And St. Nicholas was here!" Harriet cried, waving the stocking. "Get up!"

Sawyer laughed. "I thought you didn't believe in St. Nicholas," he said, stalling for time. He wasn't wearing a stitch, and neither was Piper, which meant, of course, that the getting-up part would have to wait until the girls were out of the room.

"Now we've got proof!" Edrina trilled, exhibiting a burgeoning work sock of her own. A doll's head poked out of the top, flanked by what looked like a toy horn of some kind, brightly painted and made of tin.

"And there was a *note!*" Harriet added, her eyes huge with excitement. "St. Nicholas left us presents *in the barn,* and that's why you have to *get up,* so we can all go out there together and see!"

Sawyer thought of the two spotted ponies Clay had been hiding in the barn for three days now, and grinned. The night before, he and Clay had set the small, fancy saddles out in plain sight, on a bale of hay, and draped the bridles over them. "Go wake up your folks, then," he said.

Piper's head popped out from under the covers, and she smiled sleepily at the girls, yawned a good-morning.

Sawyer would have given a great deal for another hour alone with her, right there in the guest room bed, but he knew he was out of luck, given the combination of kids and Christmas.

"They're *already* awake!" Edrina informed him. "Hurry *up*—at this rate, it'll be New Year's before we get to see our presents!"

"Out," Sawyer ordered good-naturedly.

"Go on," Piper urged the girls, with a twinkle in her eyes. "We'll be up and around in a few minutes, I promise."

Possibly because she was their teacher, as well as their mother's cousin and closest friend, Edrina and Harriet scampered out, shutting the bedroom door smartly behind them.

"*Hurry!*" one of them called back, over the sound of rapidly retreating footsteps.

Sawyer sighed, got out of bed, and gathered up his clothes.

He went into the bathroom to dress, and when he came out, Piper was fully clad and pinning up her hair in a loose chignon.

He kissed her nape. "That was quick," he said.

"Christmas waits for no one," she replied, turning in his embrace to kiss the cleft in his strong chin. "Let's go see what St. Nicholas has left in the barn."

One year later
Triple M Ranch, Indian Rock, Arizona

The whole clan had gathered at the main ranch house, where Angus McKettrick officiated, from his wheeled chair, over a busy and memorable Christmas Eve. Even Clay and Dara Rose were there, with the children, having traveled all the way from Texas on the train.

Since all the McKettricks would have separate celebrations for their own families the next day, gifts were exchanged after supper, and even after months spent with these people, Piper was amazed by the rough-and-tumble love they bore each other. They'd taken her into their lives and hearts back in June, when Sawyer had returned, bringing a new wife with him, and she'd fallen in love with them, too.

She and Sawyer had stayed with his mother and father, Kade and Mandy McKettrick, at first, while they were building their own house and barn on a little rise with a spring and a broad view of the ranch. Mandy was still trim and agile, though she'd long-since given up sharpshooting to reign over her children and grandchildren, as well as her adoring husband.

Besides aunts and uncles, there were sisters, too, and brothers, and cousins galore.

Piper was still getting to know them all. Sawyer's aunt Katie, Angus and Conception's late-life daughter, a particular favorite of Piper's, was married to a United States senator and divided her time between Arizona and Washington. She was bound and determined to see that women got the vote and constantly pestered her husband and his associates to "catch up with the modern world" and do something about the problem.

On this sacred night, Mandy approached her newest daughter-in-law and gently touched her protruding stomach. Piper and Sawyer's first baby was due soon—she'd been hoping for a Christmas birth—but that didn't seem likely, since there hadn't been so much as a twinge of a contraction so far.

"You mustn't overdo, now," Mandy counseled. "We're a pretty overwhelming bunch, we McKettricks, especially when we're all in the same place."

Piper smiled, caught Sawyer's eye and received his smile like a blessing. He was standing next to Angus's wheeled chair, listening while the older man went on about the unfortunate changes statehood had brought.

None of them, in Angus's view, were good.

Sawyer winked, and Mandy, seeing the exchange, smiled at Piper again. "At least sit down," she said, steering Piper toward one of the few unoccupied chairs.

Chloe, a lovely red-haired woman and a teacher, like Piper, approached them, having taken a large and gaily wrapped package from beneath the towering Christmas tree. Katie and Lydia and Emmeline, the other aunts, found their way over, too, all beaming proudly.

Chloe handed the parcel to Mandy, who gently laid it in Piper's lap.

Dara Rose joined them, too. From her smile, she was in on the surprise.

"What on earth—?" Piper asked, near tears.

"Open it," Mandy urged eagerly.

Carefully, her hands trembling a little, Piper removed the

ribbon, draping it over the arm of her chair for safekeeping, and then smoothed back the tissue paper.

Inside was a quilt, as wildly colorful as the northern Arizona landscape surrounding them all, exquisitely pieced.

"We all worked on it," Katie said.

Lydia and Dara Rose took the quilt by its ends and unfurled it, so Piper could get a good look at the design. The Blue River schoolhouse had been faithfully reproduced in fabric and appliquéd to the center of what, to Piper, was a work of art. There were children embroidered here and there, frolicking in the school yard, and she saw herself standing in the tiny doorway, with Sawyer beside her.

"Sawyer told us he ruined your trousseau quilts by bleeding on them," one of the women said.

Piper's vision was blurred, but she could still make out the words stitched, sampler style, in a rainbow arched above the schoolhouse.

"Piper and Sawyer McKettrick," the thread-letters read. "Blue River, Texas, 1915."

"It's so lovely," Piper whispered. "Thank you."

Mandy leaned down and placed a kiss on her daughter-in-law's forehead. "No, Piper," she said. "Thank *you,* for saving Sawyer's life and for being precisely who you are." Mandy's gaze took in the entire gathering in one swift sweep before returning to Piper's upturned face. "Welcome to the McKettrick family," she finished.

★ ★ ★ ★ ★